Jan...

SHADOW RITES

A Jane Yellowrock Novel

Faith Hunter

A ROC BOOK

ROC
Published by New American Library,
an imprint of Penguin Random House LLC
375 Hudson Street, New York, New York 10014

This book is an original publication of New American Library.

First Printing, April 2016

For more information about Penguin Random House, visit penguin.com.

ISBN 978-0-451-46597-9

Printed in the United States of America
10 9 8 7 6 5 4 3 2 1

PUBLISHER'S NOTE
This is a work of fiction. Names, characters, places, and incidents either are the
product of the author's imagination or are used fictitiously, and any resemblance to
actual persons, living or dead, business establishments, events, or locales is entirely
coincidental.

Penguin
Random
House

To my Renaissance Man,
who kept me sane and calm
through the summer of writing,
while my brain was worse-than-usual out of kilter.
You make life worth living.

ACKNOWLEDGMENTS

Lucienne Diver of the Knight Agency for guiding my career, being a font of wisdom when I need advice, and for applying your agile and splendid mind on my writing.

Isabel Farhi of Ace/Roc for keeping me on time through the edits and copy edits.

Dan Larsen, copy editor, for a fine job at catching all the boo-boos!

Cliff Nielsen . . . for all the work and talent that goes into the covers.

Mindy Mymudes for beta-reading. For being a font of knowledge and a great friend.

Lee Williams Watts for being the best travel companion and PA a girl can have!

Beast Claws! Street Team extraordinaire!

Let's Talk Promotions at ltpromos.com for getting me where I am today.

Poet and writer Sarah Speith for giving me Jane's medicine bag. It is still perfect!

As always, a huge thank-you to Jessica Wade of Penguin Random House, the best editor I could have. You make me into a much better writer than I am capable of alone. I don't know how you keep the high quality up, book after book. You are extraordinary.

CHAPTER 1

The Fist of a Child

The prickly sensation crawled over my left fingertips, up my fingers, and snuggled into my palm like the fist of a child. For a moment it was pleasurable, and in my dreams, my heart warmed. I thought of my goddaughter, Angie Baby, and smiled in my sleep.

Then something exploded up my hand and arm and into my torso, a magical bomb going off. An electric sensation, like a burning cactus, the thorns on fire, the blooms as weapons blossoming open through me. Scorching thorns ripped through my flesh. The blooms detonated like heat-seeking missiles.

I gasped a single breath that sent a shock wave of pain through me. Opened my eyes as I woke. But I didn't move otherwise. Lying in the dark. Terror rising. The heat and power of a magical working—a spell, to the mundane world—rolled through me. *Reading me.* My heart raced. My breath came too fast.

Familiar . . . I had felt this—or something like this—before. With a tearing sensation, the working ripped out of me and across my bed. And I could breathe. The fear-stink of my own sweat filled my nostrils, tart and acerbic. My heart raced, an uneven thump against my ribs.

For a moment I knew it, remembered it, and then the memory faded, like a dream upon waking, as if the working was designed to be forgotten. But my Beast reached out and swiped it into her claws, keeping it for me.

Beast shoved her night vision into me and I saw the energies of the working on the walls and ceiling and floor as it roiled slowly, a pale green power that licked its way forward, through my room, leaving nothing in its wake but shadows. Nothing happened. So . . . it wasn't a magical trigger waiting to be set off. It looked as if it was taking a 3-D picture of everything, like a 3-D laser recording of the room. In preparation for . . . what? Nothing. Yet.

The moment it moved off the bed, I picked up the unsheathed vamp-killer and nine-mil on the bedside table, only inches from the hand where the spell had commenced. Rolled to my feet, careful to keep my soles away from the searching magics. I was dressed in leggings and a tee, both in shades of charcoal so that I could move through the house, only slightly darker than a shadow, without being seen from outside. Or inside, for that matter.

My palm, where the magics first touched me, sent a sizzle of pain up my arm when I gripped the vamp-killer. *Not lightning,* I thought, calming my racing breath. *Not lightning.* I was still getting over having been hit by lightning, but the panic attacks weren't totally gone yet. The feel of the vamp-killer hilt in my palm settled me, the crosshatched grip, the fourteen-inch silver-plated blade, the perfect balance for hacking.

Forcing calm into myself with each breath, attempting to quiet my heart rate, I tried to decide if running was smart or playing dead was smarter. Since I wasn't actually dead yet, and since the magics might have been intended to flush me out where someone could hurt me worse, I decided to stay in the house, silent.

As a skinwalker, one who also carries the soul of a mountain lion in my body, I knew not racing away, not taking the offensive, was the more difficult choice. Especially when attacked in my home. Flight or fight was more natural, but that might get me killed this time. Might get my business partners, sleeping upstairs, killed. They were human. I could heal from most wounds and injuries; humans might not. My heart raced. Breath sped. Muscles tightened.

With my Beast-vision, I followed the magics as they moved slowly through my bath and into my closet. I had left both doors open and so was able to watch as the working rolled through the spaces and the piles on the floor. Sometimes it paid to be a slob. Without a pause, the pale green energies swept over the sabertooth lion skull on the top closet shelf. But the working hesitated and hovered over the small wooden carving of a crow. The carving was positioned over my stash of magical trinkets given to me by my best friend, Molly Everhart, long ago, the crow and its working *hedge*, recharged on her last visit. The box of magical doodads were protected by the crow and its upgraded *hedge of thorns* ward, which spat and spluttered as the magics feathered their way over them. *Hedge of thorns*, renovated to *hedge of thorns 2.0*, had been tested recently. It was, so far, unbreakable, but . . . there was always a first time.

The working brightened and turned reddish, as if trying to read the spells, even encapsulated in the spelled box containing them. The magics grew brighter, a sparking purple, edging toward grape, and then back to scarlet as they tried to penetrate and read. I smelled ozone and a stink like hair burning as the sizzling increased. The meeting of two such workings might trigger something more catastrophic than the sparks and shadows I could see now. I needed to get the guys.

Whatever the working was, its attention was not on me at the moment. I drew on Beast-speed and her energy flashed through me, an adrenaline flush of my skinwalker magics. Slipping the H&K into my right hand, the blade in the other, I leaped over the edge of the pale green working where it had paused and thinned on my floor, its attention in the closet. I landed, a tingling of magic passing through me, my braid slapping my butt. But nothing changed. The scan hadn't noticed me move. Heart still pounding, I sped out of my room and into the foyer, up the stairs, three at a time, using Beast-stealth to keep my passage from creating any vibrations that the working might pick up.

It might have been smarter to go inside Eli's room and speak, but I didn't know what my partner slept in, and I didn't need to find out tonight. I stopped outside his door and hissed, the sound softer than air, but I knew Eli would hear it, evaluate it, and determine it was likely me, even in his sleep, picking it out as a "not normal" night sound. You can take the Ranger out of the special forces, but you can't the special forces training out of the Ranger.

I head a faint shushing sound, maybe a sheet rustling. "Jane?" he whispered from the darkness.

"Magical problems. Silent mode. Weapons," I said, not much more than a breath, hoping he would understand my intent.

He came out of the room barefoot, his dark skin a shadow in the night, his new weapon harness slung around his head and one shoulder. He was wearing dark pants, his dark skin making him a shadow. He put his head near mine and said, "Deets."

"Something scanning the house. Magic. Unknown source. I can see it, currently in my bedroom, interested in Molly's toys and *hedge*. It scanned me and my room on the way in. Now it smells like something overheating and it might go boom on purpose or accident. Ultimate purpose unknown. Person or persons involved unknown." Which meant one of two things: it came for the toys it had found, or it was temporarily occupied with the toys it hadn't expected to find, and would eventually return to whatever it had come to do. If curtain number two was the right one, then the toys sidetracked it. But either way, there could still be an explosion.

Eli gave a single nod and glanced into his brother's room. "Alex isn't in his bed," he murmured.

That meant the Kid, Eli's teenaged brother, and the brains of our business, was still at his online gaming downstairs or was asleep on the couch, also downstairs. I nodded. "No glow from his screens."

"Copy."

We moved down the stairs, silent. Two shadows. Automatically avoiding the steps that might creak or shift or groan under our weight. Old houses have alarm systems built into the floors.

The energies were still at work in the closet when we reached the foyer. The stink of burning hair and ozone had been joined by a stench vaguely reminiscent of iron and salt and the stink of stagnant water. Eli's nose wrinkled. Even if I had been human, it would have been horrible; as it was, I pressed against my nose to keep from sneezing at the stench.

He leaned into my room and said, "Nothing visible," which meant humans couldn't see the working. Alex was sleeping on the living room couch, arms thrown out, legs spread, with one hanging over the back of the couch. He was shirtless, wearing a loose pair of Captain America pants, the kind that kids wear, hanging on their hips, baggy at their knees. I grinned, glad of the dark, so he wouldn't see my amusement when Eli woke him. Alex was a boy on the brink of manhood, and laughter had begun to sting.

Eli touched Alex's shoulder. When that didn't wake him, Eli set two weapons on the floor, covered his brother's mouth with one hand, and shook him with the other. Alex came awake fighting and Eli avoided the flying fists with ease. It looked like long practice. Despite the magical energies in my bedroom, my smile grew wider. Eli bent over his brother and whispered into his ear. When he let go, Alex slid his feet to the floor, stood, shook himself like a dog to wake up, and made his way to his tablets.

Eli gave me a hand signal that meant, in essence, "Where's the big bad wolf?" not that I'd say that to him. Hand signals were a military thing and he took that stuff seriously. I looked back over my shoulder and saw that the working was still occupied in my closet. I just hoped that the *hedge* was enough to keep the magical attack out and that none of Molly's toys was accidentally activated. I'd hate to have to rebuild my closet. I pointed to my bedroom and made a chipping motion to suggest it was still

working there. Eli nodded before moving off to survey
the windows and doors and, through them, out into the
night.

Yellowrock Securities was a well-oiled team, everyone
with a job. This was what it meant to be family. Living
together. Working together. Fighting together. If we hadn't
been in danger, I might have gotten all teary. But this
wasn't the first time our home had been attacked by magical means in the last months. It almost felt as if someone
had painted a target on us. Or on me. Yeah. That.

I went back to the bedroom to study the magical working, standing well outside the paused line of magical energies that marked my floor. The energies were a line of pale
light through the bedroom, faintly flickering. The floor and
walls beyond, the ones that the magic had already passed
through, were unmarked, and the floor and walls on this
side were also unmarked, which, with the exception of the
pain in my palm, led me to believe that my first impression
had been right—a scanning spell. The energies were much
brighter in my closet, in my mixed puma/human eyesight,
reddish and greenish with sparks of silver flashing through
it, the gray of storm clouds.

I caught a whiff of smoke. The scan was setting something on fire. I raced back to the kitchen and grabbed the
fire extinguisher, pulling the pin, and stopping again at
the closet. A gray cloud, totally physical and fiery in nature,
came off the *hedge*. The pale green energies of the attacking scan spluttered and sizzled and I felt the heat signature
from where I stood. The sound stopped. The scan withdrew slightly. The stench began to lessen as it filtered into
the air and diminished. The smoke dispersed, a long,
indistinct tracery across the ceiling. Nothing happened for
what felt like two or three minutes. Then the attacking
magics tapped on the *hedge* and stopped when it sparked
and spat.

I had a better way to see the unfamiliar working, but I
wasn't in the mood to make myself deathly ill unless it was
life or death for my partners. The working in the closet
flashed again and the line of pale light guttered like a can-
dle going out before strengthening into a pale green hue,

brighter than a Disney night-light. It slipped from the closet and started moving again, taking in the ceiling and sliding toward my doorway.

I backed away, through the foyer into living room, watching the magic as it slithered across the floorboards and up the front wall, tracing the floor in light before passing on. It wasn't something I could hear with my ears, but I felt a sensation of popping and hissing as magical energies worked their way around and through the front door, pausing to limn it in a fairy-tale illumination that few humans could see.

I stepped away and it paused, as if it had heard or sensed me. I froze, wondering if it would follow me when I moved. If I should run. But it touched the stairs and angled up, climbing slowly.

I slid through the darkness and shadows to Eli, and when he glanced at me, I mimed it rising up the stairs, and pointed to the Kid's bedroom overhead. Eli nodded and jutted his chin out the kitchen window. He held up two fingers, meaning that we had two people out there who shouldn't be out there, doing things that tourists in New Orleans didn't do.

I leaned to the glass and studied the street, at first seeing nothing but a fine mist that hung like a slowly falling fog, a leisurely, Louisiana rain. But when my eyes felt the need to drift away from two different places, I understood. There were two human-shaped forms out there, both hidden beneath obfuscation spells, one standing at either end of the block, in shadows. Not vamps. Not were-creatures. Witches. To a human they would be no more than two blurs, a haze on the night, obscured by the mist, an illusion of shadows in the darkness between the streetlamps. The power of their magic kept me from seeing them well, but now that I knew they were there, the magic itself was something Beast could make out, at least partially.

The working came from both of the hidden forms, two separate pale lines of power that ran across the street to meet and merge just in front of the house into a stronger line of energies. One line was a smooth, weak, pale red, the

magics controlled and even and concise. The other witch's
magic was a pale green, the energies jumping and spitting,
slithering like snakes, full of power that seemed to want to
sprint away and perform all on their own. The term *wild
magics* came to me, power that was feral and uncontrolled
and seeking destruction. The red magics were meticulous
and skillful, if not so dominant; the green magics were
more potent and by far the greater danger. A yard or so
after the two lines of witchy power combined, they entered
the house through my bedroom wall.

I looked back at my partner and pointed to my eyes and
then to the backyard, asking him if anyone was back there.
He gave me a down-turned thumb. No other witches were
part of the attack. Just two witches, one extraordinarily
powerful. And if they hadn't known before, they now knew
about the magical trinkets in my closet.

Eli went to his brother and looked over the Kid's
shoulder. Alex was a former hacker, a former felon, and
currently studying for a double doctorate at Tulane, while
spying on me for some supersecret information gathering
part of the Department of Defense or Homeland Security
or the CIA. Or all three. The government wanted to know
what I was. Alex was feeding them incorrect info, and as
long as I didn't shift in public and stayed under the radar,
things would be okay. I hoped.

The Kid was too smart for his own good sometimes,
but he was exactly what we needed as intel backup. He
had the outside cameras up and running, taking digital
and tape recordings. We had discovered that digital media
worked when photographing vamps but was interrupted
by many other kinds of magic. Old-school stuff was sometimes better at capturing images that would otherwise be
hidden beneath the pixelated energies.

Tapping his tablets and putting camera views up on
the big screen, Alex whispered, "You want me to call the
police?"

"And tell them what?" I murmured in reply. "Two people are standing out front and shooting invisible X-ray vision
at the house? That would go over well. Not." I frowned hard.
"They aren't actually doing anything illegal according to

human law. Witch law, maybe, but not if the NOLA coven *sent* them."

"You think?" Eli muttered, concern lacing his voice.

"No. But I also don't think the local witches would be interested in helping me against two of their own." Witches were notoriously insular. I had made some witch friends back in Asheville, and while I had met some of the locals, I wouldn't call them gal-pals.

Still softly, Eli asked, "Where is it?" meaning the scanning energies.

I walked silently through the house to the foyer and looked up the wide stairway. The pale green glow was entering the bedroom where Angie Baby stayed when she was here, and that didn't sit well with me. I didn't like anyone or anything that might affect my godchild, and I had no idea what the spell was really doing. It might be simply a scan, as I thought, or it might be putting down the witch equivalent of napalm, or a trigger for some future spell to incinerate us all. Or worse, it might be setting up a way to get to us when the Everhart-Trueblood witch family arrived in just a few days for the Witch Conclave. These witches might be working against the assembly; there were always people who wanted the status quo instead of peace, and the Witch Conclave was gearing up to be the event when the witches and the vamps of the Southeastern U.S. signed a peace treaty of sorts (though they called it something else) for the first time ever. I didn't have enough information to make an informed decision about the purpose of the scan. As usual, I was flying by the seat of my pants, which didn't bother me when I was the only one who would pay the consequences, but it did bother me when my lack of knowledge meant the boys or the Everhart-Trueblood clan would pay as well.

The stink of iron, salt, and burned hair had grown stronger again. What did burned hair mean? I had to assume it meant danger for the Youngers and me in the present. Or danger for my godchildren and their parents, later. Inside me, Beast growled and thought, *Kits in danger.* Kill *witches.*

Beast had a much simpler view of things than I did.

Kill and ask questions later. *No can do,* I thought back at her. Deep inside, she extended her claws and milked my brain. It hurt. A lot. But it meant she was close if I needed to draw on her, so I wasn't going to gripe.

Walking back into the shadows of the kitchen, I muttered, "The scan—if that's what it is—is nearly done upstairs. That leaves this half of the downstairs. Oh." Apprehension sped through me. "And the weapons storage and the utility area." Parts of the house I seldom went into and rarely even thought about.

Eli waited, watching me. He wanted a plan of action, but I didn't have one to give him. As a rogue-vamp hunter, I had a legal leg to stand on when killing vamps—and their human blood-servants—who presented a clear and present danger to the human populace. The blood-servant ruling was a new one, recently issued by the Louisiana Supreme Court, over a kill made back in the nineties by another vamp hunter, who was arrested, convicted, and imprisoned when he killed three of a vamp's walking blood-meals while saving a family of four humans. The vamp hunter was free now, though no one could give him back his lost years. The state supreme court decision gave me certain powers, within state law, against rogue vamps and their willing dinner partners. Against sane vamps, law-abiding humans, law-abiding were-creatures, or witches, I had no more power than anyone else.

I didn't know what to do. My Beast-inspired headache was growing. One thing I knew for certain. The house was old, constructed of wood and old brick, with an antiquated electrical system. If the magics wanted to cause me trouble, burning down the house would be easy. I sniffed again, but the stink of magic-induced smoke was gone. For now.

Alex waved us over and said softly, "I took digital photos of them, but the photos don't work worth jack through the obfuscation spells." We stood behind his chair and his boy-man-garlic stink wafted up. Eli swatted him on the back of the head.

"What's that for?" Alex complained, sotto voce, rubbing his head and straining back to grimace at us.

"For being Stinky," I said. "So the digitals didn't work. Why am I here smelling you?"

He scowled at us through his straggly curls and bent back over his screen. "Because the tape is working fine. Both witches are female, natch, and though the light sucks, they might be African-American or mixed race."

We all studied the camera footage. One witch appeared to be about five-five, two hundred fifty pounds, give or take. She held herself stiffly and something about her stance suggested that she was middle-aged, dressed in a long, full skirt and turban. The other one moved like some-one younger, maybe even late teens. She was dressed in jeans and T-shirt, a skinny girl with lots of hair. Alex initi-ated some kind of electronic conversion, taking the tape to digital where he did something with the brightness and contrast and created stills from the footage.

I pointed at the younger one and asked, "Lots of long curly hair. A wig?"

"Could be," Alex said. "Or extensions. That is all the still shots can make out."

"Decisions," Eli demanded. "Stay here or leave? Call the cops? Call someone else?"

I frowned and walked to the bottom of the stairs again, to see the light of the working moving to the front of the house and the two narrow doors/windows that opened to the small second-floor gallery at the front. We never used the front gallery. I didn't even know if the doors would open anymore, what with the damp and heat, and the swell-ing and shrinking of old wood in older frames.

I needed to get close to the witches.

"No," Eli said.

I chuckled under my breath. My partner had a way of reading my mind. "I can access the Gray Between and bubble time, without much pain, if I don't try to actually *do* anything but watch while I'm there." And maybe Eli wouldn't realize that this situation might to call for more than that. The witches might have the ability to set the house on fire, so I needed to be able to disable them. And to do that, I would have to move in the Gray Between of bubbled time. The ability to move outside time was part

of my skinwalker energies, though whether it was something that all skinwalkers had been able to do, or if I was
the only one—because an angel had given me the ability—
I didn't know. I had met only one other skinwalker. And
I had killed him. And the angel wasn't talking.

Bubbling time made me deathly sick, and it wasn't
something that my skinwalker energies healed well. Moving in bubbled time had nearly killed me, leaving me afraid
to use the gift. Fear was a new emotion for me and I hated
it. But I had to be honest and admit that the fear was one
reason I hadn't made a decision yet. Fear paralyzed.

The pale green swath of light was coming down the
stairs. "Well, crap," I muttered. I was out of time. *Ha-ha.* I
blew out a breath. "Call the cops," I ordered Alex, "but not
nine-one-one. Try the woo-woo room. If someone we know
is on, tell them what's happening. Then do what they say. If
no one is in the department, then call nine-one-one."

Giving up on being discreet, I stepped into the middle
of the living room and pointed again, drawing an imagi-
nary line from one part of the house to the other. "The
scanning beam is here." It was about eight feet from Alex,
who reacted by grabbing up his precious electronic equipment while dialing the woo-woo department of NOPD,
direct. He got through on one of his backup systems to
someone in the woo-woo room, the department that handled paranormal cases.

"Talk fast," I advised him. "I suggest we withdraw to
the backyard." Which might actually work, if the witches
didn't think about scanning the grounds too. For now, they
halted again, scanning the weapons room under the stairs.
That gave us a few precious seconds.

Alex explained our situation succinctly to someone at
cop central while rushing onto the back porch with an
armful of his toys. He made three trips, the last one with
an umbrella he found in the butler's pantry/coffee bar/tea
nook. Eli and I backed slowly away and out onto the side
porch and the night mist.

Even with the noise of voices and the vibration of feet,
the scan didn't change in any way. There was no speeding
up or slowing down, no brightening or dimming or color

change, no more smell of hair burning, just iron and salt on the air, which were unusual enough as witchy scents went. All that stealth had been unnecessary.

And it told me something about the witches. Either they didn't care that I knew they were scanning my house or they didn't know that I could tell they were. I was betting on the latter. Which would then mean that they didn't know I was a skinwalker. Which meant they had been surprised at the magical feel of my body, hence the pain they might not have expected me to feel, and the magical ward in my closet. Which was way too much guesswork. But the weapons room didn't hold their interest for long. The line of light started progressing after a little over a minute.

I was still barefoot, but in the retreat, Eli found a pair of my flops. They were purple with pink plastic flowers on them and were studded with sparkles and glitter. The thongs were a gift from Deon, Katie's three-star chef and up-and-coming IT guy, as a way of thanking me for suggesting him for the job. One did not throw away a gift. Even something as ugly as the thongs with bling. I have tiny feet for a six-foot-tall woman, and the flops were way too small for Eli, his heels sticking out behind. The flowers hanging over this toes bounced with each step. I couldn't help it. A soft titter started in the back of my throat.

"Don't," Eli warned.

My laughter spluttered out in a single syllable that was half snort, half interrogative laugh. I caught it before it was more and turned both lips in, biting them to stop the giggles. I took a breath to maintain some form of dignity and managed, "Very stylish. They go so well with the vamp-killer and the nine-mil. You're so . . . pretty," I sang out. And then I dissolved in giggles, the song from *West Side Story* banging around in my head, though I knew well enough not to sing more. "Sorry," I squeaked. Catching my breath, I said, "I'll go around back and take the witch over there." I pointed downtown. "You get the one that way." I pointed uptown.

"This is not over."

"Oh. God. I hope not. I want pictures," I said. I turned on one bare foot and raced around the house. In the distance, I heard two sirens; NOPD's finest were heading toward us from the general direction of the Eighth District Precinct House.

Knowing that my hilarity had something to do with an unsupported sense of relief that nothing had exploded or caught on fire—yet—I raced to the brick wall on the far side of the yard and leaped. Beast's power flooded my limbs and she pushed off with me, adding two feet to my jump. I was glad I was no longer hiding my skinwalker abilities, because this would have been hard for a human, even one as fit and pretty as Eli, in his purple flops. The wall had small outthrust brick ends in irregular spots, making it easier to climb than a sheer face, but the brick was wet from the mist. The rain seemed to be growing stronger. In midair, I crashed into the wall and caught a brick with my fingertips, one toe on a tiny toehold. I slipped, the brick rough on my skin. Using the waning momentum, I shoved off again, catching the top of the fence. I levered myself over and dropped down to the other side.

It was what passed for fall in New Orleans, but the air was still warm and muggy, the ground damp and squishy. Only my nose kept me from stepping into dog poo. Fortunately the neighbor's ugly, hairy yapper dog wasn't out this time of night. It didn't like the way I smelled, and kicking a lapdog was bad form and downright mean, no matter how much Beast wanted to play bowling ball with it.

I hadn't been through the neighbor's yard in ages, and I slunk around under the dripping banana tree leaves until I was at the front of their house and could see the witches. The rain increased to misty drizzle and ran down my neck and under my T-shirt, and it further obscured the witches. The larger woman with her red magics was only the width of the street away, standing in a tiny patch of grass and dead flowers, less than twenty feet from me. I peeked around the wall and saw the pale green lights of the magical working flicker in the front windows of my house. The squad cars turned onto my street and moved in, blue lights flashing, sirens wailing.

Both witches looked up. I had to move.

The green and red energies of their working snapped and brightened in a blast of force. The flash of witch energies left my eyes burned and blinking as the working snapped to a close. The woman nearest bent as if to pick up something at her feet and the smaller girl slammed into her, moving fast. The rain pelted down; the girl slid. They both almost went down, stumbling from the patch of grass into the road. The rain bent around the obfuscation spells they were hiding under, making them visible as human-shaped shadows for a moment, but the splattering rain kept me from getting a clear look.

The girl screamed, "Go, go, go, go, go, go!"

The larger woman caught her balance and followed the girl, both of them running. The drivers of the NOPD units could see the shadows of them inside the rain-drenched spells, and seemed to assume that a running person was a guilty person. The cars sped after them, toward an alley between two houses, down the street from me, sirens wailing. Lights were coming on in the houses up and down the street. I could see heads peeking through windows.

Inside me, a voice repeated, *FUBAR, FUBAR, FUBAR*, and it wasn't Beast. It was me, starting to panic. Humans in danger, everywhere, all around me, if the witches intended to release some form of magical working. And to stop the witches, I might have to kill them.

As the cars raced down the street, a speaker blared, "Stop! Police. Stop, and put your hands in the air."

But the witches turned as one and the girl reached into her shirt pocket. Time slowed for me, that battle-time change that made it seem as if I could see everything and everyone, almost—but not quite—standing outside of time. Me, moving through it, faster than normal. As if I had all the time in the world, but that was a lie. I raised my gun but forced my muscles to wait. To fire at a witch was a cop call, not mine.

The NOPD units both rocked to a halt, tires screeching. One cop opened his car door, weapon leading through the crack of the unit's A pillar and the door itself. "Stop!" he shouted. "Put down your weapons. Show me your hands!"

He was young, and his voice went high and breathless. Over the noise, I heard the other officer calling for backup. I was right. We were about to get FUBARed.

Still in a stutter-slow motion, the girl pulled something out of her shirt. She screamed a *wyrd*. Or part of it. The older woman grabbed her and shook her, the girl's head snapping back and forth, the wyrd only half spoken—the powerful spell, contained in a single word, ended before it began. The turbaned older woman snapped her fingers and red sparks of power flashed out, visible to the human eye. The cops ducked.

The girl screamed, "No!"

The older woman wrapped her arms around the skinny one in a mighty hug. Threw out the fingers of one hand.

A blast of white smoke burst from her fingers and . . . the witches disappeared.

Just like that. In a vanishing act worthy of Las Vegas.

I shook my head.

Nothing made sense. And I hadn't gotten a good look at them. Dang it.

CHAPTER 2

The Nose Doesn't Lie

The cop in the car rushed out and over to the spot of the vanishing act, his gun in a two-hand grip at his side. He turned and saw me in the shadows, a weapon in each hand, and his service weapon tracked to me. I raised both hands and shouted, "I'm putting the weapons on the ground."

"Down!" he yelled back, his weapon now centered on me. "Get on the ground. Get down!"

I bent and placed the weapons at my feet. Stepped back, both hands returning high in the air. I put both behind my head and laced my fingers, kneeling, then lying flat on the wet concrete, spread-eagled, my cheek on the wet sidewalk. The rain beat down on me. The cop sped over and dropped a knee into the small of my back. I grunted. That was gonna leave a bruise. He dragged my arms down and behind me and cuffed me while I struggled to breathe.

Eli called from the shadows, "That's Jane Yellowrock, y'all." The other cop whirled, his weapon trained on the sound of my partner's voice. "I'm unarmed and alone," Eli continued. "Coming out of the shadows hands raised.

Don't shoot. Sloan Rosen is putting a call through to you on your cells about us."

Eli, still bare-chested, hands in the air, moved slowly out of the dark. He was barefoot again. *Coward.* I heard a cell vibrate, but the cop ignored the call. A moment later, he ignored his radio. So much for calling the woo-woo department for backup.

"Who are you? ID. What are you doing out here? Who were the women?" The cops talked over each other, the smell of anger and a thin thread of fear in their sweat, though both were as soaked as we were, the rain washing away scents and the tingle of magic.

Eli didn't answer, just knelt near me and let the cops cuff him too. And then, because we had no ID and chose not to talk, we were shoved into separate units and driven to NOPD Eighth District on Royal Street. Our attorney was waiting for us there, which had to be Alex, doing his intel thing. I hoped he wasn't still outside under an umbrella.

Brandon Robere was a lawyer, a graduate of Tulane Law, LLM, back in 1946, although he still looked like a man in his mid-thirties, a very self-assured man, currently oozing charisma, a confidence that was almost aggressive, and the kind of sensual magnetism that promised imaginative sexual escapades and the ability to handle anything or anyone. An alpha male at his finest.

The Onorio was lean, narrow-waisted, broad-shouldered, and former military, and was distinguishable from his identical twin by the small mole at his temple. It was the middle of the night, prime time for vamp business, and Brandon was dressed in a charcoal suit and tie, with lace-up Italian leather shoes that probably cost more than any pair in my closet. Brandon strode across the open space to us, and I watched as every female eye and most of the male eyes followed his passage.

Onorios were rare among vampire hierarchy, far above blood-slaves and blood-servants. They outranked secundos and primos. The couldn't be blood-bound. They couldn't be compelled. They needed vampire blood only occasionally. They lived for centuries. They had a magic that hadn't been explained to me yet, but was clearly charismatic and compulsive. And maybe sexual. And probably a lot of other things. The fact that Leo Pellissier—the Master of the City of New Orleans and most of the Southeast U.S., and my boss—had three Onorios in his organization gave him power among the world's vamps that I had yet to figure out.

From the front of the building, more help came. Moving with purpose in an unswerving line that took him direct to me was my sweetie pie. Not that I would ever call George Dumas, "Bruiser," that. Not in a million years. We were still figuring out what kind of relationship we had, and *sweetie pie* did not begin to describe the man. Like Brandon, Bruiser was Onorio, another of New Orleans's three. And he exuded power the way a billionaire politician did, wearing a suit and tie and his professional smile, his brown eyes finding me instantly.

Everyone in New Orleans recognized the former primo of the Master of the City, and the tension in the building changed and tightened, scenting of the kind of adrenaline that was hyperattentive and uneasy. Suddenly, for the cops, something wasn't going according to protocol and the big room fell almost silent.

George Dumas took the words *self-assured* to new depths. I felt my face warm at the sight at him. His mouth fought a grin as he took me in, in my wet PJs, barefoot, dirty from being on the sidewalk, scuffed from being picked up from said sidewalk by my bound arms, and not wearing a bra. My hair had come loose from its braid at some point and hung, kinked from the wet, down the middle of my back and over my face. I stood as straight as I could at the sight of my rescuers, and lifted my head. It's hard to look badass in your jammies, with your arms bound behind you, but I'd give it a go.

No one tried to stop him as Bruiser reached our small grouping and leaned in toward me. He pushed back my hair, exposing my cheek. It had been ground into the concrete when I was cuffed. The abrasion stung, but I'd had lots worse.

Unfortunately Bruiser was old school, the kind of gentleman born and bred in England over a century ago, and he didn't like seeing me abused. It set off his manly protective instincts and I smelled his anger. Which was just so cute.

Before Bruiser could say anything embarrassing, Brandon addressed me loudly, saying, "Enforcer." The single word had two effects. It brought Bruiser back to himself and his position, and reminded him that I had a rep to uphold. It also alerted everyone within hearing whom they had in custody. Bruiser's hand fell away, and he buried whatever he was feeling beneath the professional élan he wore so well.

The cop who had brought me in mouthed the word *Enforcer*, suddenly realizing that he had possibly miscalculated.

Brandon glanced at Eli and said, "Mr. Younger."

Eli nodded, his gaze hooded, his body far too still for my liking. This was the way he stood when he was getting ready to put a hurting on someone who had been overly rough with him. And I smelled blood. His. The cop transporting him had hurt him. I frowned, looking for the injury, seeing nothing, but the nose doesn't lie. Eli was hurt.

Brandon said, "Are you injured, Mr. Younger?" Onorios had excellent noses too, far better than humans.

"Nothing a Band-Aid won't fix."

"And did this injury take place after you were in custody?"

Eli nodded once. Very slightly. Eli was ticked off.

Brandon asked me, "Have they charged you with something? Read you your rights?"

"No, on the charges. Yes, on the rights."

He looked to Eli, who acknowledged my statements with another slight nod.

"Did you identify yourselves to the arresting officers?"

"Eli told them my name."

"I see. And they didn't allow that name to temper their actions. Interesting. Enforcer, could you remove the cuffs, if you so wanted?"

Now I knew where we were going with this. I was supposed to be the reasonable one. Bad casting, but, again, I could go with this. I nodded once. "Yes, but they'd be in pieces."

"And yet, although you could have stopped them at any time, you allowed yourself to be taken in."

I shook my hair back from my face. "All in the name of good relations with the local police. They had weapons drawn. They had just been in the presence of a witch working, and as humans, they were—" *Not scared. Not about to pee their pants. Right.* "—unnerved. I didn't want anyone to start shooting, which might have injured any possible bystanders, tourists, or people looking out their bedroom windows at the scuffle. I figured things would be worked out easily later, when the officers heard the whole story. And then they'd apologize to us for being a tad too rough." I let a small smile find my mouth. "But then someone called you guys, and I never got a chance." The Kid was getting smarter by the day.

Brandon turned on one heel and lifted his chin, saying to the cops who had brought us in, "Commander Walker will be contacting you momentarily, alerted to the situation by Sloan Rosen—who you chose to ignore—and the office of the vampire Master of the City. It is my sincere hope that when the commander does communicate with you, the Enforcer to the Master of the City and her partner, Eli Younger, are no longer in restraints."

The cuffs came off so fast the cop nearly dropped the pair on me. "I didn't know who you were, Miz Yellowrock," the officer said.

I rubbed my wrists and pushed back my hair, glancing a warning to Bruiser to show I was fine and would handle this myself. "Not a problem, Officer . . . " I glanced at his name badge. ". . . Cormier. It was night, raining, bad lighting. You took care of a potential problem. And I'll heal. Kudos to the local police.

"Do you need me to give a statement? If so, I'm happy to oblige, but if you don't mind, I'd like to go home and change clothes. Get my partner his *bandage*." I put a tiny emphasis on the word. "And come back. Would an hour work?"

"Miss Yellowrock and Mr. Younger may come back at their convenience," a voice stated from the back. Commander Walker strode into the room, a frown so firmly etched on his dark-skinned face that it looked as if iron had been melted, poured into a mold, and hardened there. "We're sorry for the trouble, Miss Yellowrock. My men and I appreciate your willingness to offer a statement. We'll all be waiting here when you get back. And an hour would be most helpful." He looked at his men and said, "Make sure they have their possessions. *Now* would be a good time."

My gun and the vamp-killer appeared on the desk nearest, still damp from the rain. Commander Walker's eyes went up at the sight of the blade, but he didn't say anything. Instead he reached out and shook my hand, then Bruiser's, Brandon's, and last Eli's. To my partner, he said, "I appreciate your service, soldier, even it was with the piss-ass army and not the air force."

"Never liked flying, sir," Eli said, relaxing in the presence of a military man who had clearly done his research into our backgrounds. "Much prefer jumping out of planes than flying them. We'll be back ASAP."

And just that easily, we were outside in a limo, where Bruiser offered us towels, unopened packages of men's T-shirts, and anything we wanted from the limo's liquor cabinet. I took the first two and pulled the tee over my wet shirt. Eli accepted all three, the last being a glass of single-malt scotch, forty-year-old Laphroaig, which I figured was expensive, both by the delight with which Eli sipped it and the amusement with which Bruiser watched.

"Tell me what happened?" he asked, handing me a beer, a Guinness, which brought a smile to my face. Once upon a time, beer had little effect on me, but things had changed somewhat since I was hit by lightning and nearly died. Now my appreciation had increased and so had my reaction to it. A tiny buzz had begun to stalk me from time to time, mostly when I was tired or stressed, and tonight was no exception.

I sipped and explained, walking Bruiser—my . . . whatever he was to me—through the last hour. At one point he took my left hand and sniffed my palm, which I thought was odd. I sniffed it too, but with the rain and fighting, there was nothing detectable, and I have a better than human sense of smell even in human form. I wrinkled my brow when I was done, thinking. "There seems like there's something else, but whatever I'm forgetting, I lost it waking up."

Bruiser released my hand. "And you never saw their faces?" he asked.

"Nope. Not once." I drained the beer and smacked my lips. "But I have a very important question. I want to know how you got the limo on such short notice."

Bruiser smiled, his eyes on my mouth, which made my own eyes fall to his. An unsettled warmth blossomed in my middle. "I was with Leo and Del," he said, "when the primo received a call from Alex Younger. Leo insisted I take the limo. He also insists on a report from you once things are settled with the police. In person."

I sighed and passed him the empty, accepting another from him when the driver pulled up to the house. "You're coming in?" I asked hopefully.

"Yes," he said, opening the door for me. "I'll walk the house and grounds and along where the attack took place, in case I can pick up some traces of magic. And then I'll take you back to the Eighth."

I slanted a look at my partner. "You going out into the rain after your weapons and your pretty flip-flops?" I tilted my gaze to Bruiser. "You should see the flops. Purple with pink flowers and bling. Eli looked so pretty in them."

Eli gave me a long-suffering sigh and stepped out, disappearing into the rain.

"Thongs?" Bruiser asked me.

"Yep. Deon made them for me. Eli was wearing them when the cops came up."

"Oh. Dear God."

Bruiser walked the house, starting in the living room with Alex, while I showered and dressed and put on some lipstick. Since I had looked so bedraggled before, I went for classic style and dance shoes, in all black. Black undies, black sheath on my thigh with a short-bladed vamp-killer, black shirt, black jacket, and black dress slacks with false pockets where I could get to my blades. Some of the new stakes went into my bun, the ones with the stylized feather and the initials *YS* burned into the handle. According to Alex, we were getting famous within a subculture of vamp fans, and owning an authentic vampire-hunting stake from us was becoming the height of fashion among them. So the Kid had designed one, had had them made, and posted them on yellowrocksecurities.com for sale. People were buying them, which was just strange.

I stuck four stakes in my hair and let them fan out like decorative hair thingies that geishas might have worn. As I dressed, I replayed the last hours in my mind, the witches, the magics, the smells, the rain . . . There was something in all the events that tied them together. Something familiar that I was missing. I needed to figure out who the witches were, what they wanted, and . . .

And I didn't have time for all this. The Witch Conclave was this coming weekend, and as Leo's Enforcer, I had vamp security measures to attend to. Yellowrock Securities was responsible for other security measures—the ones at the conclave site itself, the Elms Mansion and Gardens. Unless the conclave was what the attacking witches were trying to prevent or disrupt, they understood that taking me out would put a hitch in the security for the event. Or maybe they thought that the Everhart-Truebloods were at the house. My friends weren't arriving until later, and once they got here, the house would be warded.

So maybe the witches were getting the lay of the land, so to speak, for a future attack against the Truebloods. There was a known faction of witches who wanted the Witch Conclave to go away, so maybe that was it. Though so far, the small groups of dissatisfied witches hadn't caused any problems except heavy rhetoric in the news media and on social media—and among hate groups, of course.

I heard the shower come on upstairs, Eli's usual minute and a half of luxury. I stepped into dancing shoes and buckled the straps, ready for the cops. Moments later, we were bundled back into the limo and comparing stories. Not that we needed to make up anything or had anything to hide, but it was wise to make sure we both had seen the same things. It kept questions and suspicion to a minimum.

While we talked, Bruiser stared out the windows, not adding to the conversation. It didn't take a genius to realize he had discovered something in my house. Or on the grounds. Or on the street. When we pulled up to the Eighth, I said, "Are you going to tell us what you found?"

"Yes," he said, sounding somber and distant. "After. I'll be waiting out here. Brandon is inside. He'll take care of you."

I wanted to argue, but it was late—or early, rather—and if Bruiser was withholding info, he had reasons that might have something to do with deniability. I opened the limo door and went back into cop Eighth.

It took remarkably little time to straighten everything out in the Eighth. Eli and I were both very agreeable to share everything that had happened and that we had done, which helped. Having a high-powered lawyer there to assist didn't hurt, but the real reason it went so easy was the presence of a sleepy, irritated commander, who was still on the premises. We made nice-nice with the local po-po and were out in less than an hour. Back in the limo, which had parked around the corner, Bruiser said, "Debrief, if you please." He still had that distant, worried look on his face.

We pulled away from the curb as Eli and I filled him in, and he studied the still shots of the witches Alex had sent to our cells—and which we had offered the cops. Bruiser shook his head. "There isn't enough for me to ID them. The ward magics are too intense. Perhaps Lachish Dutillet or Jodi Richoux might be able to recognize them through the wards, though I doubt it."

Lachish was the New Orleans coven leader. Jodi ran the woo-woo department, with Sloan Rosen as her second.

"I'll get Alex to send them," I said. "And to the Everhart-Trueblood clan. Heck, I'd post them on the Web site if I thought it would help stop whatever they're up to.

"So," I said, taking charge of the subject. "Your turn. Why are you so wonky?"

Bruiser smiled, his eyes regaining some of the warmth they had lost. He was opening a bottle of champagne, his hands working as if from muscle memory, his eyes on me. "Wonky?"

"Distant, dismal, dreary, detached, drab . . . worried, apprehensive, and anxious."

"Ran out of words starting with *D*?" he asked. He poured me a glass and handed it over. I had to wonder if he was trying to get me drunk. And then lots of lovely reasons why he might want to do that leaped into my brain and I went breathless. I smiled at him, waiting. Bruiser smiled back, as if he could read my mind, his expression warm. Heated even.

"Get a room," Eli said, sounding snarly. Or jealous of our lovey-dovey stuff. He hadn't seen his honey bunch in a week.

Bruiser poured Eli a glass, passed it to him, and poured a glass for himself. The glasses were real crystal and rang when we followed his example by lifting our glasses and clinking them, then sipping. I didn't make a face. It wasn't horrible but it wasn't beer. As Bruiser might do, I lifted my eyebrows in question.

Ignoring my inquiry, Bruiser closed his eyes in appreciation of the champagne. When he opened them he said, "It's possible that the scan of your house was more than simply a scan. It was likely an initial attack of some sort, possibly for a future goal or need. And despite the witches being gone, this may not be over." He looked at me, his brown eyes hard.

I took another sip of the champagne, waiting, knowing I wasn't going to like this.

He said, "I told you I intended to do a search of the house and grounds while you changed clothes. I found no traces of magic anywhere inside or on your grounds. But in the alley where you were taken and where the two witches disappeared, I found this." Bruiser reached over and opened the liquor cabinet. From it, he removed a foil-wrapped object, about four inches by three, and about half an inch thick. He placed it on his suit-pants-clad knee and carefully removed the foil, folding back the layers that were wrapped around and around. As he worked, I drew on Beast-sight and the thick flash of magics were instantly visible. The energies were a bright glow, light green, the exact shade of the scan that had gone over my house.

When the foil was unfolded, the pale green energies glowed with power, so bright I had to close my eyes against the brilliance. With my eyes slitted against the glare, I studied Bruiser's find. It was a brooch, the focal stone a large green jewel carved into a scarab. There were peacocks to either side of the scarab, the birds facing away from the green, beetle-carved, central gem. Jeweled tails swept up and out from the birds and over the scarab, their jeweled peacock tails spreading above it.

"Are they the same color energies used by the women in the working?" he asked.

"Yeah," I said. "Where did you find it?"

"In the alley. From what you said, it was possible that they dropped it when they fled, possibly why the younger woman screamed, unable to retrieve it or keep it from being captured by the police. The older woman may have stopped her from going after. Or . . ." He turned the brooch in his hands, the long fingers brushing the edges as if reading the magic. "Or it could be bait leading to a trap."

"Why leading to a trap?" Eli asked. The limo made a left turn and the green energies wafted off to the side in a slow trail of light that even Eli could see. "The energies point west," he said, understanding.

My internal compass was pretty good, but Eli's was better. He said he had iron filings in his nose so he always knew which way was north. I hadn't laughed. He might have been serious.

"That's why it might be a trap," Eli added. "And that would make the scanning of the house all smoke and mirrors."

"More," Bruiser said. "It has a scent."

I leaned in and sniffed it. "No, it doesn't. Except for magic."

His eyes on me, Bruiser said, "You can't smell it. Because it's your scent."

Eli's eyes narrowed. I went still for the space of several heartbeats. I unfolded my left hand from the stem of the champagne glass and looked at the palm, thinking back. "I was asleep and maybe dreaming about Angie. There was this prickly sensation crawling over my left fingertips, up my fingers. It snuggled into my palm like Angie's fist. I remember being happy. Smiling in my sleep.

"Then it burst up my hand and arm and into me." I looked between my business partner and Bruiser and set the champagne glass down. "It felt like a magical bomb going off." The remembered sensation rushed through me again. "I remember thinking it was something like . . . like burning cactus, the thorns on fire, the blooms like some kind of weapon blossoming open through me. For what was probably only a few seconds I felt scorching thorns ripping through me like heat-seeking missiles. Which had been way too poetic for me."

"The actual wording of a spell, perhaps?" Bruiser murmured. "Or something tied to the brooch itself?" Studying the jeweled pin in his hand, holding it by the edges as if to preserve fingerprints, Bruiser rotated it, tilting it one way and another. Then hefted it up and down slightly, as if weighing it. He said, "There is a distinct pulling sensation to the west as well. When I move it, I can feel a directional tug on my fingers. If it isn't a trap, it could be a homing beacon. Or a tracking beacon."

Eli shrugged. So did I.

"So we're back them dropping it on purpose," Bruiser said. "To lure you somewhere?"

"It didn't smell or feel like that," I said. My palms itched and I scratched first one, then the other.

"Body language suggested the younger woman was violently angry just before they disappeared," Eli said.

"You have to report to Leo, so . . . we can let him examine it while we're there," Bruiser said. His eyes were still serious, his body held tightly, as if ready for a fight. Worried about how I would react to what he said. I scanned outside and placed the limo. We were turning onto the street at the front entrance of vamp HQ, the Mithran Council Chambers. At least I was dressed for it.

"Leo wants to collect every magical thingy he can get his taloned hands on," Eli said. "I vote no."

"It isn't ours," I said. "We know witches dropped it, and under current operating protocols set in place for the upcoming conclave, that means the Witch Council has legal claim to it. And while I'm not happy about whatever it was doing in my house, I won't let Leo confiscate just it on general principle. There needs to be a good reason for me to let him steal something." Which was as tangled a set of mores as I'd ever heard come out of my mouth.

"If you keep the brooch, and if you, in your official capacity, request me to do so, I can track the spell. You don't need an order from Leo," Bruiser said.

That statement was full of "ifs," which meant it was full of political implications for the vamps and for me. I sucked at politics, though I was trying to learn. But the statement also showed just how much Bruiser had changed and grown. There was a time when he had been so attached to the MOC that nothing came before his master. Now I came before Leo. That gave me a case of the warm fuzzies all over. "I'd appreciate that," I said. "We can always read Leo in later if needed."

"Make it so, number one," Eli muttered. I kicked him in the shin and he laughed.

Bruiser gave me an elegant nod and said, "I'll let you off and have the limo take me home to pack a few things. Provided I can find a means to photograph it, I'll send a picture of the brooch to Alex and to Leo. And I'll be in touch. You go be Enforcer."

The job that used to be his. Bruiser folded the foil around the brooch and put it in his pocket. That was when I realized he had wrapped it in lead foil to enclose the energies. When did Bruiser start keeping lead foil handy, the kind one used to cart around magical devices?

*   *   *

We pulled up to the solid iron gate at vamp HQ, more properly known as the Mithran Council Chambers, and the driver spoke, then pulled in a bit more. Eli's window rolled down in front of the security camera. I leaned in so they could see my face too, and Eli said, "Eli Younger of Yellowrock Securities and the Enforcer reporting as requested."

I sat back in my seat and considered all the new things I learned on a daily basis from my partners. For instance, Eli had called me the Enforcer. Not Jane Yellowrock. He surely had a reason for that choice. The iron gate began to roll back and Eli said to me, "Spin is everything," as if he could read my mind. "Propaganda can do wonders both before and after a battle."

"This is not going to be a battle."

Eli snorted with derision. It sounded remarkably like one of mine.

Bruiser said, "With any Master of the City, undead life itself is a battle." It had to be even more so when the Master of the City was also the overall Master of the greater Southeast U.S.A. With the exception of Florida, Leo Pellissier had the Southeast under his control and dominion, had the loyalty and gratitude of Sedona, Seattle, and a few other city masters, and was arguably the most powerful vamp in the United States.

There were two other vehicles in the circular turnaround in front of HQ, both armored vamp-mobiles. Katie and Grégoire—Leo's heir and second-in-line heir, both of whom were his dinners and his lovers (vamp feeding and sexual habits almost always combined the two), were here and were parked in front, which was strange. Eli said, again without my asking, "The back entrance is closed for security upgrades. We're still installing the new traffic spike system under the porte cochere."

"Still?"

"Problem with the timer. It'll be finished by tomorrow, EOB." EOB was end of business. Meaning by five or six o'clock p.m. Eli got out of the limo without the driver's help and shut the door. He stood with his back to us, ostentatiously studying the grounds, giving me a moment alone with Bruiser. Who gripped my upper arm and pulled me across the seat, my bottom sliding across the leather with ease.

"I've missed you," he whispered into my ear as the privacy partition rose silently between us and the driver. Bruiser's arms went around me and my head went back. The heat of an Onorio's body warmed my skin. The scent that had always meant Bruiser, combined with the new notes that said *Bruiser the Onorio*, filled my senses. His mouth opened and his teeth grazed the tendons and muscles that connected shoulder to head.

Inside me, Beast quivered with interest. Big-cats' mating rituals included the female being bitten just there, or behind the ear, and held still while the mating took place. It was a pseudosubmission that Beast would never allow unless she wanted the biter as mate.

Along with her interest was my own reaction that was never very far from me, the memory of being held down while Leo forced a blood meal off me. Bruiser was trying to help me through it, past it, and he was doing a great job, as the minuscule gush of fear had already morphed into something hotter and more demanding. I slid a leg up over his and he lifted me onto his lap, straddling him.

His cheek and nose skimmed my neck and up to my ear. "Do you remember the first time we went to a party in this limousine?" he asked.

Ohhh. Yeeeah . . . Us on the floor, one of his hands down my top and the other up my skirt. If I hadn't been wearing a weapon strapped to my thigh, we might have gotten more than just frisky that night. The weapon had sorta stopped that. I hadn't been supposed to carry a weapon into the party of vamps and their humans. "Mmmm," I hummed in response.

"Are you wearing a weapon tonight?"

"Um-hum." My mouth found his and I sucked his tongue into my mouth, pulling him close, until his need was pressed hard into the center of me. I shoved my feet around his backside and locked my ankles, nearly knocking us to the

floor. Again. Bruiser braced his legs on the seat across from
us, grabbed the back of my head with one arm around me.

"If I never told you," he growled, grinding us together,
"I hate pants on you." He kissed me so hard our teeth
clacked together, and my lips swelled with the pressure. His
heated scent filled my nose. I pulled him to me with one
hand and slid the other into his dress shirt, sending a button
flying, ricocheting inside the limo. Beast growled. The sound
came out of my throat in a vibration that demanded.

And Eli knocked on the glass.

Bruiser cursed foully, promising a terrible death and dis-
memberment to my partner. I laughed against his mouth,
my breath fast huffs of interrupted need.

The knock came again, along with a fainter click. Over
the loudspeaker the driver said, "Forgive me for intruding,
sir, but Mr. Younger has informed me that the Master of the
City is awaiting Miz Yellowrock. With some impatience." I
heard that distant click again as the driver returned us to
audio privacy. I could have sworn he was laughing.

"We," Bruiser gasped, "will pick this up the moment I
return from searching out the magical imperative of the
brooch. And I don't care if I have to drag you out of a business meeting with the Witch Council, the Mithran Council, and the governor. We will finish this." Bruiser's heart
was thumping madly against my chest. It had been a while
for us. I eased away from him, unlocking my heels and
sliding to the seat beside him. He held my eyes for a
moment, the look promising much more than any words
could, his eyebrow quirking up. Just the one. I felt my belly
do a slow roll. "You ruined my shirt," he accused much
more mildly.

"Just one button."

"Do you intend to sew the button back on?"

"Nope. I intend to destroy another one as soon as
possible."

Bruiser barked with laughter, smoothing my hair back
again. He rearranged the stakes he had misplaced in my bun.
Kissed me again, much more softly and gently. "He will
smell me on you." He was speaking of Leo, who had once
upon a time claimed me for himself, until it was explained to

the master suckhead that I was neither territory nor a slave. He had claimed Bruiser too, but that was before becoming Onorio had freed him from the chief fanghead.

"Good," I said. "Old guys sometimes need reminders about who belongs to who. Whom. Whatever."

Bruiser stilled, his brown eyes holding me. "And do we belong to each other?"

I wasn't sure what I was supposed to say to that. We were exclusive. But the relationship hadn't gotten to the three-word-phrase, four-letter-word state yet. *I love you.* Which thought totally terrified me. I looked down, straightening my clothes. "We're still finding out." With that cryptic statement, I grabbed my lipstick that had fallen out of my one good pocket and opened the limo door.

Bruiser said, "Don't forget date night tomorrow night. You and me at the Rock N Bowl. And my place afterward to address the button problem."

I closed the door and escaped.

CHAPTER 3

You Will *Not* Blow It Up

Outside, Eli wore an expression even more obscure that usual. I expected him to tease me or say something, but he simply looked me over and handed me a tissue. "Wipe your mouth and put on new lipstick. You're smeared."

"Spoilsport," I accused. "You enjoyed that."

He chuckled evilly. Leaving me behind, he climbed the steps with the measured tread of a man with things on his mind. I wiped my mouth and chin and applied lipstick, following my partner up to the entrance of vamp HQ. This was why Eli and I were such a perfect team, the ability to anticipate each other's moves, needs, thoughts, plans. It was especially effective in battle, and against vamps, battle was always likely.

"Where do we stand on the ability to prevent a shooter across the street?" I asked, looking over my shoulder at the windows there and surreptitiously watching the limo pull out of the drive and down the street. All the upper windows in the two-story building were closed, thankfully. I had been shot at recently from that vantage point, and the local law hadn't caught him. Or her.

Eli said, "Leo's lawyers are still in negotiations with the owner and the property management company, but the offer Leo made was too good for them to pass up. They'll take it. And if they don't, we'll manage something."

"You will *not* blow it up."

"Now who's the spoilsport?" He flashed me a slice of a grin before we stepped into the glass cage at the front door.

The front entrance system of the Mithran Council chambers was simple on the surface. Visitors stepped through the first "glass" door, which wasn't just glass. It was triple-paned polycarbonate bullet-resistant glass, strong enough to stop most ammunition up to a small rocket. The doors locked behind the visitors, securing them in the see-through cage, also composed of polycarbonate bullet-resistant glass and steel supports. Then, when the security person watching the entrance on camera was satisfied that the visitors were welcome, the inner doors, ditto on the polycarbonate, opened. If the person watching wasn't satisfied, the visitor would be asked to remove all weapons, empty all pockets, lift shirts, and remove shoes. Airport security measures had been incorporated too, with metal detectors built into the outer walls. As we stood inside the cage, Eli and I had now been scanned and inside HQ a quiet alarm had gone off. We didn't have to do the partial strip show, however, since we were part of the team.

Operation Cowbird was still in place, meaning that we were not just worried about attackers from outside, but were still apprehensive about bad guys already inside HQ, especially since two of the baddest of the bad were chained up in the basements, one troublemaker in sub-five and one a bit higher in a private scion lair. Neither vamp was physically capable of escaping. Neither was even coherent. Heck. Neither of them might have healed brains yet. But that hadn't stopped vamps in the past and humans had paid with their lives. Unfortunately, unlike the rogue vampires I was famous for hunting, the vamps in the bowels of the building were important bargaining chips—or would be when they healed enough—saved for the European Vampires' visit, and I couldn't behead them, no matter how many humans they had killed.

HQ's inner doors opened and the stink of vamp and blood and human rushed at us: the peculiar herbal scent of mixed vamps was peppery and astringent and reminiscent of a funeral home, with the assorted dying flowers. Humans and their blood were a permanent part of the circulating air system, always hanging in the air from feedings. And sex. Not to forget sex. Many humans, when fed upon, and when given small drops of vamp blood as payment, developed high sexual drives, while also being passive and non-resistant to advances. The perfect and willing blood-servant or blood-slave.

Something else I didn't like.

Wrassler greeted us. "Evening, Legs, Eli."

I nodded to the big guy and moved into position for the pat-down. Wrassler was seriously huge, nicknamed so because he was bigger than any World Wrestling Entertainment superstar. He motioned a woman to pat me down and took Eli himself, walking with a limp, on a prosthetic that had replaced a foot and lower leg lost in a battle here at HQ. I knew that his injury wasn't my fault, but I still felt the responsibility to help him move forward and cope with his new life. Responsibility was a step up from guilt, so, for me, that was good. I was growing. I used to try to carry the weight of the world on my shoulders. Eli and Alex had been working on me, schooling me to be fair to myself. I was trying.

The woman's pat-down was professional and non-handsy and I declared the vamp-killer strapped to my thigh. "And I have wood stakes in my hair," I said.

"No silver?" she asked.

"Nope."

She stepped back and away before I could look at her name tag. She was one of the new blood-servants from Atlanta. We were still integrating the blood-servants and blood-slaves of Atlanta's former Master of the City.

"Leo's in the gym with Gee," Wrassler said. "He's asked you to join him there."

We signed in and walked away, Eli silent in his combat boots, my dancing shoes loud and somewhat clompy. Once behind the wall on the way to the elevator, I asked, "Well?"

"Did not detect a thing."

We stopped and checked our pockets for the miniature tracking devices that were being tested in advance of the next big hootenanny in town, when the European Mithrans came to New Orleans to kill Leo and take over the U.S. That was their plan and saying no to the visit and attack wasn't an option.

It took a while, but Eli finally pulled a tiny device out of a stake sheath. He held it up to the light and it looked like part of child's toy, a red and blue plasticized square. "That was a good plant," he said. "A good location, and I didn't even notice the insert."

I, however, couldn't find one on me at all. We turned and retraced our steps to the front, and on the way, I stopped and picked it up. Eli frowned, a slight downward hitch of his lips, before his face relaxed. He said, "She slipped it into your knife retrieval pocket and it went straight through."

"Yep." Back at the entrance, Wrassler stood to the side, his hands loose and ready, as if to draw a weapon. Losing a limb could make one hyperalert. "Wrassler's insert was excellent," I said. "I'm wearing slacks with false pockets and it went straight through."

The little blonde grimaced. Well, she wasn't little. She stood five-seven, but that was several inches under my six feet, so she was little to me. Her name was Brenda Rezk and she had been number three in security in Atlanta back when. So far, here, she was feeling frustrated and tentative. It was hard to move in an apparent downward direction in anything, but she was better than she was feeling right now, and if she kept up the progress, when she went back to Atlanta, she would end up higher than number three in the clan home of the new Master of the City of Atlanta.

"Where should I put it, then?" Brenda asked Wrassler. "Jane doesn't have anything else on the outside, and I had no reason to feel inside her jacket to the inner pocket when I could do that from the outside."

"You were doing a pat-down," Wrassler said. "You should have squeezed the fabric of her jacket lapels, and dropped it in whichever pocket was empty." Wrassler motioned me against the wall, and I leaned in again, hands high. He patted me down, much less hesitantly than Brenda had, and when I stepped away from the wall, he turned me to face him and ran the jacket front between his hands, first one side and then the other, holding them each out to inspect for weapons holstered beneath each arm. He nodded to me and smoothed the shoulders of my jacket, the way a tailor might, which was intended to center my mind on my shoulders, not my jacket, leaving me that impression. Shoulders. Not jacket. "Thank you, ma'am," he said to me. "I appreciate your kindness in letting me ensure the safety of everyone who enters the council chambers. Do you need a guide to tonight's festivities?"

Festivities. Right. Wrassler was demonstrating the whole thing, which was probably a good idea. "No, thank you. I can find my way."

"Enjoy your stay. And if you need anything, you'll find house phones on each floor near the elevator, and in your rooms."

I leaned around Wrassler, to Brenda and Eli. "Which pocket?"

"I couldn't spot a thing," Brenda said.

"Right," Eli said. He had a fifty percent chance of being right. And he was.

"Good guess," I said.

"Not a guess. Wrassler's got a weak hand from the injury. He'll always use his strong hand to insert the tracker."

"Huh," Wrassler said. "He's right. And we have to assume that the European Vamps have intel on everything inside." He looked at Brenda. "Practice. You're in charge of teaching lefties and righties to be ambidextrous when inserting the trackers. You'll also run the detail handling the searches when the EVs get here."

A fleeting smile crossed Brenda's face, and her shoulders went back slightly. "Thank you, sir."

I dug inside my breast pocket and found the tracker, dropping it in the tracker can. Eli and I made our way down the elevator to the gym. When the doors closed, Eli said, "EVs. Bad influence, babe."

"Yeeeah." I drew out the word. "I heard that." Once upon a time, everyone at HQ had used full names for everything and everyone. Since I got here, it was acronyms, nicknames, and a bit more snark than most vamps were accustomed to. "I'll address it at some point."

Negotiations for the visit were still ongoing, and slower than frozen molasses. I hoped they'd last another six months, because we weren't ready to deal with the amount of magic and bad attitude the EVs would bring. Fortunately, with the EVs, any kind of negotiation took an agonizing amount of time because they didn't accept or use or probably even know about the existence of e-mail, texting, or FaceTime. Their lack of electronic sophistication wasn't something I had known going into this gig. I had expected the Visitation by Evil to take place right away, but when you live centuries, and even millennia, preparations for anything can last a long time. Time itself has no meaning when you are that old. And electronic media was something trashy done by the nouveau riche—or the nouveau fanged—and their blood-servants. For communications, they preferred and insisted upon heavy bond or handmade paper, or maybe papyrus, hand-delivered. It was ridiculous. But unless they thought they could get the upper hand by making a surprise visit, their whole stuck-in-the-past attitude was working to our advantage.

The elevator opened and I stepped out, leading the way to the gym. Eli stopped at the men's locker room and came back out with a sword belted at his waist. "Seriously?" I said. Instead of a reply he drew the sword and shoved open the door to the gym, preceding me inside. "Men . . ." He was taking this whole "being my second" a little too seriously, though it was a position he had been forced to undertake on more than one occasion.

The gym at HQ was big enough for a full-sized basketball court, but it was usually set up for fighting rings. I had damaged one recently, and the antique wood on all three rings had been replaced with a modern practice mat, the kind used in the Olympics for martial arts. They were easily replaceable, in case my claws came out again, forgiving to body slams, and less abrasive than most older-style mats. They had the classic tatami texture and smooth surface, giving better traction, but also had an antiskid, rubberized, waffle backing. The mats also eliminated odors, decreasing the reek of stale vamp and human sweat, looked better than the scarred wood, and were versatile enough for standing arts and grappling arts—meaning sword practice and hand-to-hand. Also, a final plus, blood washed out of them easily.

It was close to dawn, so there should be no vamps in the room, only humans, but I smelled Leo, the chief fanghead, and the city's Mercy Blade, Gee DiMercy. He pronounced the name something like Zjeee, which sounded Frenchy. It was the misericord's job to kill young vamp scions when they didn't cure after the devoveo, the ten years or so of insanity that every human went through when turned. Not all of them made it. Until recently, humans made a bad bet when hoping to be turned, assuming that they would survive to the sane and blood-sucking stage. The odds hadn't been great. However, things change, and Leo's scions were now waking up sane and in control years before other masters' scions did. Another reason the EVs wanted to conquer the American vamps—to gain control of the one vampire who could shorten the devoveo (the time between when humans were turned and when they regained sanity) from an average of ten years to around two. Of all the things the EVs wanted, Amy Lynn Brown might be the most important.

I didn't see Leo at first. He was sitting against the wall on the bleachers with his new personal assistant, Lee. He had taken my advice and freed up his primo for important stuff, taking on the redheaded, perky Lee Williams Watts. Or maybe the last names were reversed. I no longer did the background checks on people and so I missed a lot of minutiae that I didn't need to know, and sometimes the bigger, important stuff that I did need. Watts looked sweet on the surface, but there was something about her that said she was a firecracker when she got mad, and it wasn't just the red hair. She was a tiny little thing, but I'd be moving slowly around her until we were better acquainted. She looked scrappy.

Their heads were together while she took notes the old-fashioned way, on a spiral notebook with a pen in what looked like honest-to-God shorthand, not a skill many had these days. Her eyes looked stormy and tightly focused and she was scribbling furiously. Like an accountant with super-powers.

Eli walked a little ahead of me, to one side. I followed in his wake, passing the fighting rings where Gee was teaching two security types to fight with the sword. At the same time. A sword in each hand, he was keeping them both occupied as they tried to prevent their armor and their bodies, protected beneath, from being cut into nice even ribbons of bleeding flesh. It was like dancing, maybe some violent love child of the flamenco and the tango.

Eli nodded to Leo, a little head tilt granting Leo temporary command status. Very temporary. Eli and Leo both shifted their attention to me and I was about to speak when something changed in the air. Eli shouted, "Jane!"

I threw myself to the floor, twisting my body into a horizontal roll, taking the fall on shoulder and outer foot. Hearing my shoe crack the wood. Smelling Gee DiMercy. Feeling a sword slice the air beside my face. *I'm being attacked.* I rolled behind the metal bleachers. *Attacked by Leo's Mercy Blade.*

Ambush hunter! Beast shouted. Her fury flamed, an adrenaline rush of heat blazing through me and away, out through my hand on the floor. *Gone.* Every hint of her speed and strength flooded out of me in an instant. Which was wrong, so very wrong. It was such a shock that I nearly fell. Beast took over, shoving both hands to the floor, catching my balance, my feet sliding up under me in a move that was pure cat, but . . . still off somehow. As if pained.

And the Mercy Blade was attacking me. *Why?*

I felt as much as saw Eli toss me his sword. My right hand lurched up and snatched the sword out of the air. The hilt slammed into my palm, and my fingers closed over it. Instantly I recognized it. The grip perfect for my hand. *My* sword. Not Eli's.

Instead of forcing a partial change on me, or making time slow and bubble so we could get inside Gee's reach, Beast snarled and drew in tight, deep within, sitting, hunched, shivering. Her inaction divided my attention, for a fraction of a moment.

Clumsy, I parried a cut—rude by vamp standards—and bounded to my feet, sliding left and cutting right, an ungainly backhand cut before finding the circular form of La Destreza, also known as the Spanish Circle form of sword fighting. I spun my sword in a circle around me, backing to the wall to protect my flank. As I adjusted to the shelter offered by brick and mortar, my sword flashed left to right and right to left, steel clanging on steel, ringing bright and sharp on the air, always in an arc, the blade encompassing an oval around my body. But I wasn't wearing fighting leathers and my jacket was too tight across the shoulders for full range of motion.

And weirdly my left palm burned, the one that had been scanned earlier. My empty hand felt as if I were holding a red-hot branding iron.

Inside me, I felt Beast lift her left paw and shake it. She growled in anger. Screamed in fury. Finally Beast's strength and speed touched me, adrenaline pumping into my blood, far too slowly, but damping the weird pain and making me faster than human. Nearly as fast as Gee. But *nearly* wasn't good enough, because Gee wasn't human either.

The Mercy Blade was an Anzu, birdlike beings once worshipped as storm gods. He had centuries of fighting experience and two long swords to my one. They sketched a cage of death around him that made my weapon useless. My body bladed, I slid my hand into my false pocket and pulled the silver-plated, steel-edged vamp-killer, a shorter blade than usual.

Seeing my new weapon, Gee rotated his blades even faster, an inhuman speed of glinting, blurred steel. His swords moved faster and faster, a flashing light all around him, our blades clanging, the scent of excitement from the spectators rising on the vamp and Anzu-scented air. Despite myself, I laughed, a low growl of soft sound. Within me, Beast's four paws were pulled close in beneath her, a snarl on her face, her killing teeth showing. The growl in my laughter was hers.

The Circle was based on rotation, body angle, geometry, and foot placement, and my dancing shoes weren't giving me purchase on the slick floor. The mats were too far to reach. Alive, that is. But then I didn't intend to play fair. Though there were no rules in the Duel Sang—the Blood Challenge of the Mithrans—there was protocol and a long history of expectation. Cheating was my best weapon, but cheating only worked once.

Gee shifted his feet into an advanced move, one sword still whirling, the other a lunge, lunge, lunge as he tried to turn me away from the wall so he could circle me and force me into an open area. *Not gonna happen.* But sword fighting wasn't second nature to me yet, and Gee had probably been born with a sword in his hand. Or hatched that way.

As Gee completed *atajo* and thrust, the most basic move, I swung into the lunge with my short blade as if to begin the move *medio tajo y medio reves*. But I caught one of Gee's swords on the vamp-killer's notch—barely a quarter inch deep—below the Ricasso and above the minuscule cross-guard. I swept the sword away, into the air. Gee started to react, but before he could, I slipped inside his blades. Brought my sword up in a thrust for his neck.

My left palm burned, agony detonating up my arm as I moved. Gee's eyes blazed unusually blue, the color of the cloudless sky in the east, as the sun set in the west. Blue, blue, achingly blue.

I heard the clang of his right blade hitting the floor. In the same moment I felt the piercing burn under my right arm. Up. Inside me. I hissed in a breath that burned like ice and sleet and cutting steel. I caught a whiff of burning hair, acrid and vile.

I grunted and Gee swept his blade out of me, the sharp edge slicing into rib, the pain a frisson of shock.

Beast grunted softly. So did I.

From somewhere far away, I heard Eli say, "Jane?" Worry and shock in the tone. Then a demand, *"Leo!"*

Gee stepped back, sheathed his third sword, the short sword he had hidden in his clothes or with his glamour, and picked up his discarded long sword. His eyes were still blazing that strange, too-bright blue. *Magic,* I thought. The entire room had fallen silent, a shocked, nonbreathing silence, when you hear a pin drop.

Blood ran under my clothes, pooling in my waistband before trickling down and into the crack of my buttocks. Warm. Cooling in the cold air. A lot of blood. I reached again for Beast, knowing I needed to shift, to change into *Puma concolor,* my mountain lion form. I stretched down into the deeps of me. Beast hissed and snarled, chuffing as if at a challenge. Growling in anger. *Dalonige i digadoli,* she thought at me. My Cherokee name. *Come.*

But I couldn't find her. Worse, I couldn't find me. I fumbled deeper. I still couldn't find the twined snake of genetic material, the snake at the heart of all creatures. It had changed recently, but it had always been there, my lifeline, my weapon of last resort. But this time the RNA strands, even twisted and damaged, weren't there.

And I remembered again waking up to the tingle of magic in my fist, burning deep. The odd reek of burning hair. *Oh, crap.* What had happened?

Eli cursed, softly, far, far away.

Gee said, "*Atajo*, then step into *medio proporcional.* The European Mithrans will not allow you a trick. There is not one they have not used."

I dropped to my knees. Raised my left hand. In the center of my palm, an eye appeared. A blue eye, as if it had been tattooed in the palm of my hand. It was staring up at me. I had seen it before, when I first met Gee DiMercy. It was his watching magic. As fast as it appeared, it faded, the blues going green, the color of the witches' green magics, a green eye looking up at me, blinking, seeming to take in something about me, maybe more than I wanted anyone to know. And then it faded further, like an old tattoo, dispersing into my skin or vaporizing into the air.

A line of red soaked from my pants and spread beside my knee. The stink of burning hair faded, to be replaced by the stench of human fear and shame and my blood. *Odd.*

"Jane," Eli said. Toneless. *Combat voice.* I heard the familiar *schnick* of a nine-mil being readied for firing.

"I smell Jane's blood," Leo growled. He was suddenly standing beside Gee and Eli, vamped out. His black eyes on me at his feet.

A drop of blood fell from my waist and landed in the scarlet pool on the floor at my knee. I lifted my eyes to Eli. His face was expressionless, harder than stone. The weapon was in both hands, pointing beyond me. "This is bad," I whispered. Eli shifted his aim, a minuscule change.

Gee initiated a move, the lights glinting on his sword, his feet shifting into an advanced move. *He is trying to kill me.*

Eli fired.

Gee's body snapped, as if he had been hit with the tip of a whip. Leo shouted. And Gee simply fell to the floor beside me. I sat down, my strength draining away, and looked into Gee's face, where he was gasping, trying to find breath. I picked up the single dark blue feather that rocked lightly beside him, the only evidence that his glamours had nearly failed when he was shot. I tucked it into the opening of his shirt.

"You can't heal here, you stupid bird," I said, remembering our first conversation, the one that had told me wasn't from Earth, or not an Earth I had ever known. "You might need that feather." And then I fell over him and the light telescoped down into a tiny pinpoint of brightness that illuminated Eli's boots. They were standing in my blood.

CHAPTER 4

I Always Wanted to Shoot Big Bird

I came to in a darkened room that smelled of vamps, human blood, and my blood. I was cold, so cold I couldn't even shiver, though there was something warm wrapped around me, an electric blanket, I thought, coarse and fuzzy at the same time. Something cool and smooth was against my cheek. Something wet was wiping my side, cleaning the deadened flesh where I must be—or must have been—wounded. The pain that had been with me, even in the darkness of unconsciousness, was mostly gone, leaving a dull ache.

I sighed and my breath came easily, with a sensation that let me know I had been in agony for some time in the very recent past. But the pain was gone and my breath came and went, came and went. But I wasn't ready to face the real world. Sinking inside myself, I reached for Beast.

She was in my soul home, crouched before a crackling fire. The flames were cool, giving off no heat, and the light within them, light that should have illuminated everything around us, was muted, as if hidden in smoke, except there was no smoke, no scent of fire or fresh-cut wood, no charcoal, no scent of anything. Everything was dark, except for the flames themselves and a shadowy Beast, so dark here that I couldn't see the stone walls or the rounded stone roof, far overhead. Beast's eyes were glowing gold, watching me in the darkness. Her golden pelt was dim, as if she sat in shadow, or as if she had taken on the pelt of the black panther, the rare melanistic *Puma concolor*, her pelt darkened beneath the black hair-tips. A tremor ran through her body.

I examined myself, seeing the leggings, long tunic shirt, and the plain, undecorated moccasins that I had begun to wear here, ever since I accepted that I was War Woman. I bent toward the flame. The medicine bag hanging on the leather thong about my neck swung forward, into the meager light. The green-dyed leather caught the light and faded into darkness, caught the light and faded into darkness as it swung, in time to my breathing, slow and easy. The leather bag filled with herbs had no scent, no herbal aroma, no wild tobacco, nothing. I had a bad feeling about . . . everything.

Jane is foolish kit.

So you tell me.

Jane let ambush hunter wound her with killing steel claw.

I thought he was testing us again. Making sure there was no indication of Beast in our eyes. No evidence of our new abilities. I thought back to what I remembered of the fight. The memory was fuzzy, but the memory of the pain was fresh and startling, of Gee's blade sliding in under my ribs.

Jane should have allowed Beast to be. She drew out the last word, giving it import and heft, as though *being* was a weapon I had possessed but had kept sheathed.

I didn't stop you, I thought back. *I reached for you and . . .* I tried to remember, but my memory was sluggish, as if the moment I looked for had been washed away by a flash flood.

I got the impression of golden eyes, a flick of ear tabs, and a faint chuffing sound. *Beast was there. Waiting.*

I don't understand, I thought at her. *What happened?*

Litter mate killed him with white man guns. Yet Gee did not die. Jane was dying, but Beast was awake. Beast flicked her ears, thinking. *Leo slashed Gee-bird with claws, like male puma slashes younger males, to warn away from territory. There was much shouting and human war screams. There was much I did not understand.*

Yeah, well, that makes two of us.

Two. And one. Always. Forever. As Jane understands now and not now.

I reached for you in the fight. I couldn't find you.

Jane is foolish kit. Beast can hide golden eyes and scent. Beast is . . . She went silent and I realized she was thinking, trying to find words. She settled on the familiar *Beast is wise ambush hunter.*

Yes. You are.

We are. We are Beast.

I knelt at the fire and rubbed her ears, the pelt not as warm as I expected on my icy fingers. I ran my hands down along her jaw. Her head tilted into me and she scrubbed it hard against me, scent-marking me. I wrapped my arms around her and held her close for a moment, her pelt slightly warmer than my cold skin, her breath a steady almost-purr that was more vibration than sound. She should have been warmer. Much warmer than I was. *Puma concolors* have a higher body temp than humans. Something was very wrong here. I thought, *Are we in danger?*

No. They heal us.

In the room where my body lay, I tasted vampire blood. Leo was feeding me. I swallowed. Then I tasted Edmund Hartley's blood and I swallowed again. The vampire hadn't been here before. I was certain. Voices were speaking, the sounds angry, but the words were indistinct, as if I had cotton stuffed in my ears. I pulled away from the arguing vamps and human and went back into my solitude.

In my soul home, the flames in front of us flared high for a moment, throwing off sparks. Suddenly they held warmth and light. The walls around us brightened enough to perceive that they were dove-gray rock, smooth and damp with wet. The scent of burning wood teased my nostrils as I took a breath.

Beast stood and shook herself, her loose pelt sliding around her strong frame. She was bigger now, just as I was bigger after my weight gain over Christmas. She would soon be at the top of her weight limit, without altering some genes, turning some on or off, to increase her possible weight. And I didn't know how to do that safely. But her pelt was warmer, and her flesh beneath was warmer. That was good. My hand slipped from her and she padded into the shadows that lingered at the passageway to her niche, the ledge and shallow notch where she denned. Watching her, I stood. And I woke.

In the real world, assuming it really was real and not some dream that Beast and I lived, I was shivering. The electric blanket was turned up high and the warmth burned my naked flesh, skin that prickled and ached with dryness and age. I was alone beneath the blanket but not alone in the room. I smelled Leo and Edmund and Eli, all close, the peculiar mixed odors of vampire blood, herbal and coppery and floral. And I smelled my blood.

The pain was a dull ache, like a bruise at its worst, a feeling that was hot and cold, raw and dampened all at once. I recognized the sensation. It was the healing of vamp blood. My side and waist were heavy, as if weighted, as if I pushed against something heavy with each breath.

Vaguely I remembered the cool, wet sensation on my side where I had been stabbed. A vamp tongue, laving and healing. All without the slightest hint of sexual desire or heat.

"She is awake," Edmund said. His voice was close and I realized his arm was around me, outside the blanket, holding me close. It was a protective embrace, the kind a parent offered a sick child. A safe haven in a storm of pain.

"Jane?" Leo asked.

I licked my lips. When I spoke, my voice was a parched murmur, like leaves rubbing together in a dry wind. "Eli?"

"Yes, babe?"

"No fair," I whispered. "I always wanted to shoot Big Bird."

Eli chuckled, and I heard the relief in his tone. "He's

not dead. Lead doesn't kill his type." His voice hardened. "But it'll be a while before he gives another lesson. The day he does, you can shoot him. Again."

"Why?" I asked, and my breath failed me. I wasn't sure he would understand my question, but he did. Eli always understood.

His voice had that precise but toneless note of a military debrief. "Still under investigation. Gee screwed up or went nuts or . . ." He paused as if there was another possibility, but he didn't address it. "We don't know yet. He'd been working with students dressed in Dyneema testicle stretchers, so maybe he thought you were dressed out, until after he stabbed you and you bled all over the floor. Remote possibility is that it could have been an accident." But I could tell he didn't believe that one.

That was a lot of chatter from my taciturn partner, a sure sign he was upset. "Dyneema testicle stretchers" was Eli's term for the proper sword fighting attire, the cloth reinforced with plasticized Dyneema to repel sword cuts and punctures. We wore them during sword fighting lessons, and the thong that went through the legs, holding the chest protector in place, was amazingly uncomfortable for males. So. Accident? Was that even possible? Then I remembered the blue eye in my palm, the eye that seemed to look right at me as it turned green. A memory burned in the back of my mind, struggling to get free.

"Leo? Edmund?" I asked, waiting for the memory to rise.

"Yes, my Jane," Leo said.

"Yes, my master," Edmund said.

That "my master" stuff had to be addressed soon. Very soon. There was no way I was taking the vampire to be my primo. Vamps had primos and they were human. Skinwalkers had no primos and certainly not vamp primos. No way. I said, "Your opinion on the *accident*?"

"I concur with your second's estimate," Edmund said, "but the Master of the City is also correct. It was hubris on the part of the misericord. He . . ." Edmund hesitated a bare moment, and made a sound as if he was strangling. Or laughing. "He has *issues*."

I smiled in the darkness at the modern term coming from Edmund's lips. No wonder the words had strangled him.

"Why did you not change into one of your Beast forms, my Jane?" Leo asked.

"I really don't know . . . I was holding . . ." An eye. It had started out blue, which had felt familiar. The memory came back to me in a rush. When I first met Gee DiMercy, he had used his magic both for and against me. At one point, he had employed his all-seeing blue eye to watch me, in real life and in my soul home. I had seen blue eyes in both palms. Watching me. But this time, they had started blue and faded to the witch's green.

Gee had been spelled? With a spell like the one on me? Or the one on me had triggered some remnant of Gee's first spell and found its way back to him? Yes . . . That made a sort of sense. My breathing sped, which caused a thrill of pain to rush through my chest. I thought it through again and it all made sense.

I breathed more slowly, letting the pain ease, trying to figure out what it meant. And whether the eye in my palm was also the reason I hadn't changed shape. Nothing came to me, and Leo didn't know about my Beast, the other soul I had pulled inside with me in an accidental act of black magic when I was five years old. He didn't know about my soul home. I was pretty sure I had never told him about Gee spying on me with magic. But the Master of the City was waiting. "I was holding . . . myself too tightly. I just . . . missed it." No. It was something else. Something worse. Maybe the result of many things that were worse, all coming together in a perfect storm. That was why Eli had hesitated. He knew there was something else going on too, but if he knew what it was, he wasn't going to share it here in group therapy. I tried to put it together.

Gee's magic. Eyes in my palms.

Beast's magic growing.

The soul of Beast and my soul merging.

Attacks in my/our soul home, signs of magic in a place where nothing outside me/us should ever have been able to get in.

The stink of burning hair, iron, and salt in the scan.

And . . . I had been struck by lightning not so long ago. My hair had burned. So had my flesh. That experience had done something to me. I had shifted into my Beast since, but not in extremis. Not when I had to shift or die. Not when it mattered. And I hadn't spent much time in my soul home since the lightning strike, only long enough to glance in, not long enough to notice the cold flames and lack of light.

I remembered Beast lying in the dark, her coat the wrong color.

My father's favorite form had been the black panther.

He had died, changing into his cat too late to save his life.

Was there a connection with the melanistic coat color? Had something happened to my father's ability to shift? Had he been hit by lightning too? Had something happened to us both? Was it something peculiar to skinwalkers?

The stink of burning hair. Why burning hair?

There was too much that I didn't know, so I clung to the things I did know. I had family—Eli and Alex. I had Bruiser. I was alive. Beast was still with me. I could deal with everything else. As soon I was sure that I stayed alive. Yeah. That. I took a breath that rattled in my lungs and I coughed, a soft hack of pain.

"My Jane?"

"Not your Jane," I snapped, but it was spoiled by my raspy, gasping voice. "Your Enforcer. Not your Jane."

Leo chuckled, a vamp's hunting purr that made Beast sit up and purr back. I kept the sound inside my head, but Beast liked Leo a little too much for my tastes. "You make the chase so delightful," he said.

"Stuff it."

Leo burst out laughing, my purr buried beneath his pure amusement. "Ah, Jane. What shall I do to punish my Mercy Blade for his attack on you?"

"Getting shot was enough," I said. I remembered that Beast said Leo had cut Gee. "You cutting him was enough. And if all that wasn't enough, Eli said I could shoot him again."

I felt Leo's hand on my face, cool and smooth and utterly inhuman. He stroked back my hair, and his voice was curiously gentle when he said, "I would have been most . . . discommoded had you died."

"Yeah. That's why I stay alive," I said, my native snark coming back online, as if I had rebooted that file, "to keep you from being *discommoded*." I'd have to look that one up.

Darkness was closing in on me, the dark of sleep, the sleep of healing. I whispered, "Besides, I think it's possible that Gee was magicked into attacking me." I thought back to his eyes, blazing blue. "Something's wrong. Magic and spells and . . . stuff. Eli. Tell them." And then I was under, into a place of dreams.

It was nearly night before I woke up again in Edmund's bed in his new but still tiny room with its rich furnishings and its interior window. Previously his room had had an exterior window, an indication of a vamp's low status, and I had helped him improve his status enough to get a better room. Edmund, once a clan Blood Master, had fallen far, and no one had yet told me why or how.

I could feel my breath moving in my lungs, as if I breathed iced air, though the room was warm. My heart was beating slow and hard, a bass drum through my arteries. The electric blanket was turned low, but it felt hot and prickly on my skin. By the staleness of the scents around me, the vamps were gone. Thank goodness.

Shoving pillows behind me, I gathered the blanket tight around me and pushed myself to a sitting position against the headboard. I was naked beneath the blanket. Oh, goody. That meant I'd been naked in front of Leo and Edmund . . . and Eli, who was sitting in a delicate, dainty floral-upholstered chair at a small ormolu table, his eyes on me.

The lamp on the table was off and the room was deeply shadowed, my partner's face not visible until I pulled on Beast's night vision. Through her eyes, the room was silver and green, the details sharp and the shadows black as if drawn with india ink. Eli's expression was grim, set, and he was sitting as still as a vamp. There was a shotgun across his knees. I hadn't seen the shotgun when we got to headquarters, so either he had gone home to get it or someone had brought it to him. I was betting that he hadn't left my side and that one of Leo's security peeps had brought it to him. Probably under duress.

There was a glass of water on the bedside table and I drank it dry, replacing it on the table. I cleared my throat, which still felt scratchy, and said, "Debrief."

"That bird stabbed you. I shot him. You didn't shift."

I had thought that Eli's voice had been toneless many times in our relationship, but this was even more so. Robotic. Dead sounding.

"I applied pressure. Leo flipped you over and ripped open your shirt. Arterial bleeding went everywhere. You were bleeding out. Leo sliced his fingertips and shoved them inside the wound."

Eli went quiet again. His jaw worked, tightening and relaxing in the edged shadows. When he began again, there was no indication that he was under strain, except for the total lack of emotion in his voice. "Edmund picked you up. Leo and he carried you here. I shot a couple of vamps who got in the way or got too close. Standard ammo. They'll live."

I said nothing, just watched his face. After a long silence, he said, "You didn't shift." And this time there was a bare hint of emotion, a simple thread of . . . something.

"I couldn't. Since the lightning, I've shifted when I wasn't in trouble, in danger, but this time, when I needed to shift or die, I couldn't."

"Lightning?"

"I don't know, but . . . ." I stopped and thought before I finished, reluctance in my tone. ". . . there seems to be a correlation."

"You said the bird might have been magicked to hurt you. Why do you think that?"

"When I first met him . . . Seems like forever. He used his magic to heal me of a werewolf attack."

My partner gave a slight downward jut of his head to indicate he had heard me and understood.

"Later." I stopped. "You know the eye on the dollar bill? The one on top of the pyramid?"

Nod.

"I had one of those on each palm. Like a tattoo, the blue color of his magic. I knew he was spying on me. It was in my soul home too, watching me. The eye in my palm this morning was exactly the same eye, but green. In the fight, I saw it again in my left palm, the one the spell started in today. I think I was wrong about the spell being just a scan. I think it did something to me too. I think Gee's watching eye and the witches' eye are connected. Somehow. Water?"

Eli poured me another glass from the pitcher beside the bed. It was a cut-crystal pitcher and looked heavy. And I had no energy. I drank the water down. Then two more. I was badly dehydrated and I probably needed a couple of liters of fluid. A gallon of Gatorade might do the trick. I could get that as soon as I was finished with my tale. "In the fight, Gee's blue eye of seeing was in my palm, open. Then it faded to pale green, the color of the stronger witch's power. The scent of the spell was weird too: iron and salt and something harsh like burning hair."

Eli seemed to mull that over, and something in his stance relaxed a fraction.

I let a half smile form on my mouth, and my lips cracked. "Whatever it is, it may still be active. We need a way to thwart the spell."

"Thwart?" he asked, humor in his voice.

"Magical word. Stuff you'll learn if you hang around me long enough."

"It's what I live for," he said, a tiny bit of snark in the words. "Is it possible that the spell reactivated the trace of a previous spell in you? Maybe the odd smells were something that tied it all together?"

"Oh," I said. "That makes sense." Not that I knew what the smells might mean, but at this point it didn't matter. I needed to focus on stopping the working, not worrying about the ingredients used in the spell. That was something to deal with later. Simply having priorities made me feel better.

"But if one spell, why not more?" I asked. "And which ones? I've been hit more than once with magic of different kinds, from vamp to witch to were. Oh, and *arcenciel*," the fabled but factual and existent light dragon. "Let's not forget the weirdest magical thingy of all."

"Yeah. That is a problem, babe. One of many. And maybe one of many spells, all the way back to the fight that killed the Damours."

The Damour clan of suckheads had been composed of blood-magic witches. Blood witches. The kind who used the sacrifice of witch children and teenagers to try some really humongous workings, attempting to bring their long-chained vampire children back to sanity. They had killed hundreds of witches over the centuries, and I had nearly died saving my godchildren from them. In saving them, I had been in the presence of some pretty strong black magic.

Sometimes when one is injured in battle, it comes back in a haunting for years after. In my case that haunting was a sort of magical PTSD, which had caused complications in the merging of my Beast soul and my soul. Like what had happened today. Yeah. It felt as though we were close to figuring out the green magic scan.

"I guess I need to be checked for magical booby traps? And the house too?"

"I called Molly. She'll do some magical mumbo-jumbo on you when they get here. Check for trace spells. Check the house for same and put in the upgraded *hedge of thorns* as a ward."

I shook my head, my hair rubbing the headboard with a scratchy sound. My partner had been a step ahead of me all the way except with the last statement. "They can't stay with us," I said. "Too dangerous."

"I tried to talk him out of staying at the house, but he said hotels were impossible to ward. And they didn't want to rent a house, stay in a place they weren't used to. And they already had a permanent circle at your house that they could bring up and use to protect you, us, and them. Did you know that? That they had a witch circle at your house?"

"Not surprised," I said. "They can call up wards around the place pretty easily."

"Evan said it was a fortress. Or would be when he got finished with it."

"How about he leaves us a trigger," I asked, "so we can use it too?"

"In the works, but not something we can use every day. A 'one use' ward that will have to be restored by them. But if we'd had it today—"

"I'd still have been spelled," I said. "'One use,' remember? The spell *started* in my hand, before we could have gotten any *one-use ward* up and running. Please don't blame Evan."

"Please?" he asked, startled.

"I don't have the strength to make and enforce demands. Yet."

Eli made a sound that might have been some form of laughter, if laughter could also sound like grief or released fear. He pulled and flipped open his official cell, with its Kevlar exterior and multipurpose functions, and punched a button. Someone said hello and Eli held it out to me. "Tell Alex you're okay."

"I'm okay, Kid," I said, trying to sound stronger than I was. "I'll be home soon."

The Kid cursed worse than anything I had ever heard him say and finished with "Later." The call ended. Eli gave me the ghost of a smile and closed the cell.

"So," he said. "What do we do about this little shifting problem?"

We. Always *we.* "I need to meditate and check out my soul home. Maybe visit with Aggie One Feather. Other than that, I don't know."

"Concur."

"Are *you* okay?" I asked.

"No." He stood and walked to the door, opened it, and stopped in the shaft of light from the hallway. "I got some clean clothes from your locker downstairs. They're in your satchel." He left the room and closed the door softly, very carefully. He had said satchel. Not purse. Eli had once called it a purse. *Once.* I'd decked him and he never said it again. I do not carry a purse. But this time there was no teasing. He was fighting slamming the door. Eli was really messed up.

I turned off the electric blanket and rolled slowly to the floor, the blanket sliding across my skin like steel wool. The soles of my feet hurt when I transferred weight to them. I ached deep inside when I moved. Standing slowly to let my body accept what gravity was doing, moving things around inside me, I touched my side with fingertips that were hypersensitive and dry, as if all the moisture had been leached from them, leaving me with mummy skin over skeleton hands. I found a puckered scar up under my arm, higher than I had thought. There was no blood on me or the bed, not wet, tacky, or dried. Someone had stripped me and cleaned me. I smelled of lavender soap and a female human. Thank God for that.

The wound wasn't right, however. It felt as though it had healed with microscopic shards of glass sticking from inside the new skin. I hissed softly at the touch and tried to see the scar in the small mirror over the delicate table, but it wasn't a real mirror; it had no silver backing to insult a vamp wanting to see himself clearly and without pain. I couldn't get a good look, only enough to tell that my hair had come down from the bun at some point and hung in a scraggly, knotted half braid. I slung it out of the way, the movement making me aware of my scent and the smell of Leo and Edmund still on me, almost, but not quite, hidden by the smell of the soap.

Vampires have scent-marked Jane, Beast thought happily.

Gag, ick, and ewww, I thought back.

Beast chuffed with laughter.

Inside the satchel was my soap from home, shampoo, conditioner, and scentless moisturizer. Comfortable clothes I could pull on without too much pain. Someone knew how to dress when injured in the chest. Eli had been injured in the chest. I had never asked how because his brother had nearly gone to prison searching for that info in DOD and Pentagon databases. It was classified. But he knew how to dress for pain. I knew without asking that he hadn't left my side, so he had sent for the things. There was even a bottle of water in the bottom. Portable. Unbreakable. Nice.

Sitting on a tiny bench, I managed to get into the shower and clean myself of strong-smelling soap and vampire saliva, all without falling down and hurting myself. Again. I slathered on the moisturizer and the jojoba oil soaked in, making my skin feel nearly hydrated. I went back to the satchel.

I dressed in cotton panties and a pair of yoga pants with a soft waistband. There were a selection of tops, and I chose a very tight, seamless Lycra camisole, one that would give my wound some elastic fortification, pressing against it with a steady pressure, not letting cloth or seams rub across it. Wearing it would mean I could go braless. I didn't think I could wear a real bra, not even a sports bra, until the wound healed properly. Until I shifted into *Puma concolor* and the wound went away. I stepped into it and pulled the body-hugging cami up from my feet into place. The tight fit felt good on the wound, and the shivery feeling in the tender flesh eased. I slid into a soft gold cowl-neck sweater that I loved.

There was a brush and comb in the bottom of the satchel along with a scrunchie. And my tube of red lipstick, and my stakes that had been in my hair. And my official cell. And my thigh rig with one of Eli's nine-millimeters in it. I had left mine at home and my shoulder holster wasn't going to work, not tonight. Eli had known. His thoughtfulness was nearly my undoing. I was thirsty and shaky and tears pooled in my eyes. One fell and landed on my hand while I tried to unsnarl my braid. I remembered the blue eye that had faded green. I needed to talk to Gee DiMercy.

I gave up on my hair and checked the load on the nine-mil, set the safety, and weaponed up. The sweater hung long and I tucked the hem into the top of the thigh rig to keep it out of the way.

A knock came at the door and I said, "It's open."

Edmund stepped into the bathroom. I had expected Eli. The vamp stopped with that undead, block of marble thing they do, and he sniffed. A strand of horror in his voice, he said, "You are crying."

Which made me laugh through the tears. "Yeah. I don't even know why. I need water. Tears are a stupid waste of it."

Edmund stepped back into the room and I followed, to the far side of the bed, where he opened a small refrigerator I hadn't noticed. From it he drew a six-pack of flavored bottled electrolyte water, chilled and icy. He opened the first bottle and handed it to me with a slight nod, like a truncated bow.

"I'm not your master," I said.

"Drink. Please," he added. "Slowly, so you don't become ill."

And toss my cookies all over his fancy décor. I got it. So I drank. I finished off three bottles of water and set the empties beside the bottle I had finished earlier. The fluid made me feel better, but I probably needed more sugar and electrolytes, because the expected spurt of energy didn't come. Before I could fall, I sat on the edge of the unmade bed. It smelled of blood and spit and other things I didn't want to think about. I pulled my snarled wet hair to the front and worried at it. "Who did Eli shoot?" I asked, more to make conversation and keep Edmund from noticing the tremble in my fingers than from any real interest.

"The new cybersecurity expert, for one."

I glanced up from under my eyebrows. "New—? No one told me about this," I said. One of our last electronic security experts had died, sitting in the chair in front of his console, attacked by a vamp from behind. It shouldn't have happened. He should have been able to see the attack coming.

Edmund's lips twitched. "No. She arrived yesterday, a young Mithran named Pauline Easter, out of Atlanta. When Leo choses a Master of the City of Atlanta, she will go back, fully trained in the proper way to set up cyber protections. Stop fussing with that." He pushed my hands aside, took my braid, and levered himself on the bed beside me. I stiffened at the unexpected action and had to force myself to relax. In moments Edmund had the knots at the tip unsnarled and was finger-combing my hair. When it was free and hanging in tangled ripples, he took the comb from the satchel and began combing out the knots. I steeled myself for yanking on my scalp, but there wasn't any. And suddenly I didn't know what to do with my hands. A vamp, a creature at the top of the food chain, was combing my hair, like . . . I didn't know like what, except it felt weird.

"I was trained in the art of being a ladies' maid when I was a young Mithran, newly released from the scion lair," Edmund said, a faint, amused edge to his voice, as if he was teasing me or testing me.

My eyebrows went up and he chuckled, probably smelling my surprise. The comb slowed and stroked through my hair, smoothing it, soothing me. "I insulted my original master when I first rose undead and was sold into indentured servitude to a Mithran in Charleston," he said. "She owned a brothel, one of three in the city that catered to the most wealthy. Mithrans were cheaper than slaves," he added, his voice now edged with a trace of bitterness, like the faint tang of poison in a fine wine. "We healed quickly, we worked nights when humans were sleeping, we didn't have to be fed often, we could simply be set free on the docks for one or two nights a week to feed."

"You were starved," I murmured, and closed my eyes as he combed my hair.

"Yes. Times are . . . much better now, here, in America, for some. For most, I suppose, though the effects of slavery will stain a people with pain for hundreds of years. Eh." There was a mental of shifting of gears with the syllable. "As a human, I had been educated, overly fond of myself, and a braggart. I was also unskilled in the manners and abilities my new master required, and so was set to menial labor: hauling water, chopping wood, and heating the baths in the elegant old brothel. It was an education I was not prepared for. After a year or two of *behavior modification*," he said wryly, "I learned to keep my mouth shut and my thoughts to myself. It was that or starve into madness.

"By taking cuffs and beatings and not complaining, I worked my way up from transporting filth to the drainage ditch leading to the river, to washing dishes and setting tables, to pouring wine and mead and beer for the guests, to training as a ladies' maid. I was educated, as I said, and learned to turn my gift for words into flattery and blandishment. I developed a silver tongue. The girls liked having a man wait on them, curl their hair, trim their nails, choose their attire for the evening. Someone strong enough to protect them if they called out the safe word, though it was not called such at the time."

Edmund set the brush down and divided my hair into four sections, then divided the one over my left eye and temple into three more sections. He began to plait this small section in some complicated pattern, not a simple braid, but one where he pulled a few strands loose to hang free with each twist. It felt soft and feathery against my skin. It would never do for fighting, but for now . . . And then I remembered what we were talking about.

"Safe word? That's a modern term for"—I smiled—"a different kind of bondage."

Edmund laughed and the sound was a silken warmth that slid under my skin and eased the last of my pain away. He wasn't exactly using his gift of compulsion on me, but he was doing something. I should probably make him stop, but the sense of discomfort was easing and so I let him continue. "Back then," he said, "there was no water safe to drink. Everyone drank beer instead or, if they had an extra coin, wine. Stronger spirits were available as well, in every corner of the city. And the beer in Jacob's House was some of the best in Charleston," he said.

This time there was a hint of pride in his tone and I wondered if he'd contributed to making the beer. But what beer had to do with brothels and safe words I had no idea.

Edmund said, "The plentitude of alcohol meant that a vast majority of the customers were always drunk, and drunkards are not always careful with their tender paramours. And the management was not in a position to intrude when a paying guest became too heavy-handed. But I was not management. I was neither seen nor heard except when I needed to be.

"When a patron became dangerously inebriated and angry—the two go hand in hand oftentimes—the girl or boy could shout out a word and I would come running. I was adept at calming ruffled feathers and escorting patrons out of the premises."

"Mesmerizing them?"

He murmured a noncommittal tone.

"Like you're doing to me now?"

Edmund tied off the small braid and started on the larger one, making it too all feathery and soft. When he was halfway done, he asked, "Was I so obvious? You are difficult to charm."

Charm? Huh. "Yes, you were obvious. But it helped. I feel better."

He finished the braid and clipped a gold pin on to the tip. He placed the four empty bottles in the trash and opened a fifth bottle of electrolyte water, placing it in my hand and pointing. "*La salle de bain, pour vous toilette*, my master."

Meaning that he knew I had to pee, but much more nicely stated. I drained the water and placed the empty in his hand and, without a word, went back through the door, closing it behind me. I flipped on the light and relieved myself. Put on lipstick without looking in the mirror. When I was done, I finally looked at myself in the mirror over the sink. Only it wasn't a mirror. It was a screen with a tiny camera eye at the bottom. Its angle didn't focus on the commode or shower, fortunately. To the eye, I said, "If you're watching me through this thing, I'll break it and then every bone in your body."

"I would never eavesdrop, nor spy on my master's privacy, nor abuse her trust in me," Edmund said through the door, amused. Only I wasn't his master. And obviously he could hear me talk. He was funning me. *Right*.

I repacked the satchel, double-checked the weapon, replaced the stakes in my braids—which looked fantastic, like something like out of a fantasy movie, if I was an elf princess and not a warrior. If I didn't have to worry about someone using my hair as a handle to force me to submit. Gorgeous, stupid lustrous black hair, the two braids each with tiny tufts of hair hanging out of every segment, like feathers, wispy and elegant. I really liked it.

I opened the door and said, "I like my hair. A lot. There is no way I can wear it this way on a regular basis, but I'd really like for Bruiser to see me this way."

Edmund chuckled, a human sound, and said, "I promise to get *my master* all gussied up for the Rock N Bowl."

The Rock N Bowl was my date with Bruiser.

The *my master* form of address really had to go. Unless I agreed to allow Edmund to become my primo, the first vampire primo to a non-Mithran in . . . maybe forever. I shook my head at the faint thread of sarcasm in his tone and his insistence on that *master* crap, and slung my satchel over my shoulder. As we left the room, I called Eli on my cell. He answered, "Jane. You up?"

"Kinda sorta. Where are you?"

"In the conference room. We have an update from George."

George was my Bruiser, George Dumas. "On the way." I closed the cell and walked to the elevator, my would-be primo on my heels. The hallways were empty, smelling predominantly of humans: sweat, blood, sex pheromones, alcohol breath, and vitality. Most vamps were having breakfast.

CHAPTER 5

How Many Suckheads Got Shot

The conference room was more than a big table centered with Krispy Kreme boxes, surrounded by swiveling leather desk chairs, and a new Krups coffee machine in the corner, it was also part of the security arrangements. A vamp had killed one of the team while he was monitoring the original console, and we had updated the arrangements. Now there were two consoles in HQ itself, one off the front entrance in an armored cubby, and one down here. There was also off-site supervision at Yellowrock Securities, where the Kid could monitor and call in the Marines (or YS) if things went sour at HQ.

Soon we would also have access to the security systems at all the clan homes. Leo, the sneaky suckhead, had once maintained unauthorized, backdoor access to the other clan home systems, but when Pellissier Clan Home burned to the ground, he lost it. With the EVs coming, and the possibility of a real vamp war, we needed to access to everything at multiple sites so if one was hit, we stood a chance of maintaining an overview. Eli had made it clear that in a battle, knowing what was going on and maintaining coms was paramount. The Youngers and I were making that a possibility.

I stepped inside the conference room and looked it over. It was night, though early, so the room held only humans: Derek Lee and his security team were crowded into the large space, most of them staring up at the main, monster-sized video screen over the table. On the screen overhead, was me.

Gee and me. Fighting. In slow motion, which was the only way to see every sword stroke, with Gee moving as fast as any vamp, and me having pulled on at least a tiny bit of Beast-speed.

Gee looked like a dancer, surefooted and lithe, a small, slender man wearing black Lycra beneath black knickers and croissard, both padded with blade-resistant Dyneema. His eyes were glowing a bright blue. Mine were not glowing at all and looked totally human, if a strange shade of amber. Beast had been right when she said she could hide her presence inside me.

As we moved in slo-mo, I looked like a skinny chicken trying to dance and failing. And then dropping to my knees. Gee raising his weapon for a death cut. Eli adjusting the aim of his weapon. The glimpse of humans beyond Gee, in danger of Eli's friendly fire. If he missed. Eli firing. Gee falling in front of me. I saw me pick up the blue feather and place it in Gee's croissard. Then I fell across him and into a pool of my blood. Leo vamping out, shouting something.

The sequence replayed again, even slower, and when I dropped to my knees, the person working the console touched the screen over Gee's face and expanded that small area, to focus on his expression, just after he was shot. It was blurry at this magnification, but his eyes were no longer glowing. He looked horrified. Stunned, perplexed, and, an instant later, grief-stricken. And then he fell.

I turned away from the screen to see Derek staring at me, his dark-skinned face unreadable. Like Eli, he had a battle face, and this was it, giving away nothing. I looked from him around the room and noted that Eli was standing on the far side from Derek, his own battle face on. The two men were warriors, an Army Ranger and a Marine by training and experience, both dark-skinned, though Eli was paler, with a hint of golden in his skin, when he stood in the daylight. And right now I had a feeling that they were working together, covering the room, watching all the people standing and sitting. But watching for what, I didn't know.

Leo's voice came over the speaker system. "Girrard DiMercy. The Enforcer is now present. She has seen the proof of your treachery. All have seen the evidence of your deception and disregard for my rule." The screen blanked and a new scene appeared, of Leo's office. Gee was on his knees with his arms behind his back. I couldn't tell from this angle, but he looked bound. Hog-tied. Gee's head was down and his pretty black hair was hanging forward, against his cheeks. His clothes were bloodstained with red blood, but I knew that, without glamour, his blood was a different color entirely and evaporated instantly upon contact with the air. Ergo, the blood wasn't his. Some vamp had fed him, ensuring his healing, and left traces on his clothing. It had been a messy feeding, suggesting that Gee DiMercy had been in trouble of dying from the feeding as much as from the shooting.

Leo said, "As Master of the City, I have seen all the evidence and heard all statements except for the victim of your betrayal. I myself was at the scene and was a witness to the altercation and the grievous injury suffered by my Enforcer, Jane Yellowrock. Jane, do you choose to speak to the attack or to the assailant before a ruling is made against him, before I pronounce judgment on this accusation of crime against my Enforcer?"

I looked around for a microphone, and the man at the mass of security camera screens waved me over. I didn't know him. There were so many here whom I didn't know now. It disturbed me on various levels. Mostly because it was dangerous. The man at the security console handed me a tiny mic, the size and shape of a bendable straw with a foam pad on the end. "Yes, I have something to say," I said into the foam piece. "This is Jane Yellowrock, Enforcer to the Master of the City." Full titles, because this was a trial, and with suckheads, trials usually ended in death. "I don't know what's been said or deduced while I was healing, but

Girrard DiMercy, the Mercy Blade of New Orleans, was spelled. Look at his eyes in this screen." I pointed, and the man at the console put that one up on the main screen. "Then back up to the footage before Eli Younger, of Yellowrock Securities and my partner and my second in battle, shot Gee DiMercy. His eyes are glowing blue before. They aren't after."

The footage backed up and appeared on the screen. The still shot was cut out and placed side by side with the other one. "He was spelled. We need to talk about how he was spelled, but I have a feeling that the attack on me wasn't his fault, but was the result of something else." Like his blue eye of seeing on my palm, which turned green later. I didn't really know what had caused the attack, but I didn't want Gee punished if he had been under the influence of a spell. "That's all I have to say." I handed the guy the mic and stepped back.

Leo shoved his fingers through Gee's hair, lifted his head, and leaned in. I heard him sniffing the bound captive. "I smell . . . nothing. No magic. Were you spelled, Mercy Blade? If so, by whom?"

Gee shook his head side to side as best he was able, with Leo's fingers gripping his hair. "I have said. I do not remember what was shown on the footage. I remember only a training session. I am not innocent of the attack. I have seen that I tried to kill your Enforcer. But I am . . . not certain of anything else. Except that I am consumed by guilt and self-loathing, my master. Something took my goddess magics and"—he shuddered—"something happened that I do not understand."

Leo dropped the captive's head and said, "Girrard DiMercy, we have all now spoken. Following the attack, you did scent of error and fear. Following the attack you did appear shocked, fearful, and anguished with sorrow. When you were fed by my secondo, he did read pain and disbelief in your heart and mind. The security images—the footage," Leo corrected himself, "upholds my initial impression. I rule this, as my new security team calls it, accidental 'friendly fire,' the result of magical interference."

Leo himself stepped in front of the camera, his eyes on

Gee. He was holding a curved knife, small, easy to conceal. He bent over Gee and cut downward through the bonds. Gee's body slumped forward. Leo stood, the steel knife resting on his palm, like an offering.

I had an instant of memory, a single vision, of a hand holding a knife of similar shape, but of different construction—knapped flint set into a curved deer antler hilt and tied with a hide thong. Unlike the one in Leo's hand, the one in my memory was bloodied.

My father's knife. Too large for my small hand. As I cut into a man's arm.

My heart tripped and raced. The image vanished.

Leo set the knife on the desktop and lifted Gee to his feet. Someone had beaten the small man. I narrowed my eyes and looked at Eli, but his attention was on the screen. "You are free," Leo said. "No one will harm you for fear of my judgment. Go. Find sustenance."

Gee asked, "Is Jane Yellowrock . . . ?"

"She is in the conference room. She is well."

"Tell her I am deeply regretful."

"You may tell her yourself, when next you see her." Leo turned to the camera eye and said, "That will be all."

The scene vanished, to reveal a static view of Gee and me on the floor. I said, "Let's see the rest of it." I let an Eli-worthy smile touch my lips. "I want to see how many suckheads got shot."

For a moment the silence in the room was absolute. Then Derek started chuckling. Then the whole room was laughing, including Eli, who was wearing a wry face.

"Four," Derek said. "There are few things I appreciate more, as Leo's other part-time Enforcer, than walking into the gym to see blood everywhere, suckheads down and out, and a Ranger walking away with a smoking gun." Derek crossed the room and held out his hand to Eli. "That was fine shootin', my brother."

Eli stared at the proffered palm half a second too long before slapping his hand into it. "Booyah," Eli said, Ranger-style.

"Hooyah," Derek said back, Marine-style. Then they both turned to the screen and Derek said, "Play it forward."

Over our heads the action resumed, and I watched as Leo dropped into place beside me, rolled me over, ripping my shirt. It was so fast it all looked like one move. Considering that Leo had been a warrior on battlefields where death was frequent, up close, and personal, for more years than his security team all combined, it likely was.

The wound up under my arm pumped blood into the air and Eli dropped to his knees next to Leo, medical supplies already in his hands. But Leo didn't waste time applying pressure. He drew the little knife he had later used to free Gee and sliced the blade through the fingertips of his other hand. Vamp blood didn't often pump like human blood, except from the stump of a neck or a wound to a major artery, but Leo had been under stress and his blood spurted three feet to land in a stream of droplets on the floor. It glowed crimson in the gym lights. Leo plunged his fingers into my wound. Eli froze for a moment before shoving the supplies back into his leathers.

Edmund ripped his wrist with his fangs and pressed it to my mouth. My lips didn't close over it, and the blood of a master vamp filled my mouth and dribbled to the floor. Neither vamp seemed to notice the waste, but a young vamp on the sidelines did. She was vamped out, her eyes like black pits opening into a fiery hell, her talons an inch long and sharp as steel. She edged closer. Her mouth moved on words that I couldn't make out. Derek quoted her, "I'm hungry."

On-screen, Edmund snarled at her. Eli shot her. That must have been Pauline Easter, the new security scion. Frankly she had shown remarkable control not to fall and feast, with all the blood scents and pheromones that must have filled the air. Biologists had postulated that the scent and taste of blood released something like endorphins into a vamp's bloodstream. Shot, Pauline fell and the remaining humans ducked, covered their ears, or raced from the room. Dying vamps are noisy. Vamps who might be dying or who think they might be dying are noisy too.

Vamps themselves began racing away. A woman from housekeeping was standing in back of the shot, her mouth open, frozen with fear. Her arms wrapped around her chest as if hugging herself.

On the floor was Gee, a small human-shaped body, a faint bluish haze covering him, unremarked by the others, who probably thought it was simply the video. Gee's magic was bluish and his blood evaporated like alcohol, smelling like flowers in the sunlight. But in the gym, no one noted anything about Gee. All eyes were on me as, together, Leo and Edmund lifted my body.

Eli stood to the side, a nine-mil in each hand, watching the dwindling crowd, his eyes everywhere except on me. With his fighting leathers and stone-cold expression, he looked like death's henchman. But I could see the screaming rage beneath the surface. The impotent fury. My partner had been pissed.

The two vamps carried me toward the camera, followed by my partner. Off-scene, something happened, and Eli lifted his right arm, his hand steady as he slowed and pulled off three shots. He was close to the camera now, this one with a mic in it, and I could hear the blasts as more than muffled cracks. The small group passed beneath the camera and out of sight. Eli had been armed with standard ammo. I knew because I saw the young vamp nearest twitch, even with three rounds in her.

The video began again from a different angle, from inside an elevator as they crowded in. No sound on this one. The elevator doors closed. The vamps laid my body on the floor and Edmund lifted my head and pinched my nose, his other wrist still at my mouth. I struggled weakly and swallowed. Again. A third time. At my side, Leo removed his hand from my side. The wounds on his fingertips were healed. Vamps heal fast. Leo resliced his fingers, deeper this time, and he sliced his palm as well before sticking all bleeding parts inside me. On the floor, I gagged and my body spasmed. My flesh was white, tinged with gray. It looked as if I was dying.

The elevator doors opened again to reveal two vamps, both young scions, who vamped out at the sight of me. Eli, without thinking, acting on instinct, raised his weapon and fired. When the mag was empty, he raised the other weapon and fired three more times. The air was filled with the smoke of gunfire, a gray haze. The elevator camera showed the two vamps dropping down into a small heap together. The master vamps lifted me up over the downed vampires and carried me out and down the hall. Eli followed, implacable, changing out the mags for fresh as he paced.

The three disappeared behind a door. Edmund's door. There was a trail of blood and bloody footprints on the carpet.

The video stopped and the screen went blank except for a single camera, showing the empty gym, a single woman in it, wearing the gray of housekeeping, a bucket on rollers at her side and a mop in her hand as she scrubbed my blood off the wooden floor.

Then the largest screen lightened and a huge version of Bruiser's face filled it. He was looking straight at me. I realized we were looking at real time now and that Bruiser had a combat face nearly as implacable as Eli's. "Move closer to the camera," he said tonelessly.

I stepped closer, knowing he was looking for wounds. I smiled brightly at him, and his expression went from worry to frank disbelief. "Big smile too much?" I asked.

"Yes. That was a patently fake smile."

"True. But I'm alive. A little wobbly, but alive."

Bruiser's eyes narrowed, little creases at the corners. "We'll talk when I get back."

And that sounded worrisome, more of the "Why didn't you shift?" questions. Stuff I didn't know the answers to. I said, "Yeah. Good," and nodded, my hair moving on my shoulders, drawing Bruiser's eyes.

I could see he wanted to say something about the funky braids, but he said instead, "Update."

Eli stepped beside me and told Bruiser everything that had happened. Then he quoted Bruiser back. "Your turn. Update."

The cell phone he was holding turned to the world around him. The last of the daylight cast long shadows in a swamp scene. Stagnant water coated with green slime was everywhere. Huge trees pushed out of the water, cypress knees poking through the scum, the strange upward-turned root knobs stabilizing the trees. In the small clearing, the ground rose out of the water, muddy and pitted deeply with footsteps. In the center of the ground were two wooden doors, flush with the earth. Around the doors were arcane symbols drawn inside a witch circle. In the distance gators roared, the primal sound of reptile combat.

Bruiser held out a hand. In it was a length of crumpled, oft-folded foil and the brooch that he had found in the alley, the scarab and the peacocks, pixelated with digital failure. "This is where the brooch led. We can walk across the witch circle and nothing happens, but the feel of hidden magics is quite strong, and there must be a trap inside the doors cued to their opening.

"By the scent there is a vampire inside the door, in the ground. We will open the doors tonight and discover what we may. I'll have more to say after sunset." The communications went dark. From beside me, Eli said, "So much for date night, babe."

"The Truebloods will be here tomorrow morning," Eli said as he parked down the street from the house.

Technically and legally it was *my* house, as I had won it from a vamp in service to her, but we all lived and worked there, so it in reality was *our* house. I'd come to New Orleans with a motorbike and the clothes on my back. Now I had a house, full-time work, a business with partners, and a man in my life. I had *roots*. I belonged. Everything was new and strange.

And because of the new things and people and lifestyle, my bestest pal in the world, and my godchildren, and Mol's husband, were coming to stay with me. I could offer shelter to her and hers. Also very, *very* strange.

"I'll be ready," I said. "For now, I'll be out back."

"No meditation or shifting until you eat. Pancakes with butter and syrup and half a gallon of electrolytes. Except for the new hairstyle, you look like crap."

"I love you too."

"I know. Come on." He opened his door and stepped

out into the autumn heat and humidity. "Alex has breakfast started."

I followed much more slowly into a warm rain that felt like a tepid shower—the typical rain of the Deep South this time of year. Slow drops splatted onto my head and shoulders as I stepped to the sidewalk. "We're going to eat more food the Kid cooked? He maxed out with the broccoli and cheese. You want us *both* to die?"

Eli slanted his game face my way for an instant, his eyes moving left and right behind his sunglasses, checking out the street. "I gave him a lesson last Saturday. That was his cooking. No one died."

"Fine," I said, reluctance in the word. "I could eat." It was a lie, I wasn't hungry at all, but I also knew my body needed calories and lots of them to get me back up to speed. I needed to shift into my Beast form to heal completely, and no way was Eli going to let me go without a meal or three and restorative fluids. As long as it wasn't blue Gatorade, I thought I could keep it down.

It was a pretty good breakfast, though it was hours after normal people ate pancakes. Tied into the security system at HQ, Alex had seen all the footage in real time and had followed along with the replays, but he had to be filled in with the details, which Eli did while we ate, his words clipped and staccato. I mostly stayed silent and let them talk.

The syrup was delish, from Eli's private stash of one hundred percent maple, and the sugar rush was immediate and heady, tempting my appetite. The pancakes were fine, though the texture wasn't quite as light as Eli's. It could have been the humidity and the rain that made them a little doughy, but they were filling and easy on my stomach, better than I had expected, and I didn't feel like hurling with every bite.

Deceptively casual, his face almost pleasant, Eli said, "Let's spar, before you meditate and shift."

"Why?" I heard the suspicion in my voice. It was easier for my partner to win a sparring match when I was down and out.

"To see how well the suckhead blood healed you. You've had trouble in the past, changing into Beast to heal, and you didn't change this time when you got stabbed. And when you shift, you can get stuck in puma form when we need you in human form. Beast also wasn't able to help you with significant speed or strength, and while you're strong enough on your own, as a skinwalker, Beast gives you an edge. Correct?"

My partner had been paying attention. Close and detailed attention. Reluctantly I nodded. "She tried. The power drained out of my hand into the floor." I held up my left hand, the one where the spell had ignited. "Spelled."

Eli's face tightened, just a smidge. If he was showing that much, I figured he was terrified. He said, "We came close to seeing how you react without Beast assisting you. And it wasn't pretty."

Deep inside, I felt Beast growl. She didn't like that idea. But Eli had a point. If I couldn't draw on Beast in a fight for some reason, I'd be using my own skinwalker fighting skills and my own pain-damping abilities. I'd gotten used to having Beast as part of me. I wasn't used to fighting so alone and hoped I'd never have to find out how well or poorly I did without her totally. But in the middle of a fight hadn't been the time to find out how that situation worked.

If I had access to Beast, but needed to shift into an animal by day, I had no way to shift back until night. It was a quirk in my shifting that had proven problematic in the past. I did feel better, stronger, as much because of the food in my system as the vampire blood.

Once upon a time, drinking vamp blood was a way for a suckhead to attempt to bind me magically. I considered myself, the darkness of the cavern of my soul home, and the fact that a forced binding would never work, which was one big point in my favor. I gestured with a pancake-laden fork for Eli to go on.

"If vamp blood works well enough, it gives us an extra defensive weapon for you."

I slid a hand to my wound, feeling the thick scar tissue and muscle there. "I don't think I can take a direct hit here yet."

"Understood. Eat. Drink. Then decide." Eli shoved a pitcher of electrolytes at me.

I ate. I drank. And I felt better moment by moment. "Okay," I said when I finished my third stack of pancakes. "Lift some weights, stretch, and spar. But you go easy on me this time." It wasn't something I had ever asked of him and Eli paused with his fork halfway to his mouth, considering.

"Wimp."

"Totally. All I need is pom-poms and a tutu. Maybe a teddy bear."

Eli laughed, a real, full-on laugh that warmed my whole heart, and ate.

The room tumbled end over end and I landed flat on my back with a wham and an "Ooof" that drove the air out of my lungs and made my body spasm with electric shocks of agony. *Crap, crap, crap,* I thought, tensing against the pain.

My Beast tried to force her way to the surface to take the fight back to Eli, but I was hurting and the purpose of this exercise was to fight with her down, firmly in place and submissive. From the way she was pacing across my mind, like a cat in a cage, I understood that she didn't like our little test. She didn't like being unable to force her energies into me when I was being bruised. She didn't like not forcing a shift on me, into her form, *Puma concolor,* but she hadn't been able to do that earlier, when I was dying. Eli was right. I—we—needed to know this.

Waiting game, I reminded her as she squirmed beneath my mental hand. *We are ambush hunters.*

She growled at me, but subsided. I finally found a breath of air. It hurt going down, as if someone had yanked a rosebush into my lungs. It made a painful sucking sound too, and Eli chuckled, the evil man.

Want to ambush-hunt Eli. We are Beast. *We are stronger than human.*

Yeah, but we need to be able to hide what we are, and practice makes perfect, I thought back. *And we need to figure out what happened today when you didn't shift.*

Seeing eye, she thought. *Seeing eye and green magics.*

Some magical whammy for sure.

Jane has practiced dying many time, Beast thought at me, snark in her thoughts.

Thanks. I gave some snark back and pressed down on her, holding her still, practicing what I had been working on for the last few weeks, in the meditation exercises that had been assigned to me, holding her in place with a mental hand, not letting Beast assist in a fight, not letting her take over our form, not letting her be alpha. It was important that she learn to stay hidden, or we might end up a captive, taken prisoner, and used by the European Mithrans, the biggest of the baddest suckheads. And they'd be here in a few months. Or, if I was lucky, in a few years.

Beast subsided and I blinked the sweat from my eyes. I had missed the mat again, surely Eli's intent, and was lying halfway into the hallway. I managed another breath and dropped my hands flat to the wooden floor, faceup, staring at the ceiling twelve feet overhead. The corners were dusty. And the ceiling needed a paint job. And . . . there was a tiny attic access in the corner that I had never paid attention to. *Interesting.*

"Better," Eli said, and he tossed me a towel. It landed on my face, also his intent. "Your eyes didn't start to glow, even when you landed." I could hear the insulting laughter in his voice when he asked, "Did it hurt, babe?"

I patted my face, neck, and upper chest with the towel and left it on my belly to absorb more sweat through my workout shirt. "Oh yeah. I hurt." Eli chuckled again, and I added, "You don't have to enjoy it so much."

"Sure I do." He moved to stand over my right side, his face faintly amused, sweat trickling down his temple, his dark skin sheened with perspiration. He smelled of sweat, testosterone, deodorant, and sour clothes. In the New Orleans's humid heat, sweaty clothes soured quickly, and I was pretty sure the concept of autumn was Mother Nature's big joke this far south, leaving us in a muggy, wet hell forever.

Eli lowered a hand, palm up, as if offering to help me up, and kept talking. "I take joy where I can find it."

I had heard the story before and I finished it for him.

"One day this old soldier told you, 'Never pass a water-cooler without taking a drink, because you never know when your next one will come.'"

"Beating you is a rarity," he agreed. "So I enjoy every moment."

I grunted. Eli was talkative after we sparred, which was a pleasant change from the hard, taciturn man Uncle Sam had shaped him into. I slapped a hand into his and accepted the lift. Eli looked me over, as if checking out a prizefighter or a horse he might buy.

I grunted again and looked myself over. Sweaty and sour, as much as Eli, and sore. And bruised. My pretty braided hair was a goner. But I was feeling a lot better following the weight lifting and stretching we had done before the sparring match. Over two hours of hard activity had eased the aches and pains I hadn't realized I was carrying around in my body.

"The extra weight looks good on you," Eli said. "Five more pounds and you'll be able to stand against the next breeze."

When I came to New Orleans, I had looked like a poster child for the seriously undernourished, at one hundred twenty-five pounds. I had put on twenty pounds over last Christmas, and in the last month, five pounds more, mostly solid muscle. A little of the weight had landed in the boob department, but I'd never be mistaken for a model, more like the before photo in an advertisement for boob jobs.

"Did I pass for human?" I asked, easing my weight against the wall and letting my head rock back to it with a thump.

"As long the vamps don't get close enough to smell you, you'll be fine. Or you can drench yourself in some cheap perfume and overpower their olfactory senses."

"Pass," I said, toweling dry. I dropped the towel to the floor and used my foot to mop up more sweat. It had splattered when I landed. I took the time to stretch out the pulled muscles as I worked. "When is the help coming to move the workout room gear and set up the bed?"

"Alex and I can handle it. We decided to transfer it all into the hallway, not to a storage unit. Easier to put back when they go. What do you think about a Murphy bed in there? It would save time. I can put it together."

"Fine." I shrugged as we trooped down the stairs. The hallway was extra wide and could indeed hold the equipment. It had enough square feet to set up bunk beds if needed. My BFF, Molly, was coming, with her husband and my godchildren, to attend the Witch Conclave this coming weekend, so both guest bedrooms had to be available. Molly was spending so much time here that I should just let them move in. Which I'd do in a heartbeat if I thought they might stay, but Molly wasn't fond of New Orleans's heat, both the temperature kind and the blood-sucking-danger kind. Not that I could blame her.

My cell rang and I trotted into the kitchen where I had left it. On the screen was the pic I had taken of Bruiser. Brown eyes staring right at me. I loved that pic. I swiped and tapped the screen, answering, "Hey," My voice was too soft, not sounding like me.

I stiffened my back at my tone just as my honey bunch said, "We may have found Ming." He took a breath that I could hear over the cell, and it sounded uncertain and confused, two things Bruiser never was. "I'm pretty sure she's alive."

"Ming of Clan Glass?" I asked, confused. Because Ming of Clan Glass was Blood Master of Knoxville, and so far as I knew she was just ducky.

"No. Ming Zoya of Mearkanis."

I pulled the cell phone from my ear and looked again at the screen while my brain made a quick series of analyses on the seemingly simple statement.

Ming Zoya had been Blood Master of Clan Mearkanis, but had been kidnapped and presumed killed before I ever got to New Orleans. Her clan, under the leadership of her heir, had been disbanded recently. Her death had set certain things in motion in the world of NOLA vamp politics—things like her successor, Rafael Torrez, taking over Clan Mearkanis, practicing black magic, blood magic, with witch children to sacrifice. He was dead, but the bad things kept on happening nonetheless. Things that were still reverberating. Dangerous things.

"Okay," I said after a pause that was only a hair too long. I set the cell on speaker and placed it on the table in the clear spot between the snack plates the Kid was filling with his homemade broccoli casserole and sliced ham from Cochon Butcher. Even leftovers from two nights past, they were the best meat in the city.

Filling in my partners as we all sat for what was passing for lunch on this strange day, I said, "Bruiser says he thinks he might have found Ming of Mearkanis. The brooch led you to her? You're on speaker, by the way," I added to Bruiser, so he'd keep any lovey-dovey talk to a minimum. There was a low hum in the background of Bruiser's end that I identified as a vehicle. Bruiser was on the move.

Eli said, "I assume you mean *Ming the famous and missing* is no longer presumed dead."

What passed for famous in vamp circles was very different from and much more bloody than what passed for famous among humans. The Ming twins were famous in vamp circles for several reasons: they had both risen to clan Blood *Master* status from blood-*slave* status, something that seldom happened, and because one of the twins had gone missing, presumed kidnapped, killed, drained, and eaten by Immanuel, a supernatural creature mimicking a vampire.

I had killed Immanuel, saving a lot of lives and stopping a bigger vampire war than the one that had later taken place, but also setting into action a lot of the problems going on now.

"Correct," Bruiser said, sounding far more formal than I had expected, as if speaking to the Enforcer instead of his girlfriend. "I tracked the brooch to the west, following it to a water-filled pit in the Waddill Wildlife Refuge. I smelled Mithran when I arrived. So far as I can tell, *Enforcer*, the imprisoned Mithran, possibly the former Blood Master of Clan Mearkanis, is alive, has been starved, has been secured and chained beneath the water with silver shackles, and is most likely insane with hunger."

Using my title meant that things were grim in the extreme. "That sounds . . . bad. Dangerous. Do you need me there?" I made a swirling motion to Alex and he went to work. With one hand, he was shoveling in broccoli and cheese with the commitment and momentum only a growing teenaged boy can display. Cheesy broccoli was a new addition to his very short list of favorite foods, so much so that the Kid had even learned to make the dish. With his other hand, Alex pulled one of his electronic tablets close and brought up satellite maps of the Waddill Wildlife Refuge. It was a swampy landmass near the Comite River, near Baton Rouge.

Eli picked up his fork and placed his napkin across his lap, his brown eyes on me. I could tell he didn't want me to leave.

"No," Bruiser said firmly. "From what I can deduce, it's *very* bad. Leo has dispatched the other Onorios at his disposal to the pit, to retrieve her. They and a dozen human blood-servants are leaving in minutes on a rescue mission."

That told me even more. Onorios were hard to kill, and they did politically high-level, often dangerous, important stuff. But not usually together. That Leo was sending the two others said a lot about several aspects of this situation. "Oookaaay," I said, drawing out the word as I continued to put things together. It sounded as if Leo didn't need me to go on this assignment, which was enough to make me want to happy-dance, despite the sore muscles that were setting up residence in my limbs. Starved vamps were hazardous, blood-sucking, insane killing machines. With my skin-walker metabolism and ability to shift into other creatures to save my life, I was usually very hard to kill—even harder to kill than an Onorio—but that didn't mean I went looking for a mauling, especially right now. "So this is a call to cancel our date and tell me good-bye so you and your buddies can do hazardous, death-defying Onorio things?" I managed to stifle the plaintive note that wanted to sneak into my voice. We had been busy, and date nights had become few and far between. "Should I take you off speakerphone?"

As if he knew my reaction to Bruiser's broken plans, Eli chuckled under his breath, a sound that was remarkably wicked.

"Yes and no. Your introduction to the Rock N Bowl will have to be put off for tonight." His voice warmed slightly, "Though, I would much, *much* rather be with you, instructing you in the proper *body mechanics* of bowling, than climbing into a water-filled pit with a starving Mithran."

Me too. Especially with that emphasis on *body mechanics.* I fingered my tattered braid. I'd had such plans.

"Your own well-being aside, you are a potential liability, Enforcer." That made me sit up. "You were attacked in your home with magic, an attack that may have triggered more magic in Gee DiMercy to attack you. Until the spells targeting you are dealt with, you're a possible liability around all things magical."

"And how is that gonna be *dealt with*?" I asked, heat in my tone.

"Leo has contacted Molly Everhart Trueblood to check you out when they get there." His voice lightened when he added, "And he offered a very nice fee for her professional services."

"Oh." I sat back. "Okay. That works."

"But you aren't totally off the hook," Bruiser said. Eli's eyes tightened and he was eating with practiced, mechanical motions "I have already reported to Leo and, once the imprisoned Mithran is retrieved and safe, Leo wants you involved in the investigation, in your official capacity."

Official capacity meant my Enforcer capacity, which was why he was sounding so formal. Enforcer was a job I had taken by accident and then accepted for real, not because I liked Leo, but because regular income was important, vamp money was good, I got to learn new stuff about the supernatural world, got time to build my business, got to stay close to the Cherokee Elder who was teaching me about myself and my long-forgotten past, and I got to stay in New Orleans near my . . . well . . . near my boyfriend, or whatever the proper term was for the almost-relationship that Bruiser and I had. But mostly because I was in a position to help my witch friends stay safe; making sure the Witch Conclave went off without a hitch was a big part of that.

Official capacity also meant that I'd be enforcing Leo's will on whoever had put Ming in a hole in the ground. I'd be executioner, if that was called for. Not my favorite part of the job, but I was good at it. Very good. Usually. I slid my fingers against the scar tissue in my side. It was less ropy and stiff and far less painful. Even when keeping Beast down, as Beta, I healed faster than any human.

Bruiser said, "Once we get the pit drained and Ming of Mearkanis to safety, you'll need to bring Yellowrock Securities and work up the pit."

"Oh, hell," Eli muttered.

"Happy, happy, joy, joy," I said, knowing my sarcasm was transmitted over the cell. We'd be looking for clues to the witchy, Mithran, or human person or persons who took her, standing knee deep in mud and muck and mosquitoes.

Small biting things. Hard to catch, my Beast thought. I didn't respond, rolling up a slice of ham and chewing it.

Alex, the electronics whiz part of our team, opened another one of the tablets on the table and created a file to take notes in, typing in the location and what little information we had. "Okay," I said to Bruiser. "What else do you know so far?"

"According to the photos I'm texting you, the hole she's in is beneath a rough-cut wooden trapdoor set directly into the ground and covered with leaves. I think the Mithran is chained with silver to a cement wall set in the mud. From the scent, the skeletal remains of humans are in there with her, and if it's Ming, it's possibly her blood-servants, Benjamin and Riccard. The water table is so high that the pit is almost full of swamp water. There's no power to the site, no easy access in, despite the roads that border it and the rutted one that bisects it. We have to bring in massive amounts of pump machinery, generators, fuel to run them, and lights to work by, shovels, tools to break the chains. Maybe wood to shore up the pit," he added.

Pits didn't last long in a swamp. They filled up with mud and debris and water. Hungry vamps tended to go psycho fast, so the rescuers would need some kind of cage to secure the vamp. This was looking like a long process. I studied the sat map, tracing with a finger where Bruiser said the pit was. Mouth full, Alex nodded to show he agreed with the location.

Bruiser said, "The small patch of land centered with the pit had a dozen dead crows on it when I got there."

I didn't know what that meant, but if I was a witch, I'd be thinking about omens and such. Demons. Bad stuff. "Okay."

"This will not be easy, love," Bruiser said, his nearly forgotten British accent creeping in. "I'll call when we get the pit drained and the Mithran out. It may take two nights."

Two nights, because vamps catch on fire in the sunlight, so once they got the wooden doors open, they could work only at night, not by day. In the background I heard the unambiguous whine of a helicopter. Bruiser was being flown out, or the other two Onorios were being heloed in. I leaned in to the satellite map, looking for a landing site near the wildlife sanctuary. The most I saw was a muddy turnaround in the middle of the property where the two-rut dirt and mud road crossed it.

"Leo wants you at the Council Chambers to evaluate our photographs when we get the pit open. I'll call when we get to within half an hour of opening the site so you don't have to sit around waiting. Try not to irritate him too much. The possibility of finding Ming of Mearkanis has kept him up all day and put him in a mood. He might hurt you."

I had a feeling that *a mood* was a big understatement. "He could try. Maybe a little bloodletting would be good for his soul." *If he had a soul.* Thought not spoken. Go, me.

"Send the coordinates and photographs as you get them," Eli added.

"Of course. Take care of her." Bruiser ended the call.

Take care of her. I smiled and ate some of the Kid's broccoli casserole. I was better suited to taking care of myself than Eli was, him being human and therefore easier to damage—usually—but it was sweet. And I was learning to like sweet. The casserole wasn't bad and I said so. The nineteen-year-old grinned and served himself another portion.

Eli patted his lips delicately and said, "Adding an investigation on top of finishing the security arrangements for the Witch Conclave means our schedule will be full. Leo likes pushing you to the edge, keeping his Enforcer busy." He didn't have to add, *And this time you're injured.*

"Yeah." With Bruiser gone I might as well work. Not that I got paid extra for the longer hours. Months ago, I had negotiated a contract with Leo at a flat rate plus the Youngers' salaries and equipment costs. Of course, that flat rate was fairly hefty. "If we need help, pick out somebody, preferably two of Derek's people, one with law enforcement and one with crime scene experience, to assist at the pit," I said. "And it looks like I'll be able to join you at the Elms, after all."

"Good," Eli said.

"You both stink," Alex said, his tone smug. "Go take showers or I'll put you on veggies and meat for a week." Alex had been having hygiene issues, and food was the easiest way to get him to comply. It clearly made him happy to accuse us of the same flaw.

"Showers and change," Eli said. "We leave in thirty."

CHAPTER 6

Uncle Sam–Mandated GPS

I closed the Kevlar cover on the cell and carried it into my bedroom to shower, dress, and gather gear. The jeans and T-shirt on the bed had been perfectly suitable for bowling later on tonight but had no place in vamp HQ when trouble was brewing and Leo was in a mood. They also had no business at our first stop.

To visit HQ, I'd rather be wearing leather vamp-fighting gear, the kind with silver chain-mail armor between the outer leather and inner silk lining, and plasticized armor at elbows and groin, but I'd ruined all mine and the replacements hadn't arrived. Since I started changing into a midshift cat—one with a vaguely humanoid shape and proportions but the hind paws, claws, and pelt of a *Puma concolor*, the mountain lion form of my Beast—I'd gone through all my fighting leathers and a goodly number of boots. Fighting vamps was expensive, and today's ruined clothes just added to my financial irritation.

Clean and smelling fresher, my skin again lightly oiled with a gift Bruiser had sent me, a mixture of jojoba and coconut oils, I strapped a vamp-killer on my right thigh,

two silver stakes on my left, and slid into loose-fitting black
pants, a tight camisole, and a gold-toned, long-sleeved
T-shirt. The pants had slash pockets with holes in the bot-
toms so I could reach the weapons. Of course I couldn't
put the cell or lipstick in them, but there were pluses and
minuses for everything in life. The long sleeves of the shirt
were so the shoulder holster didn't chafe my scarred skin.
The TV shows and movies that show the female heroine
wearing tank tops and shoulder rigs are stupid. Those
things would blister a girl's underarms and side boobs in a
heartbeat, even without the injury I sported.

I added my gold nugget necklace on its doubled gold
chain around my neck. It was the one that tied me meta-
physically to the location where I had changed into my
Puma concolor form for the first time in years, after I grad-
uated from the Christian children's home where I was
raised. When I was having trouble shifting, it helped to
wear the talisman, linking me back to the past and the
power of that first shift.

I checked the .380s, making sure they held standard
ammo, since I wasn't planning to hunt vamps, but I put a
box of silver ammo, a change of shoes, and my go bag in
my leather satchel.

Sliding into the black jacket was easy, as it had been
tailored for me with weapons in mind by Melisende,
Modiste du les Mithrans. Or the tailor and designer to
fangheads, whichever works. And since I didn't plan on
shifting, even partially, I pulled on socks and the newest
pair of Lucchese boots. They had been a gift from the
master suckhead and he seemed pleased when I wore
them. Maybe wearing them would make him less moody.
I had often wondered if vamps had PMS, but I'd managed
never to ask.

I plaited my hair in its dull, boring French braid and
wrapped it into a bun, not a fighting queue, which was
much more uncomfortable and much tighter, sliding some
of the thin hair-stick stakes into it. Three wood and two
cast in silver. Just in case I needed to really hurt someone
fangy. Silver poisons vamps, especially a heart thrust.
Young ones die fast. Older ones die too, just more slowly,

unless a powerful master vamp decides to allow the dead to drink their blood. Leo had done that more than once—save a vamp I had killed. It kinda ticked me off.

I left my room and met Eli in the kitchen. He was giving last-minute instructions to the Kid, who was elbows deep in dishwater. That had been the deal. Eli cooked, Alex did the dishes, though the Kid had begun to step up in the chores department, which was helpful. He was growing up. We shared the laundry and the cleaning between visits by the housekeeping services. Mostly I did nothing and Eli and the Kid did everything, including groceries and major repairs on the house. I was a lazy bum in my own home. But it worked for us all, since they got free room and board.

Eli was dressed in fighting leathers. And lots of guns, stakes, and vamp-killers, two with fourteen-inch-long blades, none of which was suitable for the Elms, our first stop. I scanned him head to combat-booted feet and asked, "Why?"

"Not going to HQ unarmed," he said, his combat face in place. "Besides, one of us gets to look pretty. I guess that's me."

I shook my head, smeared on scarlet lipstick, and dropped the tube in my satchel. I could see Eli wanting to say something containing the word *purse*, but he refrained. Which was wise. I was feeling much stronger.

My cell rang and I opened it, my mouth falling open. My eyes hit Eli's and he muttered urgently, "Alex. Trace."

The Kid was getting bigger, but he still moved with the erratic clumsiness of a teenager. He knocked over the condiments on the table trying to dry his arms and open a tablet at the same time. He met my eyes and said, "Go."

I punched the CALL button above the Darth Vader smiley-face and said, "Reach. What's kicking?"

At the name, Eli whipped to the switches and plunged the kitchen into dimmer light. Then he started circling the house, checking the doors and windows, and out into the street. The Kid pulled up another tablet and studied the footage from those new top-of-the-line security cameras he had installed outside around the house. It all happened with practiced speed.

"Money Honey," the caller said. "Didn't know if you'd take my call."

It *sounded* like Reach. And Money Honey was what he called me once upon a time when we had done business together. Before he dropped out of sight after supposedly being tortured by a human and her vampires for the data he had collected on vamps and other supernats over the years. My mouth pulled down in a "Could be him" expression as Eli moved past, silent, predatory.

"How are you?" I asked.

"Are you serious? How am I?"

"Fine. Whaddaya want?"

He said, "They found Ming. Beware."

If he knew that much, then Reach still had his tentacles in HQ security. Or in my security. The Kid was still trying to close all the back doors into both systems but, like trying to track back to Reach's location, it was taking time. Alex was tapping on one tablet while another ran the tracer program. I forced out a laugh. "Beware?" I said. "Seriously? *Beware?* That's a little, I don't know, horror movie, puerile, don't you think?"

"*Puerile*? And you fault me for *Beware*? Money Honey, there is nothing so horrifying as reality." The call ended.

I said something that my house mothers in the Christian children's home where I grew up would have washed out my mouth for. I said it again for good measure.

"We're clean," Eli said, returning from a perimeter search.

Alex said, "Cameras are good. Premises are secure." He rearranged his tablets and continued. "I caught the call between three cell towers in Chicago. Forty thousand people live in the area. Hundreds of businesses." He tapped a screen again and repeated my curse word. His brother slapped the back of his head. "What!" Alex said, rubbing his head and pointing at me. "She said it first."

Eli slapped the back of my head, dislodging a stake, which I caught Beast-fast. I could have dodged the slap, but I had it coming. We had rules in the house, and no cussing was one of them. And I had made that one, which meant I had to abide by it more than the others did.

Still rubbing the back of his head, Alex said, "The number is a cheap burner cell, but it's one of the newer ones that has GPS, as mandated by Uncle Sam. It's turned on. It's moving. I'm tracking it."

"Uncle Sam–mandated GPS?" I asked, putting the stake back in place and checking the bun for lose hairs.

"Yeah," Alex said. "Well, the government asked for them. Politely. On the hush-hush. Most companies complied. The request came from Homeland Security, so they could trace all the cells of possible terrorists once they identified them. All you need is the number, the proper software, and access to the cell companies through the government's back doors, and you can activate the GPS."

"Alex!" Eli barked. Alex had been hacking again, and though his parole was over, all it would take was one mistake to make Homeland Security revoke it. They had the power to do anything.

"I'm safe. No worries, my brother," he added in the New Orleans patois.

"Reach would know that," I said, "so he's using one just so we can track him?"

"Messing with us. Chances are he tossed it into a passing bus."

"But you know he's in Chicago?"

"With a ninety percent certainty," Alex said, "partially based on the idea that he wants you to find him. As soon as I know more, I'll be checking nearby security cameras for footage of him."

Reach might want me to find him? Huh. "Keep us in the loop."

Eli and I left via the front door, which he had recently repaired, using a false stained glass window to keep it from breaking every time someone tried to kill us. Which happened with depressing regularity. My partner beeped open the armored SUV provided for us by Leo for as long as I worked for him and we found our way into the traffic. New Orleans traffic was always bad, but this time of day it was usually stalled in a bumper-to-bumper crush in the French Quarter. Heck. Everywhere. According to the traffic updates on the SUV's computer screen, today it was less dreadful than usual, and we made it to the site of the upcoming Witch Conclave in good time, two hours before night fell.

The witches had rented out the Elms Mansion and Garden at St. Charles Avenue and Eighth Street for the weekend for the Witch Conclave. The house was a two-story home with period décor and filled with period pieces, from marble fireplaces, delicate antique parquet flooring, swags and draperies and tassels and vases and rugs and silver and priceless antique wooden furniture. It was elegant and a little froufrou, appropriate for a conclave that would house some two hundred witches and some of their human partners and spouses for a daylong meeting, most of the witches female. If a dictionary or the tourist department needed a photo to illustrate the phrase *New Orleans mansion*, the Elms would have been perfect.

The biggest part of the security measures would be handled by the witches themselves, with wards, once they were all in place. Yellowrock Securities had been hired to oversee the off-site things, like parking and transportation, as well as the security of the house and grounds until the wards went up. The logistics of our part was beginning to look like a nightmare, which matched the nightmare of the second area of our responsibility. Or my responsibility. The part where I was responsible for Leo's safety. As Enforcer, I held the well-being of his undead un-life in my hands. He'd be there to meet and greet, to give a speech, and to share a meal with the witches, probably to indicate to them that vamps were something more than fanged and taloned killing machines with a special hatred for witches. I wondered if they would fall for it. And if they would all sign papers swearing fealty to one another. That swearing was important to the future safety of the entire city when the Euro Vamps came. There was a lot riding on this conclave.

Which was why today's meeting was so important. In every respect, the mundane security measures suggested by YS had been turned down. The house's owners had nixed the installation of cameras for fear we would ruin the hand-carved wood and plaster-of-Paris moldings. The double front doors were stained glass. Real stained glass, perfect for breaking with a grenade or a rocket launcher or a well-placed fist if the wards went down, and they had refused when we offered to replace the doors with five-inch-thick steel. Too trashy by far for the Elms.

A four-story building overlooked one side, with plenty of vantage sites for sharpshooters. The mansion's windows were not bullet-resistant polycarbonate glass and the owners had refused to allow us to replace the window glass in the room where Leo would be delivering his speech—the Grand Ballroom, with its white Italian sandstone fireplace, European tile, Doric columns, Irish linen wall hangings, and, of course, the grand piano. And lots of windows. Traffic was permitted on every street around Elms Mansion, and the powers that be in NOLA had refused to shut down the side streets even if it meant better safety for the citizens. Stupid city ordinances. All it would take was one inciting incident and this would FUBAR all the way, dead citizens and a witch/vamp war.

We parked on a side street and knocked politely on the front door for our official visit. The previous discussions and tour had been all online, so the meet and greet and real-time walk-through were essential. The woman who answered was tall, middle-aged, graceful, and elegant. Instantly I felt like a knobby-kneed teenaged girl with broccoli in her teeth. *Oh, crap.* I had forgotten to brush my teeth. I kept my lips tight against them as I said, "Jane Yellowrock and my partner at Yellowrock Securities, Eli Younger, ma'am." Eli handed her one of our business cards, gave a little half bow, which was a real classy maneuver. I'd never have thought of it.

I don't know what I was expecting from the woman. Maybe a sneer? Maybe tilting back her head so she could look down her aquiline nose at me? Instead she accepted the card with a smile, stepped back in welcome, and said, "I am Amalie. May I call you Jane and Eli?"

Eli said, "We'd be honored, Miz Amalie."

And he put his hand on the small of my back to push me inside. The door enclosed us in a wonder from another time. I had thought I'd been prepared for the interior from the online tour we had taken, but the place blew me away. I suddenly understood why the owners had said no to everything we suggested by way of security updates. The word *desecration* came to mind, with *sacrilege* and *defilement* close behind. It was so visually amazing that I hardly noted the scents of lemon oil, food, coffee, and fine cigars.

The Grand Foyer was big enough to drive a car into, with marbled and burled wooden antiques and carved wooden moldings everywhere. Directly ahead was the extravagant, curving Grand Staircase, hand-carved wooden railing, and champagne-toned carpet up the steps.

"The staff at the Elms is delighted to be hosting the conclave and will do everything possible to see to the comfort and safety of our guests," Amalie said. From the corner of my eye, I caught her giving Eli and his fighting leathers a once-over, her eyes lingering on his backside in the taut hide. She might be in her fifties, but she wasn't dead yet. She said, "May I give you both a tour?"

"Why, we'd be delighted, Miz Amalie," Eli said, his voice taking on a familiar, upscale, New Orleans accent. I lifted my eyebrows at him in surprise. He ignored me and gifted Amalie with a polished, friendly smile. One showing teeth. He never gave *me* that smile. "It's truly a beautiful place," he said as Amalie led us from room to room, describing the house's grandeur.

I let them pull a little ahead, and managed not to gawk too badly. Growing up in a children's home had done nothing to prepare me for this opulence of grace and old money. Every room was titled, Grand This or Grand Whatever, or was named after a king. And it looked like it. And every room's name was capitalized, like the NOLA palace it was. *Holy crap.* But I said nothing as Amalie and Eli discussed each room, how the tables would be set up, where waitstaff would enter and depart, and which doors would be used for guest entrance and egress. I just watched them, the armored and leather-clad man and the woman in the unwrinkled linen pantsuit and dainty heels. They seemed to get along famously, while I was the duck out of water and knew it.

When we finally reached the Grand Ballroom, which

was fifty-eight freaking feet long, Eli put his hands to his hips and studied the space. He said, "We at Yellowrock Securities understand why you would not want the windows replaced or cameras installed, Miz Amalie. But may I suggest cameras on blocks, unsecured, and resting atop the display cases along the walls?" He pointed to two locations that provided good coverage of the room. "And maybe in the Chaperone's Alcove?" He indicated an oval seating area where chaperones had waited while their charges danced and courted in a bygone era. The alcove opened to the stairway area and to the kitchen/ public toilets area. I had looked over the floor plan and it was a nightmare from a security standpoint. "We could brace them in place with blocks instead of screws and stretchers, keeping the integrity of the pieces protected. And perhaps beneath there." He pointed to cover the office and the kitchen. "And then station a few smaller cameras at the back and side entrances." Eli gave her a winning smile and finished with "All without damaging any woodwork, of course."

"Hmmm," Amalie said. "What about wiring? Electricity?"

"We can manage with battery-powered cameras for a few hours. All we'd need would be a secure, portable Wi-Fi console set up in a separate room. Perhaps on the second floor, somewhere discreet?"

I wanted to sock him in the biceps. Just for being so unexpectedly capable in the rarefied atmosphere. And then it occurred to me that he'd been in the army long enough to have stood security for embedded newspeople, traveling political types, maybe even diplomats. *Huh*. Eli had unexplored skills and abilities, and not just for making things blow up and go bang.

Looking from my partner to the area we'd be guarding, I was glad Leo had wanted to build a new clan home instead of trying to buy this place or some other old, fancy one. As the online tour and photos suggested, the Elms was remarkable, but impossible to totally secure for vamps. "Jane? What do you think?" Eli asked me, and gave me a look that said he knew I'd been woolgathering.

I tilted my head to our guide and drew on all the memories of the single etiquette class at the home. It was every bit of the meager manners at my disposal, but for once I didn't sound tongue-tied or snarly or bored or overwhelmed. Even if I was all four. "Miz Amalie, I think your home is stunning. From a security standpoint it's a challenge, but doable. We'll need names of your staff for background checks, and whatever catering company will be providing tables, linens, and food. Waitstaff. Your own security. Anything and anyone who comes from off-site."

"We'll be handling everything on-site, Jane," she said, "according to the contract drawn up by the New Orleans coven. The Elms Mansion and Gardens is a full-service venue with the capability to provide everything from flowers and sound system, to tables and linens, to catering and drinks, to cleanup, for as many as eight hundred people. The four hundred guests expected this weekend will be no challenge to our staff at all. I'll send you the final list of our people, but please know that most have been with us for years and have proven completely trustworthy." I nodded at her statement. Alex still needed to finish the background checks. "Do you also need to see the wine list and menus for the meals?" Amalie asked.

"That won't be necessary," I said. "We'll be talking to Lachish, and with you, between now and the weekend. My partners will need to get in to set up and test the security system. I'll leave it to Eli and you to find a mutually agreeable time."

Miz Amalie passed Eli a business card, a fancy one made of paper so heavy you could have used it to shingle a roof, and we made our way outside, down the walk, to the curb. There was something about old money and deep-rooted refinement, elegance, and pure style that left me knowing I was outclassed in every area.

Once we were in the SUV, I asked, "So. Who taught you to be all classy-fied?"

"Classified?" Eli chortled at my play on words, the sound deep in his throat, a sly look on his face as he started the engine. "Uncle Sam's Army Rangers, ma'am."

"That's what I figured. That's a good education, as long as no one's shooting at you or blowing you up with bombs." I glanced at his collar where the scars that had gotten him discharged from the army were hidden beneath the leathers.

"True," he said mildly. "And no."

"No, what?"

"No, I won't be sharing about the scars."

"Is that classified too?"

"Matter of fact, yes."

"Spoilsport."

"Indeed I am."

We passed a touristy shop and a few things caught my eye; I made Eli stop and did a little fast shopping. Treats for my peeps. I came back out with them rolled up in a paper bag and pretended to ignore Eli as I stuffed the bag beneath my seat. A girl needs *some* secrets.

Day was wearing away fast when we reached vamp HQ, the Mithran Council Chambers in the French Quarter. The place was lit up like a high-security prison, and discreetly armed humans walked the grounds with guard dogs at their sides. After dark, the humans would be switched with vamps, who tended to live longer in battle than the mortals who fed them and many of whom had mad fighting skills acquired over centuries.

We went through security measures just like normal, but this time without the trackers being dropped on us, and ended up back in the windowless conference room. Leo stood in the center of the room, booted feet spread, arms crossed, head back, his hair a black gloss in a queue. He was powerful and cold and in control, every bit the Master of the City of New Orleans. I could feel the sting of his power in the air and across my skin beneath my clothing. It hurt, like the prickle of sparklers and the rough scrape of acanthus thorns. The sensation told me that although he hadn't slept, he had fed well.

"Ming Zoya of Mearkanis is in a pit," he said, without turning. His voice was icy, laced with fury. "The Onorios will remove her at dark and bring her here. We have prepared a safe lair for her."

"Yes, sir," I said, stepping up beside him. On the camera, I could see Bruiser and his fellow Onorios, the creatures who were no longer human, but who hadn't been turned either. Changed into something else, something so rare there was nothing—nothing at all—in the histories, vamp or human, about them except the name.

On the screen, Bruiser was knee deep in swamp mud, his body braced and his back torqued as he guided a large rectangular box to the ground from above. I could hear the roar of the helo and the calls of the humans around him. The box was oddly shaped, tapered on one end, like a coffin. Wisely I kept that image to myself, and asked instead, "Is she struggling in the hole? Aggressive?" Meaning is she sane, but not saying it.

"No," Leo said. "Ming is compliant, so long as George stays close to her. We think it is due to the magics on the brooch he carries." Leo made an abrupt motion and the volume was muted, leaving the room silent but for the air-conditioning. He tilted his head, his braid gleaming under the lights. "The brooch you were attacked with. Are you well, my Jane?"

"I'm just ducky."

"You have not slept."

"You neither."

He have a modified shrug that tilted one shoulder forward, unconcerned.

"We went to the Elms to see to your safety," I said, my eyes on the screen overhead, "so I haven't had time to sleep." I changed the subject. "The pit's in the middle of nowhere and whoever put Ming of Mearkanis there had to know the location in the first place. Is it on any map?"

Leo's scent altered from the peppery tang of anger to the softer scent of papyrus. He breathed, the sound alien and out of place, and his tone mutated to amusement. "I had hoped it was possibly an old pirate treasure pit," he said, "though I fear that the pit is not nearly so ancient and that what is at the bottom is not gold bullion." A faint smile twisted his lips up. "However, if I am wrong, I shall have George bring you a doubloon to wire and wear on your necklace along with your gold nugget." He glanced at my chest where the nugget rested on my shirt. If he thought it odd I was wearing it again, he didn't say so.

On the screen, Brandon and Brian, the other two Onorios, identical twins, were stripped to the waist and covered in mud. The three men looked as though they should have been on TV, in an action series, saving the world, muscles ripped and sweaty. From his scent I knew Leo was enjoying the show. The boys *were* pretty, and it occurred to me that I might be able to do something to help the last of Leo's ire dissipate. It wasn't something I had ever tried, but if it helped, it might be a new weapon in my vamp-fighting arsenal. Wondering if my scent would work to mute Leo's anger all the way to calm, I let my own appreciation of Bruiser's sweaty, mud-crusted body free, knowing that vamps can detect scent change.

Leo's shoulders relaxed and his lips lifted with amusement. He slanted a glance my way. "A girl can look," I said coolly. Eli slanted an enigmatic glance at us.

On the screen, the Onorios and humans were now working with a small pile driver, one with four wide tires and a tall central tower, the cage a safe place for the human operator to sit, a sudden hard rain sluicing off him. Beneath the dark brown swamp mud, the machine was orange, the driver mechanism working up and down, the sound a basso thumping over the speakers, shoring up the ground around the pit with new pilings. It was messy, filthy work. And when night came, things would get a lot more treacherous.

With Leo calmer and me exhausted, I said, "We'll be back after dark."

Leo didn't look my way, his Frenchy-black eyes on the screen. "For now, get some rest. You were grievously wounded earlier today and I would not have my Jane weak or in peril."

Back home, I again changed clothes, this time into a stained loose T-shirt and stretchy pants for meditation, so if I decided I could shift, I wouldn't ruin my clothes. Even in mountain lion form I could get out of the shoddy duds.

Outside, on the back corner of the porch, I curled on the wooden floor, legs in guru position, my spine against the post holding up the porch. Mosquitoes buzzed around me, annoying. In the mountains they would have been mostly dormant by now, the early frost in Asheville killing them off, but here, they were a year-round nuisance.

I blew out a breath that didn't hurt and relaxed against the post. Though I would rather be sitting on the pile of busted boulders in the back, the rain was falling faster, the storm still coming off the Gulf of Mexico, with lightning flashing across the sky and the roll of thunder. The Truebloods were driving through this and would be here by morning, if not sooner. Neither Molly nor Evan was a water witch, and it would make sense for them to drive straight on through instead of stopping for the night. Though Molly, newly and unexpectedly—to me—pregnant, might need to stop and rest. Selfishly I'd like them to be here as soon as possible, and not just for the company of friends I missed. I could use their opinion on the scan of the house and the magical thingamabob eye on my palm.

Flash floods weren't uncommon in the flatland of Louisiana, but I knew that Big Evan, Molly's husband, could handle most anything that happened around him, in the real world and in the metaphysical world of magic. They would be fine. I shouldn't be worrying about the big bad magical witches who could take care of themselves better than I could.

Lightning slashed the sky open again, striking close. The ground shook, and all around me lights flickered. A shiver raced through me, reaction to the electric energy of nature, and if I was honest, a leftover reaction to being struck by lightning. I took a calming breath and exhaled. No way was I giving in to fear over a little storm. Or a little almost-died-but-didn't experience. I'd had too many to let them bother me now.

I had more important worries about the scar and the inability to shift when I was in danger and an odd feeling of exhaustion that tugged at my consciousness. But I was having trouble dragging my thoughts back into meditation, seeing the Trueblood's soccer-mom van sliding into an overflowing bayou, two witches with green merged magic working against them.

I blew out another breath and opened my left hand. It was plain, unmarked, but it was my real source of worry. The memory of the green eye in my palm. An eye similar to the magical impression of the Mercy Blade's watching blue eye, the eye he had marked me with when we first met and he healed me from a werewolf attack.

Old magic was dangerous. Traces of it were even more so, as time dulled the importance of old spells and the mind forgot the opening into the soul that could be left. The misericord had deliberately marked me long ago. Now he had harmed me, probably partly as a result of his own magic. And I hadn't shifted. That. Yeah, *that* was the problem.

Holding the old image of the blue eye in my mind, I finally let myself drop away into the place that was the home of my soul, the place I remembered from long and long ago, when I had been a child of five and my father and grandmother—*edoda* and *elisi*—had coaxed and forced me into my first change, into *wesa*—bobcat. That cavern in the Appalachian Mountains that had taken on such importance in my regular, ordinary life, a place that was all memory and healing, a place in my mind and my spirit, and in reality, though the location had been lost to me for going on two centuries. The place that told me what was happening in my own mind and heart, that showed me when I was under attack. The place I went to for spiritual healing.

The place Gee DiMercy had marked with his power over me.

The Cherokee didn't mark rites of passage on cave walls or lay claim to the caves, not like what the ancient white man did in Europe and in other places of the Americas. They didn't make handprints on cave walls. Yet Gee DiMercy had made handprints of his own in my soul home, as if claiming my place for his own.

I had been forced to cleanse my soul home with fire and spirit.

I remembered. And I slid down into the memory, like cooling smoke sliding down cave walls.

"Hands," I had whispered. *"Hands on the roof of the world."* My thoughts of that time in my soul home came clear to me.

My own memory of my own words, as I saw the hands marked all over the cave walls all around, and even up to the roof of the dome overhead. They had been blue hands in circles of white, and white-toned hands in circles of blue, pigments applied like signs of ownership fixed to the walls of my soul house.

Each kind of handprint had been made in a different way. I knew this even without acquiring the learning, as if it was part of me. For the blue handprints, the white pigment had been blown through a hollow reed onto the walls in a circular or oval pattern, and then pigments had been crushed and mixed with fat or spit. This paste had been applied to Gee's hands and the blue prints pressed against the walls. For the white handprints in circles of blue, the procedure had been different, possibly because of the nature of the pigments themselves. I never bothered to discover why the different methods had been employed. The blue pigments had been crushed and sucked up into a reed. A hand had been placed on the cave wall, and the pigments had been blown over it, leaving the unpigmented print in the whitish gray of the cavern rock.

Gee used woad to create the blue. Woad was a European herb, an invasive herb that took over gardens, and, like indigo, was used to make blue dye. Yes. That was important. Invasive herbs took over and killed all else but their own. And here each palm print was marked with a blue eye.

At the time I had first seen the claiming handprints, prints that had allowed the Mercy Blade to track me and watch me, I had also noted a pink flower. A rose, the symbol of Evangelina Everhart, Molly's sister whom I had later killed for consorting with demons and killing humans. The flower had smelled of roses and wormwood, sweet and bitter both. And it was put there with magic—witch magic.

In my memory, *I bent over the fire, the scent rich and herbal and warm, and breathed in the sage and sweetgrass. We—Beast and I—reached to the side and chose a thick sliver of wood, pointed on one end, sawn smooth on the other, one side wild and splintered, one side shaped by hand. A stake. It was dry heartwood, its cedar scent resinous and tart. Heartwood to destroy the vampires we hunt and kill. Our hand closed over it, tlvdatsi claws at the ends of human fingers. Pelt, tawny and thick, rose over the bones of our arms. We hefted it and placed the splintered, sharp end of the stake into the flame. It took light. And we rose into the shadows, the first time I ever saw my promised half-Beast, half-Jane form, cast upon the wall.*

Ohhh. This is important. This timing, I thought, my consciousness dividing, partially in the memory, and partially where I sat on the porch.

The roof at the heart of the world reached down to us, to Beast and me as one. With one knobby-knuckled hand, killing claws exposed, we scraped a woad-made eye from a palm on the damp stone. It glittered, lid closed as if sleeping, on our hand. With the other hand, we held the flame to the woad-made handprints. The fire from our torch blazed up, burning the woad, burning the handprints that had taken root. And in the center of each palm on the cave walls, a blue eye appeared, opened, and focused on us. Gee's eyes, shocked. I stabbed at the eye in the center of one woad palm print and it blinked away, but not before I drew blood. It splashed down onto my hand, copper and jasmine-scented. The woad lit, sizzling and hot. Flames raced up and over the cave, blackened the roof. I stepped away as the flames roared up hot and cleansing. All the handprints took flame, all but the one I had stolen with my killing claws. "Mine," *I growled to it.* "My place."

I crouched on the stone floor and watched as the ceiling at the heart of the world flamed and burned. And was cleansed. It took a long time. And no time at all. And when it was done, I sat at my small fire pit and fed the stake into the coals, letting it too burn away. When the smoke cleared,

*the ceiling was clean again, only the soot above my small
fire blacking the smooth rock. I lay down, folding my body,
paws beneath me. And I closed my eyes.*

But, though I had cleansed the cave by fire, perhaps
the watching eyes were still there, in some arcane man-
ner, leaving some trace of the magic. A trace still potent
enough for the green magics of an enemy to find me. Hold
me. Harm me.

Even though I had been in the presence of angelic
power since then, and had cleansed my spirit and soul with
baptismal water and had *gone to water* in the *Tsalagi* tradition and . . . had done everything I could think of to protect and purify my soul—something was still there. And I
didn't know why.

CHAPTER 7

Bad and Getting Badder

It seemed possible that the old spells were still present—dormant, latent, but filled with sleeping power, able to offer a magic user a way in to me. And I remembered something else, something more recent, a dark heart beating in the roof of my soul home, like a bird's heart, fastfastfast, beating in flight.

Not certain what to do about the old memories, or even if I should push on into my soul home to see what was there now, I eased up out of the calm of meditation and into the sound of slow-dripping water, the tinkle of rain down the gutters, the plink of large, slow drops on wood and stone. And the scent of witch child in my nostrils.

Angie Baby was sitting in front of me, her legs crossed in a mimicry of my own, red Keds on her feet, coral pants and shirt, watching me. Behind her was Little Evan, also known as Evan Junior, or EJ, her baby brother, sitting against the wall of the house, his legs stretched out and a soccer ball in his lap, steadied by both hands.

"Hey, Aunt Jane," Angie Baby said.

"Hey, Aunt Jane," Little Evan copycatted.

Around us, night had started to fall, the early dusk of storms passing. Inside the house, lights were glowing through the windows, but I heard no one speaking, no one moving around. I got an unhappy sensation in the middle of my chest. This wasn't good. I opened my mouth, lips dry and slightly cracked from the remnants of dehydration. "Hey," I said to my godchildren. Neither replied, so I asked, "Is everyone inside . . . um . . . asleep?"

"Yep," Angie said.

"Yep," EJ said.

That unhappy sensation in the middle of my chest grew heavy, like a pebble dropped in water, tumbling deep. "Okay. You have something to tell me?"

"Nope."

"Nope."

"Ask me, then?"

Angie laughed, the sound playful and childish and happy, her strawberry blond hair stirring with the motion and resettling around her shoulders. "We want to know about that." She pointed at my chest.

I looked down at my ratty T-shirt. "Just me."

"Nope."

"Nope."

"You got something inside," Angie said. "Right there." She pointed at my chest, at the scar that was still unhealed. "Why you carrying her around, Aunt Jane?"

"Her?" I asked, suddenly confused, wondering if she was seeing Beast's soul inside me.

"This." She leaned in and touched my hurting flesh, drawing out something I had never expected to see. A mote of magic, its color uncertain, one moment silver, another red, another black. And then a tint of green. "Blood black magic," Angie said with utter confidence.

"Holy craa . . ." I stopped, seeing the mote of dark power that she was drawing from my chest into the air. The mote was attached inside me via a length of dark red soul/spirit energy. My heart rate skyrocketed and my breath came fast. Pain flared along the length of the trailing energies and knotted around the healing wound. Each beat of my heart ached and trembled along the magical chain that bound the mote to me. And the mote beat like a tiny heart, but an unfamiliar tempo, out of rhythm with my own, a peculiar antiresonance to my own heartbeat.

I had seen something like it before. The mote of magical power was familiar, as familiar as old scars and fresh wounds. It was part of my history in New Orleans, from the time I saved Angie and Little Evan from being killed by black magic witches searching for more power than anyone should ever need. Red motes of raw, black magic power had invaded me. I had thought them all gone. And this one was no longer just red, it was red and black and silver and blue and green, moving through the spectrum in scintillating patterns of light and shadow.

"When you was saving us," Angie said, "one got inside. And it's still there."

From the time I fought the Damours and the blood diamond and the motes of evil energies attacked me. *One stayed inside.*

Somehow I had known this, on some deep plane, darker and deeper than I had been able to perceive on a conscious level. Hiding, along with a lot of other magical mumbo-jumbo crap. Chained inside me. I had seen it not so long ago, a black beating heart in the center of the roof of my soul.

Even with the protection of the angel Hayyel, the dark mote of power had been with me ever since the Damours.

I asked, "Angie? Can you yank it out?"

"If *I* break the chain it might hurt your real heart and you might die, Aunt Jane." Words so calm, so adult on her lips. Words no witch child so young should ever speak or understand or know.

The mote was chained to me. I remembered the chain I once had to Leo, when he tried to bind me and I had instead accidentally bound him. I had broken the chain and the binding, but that was many months ago and partially by accident. I wondered if Beast and I were strong enough to break *this* chain. A spear of fear stabbed into me from the new wound and I wondered if I would die if *I* tried to break it. I wondered if it would kill me anyway, or warp me, or drive me to become *u'tlun'ta.* Liver-eater. The final persona of all skinwalkers when we veer from the path of good into the pathways of darkness. All that thinking took only an instant and I said, "Let it go, then, Angie. Let it go back into me. But keep an eye on it, okay? If it gets wonky, you tell me. Okay?"

"Wonky," Angie giggled. "Okay, Aunt Jane."

"Wo'ky. Okay, Aunt Jane," EJ echoed.

Angie let the mote go and I felt it slide back into me through the scar and between my ribs. Into my heart. Into my spirit. Into my soul home. It hurt, sharp and cutting, as piercing as the sting of Gee DiMercy's blade. I needed to talk to the little Anzu, maybe at the point of a steel blade. And soon.

Angie stood, EJ moving with her. He tossed the soccer ball to me and laughed, his eyes alight with mischief. I caught it and tossed it back, moving woodenly, without the grace of Beast, who had been silent inside me for too long. Again.

Standing, I followed the children into the house, shutting the door quietly behind me. On the sofa, Molly and Big Evan were curled against each other, Big Evan snoring slightly, his mouth open, lips drooped against his red beard. Molly was slumped on his chest, her baby bump more pronounced than only weeks in the past, her red hair in wild short curls, a nimbus of energy that even slumber didn't abolish.

Alex was asleep at the small table he used as a desk, his head resting on his arms. Eli was sitting upright at the kitchen table, his eyes closed and jaw loose, but his posture perfect. Silent. Not snoring.

Even Kit-Kit, Molly's not-familiar cat (because witches didn't have familiars), was asleep, curled on a shelf with the television screen.

Asleep. All of them asleep. This was so bad on so many levels. "Angie. You know the rules. No magic without your parents' approval." And worse, so much worse, the last time I had seen Angie, I had been outside time. I had seen the way her parents' bindings came free and I had used Angie's own magic to bind her down, used her own potential to put her in a straitjacket that left her without power, that tied her magics around her in a sheath of binding. And now she had it all back.

The little girl shrugged, and the four people instantly woke up. No snapping of fingers, no magical *wyrds* of a spell, no wiggling nose, as in an old TV show about witches, before the workings of magic were so well-known. Nothing. Just asleep, then awake. My godchild was scary powerful. The last time I'd seen her put someone to sleep, she had used a *"Tu dormies!"* wyrd spell, one over the abilities of most adult witches, and all witch children. And at the time, only weeks past, she hadn't possessed the ability to wake up her victims. Now she did. *Crap on crackers.* Too much had changed.

Molly scrubbed her face like a child and peeled herself off her husband. Moving gracefully despite the pregnancy, she grabbed me up and hugged me. I hugged back, watching Angie over her head, as my godchild crawled into the chair beside the couch, picked up her doll, and started talking to it, too soft to hear over Molly's chatter about the trip in. "You're not listening," she said.

"Yes, I am. You were tempted to stop in Mobile, but you came in tonight because of the storms getting worse by the minute and the flash floods. I heard."

"You were meditating, so we left you out there. You okay, big-cat? You don't look so good." She patted my waist, holding on to me, her head tilted back to look up. At six feet, I looked down on most women, though not metaphorically, and Molly was no exception.

I hugged her one-armed, and then squeezed Big Evan when he gathered us both up in a bear hug. Which felt weird, the smell of sweat and car and man and magic, the heat of his body. Big Evan and I didn't hug. Most times we disagreed on everything, but he seemed genial and pleasant and I was loath to disregard that. Even if it too was the result of Angie's magic.

I didn't know what to say to them about their daughter, so I said, "I'm good. Other than no sleep and keeping vamp hours."

Big Evan stepped back, headed for the stairs, pointing to his chest. He said, "Shower. Then bed. Big day coming up. Oh. And tomorrow we check you for booby-trap spells and trace magic."

Which their daughter had already done. She must have been listening to her parents talk about searching for outside energies left inside me and done her own scan. Little girl with big ears.

"Me too," Mol said. "We ate on the road, and Eli told us how you were needed back at suckhead central, so you go. We'll set the wards and we'll be fine. To get in, just walk through. The wards will recognize you."

Angie smiled and kissed her doll on the cheek, looking sweet and angelic, like her name, Angelina. But she was so much more than that. She was perhaps the world's only homogenous witch, with two witch genes, one from each parent. She was terrifying, overwhelming, and I didn't know what to do about that. It was a problem that had been growing for years and her parents had never really had a handle on the reins of her magical potential. Yeah. Little Big Ears.

"Yeah. Fine," I said, fingering my T-shirt, feeling the pull of the black mote of power in my chest, remembering the way it slid through Angie's fingers as it returned to the heart of me.

Molly hugged me again and picked up her son. "Come on, little man. Let's get you in the tub and then in the bed." She looked to Eli. "May I bathe him in your tub while Evan's showering? It'll speed things up."

"Help yourself, ma'am," Eli said.

"Ball!" EJ shouted.

"Tomorrow. Plenty of time for play then." Molly took Angie's hand and pulled her daughter from the chair and up the stairs. My last look was of Angie's smiling face as she made the turn upstairs.

I said nothing all the way back to vamp HQ, rain sluicing down the windshield and windows of the armored SUV, rivulets that reflected the neon lights of the Quarter, turning them into vibrant, liquid lines of light. Silent while Eli adjusted the air repeatedly as the AC fought the inside condensation of the night storm.

We were late, but I didn't care, couldn't seem to find the desire to care about much of anything. He accessed security and drove past the heavy iron gate, which had been affixed with a wrought-iron fleur-de-lis to prettify the design. I hadn't known the stylized "flower of the lily" had been going up, but I couldn't complain. The gate had been awfully ugly. Eli pulled into the front drive, parked, and turned off the engine. He sat there, not looking at me, the rain isolating us from the rest of the world. After a time, his thumbs tapped on the steering wheel. "Twenty-seven minutes."

"What?"

"That's how much time I'm missing from this evening. Twenty-seven minutes and a few seconds. What happened?"

"Angie Baby put everyone to sleep so she could tell me I had a black magic mote of power stuck inside me and that I'd die if she took it out. I think Little Evan helped. I think Angie's magic is bringing his magic on early too. I have to assume that the mote made it easier for the witches to spell me. And Gee. As if it's a weak link in my soul. I think . . . " I took a deep breath that did nothing to relax me. "I think we're in deep shit."

"Hmmm," he said, probably interpreting my use of the *S*-word. "Okay. I can handle the shit. You figure out how to fix the black magic whammy."

I let a tiny smile touch my face. "That's it?"

"What else is there?" He unlatched his seat belt and stepped into the rain. Feeling oddly buoyant and more optimistic, I followed my partner up the stairs to the doors, the rain dampening my hair and clothes. The scents of vamps and humans and blood and sex filled my nostrils as we passed through two sets of double doors and out of the rain.

"Legs," Derek said to me as we shook rain to the marble, fleur-de-lis floor. To his people he added, "Make it fast. Leo's a bear."

The security measures and pat-downs at the entrance were hurried, as if they had orders to get us to the conference room pronto, and I noted that no new people were working the entrance, just the Tequila boys and the Vodka boys, Derek Lee's best and most dependable security personnel, all former military. And then we were in the elevator and on the way down to the conference room, Derek accompanying us, his hands clasped in front of him, his new work clothes looking expensive and well made. Tailored. Far different from the camo-clad man of our first meeting. Of course, I was different too. That night I had been wearing a bloody party dress and carrying the severed head of a young rogue vamp. I glanced at my reflection in the metal door, dressed again in the professional outfit of an Enforcer in conference—as opposed to an Enforcer in battle. Big difference there too. We had both come a long way in a short amount of time.

The doors opened and Derek led the way. I let him. He'd be in charge as Leo's full-time Enforcer long after I was gone. I had to let him be alpha or turn him into a kitten with no confidence—Beast's thoughts, not mine, and she knew a lot more than I did about training up a predator.

The conference room was full to bursting with vamps, humans, and that piquant, biting, provocative miasma of scents that said "vamp stronghold." The stink of too much coffee, too much testosterone, and too little sleep added it its own rich undertext to the pong and I wrinkled my nose. Voices were raised to be heard over the volume on the screens, and men and women stood, straining as if to assist the men on the screen, though we were all too far away to assist in any way.

I was just in time.

The small clearing in the Waddill Refuge was illuminated with bright lights, the kind highway paving crews worked by overnight when traffic allowed them to make real headway without bogging down commuters, slowing commercial transportation, or endangering their own lives in the traffic. Bodies were racing here and there on the scene, so covered with mud and sweat and the beating rain that they were unidentifiable. At least two generators were contending for clamor awards, and the voices of the Onorios and the humans were raised to compete. There were two cameras positioned to capture the whole clearing, the wooden doors in the ground clearly visible in the center. The doors, which were set flush with the ground, had been blown or swept free of the refuse and rotting vegetation that had covered them, and the dead crows had been removed. The doors were stark and weathered in the too-bright light.

There were white-painted figures on them, the markings recognizable as runes, sigils, symbols of arcane power. The sight of them made my skin crawl. The last time I had seen so many powered-up runes in one place had been when I fought for the lives of my godchildren.

Eli placed a cup of tea in my hand and I closed my cold fingers around the ceramic cup, smelling Irish Breakfast blend tea, the water still simmering from the steeping boil. He also waved a Krispy Kreme donut under my nose and I took it too. Ate. Drank. Watched the humans on the screen back away from the doors as the Onorios closed in, Brandon and Brian from the sides, in a pounding, splattering rain, each of them lifting a leg and stepping over something, possibly a witch circle in the ground. A hint of green flooded the screen before it pixelated out to a series of overlapping rectangles in shades of gray and green, the grinding sound of static replacing the roar of generators. The circle was still active, still full of arcane power. Magic and digital images and sometimes even cellular transmissions had trouble merging energies. A moment later, the screen cleared and a collective relieved scent filled the room.

The Robere twins looked unchanged until I got a clear view and focused on their legs, which were missing pants. The charred remnants hung to midknee, exposing lower legs, scarlet with burns and weeping blisters. Interesting. They had fought off a witch circle.

I ate and drank and wondered what power Onorios had to step inside an active witch circle and survive. Hopefully. The boys standing on the closed doors were too pretty to die in an explosion of magic.

I drank the cooling tea and finished off a donut and unabashedly Onorio-watched while the stink of vamp-worry increased in the air around me and the men on the screen worked. There were a lot of vamps in the conference room, and once upon a time, I might have been on pins and needles, ready to defend myself at any moment. Here . . . *crap*. I was one of the big cats. No one looked at me twice, no hint of challenge, no need to prove themselves against me. I had both hands full. I was eating and drinking and relaxing in the presence of the apex predators of the food chain.

I took a second donut and ate it, blueberry this time, the powdered sugar falling like pollen over my shirt as I ate. I took another cup of tea when it was offered, this time by a blood-servant, and drank a different blend, something with spice in it. I had never been waited on hand and foot. Never. But I could see why people got used to it.

I was changing.

Before I could dissect that thought, the screens showed a pixelating image of the Roberes, shuffling back, bending in tandem, each grasping a handle in the doors. Which brought me back to the night I was struck by lightning while standing in a witch circle. I had been blown out of the circle when I was struck. Lightning and magic had burned me crispy. I had no idea what that event meant to my life, my future, or my Beast, but I shook off the nagging worry.

Bruiser knelt from just ahead of the camera, his clothes soaked to the skin in the pouring rain. He was holding the foil-wrapped brooch in one hand and a gallon milk carton of what looked like fresh blood in the other. That gave me pause for several reasons, one, because, except for scions in the devoveo, vamps hate any blood that isn't instantly fresh and from the veins or arteries of their blood-servants or blood-slaves, and two, because how many humans had he bled to get a gallon of unclotted blood, and three, how did he do that logistically? I had a mental image of six or eight humans at a long table, slicing their arms open and holding them over a humongous funnel. I chuckled at the vision and took the last bite of donut, grinning and saluting Leo with the dough treat when he looked around, annoyance on his face.

The room around me fell quiet, only the roar of machinery and voices on the screen breaking the silence. The Robere twins strained and the doors lifted. I could hear the creak of water-expanded wood over the generators. The cameras that I had thought were stationary moved forward, clearly shoulder-mounted, to peer into the hole as the harsh lights fell inside to expose a watery hell of . . . not much.

Foul, brackish water, muddy and greenish with algae, filled the pit up to about a foot from the doors. Mold and slime coated the edges of the contained pool and climbed up the warped wood and crumbling concrete walls of the pit. Raindrops spattered down, making concentric circles on the surface.

Bruiser tilted the gallon bottle and drizzled some of the blood into the water. It spread like crimson ink, dropping quickly from sight. Nothing happened. Seconds ticked by and he dripped some more blood in. Something sallow rose, a yellowed-brown bowl, the color of smoked bone. A fringe of blackness floated up around the bowl. Hair. That was hair. And the bone bowl was the top of a skull. The head tilted back and a ravaged face lifted from the water, eyelids thin as paper, bluish as they opened over black eyes in grayish, yellowed sclera. A vamp. Eyes vamped out. But without the blood to make the transition to blood-drinking predator work.

The mouth appeared, lips blackened, the teeth looking human, but the augmented jaw opened too wide to be human, more snakelike, unhinged to spread wide. The cheeks were hollows with tendons clearly delineated and the skin over the facial bones was so desiccated it was mummified.

Someone near me whispered, "Is it your twin, Ming?" The man's voice continued to speak as if he had been answered, an Asian language, cursing by the tone, the syllables harsh with pain. I knew that voice but glanced back to be certain. It was the primo and Enforcer to Ming Zhane of Clan Glass, called Cai, no last name or maybe no first name. The primo of Ming Zhane was slender, dark-haired, and deadly in the kung fu, Bruce Lee kinda way. The moment I had met him I had known that he could break me into tiny little pieces while yawning. Beside Cai, a woman hissed in a breath and began to weep and whisper in the same language, Mandarin, which established that Ming Zhane was in the room, watching her sister's rescue.

The scent of horror, vampire dread, and panic began to seep into the room, a stale scent of rotting flowers and old blood. I felt Leo's power flow into the room, cold as the tundra in some frozen Arctic land. Saw him take a breath. His action repeated as every vamp in the room breathed in and out together. The tingle of vamp magic rose, itchy and unpleasant, Leo, holding it together, holding his people together. The stale scent of panic began to fade.

On the screen, the creature's jaw opened even wider and fangs nearly three inches long slowly swiveled out with a grinding sound, as if long unused.

Bruiser tilted the gallon milk bottle over the opened maw. Blood fell down and trickled into the mouth. The throat swallowed. And swallowed. And drank and drank, growing more effortless with each swallow. She drank the whole bottle of blood. Bruiser moved the plastic container away and Brandon, or maybe Brian—with the mud it was impossible to tell the twins apart—knelt beside him, a blade at his wrist. With a clean upward slice he gashed open the artery and positioned it above the blackened lips, his strong blood pulsing down. The mummified vampire drank, straining upward, taking in enough blood to feed a Naturaleza vamp—the kind who drink down and kill humans for funzies—for days. Onorios have powerful blood and they can lose a lot more than a human can before suffering the consequences, but even with that, it looked like a lot of blood to lose. The other twin bled himself next. And then Bruiser, but he lay on the ground and cradled the skeletal head in one hand, allowing the vampire to bite into his wrist. Which the fanghead did with surprising gentleness, her fangs just grazing into the artery, not sinking deeply, not tearing flesh and tendons, not breaking bone. Ming of Mearkanis, once a Blood Master of a Mithran clan, drank.

I had seen Leo after he was drained. It hadn't been pretty and he hadn't been sane for a long time after. This vamp was peaceful. Passive. It had to be the foil-wrapped brooch keeping her sluggish and relaxed. Which meant that witches, somewhere, somewhere close by, had a way to tame a vampire. Control a vampire. *Use* a vampire for something that I couldn't even imagine.

Suddenly the Witch Conclave, where the vamps and witches would sign peace accords for the first time in forever, so far as I knew, was in serious danger. This was bad and getting badder. I licked my fingers and slid a hand down to make sure the vamp-killer could be easily accessed.

Beside Bruiser, long, thick black tubes snaked into the water. The sounds of pumps came on, adding to the clamor on the screen. The water level in the pit began to go down. Inside the pit, more of the captive became visible. Bony neck that was nothing more than tendons and spiny processes and working esophagus. Shoulders and collarbone and upper ribs. Rotting clothing. Pinned to the remains of the shirt or blouse, and through her flesh as well, was a twin of the brooch on the ground beside Bruiser, this one filmed with scum, but recognizable. Through several inches of water, the gems glowed with greenish energies that pixelated as soon as the water dropped below them, leaving a series of rectangular irregularities in the footage.

As the water went down, the wood and concrete wall was revealed, the wood blackened, the shell-based concrete crumbling. Iron rings had been set into the concrete, rusty but still strong. Blackened silver chains were looped around and around them, and wound across the vampire. Where they touched her, blackened skin showed and one Robere brother set to work with huge metal snips, the kind used by rescue workers to free bodies trapped in car accidents, powered by yet more generators. The chains fell away and the vamp slid deeper into the water, reaching up with her freed arms to grab Bruiser, pulling him into the water with her, a splash we could all see but not hear over the pumps and generators and the occasional shrill calls of human voices.

Brandon and Brian lay on the sides of the pit and reached in to support the two. Behind them, in the shadow of the lights, something else yellowed and broken appeared. I knew what it was even before the shapes came clear, what they had to be. Skeletons. Human skeletons. Chained as Ming was chained. The bones had been broken, splintered, torn apart. Even across the distance, it was clear that the bones had been gnawed, the marrow sucked clean. Ming, if it really was Ming, had killed humans and eaten them, which meant she would be mad, insane with rot. I'd seen it before, the madness that came to a vamp from eating dead flesh. It was bad. Really horrible.

Beside me I felt movement and turned from the screen to see Katie, Leo's heir, and all I could think was *speak of the devil . . .*

Katie had eaten dead flesh. And while she was the most powerful vamp in the land—for entirely different reasons—she was also officially nutso. She leaned to me and whispered, "I have tasted of the darkness of death, and I lived. So shall Ming Zoya of Mearkanis."

"Ummm. Yeah," I breathed. "Okay." I eased away from her vibrant energies, but she gripped my upper arm in taloned hands, too close to the unhealed scars. I felt the cutting edge of her claws through my clothing. I dropped the empty teacup; it hit the carpet and rolled. So much for feeling safe in a room full of blood drinkers.

"I will feed my old friend of the massed blood that is mine from the *gather*. Together we will find the cursed fools who did this. And we shall hunt and destroy them."

Which made no sense at all.

Leo said, "Katherine, my love. Come to me."

Instantly Katie let me go and practically slithered into Leo's arms. Across the way, Grégoire, Leo's secundo heir, watched the two, his face impassive. I had no idea what was happening between them; the ménage à trois had never made any kind of sense to me.

On-screen, Bruiser was trying to remove the brooch pinned to Ming's flesh, but the slightest touch caused her to writhe and rave in pain and madness. Bruiser stopped attempting to remove the ornament and stared at the nearest camera as if searching out Leo. The Master of the City leaned into a mic and said, "Bring her home. And bring the chains that bound her, that I might scent of them."

And in that moment I accepted how dire things might really be. If a witch had done this, Leo would know. If a vampire had done this, Leo would know. If a were-creature, Leo would know. And there would be vengeance and retribution. No matter who had imprisoned Ming, nothing good would ever come of it. New Orleans vamps had been through one war already, a war that had resulted in the destruction of half its clans. There was no telling what might happen if there was another vamp war so close to the Euro Vamps arriving. Or if the vamps and witches went to war. Whoever had done this had been brilliant. Sadistic and brutal, but brilliant. Everything I had hoped for, worked for, sacrificed for, to keep my godchildren safe, to keep the human population of New Orleans and the greater Southeast safe, to keep all the witches in the U.S. safe, was about to unravel all at once.

Plots within plots, schemes within conspiracies within intrigues. The vamp way. And I had little hope of figuring it out and stopping it in time.

Something sharply angled appeared at the top of the screen and was lowered into the pit. It was the wooden box that looked way too much like an oversized coffin for my comfort. To keep from saying so, I picked up a donut, stuffed it into my mouth, and chewed. When the transport box settled into the muddy bottom, Bruiser lifted Ming in his arms and placed her inside. Then he climbed inside with her, holding her like a lover, as a winch lifted the big box slowly out, the pseudocoffin wanting to swirl and twist, but held steady by the Roberes.

When the box rested on the churned-up land, lying flat in the mud, the twins rinsed the two figures with clean water from blue five-gallon bottles, the kind people drank from in doctors' offices and in places where clean drinking water was scarce. The rinse water drained between the slats of the boards until it ran nearly clean. When they were finished, the boys handed in what looked like a foam mattress pad and pillows and blankets, tucking everything around the woman as Bruiser, his wrist still in her mouth, eased his body out. He whispered something to Ming of Mearkanis and she released his wrist. Quickly a human crawled into the box and settled beside her, offering his wrist. Another human crawled in on the other side.

No way would I have done that. No freaking way. Humans were crazy.

"How long, George?" Leo asked, his voice deceptively soft. "How long has Ming of Mearkanis been in the pit?"

Bruiser gestured off to the side, and the pumps went silent. One generator went dead, leaving only one to speak over. He tapped a mud-crusted earbud I hadn't noted and repeated, "How long?" He looked at the camera and leaned into a mic held by the operator, the screen falling off to an uneven angle as the human operator did double duty. "I would say perhaps two years. No more."

Leo shook his head and the scent of anger grew again, spiking high in the overcrowded room.

"*Dominantem civitati*—Master of the City and Hunting Territories of New Orleans," Bruiser said, his words and tone formal and low. "It is unlikely that the witches who attacked your Enforcer are responsible for this horror. Not alone. Not without help. Even with magic, two strong people would not have the physical strength to accomplish this: Digging a pit. Reinforcing it with concrete and magic. Kidnapping a Blood Master and putting her here. This was done by heavy machines and a *group* of people, humans and witches, working in concert, over time."

I nearly dropped my donut in surprise.

Leo's eyes landed on me, his expression telling me to be silent. I wondered if it was polite to be filling my belly while watching the rescue. Probably not. Probably rude as heck. Feeling peevish, I finished off that donut and took another. Leo's expression morphed into feeble amusement before he turned back to the screen.

"But," Bruiser went on, still speaking formally and carefully, as if by rote, or as if he knew how fragile everyone here was, watching and not being able to help or retaliate, "witches have been here. Two witches. The scent of their magical energies are everywhere, in the runes, the sigils, in the water, and on Ming's flesh. They may not have instigated the crime, but they have perpetuated it and maintained it. Ming has been repeatedly bled, by knife to her throat, to feed one who felt no bloodlust and was not overpowered by compulsion. In fact, Ming of Mearkanis is not able to mesmerize at all at this time. It must be the effect of the brooch, and I cannot remove it alone. It must be done by the Master of the City, under controlled circumstances."

I thought about the brooch pinned through her flesh. Magic working on a vamp. Not good. In fact, very bad.

Bruiser continued with his report. "The two humans in the pit with her have modern dentistry, ruling out them being her primo and secondo blood-servants, Benjamin and Riccard. Whoever these humans are, it's unlikely that they signed papers to serve the Mithrans. We have taken photographs of the skeletons, which we have sent ahead. Local law enforcement will need to be called, quite soon, sir."

Leo's lip curled at the idea of human law enforcement, but his gaze narrowed and he said, "As soon as Ming of Mearkanis is in flight, you may contact the parish authorities and tell them that the *pirate pit* revealed something other than treasure. There will be no mention of Ming. The identity of the humans may lead us to the perpetrators."

Which totally let Eli and me off from having to do a crime scene workup on the pit. A sense of relief filled me, making me know just how much I had not been looking forward to Yellowrock Securities being involved in that.

"Yes, sir," Bruiser said, his tone impassive.

"Well done, Onorios of New Orleans," Leo said. "We await you and your precious cargo. Godspeed."

Which made my eyebrows go up. Godspeed? For a vamp? Weird and weirder.

CHAPTER 8

Eww, Ick, and Grody

It was early by vamp standards, but I hadn't slept and if I didn't get some shut-eye, I was in trouble, so Eli and I went to the break room. I spent little time in the room, mostly because on one memorable occasion, I met two heavily tattooed men who later tried to kill some people. And succeeded. More vamp machinations. In the back of the room was a small door, set flush with the wall, a door I hadn't known about back when. Behind the door was a small bunk room, available to anyone, human or vamp, seeking a place to sleep. There were twelve double bunks in a row, so close together that any hope of privacy was long lost. But it was better than asking to bunk in with a vamp.

Three of the bottom bunks were inhabited. A greater number of the upper bunks were being used. The room stank of sweat, old beer, bad breath, and the sort of bodily gasses that tended to accumulate around people who ate a lot of highly spiced food. I didn't care. The sheets were clean and the room was dark, so I crashed on the bottom bunk closest to the door. Eli swung up into the one above me.

With Leo's clan home still not finished, and stuck in the

peculiar hell of seeking a certificate of occupancy permit while not really being ready to be occupied, HQ was stuffed full and the room was seeing a lot of action. Too many humans in one small place meant very restricted sleeping arrangements. Leo had thought he could speed up things in his clan home by offering a building inspector a little cash flow and had the misfortune of meeting up a parish employee who had an unbreakable moral code. Or who hated vamps. The guy had turned Leo over to the police, who'd had no choice but to file charges. Leo had been ticked off. I'd had the wisdom not to laugh. Go, me. On that self-congratulatory note, I fell into dreams.

There was a new dream, but familiar to me. A green eye in my left palm, opened to see me, to read me. The feel of energies scanning through me, learning who I was, what I could do. And then the dream was gone, as if it never was. I dropped deeper into sleep.

It was after midnight when Eli woke me, his watch making a tiny beeping noise, too soft to wake the others. I had kicked off my shoes in my sleep and I pulled them on, stretching before following my partner into the break room and the hallway beyond.

"I got a text from Alex," he said. "Ming of Mearkanis is in the special lair."

"Okay," I said, counting and resetting the stakes that had come lose in my bun. "Special lair, as in the one between floors where Leo keeps my favorite redheaded psycho, Adrianna, the so-far-immortal vamp Leo won't let me kill?"

"One and the same."

"You know it ticks me off to wake up from a nap after too little sleep, to see you looking so wide-eyed and bushy-tailed," I grouched.

"Babe. My tail is not bushy. Syl says it's slick as a baby's butt."

I almost said I wasn't touching that with a ten-foot pole, but thought better of it. Instead I made a gagging noise and let him lead me down the hallway to the elevator, and then down more hallways, some steps, and finally to the special scion lair.

The guard, a tall, slender woman with prominent shoulders and a narrow waist, let us into the lair. The room was small, white, and featureless with one door and no windows. The floor was smooth and sloped to a drain in the center, presumably for hosing off the inmates, though the opportunity to use it for torture had occurred to me. Vamps are treacherous, double-crossing, unstable creatures. Torture would seem to be right up their alley.

Tonight there were six steel mesh cages, like small jail cells. Each made of woven steel strands, making the walls and floors of the cages pliable but strong. In the bottom of each cage was a stainless steel, traylike bottom. The edges of the trays were cupped to hold whatever the chief suckhead wanted to put in it—mixed blood to speed healing, some newspapers to catch droppings, bird kibble, whatever. For now, there were only two occupied cages, one imprisoning Ming of Mearkanis, who was sleeping on the filthy foam mattress that had been in the transport coffin, and swaddled in a mass of linens and an electric blanket. To say the former clan Blood Master stank was an understatement, but I had to guess that sleep was more important than a shower.

At the door to her sister's cage stood Ming Zhane, the Blood Master of Clan Glass in Knoxville, not breathing, heart not beating, something my kind can hear. She was doing that motionless, more-immobile-than-a-marble-headstone thing vamps do when they aren't trying to ape human. I had been around vamps for a long time, but it still unnerved me.

Ming of Glass was wearing black from head to toe, some kind of tone-on-tone-striped, silky fabric pants and a Mao jacket. Her black hair was up in a tight bun and her claws were out, suggesting that she was close to vamping out. She was holding her own wrist and when I caught a whiff of fresh vamp blood, I knew that she had fed her sister. I stayed at the door to give the Mings some privacy.

The room's other occupant was Adrianna, my nemesis and a vamp I had killed several times. Leo kept bringing her back to undeath, and while I didn't understand it, I figured he had his reasons and I'd figure them out about ten seconds before Adrianna tried to kill me again.

The last time I'd seen the blue-eyed, nutso vamp, she was an unbreathing, lifeless, naked body lying in mixed vamp blood like something a chef was about to barbecue. At the time she had a hole in her head made by a silver stake, and gray matter had been seeping from the head wound. A horror movie trope. Now she was sitting on a beanbag-style cushion, her head appeared healed, and she was fully dressed, wearing Lycra yoga pants and a stretchy top, her feet in soft fuzzy slippers. Her scarlet hair was up in a French twist and she was wearing makeup, something sparkly like mica on her cheeks, mascara, and coral lipstick. She looked fantastic, but her blue eyes were still mad as a hatter, and she laughed as if she found me amusing and a bit silly, like a younger sister who needed to grow up.

I turned my back on her as I stepped into the room. Adrianna was more dangerous than an atomic bomb and no way was I giving her any kind of attention until Leo allowed me to behead her. Even he couldn't bring a vamp back from that.

"Jane Yellowrock," Ming Zhane of Glass said, without turning, knowing me by my scent from when we met in Knoxville. From when I rescued her scion from a group of cultists.

"Yes, ma'am?" I took three steps inside, my shoes loud on the smooth floor, but I kept my distance from the vamps. The mixed scents told me that Ming of Glass was emotional, and no way was I getting closer unless I had to.

"You will find the persons who did this to my sister," she said, her tone so low it was hard to hear, even with me drawing on Beast's hearing. "You will bring them to me. Do you understand?" It wasn't a question. It was more in the nature of a threat. And I didn't work for either of the Mings, I worked for Leo, so it wasn't as if I could agree to her orders. Beside me, Eli drew two vamp-killers, not trying to hide the sound of steel-edged blades leaving leather sheaths. Someone stepped into the lair behind my partner and I knew it was Cai, Ming Zhane's primo and Enforcer, without even turning. I lifted a single finger to Eli, knowing he would understand the cautionary gesture. But I had waited too long to answer and had been unintentionally rude. Ming Zhane was turning her head to me, a slow, controlled swivel like a doll's head, but too far, inhumanly too far. Her eyes were vamped out, though her fangs were still in place. I had a chance to fix this. One.

"Blood Master Ming—" I started.

From the open doorway Leo said, "Jane will bring the culprits to me." Ming whipped her entire body to him, vamping out so fast I missed it altogether. Leo didn't seem distressed by her emotional reaction or her three-inch-long fangs, however, stepping in behind me, saying, "Together we will decide their fates, my old friend, you and I. Together we will mete out justice. Allies, as always."

Ming's shoulders, which were hunching up under her black jacket, halted their rise. A moment later she said, "You will not withhold from me the right to vengeance."

"No. I will glory with you in vengeance against our enemies. Together, in the way of the Vampira Carta, by rule of law. As always. But for now, come, you and your bloodservant. You scent of hunger and blood loss and your sister sleeps."

Ming seemed to be on the verge of refusal, but after an interminable time, her shoulders drooped and her fangs *schincked* back into her mouth. Almost visibly, she pulled the power and dignity of her Blood Master status around her and said, "The hospitality of the Master of the City of New Orleans has always been most exemplary." She gave Leo a small bow, her elegant and perfect face a total contrast to her sister's cadaverous one. "I am honored."

"No, it is my clan that is honored," Leo said. "Come. I have a small repast set aside for you, one who has been known to bring healing to the long-chained."

"Ahhhh," Ming said. "I have long desired to taste of this Mithran scion. My master," she said to Leo, "will the Mithran, Amy Lynn Brown, be offered to my sister as well?"

"The very moment it is deemed fully safe. Until then, Katherine, my heir, has fed Zoya of the mixed blood of the *gather*, and your Zoya is much improved."

"You show much kindness to your old friend, my Leo."

"There is little I would not do help one of the Mings, loyal and beloved, friends, allies, and comrades at arms." Leo was pouring it on thick, but Ming of Glass seemed to take him at his words—every flowery one of them.

"For now, you shall taste of me," Leo said. "You spent much of your powerful blood to bring your sister ease, and I sense your weakness. Forgive me for saying such, but my regard is too high for Ming of Clan Glass, and I will not have a guest who hungers." His voice held a laughing note when he said, "And as tonight is a night for celebration, for rejoicing in the return of your sister, I have also chosen a young man for you, one who might fulfill the desires of the Ming I remember from our last visit." Leo took her hand and their heads bent close together, his black locks waving toward her as if with a will of their own. "Your stamina was enough for four men the last night we spent together, but I have found a treasure, who has been waiting just for you and your primo."

Eww, ick, and grody. But I didn't say it.

Together they left the room and the door closed behind them. Eli muttered under his breath, "Blood and orgies."

I said only, "Mmmm," and wandered over to the cage holding Adrianna, to stare down at her. Despite being a captive, she still managed to give off an air of stylish superiority and predatory arrogance. Her eyelids slitted nearly shut and she tipped back her head, exposing her throat to me a in gesture that said, *Come on. Try it. You couldn't take me even if we started with my throat bared.* I didn't rise to the bait. Instead I turned my back on her again and walked out of the room, Eli on my heels.

The door closed with a solid thud that said it was soundproofed. I didn't remember it being so solid last time. I asked the guard, "Why didn't Adrianna talk? She used to be big on taunting and threats."

The slender woman said, "No one's heard her speak in weeks, ma'am. There's speculation that the part of her brain used for speaking is still regrowing. And then there's other speculation that she's forgotten English. No one's bothered to spend the time with her to see which it is, or if there's something else going on.

"We haven't met, ma'am. I'm Ro Moore," she added.

"I'm Jane or Legs. Not ma'am."

"Copy that."

"Military?" I asked her.

"No, ma'am. Alabama backwoods hillbilly, boxer, wrestler, and MMA cage fighter."

"MMA?" I asked.

"Mixed martial arts," Eli said, approval in his tone. "Why not military?"

"I tried, but they wouldn't have me except as officer material 'cause I got a bad ear. I wanted to fight, sir."

"Hearing aid?" Eli asked.

"Had one. Vamp blood healed me. Now I got twenty-twenty hearing," she said, laughter in the words.

Eli nodded. "I'm an MACP level-four instructor. We should spar."

"I'll kick your butt," she said, totally without braggadocio.

Eli said, "It's a match."

"I'll bring snacks and beer and cheer you on, Ro. Come on, Eli. We got people to see and fires to put out." And I needed my bed, but I knew that was unlikely until after dawn.

The elevator doors opened on the conference room level, and I saw Bruiser. He was leaning against the hallway wall, one hand in a pocket, the other dangling. He looked nothing like the mud-spattered man in the video screens, but was dressed in brown cuffed pants, brown belt and shoes, and a white dress shirt with the sleeves rolled up to reveal his forearms. I had developed a serious appreciation for his arms, the veins corded, muscles long and ropy beneath lightly tanned skin, the hair thick enough to make me want to run my fingers through it as I slid my hands down his arms. Bruiser was no waxed and smooth man, and I loved that about him.

"Hello, love," he said.

"Bruiser," I said, not running to him like a sixteen-year-old with her first boyfriend, but letting my happiness show, not hiding it. I didn't know what we were to each other yet, but I liked it, whatever it was.

"Get a room," Eli said.

"We have a room," Bruiser said, a half smile warming his face for a brief moment before falling back into solemnity. "And we have a problem. Is the Enforcer available to talk?" I saw the headset he was wearing around his neck. Business, not fun and games, then.

"That sounds ominous," I said, sharing a look with Eli as we followed Bruiser into a room off the gym. The room had a small sofa, chairs, and a few tables, and reminded me of a private waiting room in a hospital, the place where they put a family for a private chat with a surgeon who was about to deliver bad news. I sat on the couch. Bruiser and Eli both took chairs.

"Before I left the pit where we found Ming, I called the local parish law enforcement agencies and PsyLED," he began.

"Okay."

"An experienced forensic pathologist or medical examiner will see the bones. The damage to the bones will eventually point to a vampire."

"Okay," I repeated.

"The last vampire who was known to eat humans was Immanuel, and law enforcement has his teeth imprints on record from the postmortems on the police officers he ate."

"And the imprints won't match. So now they'll assume that vamps killing and eating humans is common," I said.

"When it is not at all," Bruiser said.

I let out a tired-sounding sigh. "I'll notify Dell to prepare a PR response to those potential problems. And Jodi," I added, "just in case someone calls her about the cop-eater vamp."

"The second item I need to share with you," Bruiser said, "was something that we found at the bottom of the pit. A small gold knife that once belonged to Edmund

Hartley. He claims that it was lost during the time he moved from clan Blood Master to minor scion."

"And since no one understands how a freaky powerful vamp like Edmund lost his clan to a weaker vamp like Bettina, that makes him suspect in some machination to overthrow Leo or cause trouble in general," I said. "Got it." I might not like vamp politics and quarrels, but I was getting a handle on them, even the quarrels that went back centuries.

"Edmund has been bled and read to verify his claims."

Bled and read. I liked that. "Has Bettina been asked to HQ?"

"She has, and she arrived some hours ago. She has refused to be questioned about the Blood Challenge that led to her taking over Clan Laurent, Edmund's old clan, however, so Leo is simply serving strong vintages to her, to Ming of Glass, to Cai, and to Shaun Mac Lochlainn, Bettina's anamchara, in a party room, in the hopes that some verbal insight might be allowed to slip out in the gaiety." His tone was droll, and I knew that *gaiety* meant way more than party hats and balloons. Strong vintages meant that the humans the vamps were drinking from were terribly drunk on expensive liquors, making it possible for the vamps to enjoy themselves as well. Sex and blood, as Eli had said.

I was too tired to put what it all might mean together without banging my head on the nearest wall in frustration, but Bettina had once been clan master of Rousseau. She had been taken down by rivals within her own clan, not according to vamp law, in personal sanctioned combat— Blood Challenge—but outside proper channels. Clan Rousseau had been ruined in the war and the claimants to her title had died. Then Bettina called the sire of Clan Laurent, the powerful and charismatic Edmund Hartley, to personal combat and she had bested Edmund.

Bettina, a beautiful, tiny, curvy woman, was of mixed race heritage, mostly African and European, and while her sexuality could make the air burn, she hadn't appeared that powerful in other vamp gifts, as least not to me. Vamp one-upmanship stuff wasn't my department, but I said, "Okay, so we have two witches." I raised a finger, counting. "Ming in a pit with dead humans." A second finger. "With Edmund, who wants to be my primo, and maybe Bettina, who is keeping secrets, and a Witch Conclave coming up." I had five fingers in the air. "Just five little things to deal with. So far."

"So far," Bruiser agreed.

I dropped my hand. "And two, count 'em, two, magical brooches tying them all together. Were there fingerprints on the brooch you were carrying?"

"Yes, but no matches with AFIS or military databases. The brooch that was on Ming of Mearkanis had been underwater, so no prints there at all."

"May I see the brooches?" I asked. "Together?"

"Yes." Bruiser slid the headset up and into place, switched it on, and said, "Bring the brooches to me." He gave his location and said, "And please bring the small repast I requested. Tea and some scones for the Enforcer. Coffee for Eli Younger and myself." He switched the set off. Eyes twinkling, he said to me, "In case you didn't get enough donuts while I worked in the mud to . . . satisfy you."

I flushed slightly but held Bruiser's eyes and said, "I was satisfied at the time, but there's always room for more."

"Room. Room, you two," Eli said, sounding long-suffering, keeping his eyes on the far wall.

Bruiser and I sat silent, waiting on the brooches and the *small repast*. So dignified, that. Way better than a snack.

Following a discreet knock, three blood-servants entered the room, one carrying a tray with a carved wooden box on it, the size of a child's jewelry box. The other two blood-servants brought in the repast and a tea table with folding legs, which they set up in the center of the room. "That will be all," Bruiser said. When the door closed, he poured my tea into a porcelain teacup so fine I could see the tea through the cup, and placed it on a saucer. Moving gingerly to keep from breaking the expensive china, I added sugar and real cream and stirred with a sterling silver spoon while Bruiser and Eli helped themselves to the carafe.

When I had sipped and eaten, Bruiser slid the wooden box across the table to me. The wood was unfinished, the top and sides roughly carved in lotus blossoms. The wood was unfamiliar to me, but the tingle of magic when I reached for the box wasn't.

I opened the top and caught a single glimpse of the gems. A bright greenish magic slammed into me, sizzling into my left palm like a red-hot branding iron. The light in the room telescoped down to a single pinpoint of light. And then even that went black.

I came to, ears-first, hearing the conversation around me.

"She's breathing."

"Heart rate one eighty-five. BP two fifty-six over one twenty-seven."

"Too high. Too high. Stroke territory."

"How do you know what a normal blood pressure is for a . . . whatever she is?"

"Skinwalker. Cherokee skinwalker." That was Eli. He sounded pissed. "And it's too high no matter what species she is."

"O^2 level is ridiculous. Two fourteen. I've never seen one that high except in a full code."

"I have," Eli said. "It isn't a problem. The only thing I'm worried about is the BP and the partial shift."

"When she wakes up she'll finish the shift. What's the big deal?"

"If you don't get him out of here, I'll shoot him," Eli said, using his combat voice.

I heard a door open and close. I wanted to chuckle, but my body wasn't responding. And my left hand was in misery, feeling as though it was in the middle of becoming a paw, all the bones expanding and breaking and reforming, but in slow motion. Stuck. They said I was stuck mid-shift. "Well, crap," I whispered.

"She's awake."

"Mr. Obvious," I muttered, taking a breath that stank

of blood—mine—and magic—not mine. A stink of burning hair and ozone had filled the small room, and beneath it was a faint, distant reek of old iron and salt. The smells of the green magic that had scanned my house. And me. I remembered. In the moment of waking, I remembered what the scan had spelled me to forget. The familiar awareness of the reading. I had been read exactly that way once before, when I first came to New Orleans, by a magic user named Antoine. Antoine was dead, killed by the creature who had taken over the form of Immanuel, Leo's son. A skinwalker, just like me, but one who had gone to the dark side and started eating people.

And the green eye in my hand allowing Gee DiMercy to keep tabs on me, because he thought I was a *little goddess*, whatever that was. It was all tied in together. Somehow. And it was too much going on. "I need Gee DiMercy. And I need to talk to Rick LaFleur," I said. "And make it snappy before I pass out again and forget everything I just figured out."

My mouth wasn't working well, but Eli understood me and rephrased my orders, adding, "Get George back in here. Jane, do you need Edmund?"

He meant to drink from to help me heal. "No. Just . . . Just Gee."

I must have passed out again, because suddenly Gee was in the room, the smell of him pine and jasmine, like lying in a cold waterfall surrounded by a conifer forest and a garden in bloom. "Sit me up," I said, speaking louder this time, my voice a croak. I got my eyes open and when I was halfway upright, my spine pressing against the sofa foot, said to Eli, "Everybody out but Eli, Bruiser, and Gee."

"And me," Leo said.

"Sure. Whatever."

When the door closed behind the others, giving me some oxygen to breathe, I said, "Call Rick LaFleur's number. Y'all need to hear this."

"It's the middle of the night, Jane," Eli said, cautiously, as he found my cell in my pocket.

Bruiser said nothing and his scent didn't change, but I read between Eli's words and said, "I'm in my right mind.

Rick was in town when something similar to this magic hit me once before."

Eli tapped the screen and held the cell to my ear. The number rang. And rang. I heard the line open and on the other end, a door closed. "Jane," Rick said. The one word. Toneless. Waiting. Knowing that I wouldn't call him except for business. Not anymore. Rick. My onetime boyfriend, who had publically dumped me for a black wereleopard, and who now worked for PsyLED, the Psychometry Law Enforcement Division of Homeland Security. My life was so weird.

"Sorry to wake you," I said, my tone matching his. "Speakerphone."

Eli punched a button and set the cell on the table nearest me.

"You sound like shit," Rick said deliberately, to annoy me, because he knew, good and well, how I felt about cursing, even when I was the one who cursed. "What happened."

"I think I was spelled. It was a similar spell to the one used by Antoine, your friend who ran the diner. The one you took me to meet, so he could tell you what I was."

"Antoine's dead," he said, but I heard the undercurrent of interest in his voice.

"Yeah. I was there. But in the diner, when he shook my hand, he scanned me. Read me. *For you.* Who was Antoine? What was Antoine?"

"Antoine No Last Name. He wasn't in the system. No prints on file. Went by the name Antoine Busho, an alias, as far as I could tell. Shaman. Originally from the Pedro Cays, underdeveloped islands south of Jamaica. No running water, no sanitation, no electric, no schools, no nothing but people living on the edge. I don't know anything more about his magical system or who trained him. Except . . ." Rick paused, and I could almost see him tilting his head, thinking, remembering. "One time he said something about apprenticing to an African priestess for a summer. If he ever said the name, I don't recall. How bad are you hurt?"

Not are you hurt, but how bad, as if the connection we

once had was active even now. Dang it. "I'm still breathing. Antoine said something about a wife. Marla? Maria? Marion? Something with an *M*?"

"That was a joke in the diner. Something to lure in the tourists. So far as I know he was single. That's all I got."

"Thank you for the information," I said.

"Take care." The call ended.

I nodded to Eli, who was already texting Alex with the info and the name to see what the Kid knew or could dig up about Antoine Busho. He spelled out, "Busho, Bucho, Buchoux, Boucheaux. Maybe a dozen others. There are so many names pronounced that way." We heard a ding and Eli said, "Alex is on it. He'll get back when or if he gets something."

It hurt like heck, but I got my head to turn on my neck and focused on Gee DiMercy. The small man was sitting on the chair farthest away from me. He was no longer bloodied and beaten. No bruises. No cuts or abrasions. The Anzu could heal others of most were-bites, if he got to them in time and was given enough time to work his magic, but he couldn't heal himself. Someone had fed him vamp blood to heal.

"You look better," I said.

His eyes flashed to my left hand and away. I still hadn't looked at it.

I said, "When we first met, you tagged me with a magic something-something. And I took it for my own somehow. Tell me about that spell."

"It wasn't a spell," Gee said. "It was part of the goddess's power, the remnants of her curse that touches all weres and the remnants of her personal power, the energies that generated all skinwalker archetypes and all shape-shifters. That you made my magics your own said only that you were of her get. That she was responsible for your being. It made you easy to track, to follow, and to offer assistance had you needed it."

"The one you call a goddess. Artemis. Was she, like, an angel?" I had a feeling that she had been an *arcenciel*, but I had never gotten evidence to back up my hunch.

"No. Angels are all male, in every scripture and history.

No females existed. Ever. Despite the pretty sculptures in graveyards and paintings that Christians hang on their walls."

Which I knew. I wanted to ask how angels procreated with only one gender, but that wasn't germane to this discussion. "So she was, what? And this time, don't blow me off, Gee. I need the answer."

The slight man shrugged. "She belonged to the tribe that eventually became the Greeks. She was a prototype to modern-day witches but with the ability to charm and control any animal on Earth and in the sea. She was a legend who was elevated to the status of goddess by the worship of foolish humans around her. She was grace and beauty and power and wisdom."

I said, "Was. She. *Arcenciel*?" I enunciated.

"I do not know, *Enforcer*."

My title, being used to call attention to his purpose. I asked, "How did something get hold of your magic and make you attack me? Who has that kind of power?"

He looked at me from the corner of his eyes. "There are few who might wield such might. Perhaps you, skinwalker?"

This was getting me nowhere. I felt like I was dancing around the rim of a fire pit, almost on the edge of being scorched, almost on the edge of nothing at all. And the pain in my hand was growing steadily worse. I could smell my blood on the air. Eli knelt beside me and placed a linen tea napkin below my hand to absorb my blood. "You told me once to ask one of the Old Ones what it meant to be goddess-born. What is an Old One?"

"One of my kind would do. One of the old *arcenciels* would do. You might ask Thales, Arcesilaus, Socrates, Plato, or Aristotle. Even Hegesinus of Pergamon might know."

Recognizing some of the names, I said, "They're all dead."

"True. The oldest of the weres might know. Alas, I do not. I am only a few thousand years in age, not as ancient as the maker of were-kind. But the witches of old were different from the witches of this day. They were the first of the magic users, and they"—his head tilted from side to side as he searched for a word—"are our forbearers. The term *goddess* came from them, the women of power."

I closed my eyes and leaned my head against the sofa. "Yeah, yeah, yeah. Fine. I accept that your magic is something more intrinsic and less ritual-based than modern-day witch gifts." I opened my eyes, focused on Gee, and said, "Tell me about the spell of watching that you put on my palms and in my soul home when you healed me of the were-taint."

Gee sat bolt upright and I caught a hint of blue flaring light, like an aura, the action of his magics, the layers of glamours that hid what he was to the world.

"Tell me about the blue eyes and handprints that claimed me as your own. Molly Everhart Trueblood said I stole your watching magics. Then I burned them off and out of my soul home. And then I used the last eye I had scraped of the walls to track you down."

Gee stared at me, his face unreadable. A waiting silence stretched between us before he said, "You should not have been able to find me through my own magics. You should not have been able to burn them away. No one should. No one but Artemis."

I gestured with my right hand to Eli and the small carved wooden box on the table near him. "The person who used the magic on the brooches used a form of the watching magics to spy on me, to read me. I think they got to me so easily though the remnants of your original spell. I think that because they used the same seeing eye on my palm, but greenish, not your woad blue. We're going to open the box, and you are going to tell me what you can about the energies on the brooches, and how their magic worked on your spell."

"Should we take the box elsewhere to open it again?" Bruiser asked.

"No," I said. "He should see what happens if it happens again. He can maybe tell us something about it."

Slowly, as if he was defusing a bomb, Eli opened the box. The stink of iron, salt, and burned-hair magic filled the air, nose curling even to Eli. The energies of two brooches were far more than simply the sum of their magic. It felt like the magic squared. I wanted to take them home and have Molly and Evan inspect them. But for now I watched as Gee DiMercy sniffed the brooches, then extended a hand over them, as if feeling for radiant heat. Finally he picked one up and hefted it, as if checking the weight, held it to the light overhead. Then he placed it back in the box. "It is unlike my magics. It is purely witch magic, but a working that draws from many doctrines and follows more than one set of principles. It is my feeling that it was constructed specifically for you, not me, Enforcer, and that you are correct in saying that it passed to me through the old healing I performed when we first met. Its purpose is to read and understand. To control. To pacify. And to enslave."

That was nothing new.

"But the main peculiarity of the workings contained in the brooches is that they can fuse the energies of differing magics and use them. If the magics found a place in your spirit that was still touched by the memory of my magics, it was able to read that and return the information to the creators of the spells, who could then craft a new working using that information. And it would be able to use any other magics it discovered." He looked again at my left hand. "Even the magics that belong to you alone. I have never seen such a thing."

"So could it also have traced back, through me to you, and used your magics against you?"

Leo said, "Girrard? Is this why you attacked my Enforcer? Because your magics were turned to another's purpose?"

Gee's face was pinched with worry, his black hair falling over his ears, tangled in front of his eyes. "It is possible. I do not recall much of the duel between Jane and me. I recall only a sense of euphoria and bliss. I do not recall other than the emotions of great joy. Until I smelled her blood. Then I began to awaken."

I needed to think, to meditate, to find some kind of healing, but my pain was too great and this was too important. I managed "Okay," thinking about other things that had been inside, or part of, my soul home. Eli poured me glass of cold water and I took it in my good hand and drank it empty before passing it back. Casually, watching Leo's face, I asked, "Do you think the green magic could reach out and control Leo?"

The expressions that flitted across the face of the Master of the City of New Orleans were too swift and too numerous for me to catch, all except the ones that rode the crest of the emotional storm. Shock. Recognition of danger, followed by fury. Realization that he had screwed up majorly when he tried to force a binding on me, a binding that might let him be controlled or attacked through me. I almost said, *Karmic payback is such a bitch,* but I held it in and let a sweet smile onto my face, waiting him out. "I will have Grégoire drink of me regularly," he said stiffly. "If there is external magic he will detect it." With those words, Leo left the room.

As the door swung closed behind him, I said very softly, "Karma's payback is a bitch." There was the barest movement of the door handle that let me know Leo had heard.

CHAPTER 9

Ðrugged Ðream in My Soul Home

The moment Leo was gone, Eli closed the box, chuckling evilly. Bruiser knelt beside me. "Jane. Your hand is getting worse."

"I noticed." I raised the hand, which felt heavier than it should, and this time I looked at it. It was neither hand nor paw, not the long-fingered, knobby-knuckled version of my half-Beast form. It was more of a club, the way a hand might look if it was stuffed into a paw-shaped and furred mitten. Something a kid might wear trick-or-treating on Halloween.

"You need to shift."

"Yeah. I noticed that too. What time is it?"

Eli said, "O four twenty-three."

I had to time to change into Beast and then shift back. But I wanted to be at home, not here. Never here. "I have time to try. Take me home?"

Bruiser knelt beside me and picked me up as if I were a small child. He stood, cradling me, just as the door to the small room opened again. In the hallway stood Leo,

Edmund, and Leo's new secretary, the redheaded scrappy-looking woman, Lee. She was holding a spiral notebook and a pen at the ready.

Leo stared between Bruiser and me. "I have sipped from and read all my scions and my heir and the clan Blood Masters of the city. All are innocent of the disappearance of Ming Zoya of Mearkanis, and her presence in the pit.

"Edmund Killian Sebastian Hartley," Leo said, and Scrappy wrote. He shoved Edmund into the room. The vamp stumbled and went down to one knee, his eyes on his master, "former clan Blood Master, once *servus minime aestimata*, lowest of my scions." When Leo used titles, it meant serious Mithran business. And Edmund was breathing fast, in fear, the stink of his terror rising on the air. I had the mad thought that Leo was about to behead Edmund, right in front of me, and I had to stop it. I struggled to stand and Bruiser let my feet to the floor, still supporting my weight, the pain in my hand feeling as if I had just thrust it into a furnace. I grunted in pain, but Leo ignored me and went on. "I hereby reassign the last nineteen years of your servitude to Jane Doe Yellowrock of Yellowrock Securities, Enforcer to the Mithrans of New Orleans and the greater Southeast United States, with the exception of Florida. Your status shall be raised to the position of Mithran primo and you will serve her well."

"No!" I said.

Leo flashed me a grin that was all teeth and fangs and bloodlust. "Yes, my Jane. It is done." He popped away in a small sound of displaced air and the door slammed.

I gasped and my vision darkened around the edges in reaction to shock and pain. Eli, the evil man, laughed again. To Edmund, kneeling on the floor at Bruiser's feet, I said, "This is all your fault."

Edmund, whose face had gone white, and his eyes vamped out, looked up to me, the pupils like pits, staring into hell. With an effort of will, his fangs *schincked* back up on the little hinges in the roof of his mouth, and his eyes bled back to human. He bowed his head to me, leaning over his bended knee. "My master."

I thought that I had avoided this, had actually thought that Edmund's request to become my primo was a ploy on Leo's part, something to delude the European Vamps that I had such strong magic that I deserved a vamp primo but was all bombast and no action. But . . . this had happened. It was serious. And with the little secretary putting it all in writing, there was no way to refuse. But I did it anyway. "I refuse. I don't want a primo."

"Then I shall face the dawn one day hence," Edmund said, his brown eyes on the floor at my feet. "I will have this day to sleep here, in the council chambers, in safety. Then I must remove my belongings and myself. I no longer have the funds to purchase a lair in such a short time period, and banks are notoriously difficult for Mithrans to deal with."

"Hotels? Boardinghouses? Acton House caters to vamps."

"I am yours. Send me where you will."

"Twenty-four hours," Eli said, sounding as if he was holding in laughter. "We have time to figure out something."

I might have slept, because when I woke, Eli was carrying me toward the sweat house at Aggie One Feather's place. It was dawn, and the eastern horizon was golden as viewed through the pine trees near her home. Eli pushed open the door with an elbow and knelt on the packed clay floor, sitting me down in front of a fast-burning fire. The sweat house hadn't been used in a while; I could tell because the air moved with the rising heat and the coolness of the wooden walls. And because there were no coals in the pit, only crackling wood, hickory and pine and cedar. I looked back to the open door to see that the rain had stopped. Mosquitoes buzzed in a cloud, kept at bay when Aggie closed the door on them.

I lifted my left hand. It was shaped like a war club, bones protruding beyond the pelt, bones that had no order or direction, as if they had been built by a toddler with sticks and Play-Doh. My wrist was now involved, the bones bulging. In a normal human wrist, there are twelve main bones. My left wrist looked as if I had twice that many, the tendons attached in the wrong places, stretching in the wrong ways, pressing apart the bones of my lower arm. I was in agony. Closed my eyes and cradled my arm against me.

"How long before the witch is here?" Aggie asked.

"My brother is bringing her," Eli said. "ETA twelve minutes."

"I've never allowed workers of magic into a sweat."

"You're gonna need them. This is a magical attack on Jane."

"We need her out of her clothes. It's going to hurt her."

"No, it's not."

I heard the familiar sound of steel sliding from a leather sheath and then Eli was cutting through the expensive clothing, undies and all. "Perv," I whispered.

"Totally, babe." He unbuckled all my hidden weapons and piled them beside me. "Miz Aggie, you got scissors? I don't want to risk the blade near her arm."

"I brought a pair," Molly said from the door.

"I am Aggie One Feather. Welcome. Have you ever been to sweat before?"

"Witch version. Not Cherokee. We'll work around it. What feels right from both practices, blended to help Jane. Yes?"

"I suppose. . . ." Aggie didn't sound all that certain.

But Molly did. "Thank you, Eli," she said. "But you need to go now. We'll handle it."

"But—"

"No buts," Molly said. "This is women's work."

"Technically, it's *Tsalagi* work," he said.

"True. But also, technically, it's *not* men's work and it's also *not* military work," Molly said with asperity. "Honestly, Eli. Your energies are all wrong. You might cause problems with ceremonial aspects of this. We can handle this. Please go away."

"You may wait with my mother, Eli," Aggie said. "She was making breakfast when you called. Pancakes."

Eli didn't reply. He just turned on a heel and left the sweat house. I could smell his frustration and worry over the scent of burning wood. And I caught a whiff of Alex on the air as well. I managed to get my eyes open a slit while the women finished ruining my clothing, and I found Aggie in my blurry vision. "No more cats."

Aggie laughed. "How is Kit-Kit?"

"She's Molly's familiar now," I said. "She adopted her." Which might imply that Molly had adopted Kit-Kit or that Kit-Kit had adopted Molly, which was closer to the truth.

"My mother said Kit-Kit was supposed to keep you alive, someday," Aggie said, reminding me of the prophecy warning.

"Mighta already happened," I said, remembering the lightning that had struck me. Kit-Kit had been there and I had survived. "Or if it hasn't happened yet, then she'll be there when I need her."

"Oh. Sorry," Molly said. "I'm Molly Everhart Trueblood, earth witch with a touch of moon magics. I am honored to be seated before your hearth. That's an old witch pleasantry, which means you're in charge and I'm your willing and helpful assistant."

"Except where Eli was concerned." I could hear the laughter in Aggie's tone.

"Men. Always underfoot."

Aggie laughed and I felt the two women move toward accommodation until Aggie said, "You are pregnant. I can't let you stay for a sweat. It's bad for pregnancy. I'm sorry, but you have to go. You can't stay here."

"I wasn't planning on staying the whole time. I'll be in and out. Mostly out." She patted her baby bump. "Casandra Evangeline Jane Yellowrock Everhart-Trueblood is demanding."

And a witch, I thought. Cassy's parents didn't yet know if she was a double-gened witch like Angie, or a single-gened witch like Molly. Either way, she would already be demanding. I remembered Molly pregnant with Little Evan. Her tantrums and emotional outbursts had been spectacular.

"It is against my best instincts, but if you are certain . . ."

Molly said, "I'm good. I promise."

"Then I offer you welcome in the sweat house of the *Tsalagi.*"

"What herbs will you put on the fire?" Molly asked.

The two women talked herbs and herbal concoctions and herbal reactions and herbal interactions. They talked ceremony. And all the while, Molly drank from a gallon bottle of Gatorade. The blue kind that always made me want to barf. Just looking at it made me all gaggy.

"I'm thirsty," I said. "But none a' that blue stuff. Just water."

"Soon, Jane," Aggie said soothingly. More tentatively, she asked Molly, "What do you know about Jane?"

"Everything," I said. "More than you do." I tried to focus on Molly, but she was blurry in the firelight. She was dressed in one of Aggie's coarse white shifts, and so was I, my once-pretty clothes in a heap by the fire, as if to be thrown in and burned. My weapons were nowhere in sight, and I knew that Eli had taken them with him. To Molly I said, "Aggie saw me half-shifted, and we've talked while I was under the influence of whatever stuff she gives me to drink, so she knows what I am. How old I am. But she doesn't know about Beast."

"Beast?" Aggie said.

"That's my story to tell, I suppose, since you're not yourself," Molly said, settling to a log seat, her baby belly less obvious beneath the sweat clothes. "When Jane was five years old, her father was murdered by two white men. They also raped her mother, all right in front of Jane. She went to live with her grandmother, who helped her track down and kill the white men. The old bat made Jane help in the killings, according to the War Woman way."

Aggie's mouth tightened in response. My story sounded so violent and savage, so cruel and brutal when stripped of the emotions and the pain of a proper *Tsalagi* telling. "I have heard this tale. Jane was not responsible for the actions of her grandmother, nor what her grandmother forced her to do. There is no judgment against her for the deeds of another."

"Agreed. But then the political world shifted," Molly said, "and they were sent on the Trail of Tears."

"So she has told me," Aggie said, agreeable, though mildly irritated. I hadn't decided if she believed me about it all. She might just think I was a nutcase.

Molly went on, relentless. "Jane doesn't remember much about it. But at one point, in the middle of a raging snowstorm, her grandmother forced her into the animal she knew best, a bobcat, and tossed her out into the snow to live or die."

"Jane has told me this, and that makes her over one hundred seventy years old."

"Give or take."

"And yes, I know that *Dalonige'i Digadoli* is a skin-walker."

"Good," Molly said. "I didn't know if you got that part yet. Anyway, she was out in the snow, in her bobcat form, and she found a frozen deer carcass. She was eating when a nursing female cougar came back for her kill and attacked Jane. Jane did accidental black magic and took both the form of the mountain lion and its soul inside with her. She's two-souled."

Aggie One Feather muttered something in the tongue of The People. It contained the word *ti*, which was buttocks, and the phrase sounded like a curse, which made me chuckle. "Yeah. Kinda the way I feel about it," I said, holding up my deformed left hand. "And it's probably the major reason why weird stuff keeps happening to me."

Molly said, "It's taken a long time for her accept that she isn't a liver-eater, but the possibility of someday becoming one still worries her."

"I understand this better now," Aggie said. "The two-souled are . . . dangerous."

"She knows. But she and Beast have come to an accommodation and work together to achieve common goals."

Which made me sound like a business merger with customer relations issues.

Molly continued. "She feels guilt for killing the two men who murdered her father and it's shaped and formed her whole personality and being. But she's been working on guilt with you, and things are better."

Aggie muttered the same words, and this time I got them. *Tsalagi* don't have cusswords or curses like the white man, but some phrases can be used in that way, according to the intent of the speaker. "*Uskanigigaluda tsi ti*," loosely translated, meant "scalping my butt." I laughed, the movement shaking my hand, and ended on a pained breath and a curse of my own.

"You know she's hurting if she's cussing," Molly said, of me. "And the little one doesn't like the heat, so I'm moving back against the wall. I'm here if you need me."

Through slitted eyes, I watched as Aggie stirred the wood and the new coals beneath, muttering in Cherokee too low for even me to hear. She now knew all my secrets, and she hadn't tossed me to the curb, which had always been my private fear. She rearranged the river rocks that would take heat from the fire, pushing them closer to the flames. She rearranged the clay bowl filled with water and the dipper, and a fired red clay tile, like one off a roof, something new that she hadn't used before, her actions and the way she was breathing indicating that she was using the motions as a formulary, a methodology, trying to settle herself, to make room inside for all the things she had heard.

She didn't look at me, not even once, keeping her gaze on the fire, and I didn't like the fact that she kept her gaze averted. Aggie was having a hard time dealing with this. With me. "Can you accept me, even knowing this, Aggie?" I asked.

Aggie scowled and, from a basket at her side, pulled a sprig of dried rosemary and held it to the fire. Rosemary hadn't been a traditional Cherokee herb, having been brought by the first European settlers, but many medicine men and wise women of the Americas had incorporated anything that worked into their ceremonies, and rosemary had strong oils that performed well with many other herbs. The scent filled the sweat house as the dried leaves curled, sparked, and caught fire. Aggie placed the burning stem in the curved arc of the red clay tile, which she had turned concave side up, perfect to hold the blazing stem as the rosemary leaves burned to ash. The stem burned as well, and the sweat house was thick with the scent. When the rosemary was ash, she slanted her gaze at me and said, "I'm your elder. Or I *was* your elder. It was difficult for me to find out you're older than *lisi*. It is doubly difficult to hear of your souls. There is no story in the histories to tell me what to do or how to help you. But it doesn't matter. I will try to help one of The People who comes to me for wisdom. Breathe."

She pulled another herb from the basket and extended that branch toward the fire as well. When it caught, she placed it too in the clay tile. The herb was something even stronger than rosemary, smelling of camphor. I sneezed three times in succession, which jarred my arm horribly. When I looked at it again, the abnormal shape-change had worsened, and now my elbow was involved, the joint trying to bend backward. I groaned in misery.

"Breathe!" Aggie demanded, and I breathed in the stink. In and out. In and out. She threw another branch on the fire, and I watched it flame and turn to ash. She repeated the command to breathe and burned small branches of the stinking herb until she had done it seven times. Then she lifted the clay tile and emptied the ash over her clay bowl and tapped it until the ashes were transferred. I had a bad feeling about what she was going to do with the stuff in that bowl.

Aggie burned three more herbs, these smelling of two varieties of mint and one that stank of creosote, adding the ashes to the bowl. She had a small pile of stinking ash, like a tiny volcano cone, in the bowl. She unscrewed a Mason jar, and the stench of moonshine filled the sweat house. She added a splash of that to the bowl too. With a whisk made of plants, she stirred the contents.

"Aggie," I said, "none of those were Cherokee herbs."

Her scowl deepened. "No. These are herbs suggested by a crazy old Navajo man. He's one who saw the photos I sent of your last spell-instigated injury. He said they might help you attain a higher state of energy, one strong enough to reach inside and pull your own shape back out. I thought he meant a healed version of yourself. Only later, I realized he had to know you were a skinwalker or a were and he was seeing a maltransformation, not simply an injury. A dark magic spell might have brought about this particular problem, but the treatment would still be the same, no matter how it was acquired." At my confused look, Aggie said, "Never mind. Maybe this will help. Maybe it won't. So breathe and meditate and we'll see what happens."

I breathed, watching as she added something bluish green to the bowl's mix; it looked like a small upside-down cup made from a wrinkled cactus, but without the spines. She took a pestle to the mix and ground it for a long time, adding more moonshine. And when she passed me the moonshine, ashes, and wrinkled green thingy, I didn't refuse, question, or hesitate. I drank it down. The moonshine was so strong, I didn't half notice the other tastes, though the texture was gag-worthy all on its own. I coughed and spluttered and thought my esophagus might catch fire, but it didn't. It hit my stomach like a bomb going off, however, heat flaming back up, and I had to swallow it down again. This time, the vile concoction didn't come back up. Instead the alcohol hit my system and I dropped down into a meditative trance, faster than I ever had. Almost as if the moonshine and other stuff pulled me down.

And down.

I fell into my soul home as if dropping though an opening in the roof and I landed beside the fire pit on all fours, Beast form. I/we shook myself, loose coat sliding across my frame.

We bent to the fire and breathed, the scent strong and warm, of cedar heartwood and hickory. Here, proper herbs had been burned on the flames, sage and sweetgrass. *Tsalagi* herbs, not that awful peyote. *Peyote.* I wasn't certain how I knew that the greenish wrinkled cuplike thing was peyote, but it was. And I was having a drugged dream in my soul home.

I sat upright, front paws together, and studied the cave that represented my own soul, my spirit, a place of refuge and safety, which, on the surface, might seem to indicate that it should never change, but it did, and often, as a reflection of my life and what was happening to me. It was like a three-dimensional representation of my psyche.

Beast growled. *Soul den. Place where Jane and Beast are one.*

Yeah. Pretty much.

It was a cave in the real world, somewhere, because I had been there when I first changed into my bobcat form, helped along by my father and my grandmother. In that long-ago past, the cave walls and ceiling had been a grayish stone, the roof melting down in drops and spirals, soft and puddling, like melted candles, the rock seeming magical. The cave roof had cried the tears of the world in soft plinks, the sound of falling water merging with the drums and flute of my first change.

Since, it had become this representation, where I saw myself as I was, moment to moment, sometimes standing on four legs, sometimes on two. The shadows on the walls merging often into one, a form with no certain shape, both cat and human, furred and skinned, four-pawed and two-footed. A shadow shimmering with black motes of light.

On one wall I had once seen circles and swirls painted in soot and fat and crushed pigments. Carved into the stone were arrows pointing to the right. Lines parallel. Lines like waves—the symbols of The People. And there had been paw prints. They padded across the rounded stone roof of the world, big-cat paws in the red of old blood. Human footprints walked beside the paw prints, up and over the roof of the world. Side by side. Like Beast and me.

There were also white man symbols, brought here since we had lived in the modern world, diamonds and stars, signs and ciphers, and an image of a cross that burned. And of course, there had been the blue hands in circles of white, and white hands in circles of blue. Pigments, signs of ownership applied to the walls of my soul house by Gee, who had thought to use me.

Cleansed by fire.

"Mine," I growled. "My place."

Until I had been hit with a spell by the Son of Darkness. Then I had seen above us, in the dome of the roof, red lines, like blood vessels, veins, and arteries pulsing with silver and black and red motes of power and full of blood. Magic that hurt us was black magic. Blood magic. Like the magic of witches turned to darkness. Like blood magic stored in stone. The blood diamond had such magic, magic that sent out red pulses and motes of power. But in my soul home the vessels had looked clogged and bruised, full of clotted and dying blood, and they had been leaking. It was what I understood a soul might look like when under attack from vampire blood.

Later, the walls had appeared blackened as if by fire, the smell of sour smoke hanging on the damp air. It had smelled unused, had sounded silent, had felt cold and empty. My cavern had been damaged, as if fire—or lightning—had left soot and char all over it, black and gray and dirty, with the undamaged wall showing through in places, white and the palest of greens and creamy grays in what looked like strange symbols, nonpatterns that I didn't recognize at first. I had walked around the pit, studying the shapes, and they had resolved into hundreds of representations of the Blood Cross scorched into the walls at every angle, as if the lightning and the cross had been spinning around, engaged in a dance—or some arcane form of combat.

More recently there had been a vision that had worried me more than any of the others, even more than the burned, lightning-struck vision. The cavern had no longer looked sooty and burned, its walls creamy gray, tinted with greens, but directly overhead had appeared the shape of wings, white wings and dark wings, as if a snowy owl and a crow fought there. It had seemed a symbolism of danger, as if forces of light and dark engaged in combat for my soul.

And lastly, there had been wings, possibly angel wings draping across the roof of the world. And there had been that black mote pulsing beside it, like a heart of darkness, full of power. The angel wings were still here, in this peyote dream, draping across the roof and down the walls, the flight feathers resting curled on the floor. The dark mote was still there, where Angie Baby had pointed it out, up high, near the joining of the angel wings, where the heart of the angel itself should be.

I stared at the place overhead, straining to see the dark mote clearly. Where the angel wings joined together, the mote was shackled with a large blue ring the color of woad, and from the other side of the ring fell a triple-linked chain, in style like an ornate necklace chain. The links draped along the wings, following the shape of the roof, until it came to a stalactite, thick and strong, one that had been forming for millennia, long enough to meet the stalagmite below it and merge into a single column that reached from ceiling to floor. There the silver chain looped loosely around the pillar down to the ground to lie coiled like a woman's necklace dropped and forgotten in the shadows.

That chain was what Angie Baby had used to pull the black mote from my chest so we could see it together. The chain she said might kill me if I broke it. I padded to the pillar and sniffed the chain. It smelled of metal. And ozone, like the aftermath of lightning. And it smelled of blood. Vampire blood. Beneath that stink was the reek of burned hair. I sat down again, studying the chain. It was thinner near the floor, and the way it was curled, it had taken on the shape of a flower. A rosebud, which seemed significant but I couldn't remember why. Overhead, as the chain fell downward, the links were thicker, and the higher I looked, the more organic they appeared, less perfectly made and heavier, as if the chain was alive and was growing and the roots were overhead, like a plant growing upside down, to flower on the floor.

I extended my claws and poked at the bloom, pricking it. The bud opened, fast, like the special photography showing the "pop" of some flowers opening. Inside the petals, where the stamen should be, was an eye, green and blurry and unformed, but looking at me.

Every time I've been attacked by magical means, it left a mark, I thought. *Like a crack in a piece of pottery that allows water to slowly drain through, continuing to damage the dish.*

Jane is not dish. Jane is not in cage. Jane is free, Beast thought back, which didn't sound like a reply to my comment, but an altogether different observation.

Okay. I'll think about that one. For now, we need to fix my hand.

Jane can fix hand. Jane is not in cage.

I chuffed out a breath. Lay down and thought about our twined and twisted double helix of genetic material, the double spiral that once was, a double helix for Beast and a double helix for me. But like the last few times I tried to find one or the other, they appeared together, a tripled helix of tangled DNA polymers. The nucleic acids held together by nucleotides, which should base-pair together, were instead in rows of three, twisted back on themselves and knotted in odd places. I had read as much as I could understand about how the helix should work, but it wasn't enough to separate the strands.

Chain and mote and flower eye, Beast thought. *Three links.*

Tripled links, I thought back, and examined more closely the chain that hung from the roof of my soul home. I had thought it looked organic and it was. The chain was the spiritual representation of our twisted genetics. Twisted by all the strange magics I had come in contact with over the time I was in New Orleans. Just as radiation forced mutations on genetics, so the magic had forced a change, a mutation. And that mutation was tied to the dark mote of power at the heart of my soul. And was part of the eye-in-my-palm spell that was tied to me. Through my RNA and DNA. It all made sense, here in this place.

Beast extended all our claws and gathered herself.

Beast, what are you—

She shoved off the floor of the soul home with all four powerful legs and leaped high, catching the pillar in her claws the way she would sink them into tree bark. The pillar should have been slick and slippery as water-smoothed stone, but there were rough edges and a spongy feel to the mineralized column that allowed my claws to sink deep. Beast climbed the pillar just as she would a tree. High, to the top of the cavern. I didn't look down, but Beast chuffed a laugh at my fear. *Beast has leaped much farther.*

Fine. Okay. But what the crap are we doing up here?

Beast set her claws and held on, her nose only inches from the woad blue link and the dark pulsing mote as she sniffed, drawing the air in over her tongue and the scent sacks in the roof of her mouth in flehmen behavior. The smell of vampire was stronger here, as were all the scents. And the stink was a mixture of Leo, Gee DiMercy, Joses, the Son of Darkness, and . . . Bethany.

Bethany. Holy crap. When she healed me the first time, she left something inside me . . .

Vampire! Beast snarled. *Ambush hunter!*

Faster than thought, she snapped at the woad ring. It was the striking of a big cat on prey, canines sinking deep and ripping out. The blue link broke and she yanked it free of the pulsing mote. The edge of the mote burst outward in a shower of blue and silver and scarlet sparks. The chain slid free and fell, slithering around the pillar. The blue link crunched and bled, a bitter taste like the drink Aggie One Feather had given me. And the stink of iron, salt, and burned hair.

Below me on the floor, the silver chain piled up as it fell, rattling like snake scales, a sliding shush of sound that was nothing like the metallic ringing chimes it should have been.

The woad ring in her teeth, Beast backed partway down the pillar and then leaped, free-falling toward the cave floor twenty feet below. Where a silver snake with one huge green eye was coiled, looking up at us, ready to strike.

CHAPTER 10

You Can Try, Witch

Midair, Beast whirled her heavy tail and torqued her body, pushing off the pillar with her back paws, launching herself out and to the side. In a movement worthy of a kung fu special effects movie, she spat out the ring and whipped her body around, catching the snake behind the head. She bit down. Metal and bone crunched, green blood splattered and filled her mouth. Beast whipped her whole body side to side, lashing the snake, thrashing its head against the floor, breaking its spine in a dozen places. Death tremors twitched through its long tail. The emerald slit pupil in the single green eye widened and went still.

The woad ring had gone dull and grayish. The stink of burned hair disappeared. The snake was dead.

Just to be certain, Beast ripped out the snake's vertebra and spat bone, green blood, and silver scales to the floor. She settled to the cave floor to groom herself. Her tongue was rough and coarse, and pulling green blood and blue woad off her pelt.

Oookaaay. I can't complain.
Beast is best hunter.

Yes, you are. But we're still left with my hand all bent back and broken. And what is with that stink of burning hair?

We can shift now. We can become Beast. The Gray Between is ours again, she thought.

I studied the ceiling. The dark mote was still there, but instead of a strong pulsing, it was fluttering, as if Beast's rough treatment of the woad ring and removal of the chain had damaged it somehow. I remembered it spurting, as if it was alive and had been injured. I pushed to our feet and moved slowly to the other side of the fire pit, to see the mote from that side. There was a small blackened mark there, like a scar.

I went back and pawed the ring. Part of it was missing. *What happened to the blue ring?*

Beast ate it.

Was that wise?

Tasted of blood of Anzu. Beast chuckled. *Makes Beast strong.*

I didn't like the idea of her swallowing the magic of another creature, but it was a bit late to argue about it. *What about the smell of Bethany?* Bethany was a vamp priestess and she took the term *nutcase* to new and whacky heights.

Bethany meant to watch, like ambush hunter. Bethany has not done so.

So she, what? Forgot about us?

Beast does not know.

But . . . her magic. Is it dead?

Beast looked away, bored with the topic. Or she didn't know the answer and wouldn't let me know that she didn't know. Dang cat. *How about the burning hair?* I asked again.

Jane has hair.

Yeah. Dang cat was messing with me. *Fine. Ducky. Let's try this thing.*

I padded back to the fire pit and lay down on the cool stone floor. Closing my eyes, I searched out, not my own DNA, but the vision of myself in my human form. I felt the Gray Between as it erupted out of my breastbone, high, near my throat, and spread around me with cool, sparkling radiance I could feel, even sightless. The shift began with my spine and ribs, bones cracking, snapping in two, and reforming. I opened my mouth to scream, but had no breath for one, my lungs half collapsed as they changed and reshaped. This change was as painful as my shifts used to be, and as slow, a ripping, tearing transformation. I opened my eyes as the bones in my left hand and arm, and even higher in my shoulder, began to reform, reshape, realign, and snapped into place. Human. *Better,* I murmured to Beast. *Much better.*

And then I remembered one of the *Tsalagi* words for the double helix of genetic material. The snake. *I-na-du.* The snake in the heart of each creature. And I had to wonder whose DNA Beast had just broken. Or healed.

I came to in the sweat house, the coals burned low, into deep red heat, the rocks discharging the same heat outward. The first thing I noticed was that I was pain free. Salt-caked. Stinking. I rolled my body over and took a good long look at my hand. Human. Mine. I checked out my feet and knees and thighs, and peeked down through the neck opening of the sweat-soaked gown. Human. *Thank God.*

My BFF was gone. Aggie was sitting against the far wall, her back ramrod straight and pressed firmly to the wood, as far from me as she could get and still be inside the sweat house with me. I cleared my throat, which felt like two pieces of chamois buffing together. I was seriously dehydrated, and when I spoke, my voice was coarse and gritty. "So. Now you know my deepest darkest secrets."

"I doubt that." She sounded wry, not terrified.

"Well, all the ones that are fit to be aired in public."

She made a sound that was part snort, part a sound like *pshaw*, and all Cherokee.

I remembered my grandmother making that sound and I smiled, or what passed for a smile made by lips dried in mummified wrinkles. With all the formality at my disposal and with my heart in my throat, I said, "Thank you, Aggie One Feather—*Egini Agayvlge i*—of the *ani waya*, Wolf Clan of the Eastern Cherokee, Elder of the *Tsalagi*."

"You are welcome in my sweat house and in my home, *Dalonige i digadoli*, of the *ani gilogi*, Panther Clan, through your father and grandmother, but also of the *ani sahoni*, Blue Holly Clan, through your mother, who must also be honored." She gave me a slow, low bow, as ceremonial and ancient in its formality as anything I remembered from my toddler years among the *Tsalagi*. The kind of bow offered to an honored guest who might come to trade or bring news from a distant clan. As formal and measured as a bow offered to one who brought news of war.

Pushing up to a full sitting position, I managed a much less graceful bow in return, but did succeed in dropping my head lower than hers had gone. As was proper to an Elder and to a shaman of The People.

She gave me a wisp of a smile in return. "Let's get you showered and inside the house. You need to eat and sleep and drink a great deal of water."

Before we left, I ate enough at Aggie's table to feed three people and drank so much water there, and on the way home, that running trips to the bathroom woke me several times, which was the only thing that kept me from sleeping away the rest of the day. Not even the squeals of running children, giggles, and Alex's teenaged irritation at the noise and interruptions had any effect. On some level, I must have heard it all, but I slept through everything, and woke at sunset, the last rays of scarlet light brightening the street outside my window. My hand was normal, my Beast was purring contentedly inside me, and I was pain free, if stiff as a board. I couldn't ask much more of living than that.

However, I shuffled to the bathroom and caught sight of myself in the mirror over the sink. I decided that the myth of zombies was really true, as the black-eyed, sallow-skinned, dull-haired, uncoordinated thing in the mirror didn't lie.

In the shower, I turned the water to scald and slid to the floor, letting the hot water beat down on me, washing away the last of the salty scum I had missed in Aggie's outdoor shower, the new stink of sleep sweat, and some of the muzzy-headedness. When there was no more hot water, I crawled from the shower, dried off, combed my wet hair, dried and braided it, and dressed, remembering the clothes that had been piled at Aggie's sweat house fire. Pretty sure they had contributed to the stink of burning herbs and roots and other scents. Being Enforcer was hard on a girl's wardrobe. Good thing I wasn't a fashion horse, a woman who loved clothes and shopping and all that stuff. My lifestyle would have left me in permanent misery.

I dressed in a loose oversized gray tee and black leggings, and pulled on socks, because my feet were unaccountably cold, before leaving the bedroom for the kitchen and whatever animal protein I smelled cooking there. I passed Molly, who said, "We need to talk and scan you for external magics as soon you can be coherent. Which, at the moment, looks like never, but I'm withholding judgment."

With a grunt, I lifted a hand in her direction as I slid into a kitchen chair. Eli was lining up a plate full of beef shish kebabs, with pineapple and onion and three kinds of peppers, heavy on the beef, which was cooked rare and bloody and perfect. I sat and breathed out, "If you weren't already adopted, I'd adopt you right now, just for this."

"That's what all the old women say. The young ones want to bump bones."

"Uncle Eli, what's bump bones?" Angie Baby asked from the living room.

"Crap," he whispered.

That woke me up. I stuffed a huge gobbet of beef into my mouth to keep my laughter hidden from my godchild. Eli swatted me with his dishrag, smacking my head without even aiming. "These are shish kebabs, Angie." He indicated a platter on the edge of the table as she walked up. "And when you remove them from the stick, and they bounce, that's bumping bones."

I nearly choked trying to swallow the beef half-chewed and not laugh at the same time.

"Uncle Eli," Molly said from the living room, censure and glee in her tone.

"Sorry," he said. "Best I could do on short notice. I'll do better next time."

"I suggest there be no next time."

"Yes, ma'am," he said. "That would clearly be the best decision on my part."

"Mmmm," Molly said. "Come back here, Angie."

"I'm bored. I wanna watch a movie on the big screen."

"I wan' watch moo!" EJ parroted.

"I'll be working in my room," Alex muttered, gathering up all his gear and traipsing upstairs.

"So, what are you going to do about the vampire?" Eli asked, trying to divert attention from his own faux pas to me. "You know. The one who wants to live here."

"What?" Molly asked, whirling to face us again.

I shoved in another hunk of beef and chewed, my eyes promising all sorts of retribution on Eli. He laughed easily, happily—that rare mirth that would have been part of Eli all the time if Uncle Sam and military service hadn't ripped all the innocence out of him.

Molly shooed Angie to silence and started a Disney movie, listening as Eli explained all about the situation with Edmund and his new, forced position in my life. Things were happening behind her intent expression, thoughts caught in her silence, reflected in her expression before she turned to me. She took a chair beside me and propped her head on her fist, her elbow on the table, red curls flopping over to one side, a little longer than the last visit, but still far shorter than I was accustomed to. "A fanghead primo isn't a bad idea," she said.

I nearly suffocated on a half-chewed globule of beef. Eli's happy smile faded away. I choked the beef back up and said around it as I chewed, "Whatchu mea'?"

"I've been studying the Vampira Carta in my spare time," she said, offhand. "Well, the twins and I have. And Lachish Dutillet."

Lachish was the head of the New Orleans coven, the woman leading the Witch Conclave, and she was in charge of vamp/witch reconciliation. She was a stout, stern middle-aged woman who looked like someone's grandmother, but was really a magical force to be reckoned with. The twins, Elizabeth and Boadicea, were two of Mol's remaining witch sisters and were always in trouble. Or making trouble.

Or stirring up trouble. Despite which, I liked them both a lot.

The Vampira Carta and its codicils contained the rule of law for the Mithran vampires and it contained protocols and rules for proper behavior between vampires, scions, blood-servants, blood-slaves, and cattle—the demeaning term for the nonbound humans whom vamps once hunted, sometimes for sport. The Carta provided proper procedures and conventions for everything, including challenging and killing each other in a duel called by lots of names: the Blood Challenge, the Sangre Duello, and the Blood Duel, to name three.

"A Blood Challenge," Mol said, her eyes squinted, unblinking in thought, "Enforcer-to-Enforcer, or primo-to-primo, for first blood, is a common proper protocol for visiting vamps. It's one acceptable first step to one master issuing a Blood Challenge to another. But if the first blood challenger loses on the first pass, they usually don't offer formal challenge to the death."

A fight to the death, with a sword, was a challenge I was destined to lose, which reminded me of the scar. I reached up under my arm and pressed the flesh there. I felt a ridge of tissue, but it was no longer sore or tender. The healing in the sweat house had given better results than I had expected, short of a true shift to another form.

"Having a primo makes you a master," Molly said, "while still being Enforcer to Leo. It would put the challenger in a difficult place protocol-wise. A primo or an Enforcer can fight that first battle for any master. Is Edmund any good?"

"Yes," Eli said. "Better than his position would indicate. He's a former Blood Master who lost his position to an inferior fanghead, inferior in terms of vampire power, compulsion, and fighting ability. We've always thought he gave up the position instead of fighting for it, for reasons that have never made sense to us."

"Interesting," Molly said, picking at the pile of pineapple and onion and peppers I wasn't eating. "One has to wonder why he fell so low, and why he's still so low. Machinations, maybe? Leo doing what Leo does best?"

"Plans within plans," I said.

"And this fanghead primo. He has no place to sleep? How about the bolt-hole/safe room you turned into weapons storage?" She was referring to the long narrow room under the stairs, hidden by a bookcase in the living room.

"We secured the entrance from under the house, but I could unsecure it," Eli said. "I could put a lock on this side of the bookcase opening so he couldn't get in through there. That would leave the house safe from him. There's enough room to put a cot there, but no place for his belongings."

"You are not seriously considering having Edmund stay here," I said.

"Why not?"

"Big Evan would have a cow."

"There is that," Molly agreed. "Evan has cows often." She pushed away from the table and wandered into the living room, where the kids were watching some animated, improbable movie, where the girls were all wimps, waiting to be saved by a prince.

Angie Baby was telling her little brother what was wrong with that scenario. "The princess would have a sword and lots of magic spells and point her magic wand and the bad man would go 'poof' and be gone." And it made me smile. Angie would never be a wilting violet, waiting to be rescued.

Big Evan was upstairs, arguing with Alex about research. The Kid's room had become a library filled with things we borrowed from the sub-four storage at HQ. Journals, newspapers, letters, diaries, vamp and human histories that were being scanned and, where possible, automatically added to our ever-growing database. I could smell the Kid's frustration from here. He wasn't used to anyone butting in on his methods or trying to change his organization. Currently he was updating info on the Mings, specifically chronicling their vamp connections through the last hundred years, hoping to find a clue on who might have taken Ming of Mearkanis. From the snippets of conversation, Evan wanted him to concentrate on the witch aspect, and right now, not later.

I transferred my attention to Eli and said softly, "Now,

why do you think Molly would be so agreeable and then walk off like that?"

Eli chuckled, the sound grim and admiring all at once. "So she can declare innocence when we do this thing. So she can lay the blame cleanly at your feet and Big Evan can get mad at you, and you can find a way to make it work without her being at fault."

I swiveled my head, watching my BFF scooch onto the couch between her kids. "Dang. Molly's sneaky. And maybe a genius."

"Sylvia assures me that all women are geniuses that way. Except you. She says you 'think like a man and don't give a good damn who you piss off,' 'scuse the language. Mostly she's right."

I was pretty sure the quote was an insult. "I think like a cat, not a man," I said, but otherwise she had me to a tee.

Eli's cell made a burbling sound. He flipped the Kevlar cover open and said, "A text from Edmund Hartley." He chuckled as he read. "He's delivered all his unused furniture from his room at headquarters to a storage unit." Eli glanced up from his cell, "According to Alex, Edmund actually owns the storage unit facility, and he personally has access to ten units. Alex thinks they're full of stuff left over from being a clan Blood Master. Or weapons of mass destruction. Or dead bodies in fifty-five-gallon drums. Or gold bars. My brother has an imaginative and warped mind." He went back to the texts. "Edmund is on the way here. He wants to know where to park his vehicle."

From the street, I heard the high-pitched roar of a four-cylinder car. To a road enthusiast, most four-cylinder vehicles sound like vacuum cleaners, but this one sounded different. Powerful. I stood to look out the window and saw a bronze-poly-toned sports speedster gleaming in the dark and the streetlamps, a car to rival my Harley Bitsa for style, design, and sheer kick-ass-ity. "What is that?" I breathed.

"That," Alex shouted down the stairs, "is Edmund's Thunderbird Maserati 150 GT. It's one of the few 1957 prototypes still in existence." He smacked down the stairs in his flip-flops and out the side door. The rest of us followed to see him throw open the side gate to the tiny alley between my house and the one next door and rush into the street. "Yes!" He pumped his fist. "*That* is a one-of-a-kind car called a *little rocket* because of its incredible power-to-weight ratio. One like it fetched more than three million at auction a few years back."

"Three mil? I thought Edmund was broke."

"Methinks Eddie lied," Eli said.

"Is that Brute in the passenger seat?" I asked.

"Yeah," Alex shouted over the sound of the engine echoing off the narrow walls as the little rocket eased into the tight alley and into the side yard, between the barbecue grill and the brick wall. "Ed's bringing Brute. Leo kicked him out of HQ for reasons unknown. I'm guessing the werewolf peed in his shoes or ate his Barcalounger."

"This is getting ridiculous," I said. I felt an itch between my shoulder blades, as if someone had a laser scope on me, a high-powered rifle aimed at a kill site. I was breathing too fast, heart beating too fast. *Crap, crap, crap.* I didn't like this at all.

Too many people in our den, Beast thought, panting hard. *Shift into big-cat and run. We find new den. Alone.*

The car went silent and Alex said, "Can I drive your car, dude?"

"No," Edmund said as he stepped from the Maserati 150 GT. The three-hundred-pound white werewolf leaped from the passenger seat and landed on the ground with a faint grunt as Edmund closed the door. The car door met the body of the car with that distinctive dead sound of the perfectly machined, airtight work of art. Edmund said, "Only my mistress-to-be may drive my car."

Inside me, Beast stopped panting, her dread stopped in its tracks. Her ears pricked up, her attention moving from the wolf to the two-seater. *Hunt cow in car. Fast car. Faster than cow. Faster than stinky dog-wolf. Car has no head. Can leap from car to cow. Want to hunt!*

"Edmund," I said, resisting the lure of the sportster. "You will be keeping Brute with you. You both will be sleeping in the weapons room. There is one bed. There is no room for your clothes or your belongings. And I don't care, so don't bitch at me about it. The only entrance to your room, available to you, is under the house." Edmund's eyes flared, the white sclera going scarlet, though his pupils stayed almost human small and his fangs didn't snap down. "Right," I said, stepping closer until my arm shoved against his. I towered over him. "Understand me, fanghead," I said, prodding, pushing. "You and the wolf will *not* be sleeping in the house with my godchildren."

"Isn't that racial and species profiling?" Edmund asked, deliberately goading back.

Yeah. He was pushing this. I had to wonder why he was picking now to challenge me, but I didn't really care. I was suddenly in the mood to hit something, and the vamp was available. I leaned in and sniffed him, picking out the floral reek of the undead and the stink of lies, secrets, and underhanded vamp crap. I blew out, my breath ruffling his hair, letting my anger grow, letting the stink of it fill the backyard. And I started to growl, low in my throat. Molly grabbed both kids and backed away slowly. Eli took Alex by the arm and pulled the teenager away, back to the porch. Molly and Eli were smart. Edmund, not so much. He turned his eyes up to mine, meeting my challenge.

"Vamp profiling? Could be," I said, showing teeth in a smile that had no humor in it all. "Not that I care. I don't dislike you, but I don't want a vamp here. I don't need a vamp here. I don't want a primo or an Enforcer or the responsibility to take care of and for another being. I have too many people I have to take care of as it is. I am not adding a fanghead and a werewolf stuck in wolf form to the list of people I have to protect and can't."

The backyard went silent.

After the sound of the words died away, I actually heard them.

Beast snorted, *Jane is stupid foolish kit.*

I saw Eli and Alex on the porch. Eli looked severely ticked off, eyes narrowed, mouth a forbidding line. Alex looked scared. Molly and Evan stood in the open back door and Molly was mad, her eyes spitting sparks. Evan was gathering power, witch power. I heard it in the low hum of the basso note that came from his throat, a note so low it was little more than a vibration, making his red hair and beard stand out around his head in a corona of energies like something Tesla might create. Molly took his hand and her curls lifted, swirling in a breeze that wasn't there. "Ummm. That's not quite what I meant," I said.

"Yes, it is. That's exactly what you meant and what you believe," Molly asked. "In some sick little part of your stupid brain, you believe that we come here to be *protected*. That you are *responsible* for us all." She dropped Evan's hand and strode out of the doorway, pushing past the Youngers, her energies gathering, her anger growing. "I'll have you know that Evan and I are perfectly capable of taking care of ourselves and our children, born and unborn, against all comers. We are capable of taking down Leo and his entire council. Just the two of us. We don't need you, you stupid *cat*. We love you and want to help *you*. Or I did until you said that load of horse hockey."

I turned away from my friend and looked at the ground. I didn't know what to say. But Eli did. His anger falling away, he said, "Not horse hockey. Somewhere, deep inside, Jane *needs* to take care of the people she loves. But her family is growing too fast and it's creeping her out."

Molly considered that, the magics sparking into the air easing off. She said, "Because they get murdered or raped or killed or disappear into snowstorms. Or they take off with a cat in heat and leave her alone." I felt the heat magic dissipating. "Well, da . . . ang. I get all that, big-cat. I do. But we're a team, not your dependents. Not your parents. Not your kittens. Not your housemothers or the children you protected from bullies at the children's home growing up."

I looked up at that one.

"Yeah. We all know about that," Alex said. "Reach got hold of your records from the home and I . . . kinda shared them. You know. Once we met Misha we sorta kinda knew anyway."

Misha was an untrained witch whom I had defended from bullies in the Christian children's home where we both were raised. I closed my eyes. "Oh, crap."

Molly said, "We're also not your responsibilities to worry over or provide for. We're your friends. Your family."

"Ditto," Eli said. "And if you need reminding, I can still kick your butt when I have to. Admittedly I have to cheat to do it, but I can."

"And we can deal with the fanghead and the wolf," Big Evan said. "If he tries anything, Mol can drain his undead, unlife-force so fast he'll be true-dead on the floor before he knows what hit him."

Edmund tilted his head on his neck in one of those birdlike motions they usually try to hide, a gesture that proves they aren't human anymore. "You can try, *witch*," he hissed.

"This. This is why I don't want you here, Ed," I said. "I can't deal with your silly, vamp lack of emotional control." *Good. Direct the attention off me and my big mouth.* "And I know you can take care of yourselves," I said to Molly and Evan. "It doesn't stop me from feeling responsible for you and your kids and your sisters and every witch in the world, including the sister I had to kill to save you." And the effect her life and death had on me. Which might include the flower that morphed into a snake head in my soul home. Evangelina's scent and favorite flower had been a rose. Something to worry over later, when I had finished trying to destroy or save my relationships. I wasn't sure which I was actually doing.

"And you?" I said to Eli and Alex. "You're my baby brothers. Get used to being protected. It's what big sisters do."

Edmund, who looked human again when I slanted my eyes at him, seemed to be thinking, his gaze holding a faraway stare. Without warning, he dropped to one knee and said, "Jane Yellowrock, Enforcer to the Master of the City of New Orleans, rogue-Mithran hunter, bravest woman I know. I, Edmund Killian Sebastian Hartley, do hereby swear fealty to you and to yours, to your entire extended and many-peopled and many-creatured family and Yellowrock Clan. To provide, protect, care for, fight for, and to die true-dead as you may need. I place all my needs second to yours *and* to theirs. I place my hunger second to yours *and* to theirs. I place all that I am and all that I can be and all that I can do at your disposal, into your hands, for the duration of the next nineteen years. I am yours in life and undeath and in true-death."

Yellowrock Clan? I opened my mouth to stop this, but he swiveled his body, the knee on the ground at my feet grinding in the grass. "And I swear fealty to the Everharts and Truebloods, for as long as Jane Yellowrock is yours and you are hers, one clan, placing my own well-being beneath your own, and with the promise that I shall protect your children and your children's children unto the laying down of my own undeath." He turned back to me. "You no longer must protect me, my mistress. My blood is yours to spill."

"Holy crap in a bucket," I said.

Primly he said, "The correct response is 'I accept your fealty. In return I offer you a place at my side, to share my life and my holding, and the promise of a true-death most glorious.'"

"Good by me," Eli said, his equanimity dropping into place like a veil over his real emotions. "Say it, Jane. Because if you don't, then I will for you. As your second and your brother according to the *Tsalagi*, I have the right to go to war with you." When I stared at him and then around at the group in my tiny yard, he said, "Say it," in a tone of command.

Something weird and heated flared up in me, something unexpected. Something that felt like a healing when I hadn't known I was sick or broken. It roared through my body and out my mouth. "Fine," I shouted. "I accept! You still sleep in the weapons room with a werewolf!"

"Agreed," Edmund said. "Accept my service."

I repeated the words "I accept your fealty," and a strange frisson of trepidation crawled beneath my skin and through my bones, accepting Edmund's service in the vampiric way. *Fealty.* Dang it.

"So witnessed?" Ed asked.

"So witnessed," Eli and Evan said together.

"Coolio!" Angie said from behind her father's knees. "So witnessed!"

"Coweoo. Sho eness," EJ said.

"What just happened?" I asked, fighting tears that made no sense at all.

"You just adopted a vampire and werewolf," Eli said, "to go along with your brothers and your witches."

"We need a bigger house," Alex said.

From the house came the words "You are my dark knight, Vampire Edmund. I will take care of you too." It was Angie's voice. At the words, something shifted inside me. Something dark and light, heated and icy. My world shifted on its always precarious axis.

"Angie?" I asked.

"Oh, *hell* no," Evan said.

CHAPTER 11

Everything's Better with Bacon

I wasn't sure what happened in the next few moments. Other than the witch adults and the vampire all agreeing that Angie was too young to make or sign contracts, and that until she was eighteen, she couldn't swear to anyone. Which seemed like a good compromise to me, but left Angie mutinous again. The entire household was in the living room: the witches, the children, the humans, the vampire, the werewolf, and the grindylow, whom I hadn't seen appear but was making itself at home with the nonfamiliar cat, all three beasts curled on the rug in front of the couch. The children were on the couch only feet away, again watching the improbable Disney movie with dreadful gender role models but great hair. And the witches were chatting with the vampire.

My world was . . . not falling apart. Was becoming something I had never been able to conceive. Never would have believed.

"You need to put on some makeup, babe. We're expected at vamp central and you look like death warmed over. And not in a vampy-undead-pseudo-sexy way. More like in the *Walking Dead* way."

"Dear God, yes," Edmund said. "Shall I work on your hair?"

"I saw in the mirror," I said. "No. I can do my own hair." Not sure how all this had happened, I walked away from the gathering to my room to change clothes. And do my hair. And put on makeup. To go to vamp central and do . . . do whatever it was I did there.

I was dressed in black, natch, when I smelled Molly at my door. "It's open," I said when she didn't knock. She entered and closed the door behind her, standing with the door at her back, her hands on the knob. "You look awful," she said. "Are you sure you should go out?"

"No, I'm not sure. But I have a job." I sat on the bed and rebraided my hair, fingers working on their own.

"Big bad vamp hunter and vamp Enforcer," Molly said. "A contradiction in every way."

"What's up, Mol?"

Molly made a sound that was part exasperation and part uncertainty. "I have a concern. About the conclave. And you."

"Okay." I twisted my braided hair up in a tight bun, just in case I had to fight someone again at HQ. I shoved silver stakes into the bun.

"Evan and I took a ride out to the vampire cemetery today."

My eyebrows went up and an unanticipated shiver of panic went down my spine. The vamp cemetery was where I was struck by lightning during a witch working. I still had the occasional nightmare about that. "Okay. Why?"

"You were struck by lightning during a working. It's never happened before to anyone I know. Evan and I think it wasn't an accident. That it wasn't a fluke. That the storm was attracted to the power on the ground, and that someone used that to direct an attack against you."

She waited for me to speak, so I gave her a shrug and went to the bathroom. She was right. I still looked awful. I pawed through my meager makeup, which I kept in a tackle box, and removed some concealer and powder and seven tubes of scarlet lipstick. "Okay. And?" I started dabbing the concealer onto the rings beneath my eyes. I wasn't good at putting on makeup, but anything would have made me less corpselike.

"The lightning strike was probably a *deliberate attack on you*." She enunciated the last words as if I was too dense to understand them.

"Okay."

"That's it? Okay?"

I shrugged again and applied powder over the concealer. Then chose a tube of red lipstick, one with a hint of yellow in the tint, and put a couple of dabs of the lipstick on my cheeks and rubbed them in. I could have used some blush, but I had never been adept at getting blush shades to match my lipstick, and my face usually ended up looking wrong. With the lipstick on my cheeks, I looked marginally better, so I smeared some on my mouth and dropped all the tubes into the tackle box. "Molly, I've thought it through too. I figured it had to be a premeditated, well-planned attack. But I've made so many enemies in this town, there would no way to pick out who might be behind it."

"A witch at the scene is the most likely offender."

And Molly had told the witches some things about me. Not secrets exactly. Probably all in innocence, but . . . still. It had hurt. "Yeah. I know." I blew out a breath and sat back on the corner of the bed to slip into the shoulder holster and secure the matching Walther PK .380s. With my best friend in the world watching, I pulled on boots. I was wearing the fancy-schmancy ones Leo had given me. Lucchese, hand-stitched, one-of-a-kind, gorgeous boots, which I loved to death. Grunting, I said, "I figured that out back when the lightning happened."

"All an attacking witch or witches would have needed was something of yours—hair, fingernail clipping. If they had that, the assault could even have been long-distance, directed to the working and targeted on you."

Keeping my voice carefully expressionless as I slipped

into my lightweight jacket and tugged it to fit over the weapons, I said, "I clip my own nails. I've never had my hair cut. The likelihood of someone getting genetic material from me by going through my garbage isn't impossible, but it also wouldn't be easy." I hesitated before saying the next part, but it needed to be said, to clear the air between us. "Unless you're telling me you gave them something of mine, which I don't believe." I dropped my gaze to the floor, not wanting to look at Molly. "But you did tell the witches things about me." I could hear the hurt in my voice, and knew that Molly could too.

"They asked me about you. I confirmed things that were readily available on the Internet and on your business Web site. I never told them *secrets*. And I never gave anyone genetic material. You *know* that I would never do that." Molly gripped her skirt in her fingers, a new, nervous habit. "Don't you?"

And I did. But *knowing* it intellectually was one thing; hearing the truth in her words, smelling the truth on her body, made me feel better. "Yeah. I do," I said. "Wait." I blinked slowly, eyes closed, letting memories stir together inside me. Beast had said, *Jane has hair.*

"That was back then," I said, the words coming slowly as my brain flew through possibilities. "Now, with this witch scan spell, I keep smelling burned hair."

Molly's perfect bow lips parted.

My hair? Yes . . . maybe it *had* been my hair. And if so, then it was a very specific spell, a black-magic spell tied to my genetic material. If Molly was right, then the people at the lightning debacle in the vamp cemetery were part of what was happening now. "What if . . . What if you're right and they burned *my* hair? That would explain why the spell was so specific, and so deeply attuned to me. Then and now."

"No one does DNA-specific spells anymore except for healing spells, and they take a coven of at least five well-balanced witches. Without that, the workings are too delicate and fall apart too easily. They're unpredictable and end up flying." When a spell didn't work, Molly made a paper airplane and flew it across the room to entertain the children. Her eyes traveled left and right slowly as she put that together with what we knew. She said haltingly, "Until I met you, I thought I understood magic. But now? Anything is possible."

"But if we're right, where did they get my hair to use in a spell? Unless someone else is involved. Like, maybe someone took a hair sample from a workout mat or skin scraping or blood from HQ after a battle or sweat after a workout or a spar." I gave Molly what might have been a small smile and she nodded, the motion jerky, not happy. "It's possible. I'm putting my money on a disgruntled vamp working with the two witches who attacked my house and me. If Edmund hadn't just sworn to me, I'd say he was a perfect possibility, having lost his status and wanting to get back at the whole vamp power struggle. But . . . someone like him."

Molly pulled a piece of paper from her pocket and walked to me. I didn't want to, but I took the paper and unfolded it to see a list of nine names. Only Lachish Dutillet and Molly and the two witches who went by akas were familiar to me. Some had no last names, which was odd. She said, "Lachish says you never asked her for a list of the witches who were there, in the cemetery, that night, so I asked for you. This is all of them. All of *us*."

No last names. I didn't know how to point that out. When I didn't say anything, her scent spiked with adrenaline and grief pheromones. She asked, "If you thought it might be a targeted attack, why didn't you ask *me* for the names? Did you think I would pick witches over you?"

"I didn't want to . . . put you on the spot?" *Make you choose.* That was what I meant, and Molly seemed to know that. Her scent spiked, hot and peppery with anger. Again. Pregnancy emotional swings.

Tears of frustration gathered in her eyes. "You're my friend, damn it. Damn, damn, *damn* it! I *put you first*! Before *witches*. Before *everybody*!"

I smiled. Molly had just cussed out loud, where her kids might overhear, which she never did. I said, "I know you do. And I love you too." At which point Molly's tears pooled over and spilled down her cheeks. I was making everyone cry. I sat and patted the mattress and she fell on the bed beside me, doing the pregnant-woman boohoo at a loud wail and with full waterworks. I put an arm around her and gathered her close. Big Evan opened the door, took us in, and closed the door, leaving her to me. *Coward.*

I held Molly and rocked her while she cried and moaned and said things like "You can trust me." And "I'm not a death witch anymore." And "I love you. I love you. I love you. You're my bestest friend in the whole entire world!" And "I never held Evangelina's death against you!" And a dozen other things that may have been in Gaelic, but were sure not English, and made no sense. At all.

When she calmed a little, enough that I thought the baby might not suffer from the emotional overload, I said, "I trust you, Molly. I've always trusted you. Even when the death magics rode you so hard."

"You do? You have?"

I patted her shoulder even while I eased her away from my now-drenched clothing. "Yes. I do. I have." I patted a time or two more, wondering if this was enough physical contact or if Mol needed more. I wasn't good at this stuff. After a few more pats, I said, "So, while you're up close and personal, can you check out my hands and body for any spells and crap that may be clinging to me?"

"Spells and *crap*?"

I gave an overly nonchalant shrug. "Workings. Come on, Mol."

Molly wiped her eyes and dried her tears on her skirt. She took my hands, turning them over and inspecting both sides. I felt a tingle of power, of her magics. They feathered across my palms, delicate energies, a soothing warmth, and then stronger, like the hot/cold electric touch of sparkler fireworks when lit. Oddly similar to a master vampire's magics, cold and hot all at once.

I pulled in a breath, sharp and quick. "I guess you're inspecting me for the spell."

The ghost of a smile touched her lips. "Gotta bring home the bacon. And to that, I gotta have a bill to hit Leo with.

Now shut up. I'm working here." She set my right hand in my lap and held my left, her fingers tracing across my palm. The sparkler heat changed and she pressed her fingernails into the pads of my palm. A branding iron of heat shot into my hand. Into my nerves. My bones. It was all I could do not to jerk away, but I bared my teeth and my breath hissed. "Oh," Molly muttered. "This may hurt a bit."

I breathed through the pain. *Hurt a bit*, my butt.

After what seemed like an hour later but was more likely only ten minutes, Molly shook her head. "I can see leftover energies. Nothing more. If there's anything here, I don't know what it might be."

"So there's no chance it'll explode and blow us all to smithereens?"

Molly laughed, a happy, healthy laugh, and rewiped her cheeks. "I never said that. There is always a chance for destruction and violence, big-cat."

She had a point, but I still felt better, and by her scent, so did Molly. "I gave you the general descriptions of the witches who attacked the house. Do any of the names match the descriptions?"

Molly's tears had stopped; her eyes were still red and watery as she said, "Several of them are large women, but only one matched the little woman. This one." She pointed to the name. It was only three letters, no surname. "It might be a nickname."

"Tau," I said. "Okay. Thank you. It's a place to start. But I havta ask. Why no last names?"

Molly shook her head. "Lachish says that after the coven couldn't stop hurricane Katrina, the anti-witch sentiment was so bad that most witches went underground and stopped using family names. To protect the humans in the families. She refused to give me more."

Which made sense and eased away some of the worry that clutched my spine. But only some of it. Witches might have tried to kill me. Why not give me the full names to protect *me*?

Later, on the way out of the house, I left the list with Alex, with the request "See what you can find?"

"I heard," he said, taking the folded paper and snapping a photo of it on his phone before handing it back. "We all heard. Emotional women."

From upstairs Molly shouted down, "You try carrying a baby for nine months while chemicals and hormones run through your body making you nutso and fat and swollen and then push an eight-pound lump of squalling human out through an opening big enough to fit a straw in and see if you don't react from time to time. Until then, *shut your trap*."

Wisely, Alex did.

On the way to vamp central, I wondered again how I survived the lightning that struck me. And if the angel Hayyel had saved me in a far more concrete way than I had originally thought. Did God want me alive for some reason? Did the angel work deliberately and independently to stop the witches trying to kill me? Are angels even allowed to interfere? If Hayyel acted to save me, was he in trouble with the Big Guy Upstairs?

If anyone could do something with the list of names, Alex could. Maybe he'd have something for me when we got back. Like full names. Photos. Their social media pages. Or their favorite things—walks in the rain, puppies, honesty, and laughter. Oh! And using magic to try to kill Jane Yellowrock and start a vamp-witch war.

Maybe not. I was good at the moment, no matter what he discovered. Mostly because of Edmund's words "Yellowrock Clan," which still reverberated through me. *Yellowrock Clan*. Yeah. I could live with that.

We went through security measures at HQ, much more stringent than the ones we had been through before. We were issued the brand-new, updated headsets, each with a small built-in camera. They were heavier, more bulky than the older models, not only so we could communicate with the security team while we were on the move, but so we could see what they saw if the poo hit the prop. I didn't care for the extra weight, but for the upcoming events—all of them—the portable cameras might come in very handy proving innocence on the part of the team.

While we were still at the front entrance, Wrassler limped up and delivered to Eli the carved box holding the brooches. "Courtesy of Leo," Wrassler said. "He knows you have the Truebloods at your house. He wants you to have them inspect the magics on the pins and see if they can track the witches on the other end."

"Sneaky," I said. "Pit the Truebloods against the witches who probably want the conclave and the witch-vamp parley to end before it begins. Divide and conquer. No wonder Leo's so politically successful. What did he do? Study under Machiavelli?"

Wrassler rubbed his hand over his shaved skull and gave the old grin, the one he used back before he'd been so terribly maimed under my watch. Seeing it made my heart tumble over. "Not exactly. But it's my understanding that the MOC owns one of the few copies of the sixteenth-century political treatises, in the original Latin, by the Italian diplomat and political theorist Niccolò Machiavelli. It's *possible* that they were pals. I never asked." Wrassler winked at me, turned on his prosthetic leg, and disappeared into the bowels of HQ.

Eli tucked the box under his arm. "One should remember the source when making fun of fangheads," he said to me.

"True. Let's check in with HQ's security arrangements for the conclave and get outta here. I'm still beat."

The meeting with the security team covered every planned moment from the time Leo left his private rooms, walked through the building, exited under the porte cochere, and was whisked into his limo. It covered the two other teams in similar limos who would leave at staggered times to throw off any bad guys or media types who might be watching HQ through telephoto lenses or drones. It covered the armored and well-armed SUVs that would keep pace with Leo's limos. And it covered the motorcycle backup, crotch rockets carrying armed guards, most of them in white riding leathers and with full radio coms beneath the white helmets.

Weekend traffic in New Orleans wasn't horrible, but it wasn't good either. I had learned firsthand how trapped a car could become. I still missed my bike and the ability to weave between cars, take one-way streets the wrong way, outsmarting traffic and never being late. I had big plans to head to Charlotte the moment the Harley was repaired enough for a test drive. Until then, I was making sure that Leo had motorcycle backup among his guards and among the police.

We also discussed with Derek which shooters would be utilizing the rooftops surrounding the Elms Mansion and Gardens, what ammo and equipment they would have access to. And who was in charge of their taking a shot. If our people shot anyone—even an attacker—there would be hell to pay, not only with the legal system, but also with the political situation. The smart thing, and our second choice, would be to have observers only, no weapons, but if our men saw a bomber or witches casting a deadly spell, and they didn't intervene, the consequences could be even more lethal. The third option placed off-duty NOPD officers on the roofs with high-powered rifles. There were dangers in each of the three options. It was such a dicey discussion that by two in the morning, we called Leo and Grégoire in on it.

The two joined us in the conference room and sat side by side, listened to our proposals, and studied the photos of the Elms and the surrounding buildings and streets. When we were done, they conversed in low voices, in ancient French, the black-haired Leo leaning often to listen to his blond, blue-eyed bestie and secundo heir. They looked like very young, elegant, princely, educated, moneyed, metrosexual men who lived in a constant state of ennui, but they were also fighters with over nine hundred years of warfare and politics between them. Finally Leo sat upright and asked, "Jane, which option do you prefer?"

"I've become a control freak working for you, so I think we need armed men, our men, and that Derek should run things."

"Eli Younger? You are the most currently experienced warrior in this room, even more so than my own men, with the most up-to-date knowledge of electronic warfare. What say you?"

Eli glanced sidelong at me and said, "If we were on foreign soil, I'd be all over Jane's choice. But I'm torn between using our own men and using police. They might not take a shot our own men would, but they would also be responsible for any political fallout."

"Derek?" he asked his soon-to-be-full-time Enforcer.

"I don't want any of my men facing charges," he said. "I say use cops."

"And, Grégoire? Your thoughts?"

In a languid tone Grégoire said, "We could use off-duty police officers in tandem with our own men, and put them all under the control of Jodi Richoux."

Which was bloody brilliant. It put all the responsibility under the wings of an NOPD officer, it divided the responsibility of whether to take a shot or not, and it placed any political or legal fallout in the hands of cops. I started laughing. So did the small team gathered there as they understood what the implications were.

Leo said to me, "And so you see the benefit of a few centuries of political strategizing. I'll have my Enforcer, Derek Lee, contact Detective Richoux when she goes on duty this morning. We will allow her to choose the men and women she wants on the roofs. Derek, it will be up to you to assign men and women who will work well with the people Ms. Richoux suggests."

"Yes, sir," Derek said. "I'll handle it and bring the full team in for vetting and instructions. Unless you think that should take place off grounds?" he asked Grégoire.

"If you could arrange that meeting for NOPD Eighth District, that would be preferable." Grégoire sent me a smile, the kind that belonged on the face of the teenager he looked. "I do believe that Jane and George Dumas have recently met the police commissioner?"

"Yeah. Go, me. You meet all sorts of people when you get handcuffed and taken to the pokey."

Grégoire looked at Leo and they smiled together. "The pokey," Grégoire said.

"She is charming, is she not?"

"Yeah, whatever," I said. "I'll call the woo-woo room

and see if I can get you on a conference call before you go
to bed in the morning."

"Excellent," Leo said, standing. "Shall we?" he asked
his secondo heir, and led the way out the door.

When it closed, Eli said, "And that right there is why
fangheads scare me. Three moves ahead of us on the chess-
board."

"At least," Derek said.

"Later," I said. "I need my bed. Almost dying takes a
lot out of me these days."

"Wimp," Derek said.

I just shook my head and left the room for the outdoors,
dialing NOPD, the in-house number of the woo-woo
room, the Paranormal Cases Department, headed up by
Jodi Richoux. Eli was close on my heels as I set up a conference call between Derek and the woo-woo cops. I could
mark one conclave responsibility off my shoulders.

The lights were on in Bruiser's apartment when Eli deliberately drove slightly out of our way and pulled into an
empty but illegal parking place on St. Philip Street. He
didn't look at me, staring out the windshield, his thumbs
tapping out a slow, syncopated rhythm on the steering
wheel. "Fine," I said.

"You've been saying that a lot lately, usually when it
isn't fine. Wanna talk about that or you wanna go bump
bones with Bruiser?"

I yanked my cell out of my pocket and texted Bruiser,
Out front.

He didn't text back. Instead he stepped onto the third-
floor gallery of his apartment, unit eleven, and leaned
out, hands on the iron railing. He was wearing a pair of
loose pants. No shirt. Even through the distance and the
armored glass, I could feel his eyes on me.

"Fine," I said to my partner. "I know when I'm out-
smarted." Not that I didn't want to go up. It just sounded
so much like a booty call. Which wasn't necessarily a bad
thing. I opened the door and stepped into the fall heat
and the cooler night breeze. The winds changed direction

often, the Mississippi, the bayous, Lake Pontchartrain, and the Gulf of Mexico creating their own unpredictable weather system. Eli pulled away from the curb, the car door shutting on its own.

Heels tapping louder than I wanted, I went in through the wide hallway-like entrance and climbed the stairs to the top floor. I smelled Bruiser before I saw him. Man and Onorio and heat and that vaguely citrusy cologne he wore. Just a hint. Not too much to mess with my sensitive nose. Saw the light pouring across the floor, angled to indicate his door was open. I climbed the last steps.

Bruiser was waiting in the doorway, one shoulder on the doorjamb, still shirtless, barefoot. His pants rode on his hips, abs ripped in the angled light, the line of hair pointing down from his chest, to disappear beneath the low-hung waistband. There was heat in his eyes, though his face showed nothing. No emotion at all. I didn't drop in often. Okay, never. Except for that first time, I always waited to be asked. Waited to be invited. This was different. I could feel the Onorio heat of his body when I slowed two feet away.

On the music system, something classic R&B with a hint of rambunctious country in the instrumentation was playing, a musician I didn't know. The lyrics flowed out into the hallway.

*"Blindsided by love, with no chance to put up a fight.
Well, I never saw it coming. I know I can't recover. I'm
    a victim of the night. . . ."*

The words were perfect for Bruiser and Leo. Or for Bruiser and me. *Ohhh,* I thought. Bruiser and me. I realized I had stopped moving and forced my feet to take the last steps. Right up to the man in the doorway. He smiled at last, and when he did, he caught me up in his arms, one arm like a vise across my back pulling me to him. The other hand slipped up to cup the back of my head. His brown eyes sparkled with laughter and a curl of dark hair dropped forward, to tangle in his eyelashes. The lyrics continued.

"Blindsided by love. Yes, I'm a victim of the night."

His lips hesitated before they met mine, a millimeter of space between our mouths. I let my lips curl up and felt the tension slide away from me. I lifted my arms to his shoulders, wrapped them around him, wanting out of the shoulder holster that was suddenly constricting. "Blindsided, huh?"

"Everything's better with bacon," he whispered. And that was the last thing either of us said for a very long time.

On Bruiser's gallery, we drank tea and ate French toast that had been delivered exactly five minutes after I woke. Wearing his shirt and nothing else. My ankles were crossed, resting across Bruiser's legs, and we were nestled close on the love seat that hadn't been there the last time I visited. He leaned in and licked syrup off my lips with a quick flick of his tongue, reminding me of other things he had done with that tongue during the night.

I made a small "Mmm" of pleasure and he chuckled, that manly, exhausted sound they make when they know just how well they have pleased. The vibration of the quiet laughter shook his chest. I rotated my head to rest it on his shoulder, my body in a C shape that should have been uncomfortable but was instead cozy.

Bruiser was one of very few men taller than I was, tall enough to make me feel small and delicate sometimes. Like this time. My hair slid across him and he gathered it up, smoothing it back.

"I love the way your hands feel on my hair," I said on a sigh.

"And I love the feel of your hair," he said. So far, that was the closest we came to saying the three magic words. After the debacle of Ricky-Bo's betrayal, I wasn't ready to say words that were more . . . sugary. And Bruiser acted as if the words were not even in his vocabulary. Which suited me just fine. Really. It did.

He freshened our mugs and I added more sugar and cream to the extra-strong English Breakfast Blend. It was the perfect start to a day destined to be anything but perfect, because the conclave was soon and the final preparations had to be honed and refined and today was the day for hundreds of details to be dealt with. Already a few witches were descending on the city and taking hotel rooms, gathering in cafés, chatting informally in bars. Starting the political yammering and lobbying and scheming and intriguing, trying to firm up or change the agendas. Trying to create or destroy alliances. Stuff I hated. Stuff that would change the world as I know it.

Yet, around us, the night lightened, graying the world through a rare fog, misting its way off the Mississippi River and through the Quarter. The fog made everything seem personal, intimate, as if we were the only people left in New Orleans. Bruiser tickled my soles and I kissed his scruffy chin. It was a rare, peaceful moment and I so totally owed Eli for making it happen.

Behind us, framed in a shadowbox and hanging over the bed, was a brown, yellow, and pink T-shirt, ugly as all get out except for the cute pig on it. And the logo BACON IS MEAT CANDY. It was the T-shirt I'd worn the first time I came to visit him here, bringing lunch from Cochon Butchers, and had ended up staying for more than lunch. As long as my T-shirt hung over Bruiser's bed, I knew we were good, no matter how bad things might get in reality.

The fog heralded cooler air, the first hint of real fall, and promised rain soon. No surprise there. New Orleans got an average of sixty-four inches of sky juice a year, and had no rainy season. Or, rather, it was rainy season all year long. In the distance, I heard a tugboat sound, long and low, and the fainter roar of traffic starting. Not even dawn and it was starting up.

My cell tinkled. Bruiser handed it to me and I answered, "Morning, Molly."

"It's Angie," she said, tears in her voice. "Something's wrong, Aunt Jane." And then she dropped the phone. I heard it clatter.

"Angie," I whispered. "Angie!" I shouted.

Bruiser was already moving. I whipped my entire body through the long narrow doors and inside, gathering up my clothes and weapons in one arm. In a single lunge, I leaped for the gallery and landed on the street three stories below. Bruiser hesitated a fraction of a second before he threw a satchel at me. I caught it one-handed, hearing the clank of weapons and gear. He gripped the railing on his gallery and swung to the railing one floor below him, then leaped to the ground. He beeped his car open while he was still in the air.

I was still dressing when a half-naked Bruiser peeled us out of his parking space and made a tire-screeching turn the wrong way up a one-way street. I had only two vamp-killers, a few stakes, and the two matching Walther PK .380s, loaded with standard ammo. No silver. None of Molly's preset spells. And, "How did someone get through the wards?"

"What's new at your place?" he asked as he took a turn too fast.

"People. Witches, a nonfamiliar cat, a vamp, a were-wolf, and a grindylow. Pretty much everything," I said, pulling on last night's pants under Bruiser's too-big shirt. I slid my arms through the shoulder holster, which was permanently sized to me, handmade of nylon and leather, the grips turned out, for a fast two-hand draw. I didn't bother with the jacket. "Oh. Wait. Crap. Leo gave us the brooches to have Molly and Evan look at them, check out the spells on them. Eli would have taken them inside, but it was too late to wake the Truebloods. If it's the same two attackers—"

"They got in with a *Trojan horse* spell." Bruiser braked hard and the antilock brakes stuttered on the wet pavement two blocks from my house. The fog was thicker here, the SUV's lights vanishing into it only inches from the front bumper. The streetlights were off the length of the street. So was the electricity. I remembered the scan spell. The entire street hadn't lost power, then. Bruiser pulled into a parking space and killed the motor. "Can you see the wards?" he asked, opening the door and dressing fast while standing in the street.

"Yes." In mixed human and Beast-vision I could make out the wards, the overlapping color stamp of an Everhart Trueblood working, red and blue and bright emerald green, sparking through with rainbow-hued motes of power. "I can't tell much through the fog. They look fine, but . . ."

"But you know they aren't," he said, stamping into combat boots. "The ward is keyed to you. I won't be able to get inside."

"If it's the same two witches, they took up places under two streetlights across the street from my house."

"Got it."

I got out and we closed the doors softly, simultaneously, though the sound of them slamming would have been swallowed by the fog. A form swept at us through the night and Bruiser was suddenly standing in front of me, a sword I hadn't seen him strap on in his hand and held to the intruder's throat.

The man made a small "Eeep" of sound, his arms out to the sides to indicate a lack of weapons, before saying, formally, "It is Edmund Killian Sebastian Hartley, the Enforcer's primo."

Bruiser dropped the point of his blade and Edmund moved to me. He was fully vamped out, fangs, talons, and the blown black pupils in scarlet sclera, but he was in complete control, calm, which was something I seldom saw a vamp do. His power sparked along my skin, frigid as sleet. "There are two witches, under strong multiple wards, obfuscation workings, keep-away workings, and something I have never seen before, which strikes fire and burns hot. I saw a rat incinerated and I backed away."

"Did they see you?" I asked.

"No. They do not know any of us are here. But their workings are attacking *inside* the wards, and the True-bloods have not keyed their protections to me," he added with a snarl. "I may only enter when they permit."

"I'm going in." I heard the men talking as I dashed to my house, but their voices were swallowed by the mist. I raced ahead, nearly tripping when a curb appeared where I hadn't expected one. I ran through the ward, a heated zip of power. Silently I opened the front door. A pale greenish liquidlike gas roiled at my feet and out the door. I left the door open and it poured into the street. I slipped inside, and the smell hit on my first attempted breath. Something bitter and so pungent it stole my breath.

Poison? A magical equivalent of poison? I left the door open and the spell flowed into the street. Forcing my lungs not to cough and therefore inhale a deeper breath, I raced up the steps and into the kids' room. I threw open the windows in their room, grabbed both of my godchildren up, Angie off the floor and Little Evan off his bed. Molly's cell phone clattered to the floor. As it hit, I saw something in the shadows that didn't belong there, but there wasn't time to examine it. I raced back down the stairs, lungs burning, oxygen starved, fighting to take a breath. Desperate for air, I lowered a shoulder and shoved through the side door, banging it open, hearing wood splinter and snap. Through the ward again, I stumbled into the backyard, where I started coughing and sucking fresh air. The sound was dry and rough and I wanted to throw up, feeling weird, as if I couldn't get enough air, though I was hyperventilating. I pulled on Beast to make it to Edmund's car. I opened the driver door and laid the kids on the seats.

Edmund dropped from the air to my side, having leaped over the tall brick fence. As I practically coughed up my diaphragm, he said, "Poison gas. I have notified Leo, who is calling in Lachish Dutillet and a magical Haz Mat team to deal with the gas flowing into the streets. We have to get them all out, strip off their clothes, get them oxygenated, and wash their bodies." While speaking, he had been stripping Little Evan and laid the child in the grass. He leaned over and began artificial respiration on the little boy while scooping Angie to him and starting to strip her as well. Part of me wanted to stop him—it felt wrong to see the adult stripping the kids, but he worked with almost military precision and there was no yuck factor. And I was pretty busy, hacking up my lungs, coughing with an awful tearing, wet sound, pulling on Beast for healing. It was surreal and awful and— "Jane!" Edmund barked. "You can breathe later. Get the others. Now!"

"I'll drop them down to you," I said. Turning, I raced

back through the ward, inside, forcing myself to hold my breath. *Breathe later. Right.* Tears streamed down my face as the poison magic stung my eyes. My lungs burned as if they were melting, but I held the coughing in.

The wards were air-permeable. Therefore they were gas-permeable. Open to any spell that used air to attack, and with the brooches here, the witches had a focus to use to set the spell. Stupid, stupid, *stupid*, each and every one of us.

CHAPTER 12

Licked Alex's Head

Halfway up the stairs, I had to breathe and sucked the gas into me. Beast threw herself at me in a panic, her claws ripping at me. "Fine," I said to her between coughs. The Gray Between erupted out of me, my skinwalker energies started healing me, and I slid into the place where time slowed. The poison mist around me developed visible layers, much more pale and gauzy at the top of the stairway where the concentration of the heavier-than-air mist was beginning to clear. I managed not to breathe until I reached the second story, but I still went light-headed when I sucked in the breath.

I stumbled into Molly and Big Evan's room, opened the windows here too, and grabbed Mol's arm, rolling her into a fireman's carry, to stagger across the hallway, through Alex's room. Once again, I rammed the door with my shoulder, breaking the window glass, which started to fall as I shoved past, then hung in the air, as the Gray Between followed me through the broken door, between the striating energies of the wards, and out onto the second-floor gallery. If we survived this, there would be a lot of repairs.

I let go of the time change and alerted Edmund, by coughing, that Molly was on the way down. When he looked up from where he was washing the children's bodies with the garden hose, I tossed Molly through her own ward. In a pop of displaced air, Edmund was suddenly below her and caught Molly. She was not going to be happy when she woke up naked in the backyard, but I could live with her anger as long as they all lived.

"More coming," I managed, and bubbled time again, as I staggered back, into Alex's room. The taste of acid and cooked blood was instantly nauseating, but I bent and pulled him over my shoulder too. I stood and carried the heavier-than-expected teenager out to the gallery and threw him off. He hung in midair just as Edmund started to look up and I knew the vamp would catch the Kid. Fang-heads are fast.

I staggered across the porch to Eli's room and tried the door handle. It was unlocked and why not? Why worry about security? The wards were up. I pulled the elder Younger up and over my shoulder and out to the gallery, where I propped him over the railing. I let go of the time bubble and focused on Edmund below me as he caught Alex and laid him on the ground beside Molly.

"Next," I said, and let Eli go.

Eli windmilled, arms and legs flailing limply, but Edmund caught the much heavier man like a baby and laid him on the grass, but Edmund didn't have to strip him. Eli slept commando. Who knew? Beside him on the grass, Angie Baby and EJ were coughing and shivering, waking up, cold and crying.

I pulled the Gray Between of no time back over me and nearly hit the floor as pain cut through me like a dozen blades all at once. Limping back inside, I coughed so deep I thought my intestines might be involved. The pain of bending time started there, low in my belly, that hot, churning misery and the taste of my own blood rose up my throat. I had never gone back and forth between real time and no time so many times in succession, and it wasn't helping my digestion. The pain sliced deeper, and I was having trouble drawing a breath.

I pulled on Beast and she flooded my system with adrenaline and pain-relieving endorphins as I made it back to Molly and Big Evan's room. The big guy was six feet six inches tall and weighed in at an easy three fifty. I was strong, but . . . I bent my knees, grabbed his left arm, and put my shoulder into his middle. I let his own weight roll him over me as I squatted low to the floor and took his mass onto my back and shoulder. I barely made it to my feet and when I did, I felt something tear in me, a long, linear pain down my abdomen, from the bottom of my ribs, down along the right side of my navel. Acid rose in my throat, tasting of sour, cooked meat, of blood seared in stomach acids. I staggered across the wide hallway, seeing a glimpse of someone near the front door. I made it to the gallery before letting the Gray Between snap away. I rolled Evan's butt to the top of the railing and was absurdly happy he slept in boxers as I let time go and watched him fall toward Edmund.

The vampire grunted as he halfway caught the much bigger man, but momentum allowed Evan's leg to whack on the ground hard, twisting his knee. He'd have an injury. I caught my belly, feeling the twisted agony of torn abdominal muscles beneath my fingers as I turned to go back inside and Edmund called up, "That's all of them."

"I don't think so," I said, and returned to house.

"Jane!" he shouted. But he was outside the ward.

There was a slow breeze blowing through from the opened windows and doors, and the gas was nearly gone on the upper floor. I was coughing but I could breathe.

Sick and trying to die, I went back to the children's bedroom and the strange thing that shouldn't have been there. Brute and the grindylow, stretched out on the floor near EJ's bed. There were claw marks in the wood of the floor between the doorway and where the werewolf lay. The werewolf had been trying to claw his way to the bed. To save the kids? Yeah. He had waked Angie and sent her to get the cell phone and then had come back for EJ, Angie following, talking to me.

I tucked the neon-green baby grindylow beneath an arm, grabbed Brute by his back paws, and dragged him down the stairs. His head bumped each time I took a step, and I knew he'd have a headache, but no way could I lift another three-hundred-plus-pound anything over the railing.

I plucked the cat off the back of the sofa, hoping her nonfamiliar magics had kept her alive in the heavier, denser poison, and pulled Brute to the side door, which was hanging off its hinges, and out onto the side porch. "More," I said, my voice breathless.

"I am not giving mouth-to-snout resusitation," Edmund said, sounding prudish.

I managed a laugh, two syllables of amusement that ended up in a cough so deep it sounded as if my lungs were coming up in chunks. And I threw up. Blood went everywhere. I fell, the wooden porch floor rising to meet me with a wallop. I succeeded in saying, "Yes. You will. Dog and cat both. Your word." And everything went sparkling gray as Beast reached into me and forced me into the change. My tendons snapped, my bones popped and broke. Pain cut through me like razors flaying sinew from joints. All I could think was *It's about dang time*. Because if this wasn't changing in extremis, nothing was.

The change was swift, but I caught a glance of Angie Baby, standing in the grass, wrapped in a silk sheet. She reached a hand out to Edmund and placed her fingers in the gash on his wrist, taking away bloody fingertips. "As you have sworn, so I swear to you, fanghead. I'll take care of you for as long as I live."

No! No! But the words didn't come. And the shift took me as the wards fell.

It was daylight. *I am Beast. I am Beast all day.*

"I am done," Edmund growled from the shadows of the gallery porch. "They will all live."

I, Beast, yawned, showing killing teeth to Edmund as he raced inside, his skin smoking with the rising sun. *Stinking vampire skin smoke. Does not smell like food. Smells of rotten meet from old kill.* I followed vampire to see where he would lair.

Edmund shoved open the shelf door, rushed into weapons room, and pulled it closed behind him. He did not take lower entrance to vamp-lair as Jane had ordered. Jane would be mad. But he had saved witches and humans. Vampire had earned access through inside of house, through weapons room bookshelf door. Vampire had become litter mate. Litter mate would make Jane mad too. Beast chuffed with humor.

Beast stretched, from front paws, along front legs and with deep dip of spine, through hips and back legs to back paws, scratching with claws on wooden floor. I shook pelt, feeling it slide over bones and muscle. Beast padded outside to Brute. Brute was on ground, licking vampire blood off jaw. Smell of Edmund was strong in yard. Vampire had fed each of them. Vampire had given much blood. *Vampire is good hunter and good mother to kits.*

Inside us, Jane laughed. *I'll be sure to tell him that.*

Beast walked to face Brute and reached out with front paw. Patted dog on nose. Leaned in, nose to nose, and breathed his breath. Shared breath with Brute. Breathing. Breathing. Bonding. Brute made sniffing noise. And licked Beast nose. Tongue tasted of vampire blood. Stupid dog. I sneezed, sharing snot with dog. Dog licked Beast snout. Not dog. *Wolf.* Brute was good . . . *wolf.* He licked cat snot off his nose and licked Beast nose again. Brute tried to save EJ. Was part of litter mates now. Did not like werewolf being part of litter mates. Would have to think of this.

Lay down on wet grass beside Brute and stared at Molly. All litter mates were wearing sheets, sheets that smelled of Edmund. Looked to Edmund's car. Trunk was open.

Edmund used his sheets. Silk sheets, Jane thought. *Very* expensive *silk sheets, to cover them. To give them a sense of privacy.*

Better to have pelt, Beast thought.

Grindylow crawled from Brute to Beast and groomed Beast's back. Felt good. Needed cow meat to eat, but grooming felt good. Looked at car. Wanted to hunt cow in car, but Edmund would not wake until dark.

Molly said words and ward fell in shower of sparks. Molly said other words under breath so kits did not hear, but Beast heard, and chuffed with laughter. Molly turned to kits and saw Angie with blood on her face, blood on her hands. Hissed like mother big-cat. "What have you done?" Ran to Angie, holding sheet under arms. "Angie. What did you do?" Molly turned Angie face to light of morning sun. "Son of a witch on a switch," she said.

Beast studied Angie Baby. Angie had blood across face in lines. Beast could count to five. Angie had five lines of blood. Vampire blood. *Angie swore to vampire.*

A blood vow. Holy crap in a bucket, Jane thought. *Molly is gonna kill me.*

When all humans and witches were awake, Beast was more than hungry. Was dying of hunger. Eli was thawing cow meat in little noisy box that made meat run in circles like stupid cow-prey, around and around. Big Evan, still wrapped in sheet, went to front of house and out into street. Beast followed Evan, to watch from front porch. Fog stretched in long streamers, moving like water in street, hiding Beast from human eyes. Evan went to far side of street and bent down, big butt in air. Looked like prey, backside of bull, but was litter mate. Remembered litter mate. But was hungry. Smelled cow on air.

Bruiser was with Evan. Both looking at ground.

Walked out of house to Evan and Bruiser. Not stalking. Not stalking. Not stalking big not-cow-butt. Walking. Sat near Bruiser's feet and looked at ground where Evan looked. "What do you think, Jane? These small patches of ground that have been disturbed. Shall I dig in it?"

Beast sneezed. *Am not Jane.*

I'm here. And I see it too. Jane lifted paw and placed it over spot in ground where grass had died. Magic stung Beast like bee. Jumped back. Beast growled at bee that was not bee. Was dirt. And magic. Shook paw. *Hurt!*

"Be careful," Bruiser said. "I smell magics still working."

Jane thought, *I forgot about Bruiser when I went through the ward. Molly needs to cue them to him so he can get through, though I guess he might be dead now from poison if he had gotten inside. There is that.*

Beast ignored Jane, watching Big Evan dig in stinging ground. Smell of magic grew, like smoke from white man's fire that got away, into woods, into downed trees. Big Evan jumped. Was saying words Jane did not like, but Jane laughed. *Yeah. It hurt us too,* she thought.

"I think these might have been here since the first attack, the scan Janie told us about. The magic is still active, painfully so. *Arrrg!*" He cursed and swore and Jane laughed again. Bruiser stepped away from the digging. Bruiser was smart. "Yeah," Evan said. "These have been here awhile. They were buried several days ago. Which means for certain that the attack tonight was brought about by the two women who scanned you earlier, Jane." He pulled something green from the dirt. It looked like leaves, but it smelled like iron. Iron and salt.

Evan shouted to Molly and she came into street. Was dressed in Molly clothes, but still smelled of Edmund blood and stink of poison. "What in heaven's name are you doing in the street in a sheet? Wait. What's that? It looks . . . It looks dangerous."

"It is. And if I'm guessing right there will be another one down there," Evan said.

Beast trotted down street, nose to ground like stupid dog. Found witch magic stink and sat, front feet together.

"Yeah. Good girl, Janie," Big Evan said.

Snarled at Big Evan. *Am not Jane. Am Beast. Am hungry.*

Big Evan dug in earth and pulled another iron magic thing from ground near Beast feet. This one was green, and stank like blood. Like blood of human. Evan made strange noise, like kitten. Dropped sheet. It slid to the earth, leaving Big Evan standing naked.

"Evan?" Molly said running over. "What—" She saw what Big Evan was holding. Molly raised doubled fists into air. Hit blood-magic iron and it fell from Evan's hands. She pushed Evan away. Wrapped sheet around him.

Evan touched blood-magic iron, Beast thought.

He's spelled, Jane thought. *Not good.* Big Evan dropped to ground and head bounced on grass. Molly shouted for Eli. Jane and Beast trotted close and sniffed iron thing. *They're shaped like ovals—carved like scarabs, like the center gem of the brooches.*

Destroy iron things and spell will stop? Beast thought.

*They are focal icons—things that carry witch power—
that can be used to harness energy and power for spells,*
Jane thought, trying to make sense of it all. *Iron is abnormal
for a spell-power focal item, but . . . I don't know. Something's hinky here. These have been used in ways similar
to a permanent witch circle.* Jane looked up and down
street.

Beast thought, *Sun is rising. Want cow meat.*

In a minute. Jane watched Molly, Bruiser, and Eli roll
Evan onto large board and drag Evan across street to
house. *The focal items are set to magnetic north and east of
north, with the house at south, the front door in a perfect
ninety-degree triangle. The mathematics are excellent. Yeah.
We need to tell Eli to try and burn them. Destroying them
was a good idea.*

Beast is good hunter.

Yes, you are. Jane pushed Beast to feet and trotted to
house. *Now let's see how good you are at writing.*

Beast cannot write.

Wrong-o, Jane thought. Jane led us to Alex. He was
sitting at kitchen table, eyes closed. We stared at young
human male. He looked bad. Like sick prey, ready to die.
Took Alex hand in teeth, gently, like Beast carried kits,
and pulled toward living room.

"Whaddaya want?" he asked, trying to pull hand free.
Tightened teeth. Alex yelled, "Ow! Stop that!"

"Do what Jane wants," Eli grunted as he and Molly
pulled Evan through open front door on wood. Bruiser
pushed from other side.

Bruiser is strong. Good mate for Jane.

Yeah, yeah, yeah. Whatever.

"What?" Alex stood, smelling angry and afraid, but
let Beast pull him to desk in living room. Pushed Alex to
chair. He sat and Beast butted Alex with head, stood up
on back paws. Licked Alex's head.

"Gross. Okay. I'm awake. What do you want?"

Stayed on back paws and hind legs. Put front paws on
table-desk. Scratched gently at keyboard. Alex frowned,
using big brother's frown. Jane tapped keyboard with
claws again.

Alex's eyes went wide and heart thumped into fast speed. "You want the system on so you can type something?"

Jane dropped head and raised it. Alex pulled keyboard out and system came on. Jane thought, *We did this once before, at Leo's house, before it burned to the ground.* Jane pushed Beast away from alpha. Extruded claws. Touched key with claw. Another key. Another.

Alex shouted, "Eli! Jane's typing!"

Not Jane. Beast. But Alex did not hear.

Eli read over Beast shoulder, "Burn focals with fire. Torch." Eli bent close to Beast face, met Beast eyes, but not in challenge. "Burn the metal things with a torch? Welder's torch?"

Beast dropped head in human nod. Jane typed. "Hot."

"Will that stop the spell on Evan?"

Molly said, "That's genius. Yes. It should stop it. You have a welder's torch?"

"Acetylene. Best I can do on short notice." Eli patted Beast shoulder and said, "Steak on your plate. If this works, I'll take you hunting."

Want to hunt cow in Edmund car. But Eli did not hear. Padded to kitchen, place where Beast ate cow meat. Steak was hot and stringy on outside and cold inside. But cow meat was good. Ate all of steak and licked plate clean. Satisfied, Beast trotted out broken door and into yard. Jumped into Edmund car. Car chairs were made of cow skin. Would hunt for more cow with Edmund and Eli, but would eat cow skin, not make chairs.

Turned around one time. Lay down. Closed eyes. Dreamed of hunting in car, chasing cows, many, many cows.

Beast woke up when bad burning smell stung nose. Stretched in cow chairs and slowly padded from cow-hunting car. Day was cool, good day to lie on rocks in sun. Padded around Eli to Jane's rocks in back of house and climbed to top. Jane and Beast watched Eli with fire, burning iron. Eli in strange hat.

"It isn't going to be hot enough," Molly said.

"You want hotter temperatures, we need a two-tank

system, oxygen/acetylene," Eli said. "Ambient air is less than twenty-one percent oxygen. Pure O^2 burns hotter."

"You trying to tell an air witch about burning things?" Evan grunted, a low growl in his voice. He was sitting in a chair, dressed in human clothes. He smelled like iron and salt and sickness. Was spelled, but he could talk and move. His face was red and his body smelled of frustration, like big-cat hunting with no prey in territory. "No one knows burning things like an air witch."

Jane laughed inside. Beast did not understand why Jane laughed, but she sat back and let Beast stay alpha.

"No," Eli said. "I'm suggesting we get a different system or take the iron focals to a welder or to a structural steel fabricator." Eli pulled his hat off his head, took his cell from his pocket, and punched fingers across surface like Beast sliding paws across ice, with fish swimming beneath. "Thanks to the port, there's more than half a dozen iron fabricators in New Orleans, most within an hour's drive."

Molly was sitting in rusty chair, cold glass of tea in one hand. "What if you just take a sledgehammer to them?" she asked.

The men looked to her, smell of surprise on both. "I could create a ward that would let the sledgehammer in but not let magical energies escape," Molly said.

"Yeah," Evan said, his words slow with thought. "That would work."

Molly nodded. "Evan, you'd make a separate ward. Add filters to the ward to allow only oxygen through the filter. Increase the outer air pressure, forcing the O^2 into the ward. Scientifically it might work."

Eli said. "You set the ward. I'll get the sledgehammer."

"You got a sledgehammer here?" Evan sounded surprised.

"Never know when you might need a good sledgehammer."

Mr. Prepared, Jane thought. *Let's sleep. Things might get rough tonight.*

Beast closed eyes and slept in sun, waking only to see Evan break iron into tiny pieces, and magic smash against ward like bomb going off. Fire, too bright to look at, was inside ward. Did not smell blood, did not smell iron or salt or Jane hair, even with men shouting and jumping around like kits. *Silly men.*

I rested and slept and ate raw roast and steak all day. Eli was best litter mate.

It was dusk when I changed back, hidden in my own room. I stretched, fully human, on the bed. While I was starving, needing to replace the calories used to power my shifts, I hadn't felt so good in a long time. I had successfully shifted when my life was in danger, had stayed in Beast form all day, sleeping on heated rocks, had no new scars, and my old ones were faded to pale pink lines. And from beneath the door came the scent of the grill all fired up and loaded down with more beef. I dressed quickly in Bruiser's wrinkled shirt and a pair of leggings and went to the table.

Eli had prepared me a fourth chunk of meat, this one a thick steak grilled to rare and bloody perfection, with beer-batter-fried onion rings, asparagus sautéed in bacon drippings, which was out of this world, roasted sweet potatoes, and green salad with crispy bacon on top and hot bacon dressing. "Holy moly guacamole," I said, taking my seat and digging in. I was half finished with the steak when my hunger was satisfied enough to look up. And came to a total stop.

The whole family was eating together. Everyone but Bruiser was here. Tears filled my eyes and Eli passed me a bread basket, saying, "If you get all sappy and cry, it will ruin the ambience. Plus, all the girls will have to do a hug-hug, kiss-kiss moment and the food will get cold."

I took three slices of Molly's homemade bread and blinked back my tears. "No way am I stopping eating just to cry and hug my friends. But you know I love you all, right?"

They all spoke over one another: "Yes." "Totally." "Yes, Aunt Jane." "Wessh A' Ja'." "Back atcha." "Whiny girl stuff." And Brute whuffed.

I stilled, turning to see the werewolf stretched out on the floor, two empty plates near his feet. One was Beast's plate. One was new. I thought back through the day. I remembered the claw marks on the floor at EJ's bed. And Beast making nice-nice with the wolf. And the grindylow grooming Beast's pelt. Around the table, my friends and family were deliberately paying attention to their food and not to me or the wolf. "He's moved in?"

"He's my werewolf," Angie said.

"He's ma wrolf," EJ said, waving an asparagus spear in the air.

"He tried to save my son," Molly said, taking the green spear from Evan Junior.

"The grindylow seems to think it's a good idea," Eli said.

"No," Big Evan said.

I went back to eating, knowing that a family had to make tough decisions all the time and that, oddly, I wasn't in charge.

"How much do you remember from today?" Eli asked, after an uncomfortable silence.

"Why don't you start at the beginning?" I said. "I caught up on a lot of sleep today." Which was how I heard what they had done all day, starting from the time Eli successfully beat the iron focals into small pieces and Evan's working burned them to ash, releasing the last of the spell that was wrapped around Evan, which, fortunately, had been a simple knock-out spell, but had been geared to a human male, not an in-the-closet witchy man, allowing him to find consciousness and help with the spell-breaking.

Molly had done research on the witch names on her list. Alex had done research on Molly's research. Eli had spent hours with Jodi Richoux, having missed the dawn conference call with Leo, and had made nice-nice with everyone on the security team, especially Derek and the men he chose to work with Jodi's off-duty cops who would be on rooftops before, during, and after the Witch Conclave.

Evan and Molly had come up with what sounded like a contract with Edmund, to cover the blood vow given by their underage daughter to Edmund Hartley. I kept my mouth shut about that one, still bothered by the similarity to what I had done as a child, when I took a blood oath to kill my father's murderers.

And they told me about the package that had come while I slept on the rocks in the back. They all seemed eager for me to open it, but until I finished the food, I was going nowhere and doing nothing. Because the food was OhMyGosh too good for words.

After dinner, while the sun was setting in a red sky, I let my godchildren drag the package to me across the floor. It was huge, big enough to ship a chair in, but weighed little by comparison to the size. The box was postmarked in Louisiana and it had a return address I recognized. I ran a hand over the cardboard, feeling a hint of icy magic from within, and smelling the scent of leather.

"I haven't ordered anything from this company in ages," I said, "and I feel magic." I glanced at Molly and said, "You didn't feel anything?"

Evan answered for her. "No. Neither of us."

"Open a ward over me and the box?"

Evan and Molly stood to either side of me, at north and south, and Molly said, "Inverted *hedge of thorns*." The magic snapped over me and the box with a sizzle of familiar energies. The inverted hedge kept magics inside, rather than keeping an attacker out. Which meant if the box blew up, the family and the house were safe, though my insides might be splattered across the ward like some kind of gross, bloody artwork.

Feeling uneasy, I slit the packing tape open and pulled out long lengths of big green bubble wrap. My uneasiness was warranted: the feel of magic increased with a tingle that burned and ached along my skin. Beneath the bubble wrap was an envelope. Below that, I could see black leather, the soft gleam of the leather itself suggesting that it was high quality. I peeled back some of the plastic to reveal a set of fighting leathers, far nicer than any I had ever been able to afford.

Before I removed the last layer of plastic and touched the leather I opened the envelope and read the paperwork. The leather was described as top-grain, armored with sterling silver-over-titanium chain mail and flexible plastic (to repel talons and fangs) and Dyneema (to repel blades), and it came with top-quality, heavy silk lining. More important, the leathers had been treated by the Seattle coven to repel magic. Just the jacket had to go for upward of two thousand bucks, and the box was way bigger than one used to ship a leather jacket.

There was a card with the paperwork and the leathers' description. My trepidation growing, I placed the descriptions on the floor beside my knees and opened the card.

The leathers were from Leo, the card reading, "A gift for my Enforcer, that you may shine among the Enforcers of the Europeans, and that we might appear as worthy opponents." And it was signed with Leo's calligraphy-style siggie, all swirls and fancy curls.

This was vamp politics. Which meant I couldn't say no to the gift. Not that I wanted to. Some girls want jewelry. I wanted stuff like this.

I peeled away the last layer of plastic. The leather itself put out an icy-cold magic, sparking blue and silver to Beast-vision. The texture of the magic meant the jacket was spelled for temperature control as well as being spelled against attack magic. I'd heard of such spelling. It was offered to the mundane world by the Seattle coven for mucho dinero. From outside the ward, Molly and Big Evan heaved oohs and aahs at the sight of the magic on the jacket.

These were the best leathers I had ever seen. I lifted out the jacket and the pants beneath. And the custom-made, matching leather combat boots, ones with expansion seams on the sides, held in place with leather straps. The boots would not be water-resistant at all, but they would break outward on the sides if I shifted to my half-Beast form. I had no idea how much these fighting leathers might cost. Ten thousand dollars? More?

Beneath the black leathers came a magical glow, and I realized that there was more in the box. I placed the black leathers on the floor by my knee and removed more packing paper. Below the paper was another set of leathers. My breath caught. This set was of dark gold leather, the color of my eyes when I was human, an amber gold with darker striations, almost like a . . . like a pelt. I lifted out the jacket and the pants beneath. Instantly I could see the leathers worn with the fancy ornamental gorget Leo had given me. The boots beneath were black, exact copies of the other pair.

And there was more paper below that one.

"Holy crap," I whispered. I pulled out the next layer of paper, to see a flash of red. The third set of leathers were scarlet, my favorite lipstick tint. The magical power signature on this set was brighter, hotter, and I knew without testing them that the magics in this set were particularly strong, maybe with double rebound magic, so that any attack spell that came at me rebounded on the sender. A third pair of boots was beneath the red leathers. In the bottom there were three sets of matching grips for my .380s and for the nine-mil handguns. There were also new stakes, wood, the handgrips burned with the new Yellowrock Securities logo, the tips all silver. The blunt ends of the stakes each had a cabochon gem in the end, blackstone, garnet, or citrine, matching the leathers, four stakes in each gem color, to wear like jewelry in my hair. Jewelry deadly to vamps.

But there was still more. In the bottom was a second box, this one sealed and marked with the name Eli Younger. I indicated that the inverted *hedge* could be dropped and I lifted out the box, holding it up to Eli.

He accepted it, standing over me and my pile of fighting finery. He knelt beside me and sliced through the sealing tape. Inside, wrapped in matching packing paper, was a set of leathers, matte black, as befitted a second.

From the living room Edmund said, sounding droll, "They match mine, which were given to me by Leo before he kicked me out. They are hanging in the storage room, in a garment bag. I do hope they aren't in the way." There was something snide in the last line, but I ignored it, my thoughts on the time schedule for ordering, measuring, cutting, sewing, shaping, and spelling so many sets of leathers in so many different colors and sizes.

There was a smaller, bright red cardboard box to the side, one I hadn't even noticed. It had no address on it, and had been hand-delivered. I looked the question at the boys and Edmund said, "From George Dumas." More snide, which I again ignored.

I opened the box and peeled back the tissue paper inside. And I lifted out the thing on top.

"Niiiice," Eli said. "Custom Kydex holsters for all your gear." He flipped a card over and handed it to me without reading it. The note said, "Jane. The gift isn't roses, nor so valuable as a lovely Moghul blade, but they are practical and they match your new leathers. They are custom-made by the Green River Holster Company. George." There was a business card attached that said GRHolsters.com.

I retrieved three weapons from my room and slid a fourteen-inch-long vamp-killer into a holster shaped like a blade. It clicked when it was seated, a soft snap that said the weapon was secure until I wanted to free it. The nine-mils clicked into place too. "Cool," I said, knowing there was a silly girly smile on my lips. But a guy who knew how to buy the perfect present tended to bring on a lot of such smiles.

My cell rang and I instantly knew who it was. I met Eli's eyes, and his squinted just a hint. It was his ticked-off face. He knew too. The time proved that we were being played, part of the vamp politics. I flipped open the Kevlar cover and said, "Leo."

"You have received your gift, my Jane?"

Toneless, I said, "Yes. They're beautiful. This stuff is for the Euro Vamp visit, yes? What are you planning? And for how long have you been planning it? And am I supposed to be dead when it's over?"

Leo chuckled, that silken laugh they do that sends shivers over my flesh, that come-hither sound that makes them the apex predators. "I have known this was coming for a very, *very* long time, my Jane. I have planned this from the moment you killed my enemy, de Allyon, shifted into a puma in my limo, and shredded the seats with your claws." The call ended.

CHAPTER 13

It's Too Dark to See,
But I'm Rolling My Eyes

Not long after dark, Eli and I drove up to the Elms Mansion and Garden and parked on a side street. I was in street clothes instead of the new gear, because the smell of the leathers was too much for my sensitive nose. I had tried them on, however, and they were luscious, but not luscious enough to wear without a really good airing out.

The weather was cool, the humidity was low for New Orleans, and the sunset had been spectacular, a red wash across the western sky. As we walked up, we saw five witches warding the grounds: Lachish, her gray hair like steel in the garden lights, Molly with her glorious cap of curls, and three others. One was Bliss, and the young woman had changed a lot since she accepted that she was a witch and began training. She was still ethereally beautiful, with very pale skin and black hair, but she no longer lived at Katie's Ladies, no longer serviced vamps and bigwigs in town by donating blood or other services. And she no longer went by Bliss, but by her given name, Ailis Rogan. I inclined my head, letting her know that I recognized her, but didn't go over. I wasn't sure how much of her past she had shared with others. There were two more witches I had met before, Butterfly Lily and her mother, Feather Storm. Neither was a powerful witch, but they were useful to route magical workings through, when a full coven of powerful witches was unavailable, as for this test.

Big Evan stood to the side. In order to protect his children, he hadn't outted himself, and he was here incognito, wearing a ball cap and sunglasses, looking like a bored human husband, but watching everything with a keen eye.

The five witches had drawn a witch circle that covered the house, the extensive grounds in back, the large central patio directly behind the house that lined up with a gazebo and a statue, the garden areas, the trees that lined the property, part of the sidewalks, and the curb at St. Charles Avenue. In back, the witches were standing at pentagram points with Lachish at north, and the two weaker witches standing in between the stronger witches. Moving sunwise, it was Lachish, Butterfly Lily, Molly, Feather Storm, and Ailis/Bliss. By pulling on Beast-vision, I could see the working as it unfolded, rising very slowly from the circle and beginning to lift to cover the house and grounds.

Jodi and Sloan Rosen were standing outside the house grounds and the warding, watching the witches work. Jodi was a small, curvy blond, who was the public face of NOPD's paranormal department, while Sloan spent most of his time in the bowels of the woo-woo room in research. Not that Sloan couldn't do the same job as Jodi, but he had a huge price on his head, put there by the local chapter of some big gangs. Sloan had been undercover with them and had barely gotten out with his head—and loads of info on the gangs. If it hadn't been dark, I doubted he'd be in public.

In the middle of St. Charles Avenue, in front of the Elms, Derek and his small, loyal, most experienced team of men were working on issues related to parking and witch safety during and after streetcar transportation up and down the major thoroughfare. Safety for the streetcar was paramount, as so many out-of-towners would be using the streetcar for transportation between the Elms and nearby or French Quarter hotels.

"Jodi," I called out. She started to reply but snapped her head to the circle. The sizzle of magics interrupted, of a working shattering, swept over me, scorching hot, lifting the hairs on my body and up my neck. I inhaled and caught the stink of ozone, the smell of smoke.

In an instant, everything went wrong, in overlapping impressions and sensations.

Big Evan roared with pain. He threw his head back, spine arching, and cartwheeled *into* the circle, through the rising magics, to land on the grass. Fire flared from one arm and both legs, the stink of burning flesh on the air. Smoke rose in puffs and spirals. The circle and warding began to fall.

And the faint stink of old iron and salt came from all around.

Along with Eli and Jodi, I raced for Big Evan. But the working hadn't completely fallen and I caught the others, holding them back. "It's not down yet," I said. Eli jerked free and sped into the dark, for what, I didn't know. I pulled Jodi away, and signaled to Derek to keep his men away, watching helplessly as Evan rolled in the grass, trying to put out the flames. Roaring with pain and anger.

I could enter the Gray Between and crawl through the falling energies, but at the thought, my belly wrenched with what I hoped was only phantom pain. I might die before I ever got to Evan. I ground my teeth against the fear and reached inside myself to touch my skinwalker magics, gathering them. Just in case.

Jodi pulled her radio and identified herself and her twenty, which was cop-speak for location, as she gave the Elms' address. The witches in the working struggled to hold the degrading circle, trying to keep it from exploding or imploding or whatever was trying to happen.

Molly shouted her husband's name, but didn't move from her place as she and the other four witches gathered the energies of the circle and the incipient ward, as if pulling huge cables, coiling them on the ground, lowering the power into the earth, grounding the energy. From Evan, broken energies sparked and sizzled and flew into the air. Though he had to be in horrible pain, he was trying not to use his air magics to put out the fire, which would have been a snap. But not today, not in front of witnesses, and not against the green flames.

"—Medic!" Jodi demanded, and I realized she was still speaking into her official police radio, words fast and clipped. "We need an ambulance at the Elms on St. Charles and Eighth. Single burn victim. Paranormal injury, accidental or criminal, unknown. I want marked cars at Seventh, Eighth, and Harmony streets to keep the public back."

Someone said, "Ten-four, Detective." There was a click and to me Jodi said, "Did you see what happened?"

"Something went wrong with the circle, and then Evan jumped inside it, which is either the height of stupidity or something heroic," I said, trying to figure out why Evan had thrown himself *into* the ward. He had to have seen something dangerous inside, but I couldn't spot anything.

Evan was still rolling, and with Beast-vision, I could see gold energies cocooning his body as he drew on his personal protection magics, but the flames weren't going out. Green flames. Green magic, attacking Evan. "The fire has weird green tints," I said. "It isn't an ordinary fire. It's magic." And it was attacking Evan.

"It's a targeted spell," Jodi added grimly, drawing the same conclusion.

I pulled my skinwalker energies out, a gray and silver cloud of my magic, the Gray Between, laced through with darker silver-gray motes of dancing power. I wasn't planning on bubbling time, but already my guts twisted, a taste of blood in the back of my throat.

The ward fell. Molly dropped the powers she had been holding and raced toward her husband, her hands doing something, too fast to see. Eli sprinted in from the side carrying his medical gobag, a blanket, and a fire extinguisher. He tossed the bag and extinguisher to me and shook out the blanket on the run. He threw it on Big Evan and rolled the much larger man in it, applying his own body weight and slapping with his hands to smother the weird green flames. The purely mundane remedy was working. I let go of my own power, swallowed back the vile taste of blood, pulled the pin on the bright red extinguisher, raced forward, and aimed carbon dioxide at the burning grass, the white cloud suffocating the last of the fire. It took longer than it should have to kill the flames on the grass, and the stench of ozone mixed with iron and copious amounts of salt hung heavy on the air by the time the last flame died.

Molly and Eli were kneeling beside Evan. Lachish stood at his head and Bliss/Ailis at his feet, already working to dampen his pain and speed healing, which was Ailis's special gift. I could see the brilliant energies, blues and purples, blending into a dark but vibrant working.

Big Evan sighed as the working descended and his pain began to ease. Tears and mucus glistened on his face. "I'm okay, Mol. Let me see."

"No! Don't look."

He caught both of her hands in his one unburned, catcher-mitt-sized hand, and the blanket slid down. "You know I'm going to look," he said with a pained version of his old smile. He did. The shreds of his clothes were charred; his left arm and both legs looked like raw meat; the red body hair and outer skin were gone, as if blisters had formed and burst, exposing cooked muscle and blackened, ropy veins. "Well, dang. I won't look so pretty at the beach next summer, but at least I still have my limbs." He let Molly go and touched his face, sounding mournful. "It burned off part of my beard."

"Evan!" Molly was crying, but not tears of fear or worry. Molly was mad. Which was dangerous on all sorts of levels. Molly had death magics to control and hide, and being angry tended to bring them to the surface.

"I'm fine, sweetheart," Evan said. "Breathe."

"You breathe!"

Evan laughed, the sound pained and a little wild. "I am. That's the important thing to remember. I'm still breathing."

"Nothing a little vamp blood won't heal," Eli said. Four of the witches whipped their heads to him, clearly scandalized. "Not that your spells aren't great and all, ladies, but I know this vampire? And he'll be happy to heal. He even swore an oath to do anything necessary to help." Eli gave me an evil grin. "Perfect time to test out that primo promise."

"Right," I said, relief scudding through me. "Get Alex to send Edmund here." I stopped, thinking about what I had just said. I was treating Edmund like a blood-slave, which made me no better than a vamp. I rubbed my head and drew on the hard-taught manners I so seldom used. I rephrased, "Please ask Alex to please request the presence of Edmund here."

Eli gave a half-smothered, derisive breath at my polite words.

"Molly, remember what Edmund promised. Evan will be fine. He'll see it happens. But what we need right now is for you, all of you, to tell us what happened."

"I'm breathing," Evan said, his voice tight with pain, "so I can talk." In the distance multiple sirens sounded as police and ambulances closed in from every direction.

"Okay," Molly said, though it was a lie. She wasn't okay at all. But the word meant that she was reining in her anger.

I knelt beside Evan as Molly lent her Earth magics to helping Evan with pain relief, tears drying on her face. "Evan," I said, "you were outside the circle, and Jodi and I smelled a spell go bad. And then you jumped into the circle. And then we saw that you were on fire. Did you go on fire before you jumped into the circle or after? How do you remember it?"

"I didn't jump inside. I'd have broken the circle."

"You did jump," Lachish said. "The circle didn't break and it should have."

"No, no," Jodi said, her eyes holding a faraway stare. "There was the circle you had already raised, and then the ward you were starting to raise. And there was a third working. Something outside that was activated before Evan jumped into the circle, before he caught on fire. And it wasn't your workings. I smelled something odd." Jodi pulled out a psy-meter and started scanning the grounds.

"Iron and salt," I said. "And here all along I thought that salt and iron were the antithesis to magic."

"Nothing is ever an absolute," Jodi said. "So that

means the circle itself may have been a target instead of a bystander. Is that even possible?"

"It's possible," Lachish said, drawing out the word, sounding uncertain.

"Explain," I said.

"There are two ways it might work. One: a group of witches were nearby with a working in process. Then our working triggered it, attracting it to us. The timing and similarity of energies being raised would have to be impeccable, which, to my mind, rules out an *accidental* merging. Two, which is much more likely: there was a booby trap working on the grounds, and when we raised the circle, and triggered the *hedge of thorns* ward, our actions activated the concealed working. The explosion was close enough to Evan to propel him into the circle."

"That's it," Evan rasped. "The magic was under my feet. It exploded upward and threw me inside."

I remembered the spell that had knocked Evan flat to his back earlier in the morning. That might have made him more likely to be hit again, but I didn't want to say that aloud. "Okay. Assuming door number two," I said, "and assuming Evan was an accidental target instead of the intended target, what would be needed for a booby trap?"

"A focus is the easiest method," Lachish said.

"That's it," Big Evan repeated, now sounding dreamy, as Molly's and Ailis's magics pulled his pain away. I wondered if the young, untrained, and inexperienced witch could tell Evan was a witch, but she didn't act odd, so I guessed not.

Emergency vehicles closed in on the Elms, the sirens doing that house-to-house fast echo of a neighborhood in the muggy South. "Yeah," Evan said. "I saw a green leaf iron . . . focal." And he was suddenly asleep, knocked out by the healing spell.

I knelt and checked his palms. Nothing there except blisters on the burned one. Eli said, "Jane, my cell just went out."

"Lachish," I said, pulling my own cell, "we need to keep everyone away from here, away from Evan, away from the circle. You know that my house has been attacked twice, by two witches using iron focal items. So was I, personally. Evan got some of the backlash." I took a surreptitious look at my left palm, which was unmarked, no green eye there. Thankfully. I scrubbed my palm on my pants before opening my phone. "Alex sent you the photos. Did you recognize anyone through the pixelated-out mess?"

"No," she said. "Their body shapes might have been any of dozens of witches in the state. But there was nothing visible of their faces." Which I knew.

"My phone's out too," I said to them, poking at the dead screen. "Proximity to the broken circle?"

Lachish said, "It could be. Or it could be a multilayered spell with interrupted communications as part of it." She looked at Jodi, who immediately started barking orders at the officers, to cordon off the whole block. Too many things were going on, going wrong, and I tried to think, while Jodi, standing on the patio tiles, waved the approaching ambulance into a parking spot. I could hear the voices as they explained to the cops and the paramedics what the witches were doing and what the holdup was. The cops checked their cells, to discover that they were out. Even their radios were nonfunctional, though the car engines themselves were seemingly fine. While the human cops cordoned off the area, I walked around the healing working and murmured to Molly, "Where are your kids?"

"Being watched over by a teenager playing World of Killer-Death-Something, and a *werewolf*." She sounded wry, as if her life had taken off on an inexplicable tangent and nothing made sense anymore.

"Can you find any other icons that might be on the grounds?" I asked, not adding, *Like Evan did*.

"Yes, I think so." To Lachish, she said, "I think he'll sleep now. The ambulance is here. We should clear a path from the street to Evan first, and get him to the hospital, where the vampire can help heal him."

"I wouldn't let a fanghead touch my—" Lachish stopped. "Never mind. Things change. Maybe the suckheads have changed too." More reluctantly she added, "And if it was my husband there, hurt, I'd strip naked and slow-dance with a vamp for the chance to get him help. You're right.

We need Evan in a safer place so we can tackle the whole yard."

"Good enough," Molly said, tension leaking away, making her shoulders droop. "And by the way, you and Jane need to go over the list of witches who were at the cemetery when Jane was struck by lightning, and add a few last names. She has a right to personal protection. She has a right to see which witches might be responsible for the attack on her."

"None of my coven would be involved," Lachish said, her chin up and shoulders hunched in what looked like a pugilistic stance.

"You're probably right," Molly said, her tone composed and serene, "but it's smart to consider everything. No stone unturned, you know?" she said.

Lachish didn't like it, but she gave me a curt nod. She gave Molly a small *come this way* gesture with her fingers and said over her shoulder, "We can start at the ambulance and work our way to Evan. Then once he's in the ambulance, we can clear the yard, beginning at the area where your husband entered the circle. We need to find out what attacked him and how he was able to enter without breaking the energies. The circle should have stopped him."

Molly's expression didn't change, but her scent went to panic, fast. Lachish didn't know that Big Evan was a male witch—whose magics had never been studied—and this wasn't the time to explain it all.

Speaking loud, I said, "It could be part of the focals' working. First disrupt a working and its ward, and then allow people in to attack. All you have to do is figure out how to defend against both parts. Or it might be because he was in the backlash of the same kind of magics today."

Molly blinked and said, "Exactly," maybe a little too emphatically, but Lachish was already on the far side of the patio, bending over a place in the grass, a spot of browned grass similar to the ones at my house.

Lachish said, "There's something here—"

"Don't touch it!" I shouted.

The explosion threw the witch across the grass, toward the ambulance. Dirt and grass and two tree branches blew outward. Beast shoved me into action and I threw myself over Molly to protect her. Eli hit the earth. So did two of the uniformed cops. Jodi and all the other officers drew their service weapons. One raced to unlock bigger firepower and came out with a city-issued automatic rifle.

"Get off me, you big oaf," Molly said, pushing at me. "I'm suffocating here."

I rolled to the side and got to my feet, pulling her with me and running my hands over her and her baby bump, leaning in and breathing her scent deep. Molly wasn't fine, but she wasn't bleeding or leaking amniotic fluid from the concussive release of magic. Lachish, however, wasn't moving. "Lachish is hurt," I said. "Stay with Evan and keep his healing wards up. Don't wander." I spotted Bliss—*Ailis*— standing in the shadow of the back door, with a hand over her mouth, her eyes wide. The elegant hostess, Amalie, stood beside her, face pale and drawn. "Ailis," I said.

"The explosion shut off my cell phone," she said. "I don't know how to summon yet, so I was going to call in some more of the circle to help, but the phone is fried."

"I know. I need you over there." I pointed at Lachish, whose blood I smelled on the air. I walked slowly across the lawn toward Lachish, my eyes on the ground. But it was getting darker and even pulling on Beast-vision I couldn't see well enough to step safely. "Watch the ground for any indication of dead grass or magics."

She came, feet uncertain, eyes wide, watching the ground, and followed in my footsteps to Lachish. The coven leader was bleeding from the mouth, her left arm looked as if it had an extra elbow above the wrist, and her lower left leg was deformed. Both leg bones were broken, not quite compound fractures, but close. But she was breathing and her heart was beating. "Don't touch her until the paramedics can get here. Set a healing circle," I said, "and"—I looked around—"where are the two aka witches?" I asked, meaning Butterfly Lily and Feather Storm.

"They took off the moment the circle was down."

"Guilty or afraid?"

"Terrified," Ailis said. "I have the healing circle up. I can hold it for a while alone, but I'm not used to using my gifts, so . . ." She opened her lips to drag in a deeper breath, and finished, "So I can't promise anything."

"You didn't run," I said. "You could have. I'm proud of you." Ailis sent me a smile that suggested I shouldn't be proud just yet because she might still run, but she returned her attention to Lachish.

Carefully I walked to the side street. "Eli," I said as I neared, speaking softly, "the magic may have been intended to interfere with communications too."

"You think we set off a prepared working early. As in, this was probably supposed to happen after all the witches were gathered in one place. Which would mean the witches who set it weren't on the inside of the plans."

"I think so. Maybe. But multipurpose spells are difficult to craft, harder to power, and tricky to activate and deploy." I lowered my voice even more. "I have no idea what the double exposure to the green energies will have on Evan, or have on the spells here, for that matter. But we need to get Lachish and Evan to Tulane."

"Suggestions?"

"I find the icons, and you shoot them?"

"Anything with explosions—where people don't get hurt—is fun. I'm in. I'll tell Jodi, and she can tell the cops what we're doing so they don't shoot us."

"Good idea. I always like not being shot at."

"But the adrenaline rush is such a high."

"It's too dark to see, but I'm rolling my eyes."

"Love you too, babe. I have a .22 target pistol in the SUV. I'll be right back."

It didn't take Eli long to talk to Jodi and get his pistol, and bring the cop she insisted go with him up-to-date. The officer was a recently discharged boots-on-the-ground soldier, and the two army boys bonded immediately over weapons and blast radii and other weapons-porn, and discussed what they needed to take cover behind to be protected. I let them talk and make decisions and move the other cops back and generally handle all the details while I studied the grounds with Beast-vision.

The night grew deeper and artificial lights came on from all around, throwing long grayed shadows and shorter black shadows, which interfered with my Beast-vision and made it harder to find the pale greenish energies I was hunting for, buried beneath the grass or in flower beds. I found three probable sites of unexploded focal icons in the backyard, one to the very back of the property, and the other two out to the sides of that one, positioned halfway between it and the exploded ones. There were probably more in the front yard, and since magic was mathematics and geometry, there would be a specific number and place-ment of them, oriented along specific lines and compass points. We had blown two, with injuries, at east and west, near the house. With three more in the back, that was five, and covered a shape that might be a triangle, which would intersect with similar shapes in the front yard. However, the front and side yards were minuscule as compared to the back. The mathematics were going to be either mag-nificent and complicated or overly simplistic and imbued with raw power. I was going with curtain number two, but none of the witches were available to help me with my speculations.

"Jane, we're ready," Eli said.

"Okay. Here's how it will work. I'm going to walk up close to a location that looks likely to hold a focal item, point at it, and then I'm going to back away and you are going to shoot it. There may be an explosion or there may be nothing. If it explodes we'll know we were successful. If it doesn't we won't know diddly-squat and we'll have to figure out something else."

"How come you can see the magic stuff?" Eli's new partner asked.

"She's Supergirl. She has X-ray vision," Eli said.

"Rolling eyes again," I said, checking out the cop's name badge, which was P. Nunez. In any other part of the coun-try, that would be a Latino name. In this part of the world, it was just as likely to be Cajun. "How close do you need to be to hit a target about four inches across?" I asked.

Eli said, "Distance on this property won't be a prob-lem, but the angle of shot might be, if the target is buried. If you can tell me how deep, I can make adjustments by climbing trees or on top of the gazebo."

"Okay. Gazebo first." I pointed to a place behind the ornate columned gazebo. "Maybe four inches deep. The apex focal is there. Nunez, we can boost him up."

The cop's eyebrows went up and Eli said, "She's stronger than she looks. Supergirl, remember?" At the base of the gazebo, the guys put weapons on the patio tiles and I took off my jacket, laying it near the firepower. Nunez made a cup of his joined hands, boosting Eli up about eighteen inches. My partner caught a column to hold his balance and I stepped close and bent, hands to knees, offering my back as a step stool. He transferred his weight to me one foot at a time.

"Next time, take off your freaking combat boots," I said. "The treads are getting grit on my shirt."

"Such a girly comment," he said as he stepped onto Nunez's right shoulder and I stood, taking his other foot on my left. Nunez was shorter than I was and when Eli bounced up off us and pulled himself up to the gazebo roof, it was an ungainly leap, but it was sufficient.

I brushed off my now-dirty shirt and called up, "When you hand-wash my shirt, be sure to let it soak, you thug."

"Yes, dear," Eli said, accepting his weapons from Nunez, who clearly didn't know what to make of us or our relationship.

"He's my brother," I said to Nunez. "You can see the resemblance in the jawline and the snark line."

The cop shook his head and called up, "Target?"

"Acquired. Back off at least fifteen feet. That's about ten feet father than Lachish and Evan were thrown." We walked back and hunkered down, kneeling on the patio. Louder, Eli called out, "Everybody down. On one." He counted down, "Three. Two. One."

The shot and the explosion seemed to happen simultaneously. A frisson of magic spiked the air and shivered across me. I was expecting it this time and I was holding my left hand open. An eye appeared there for a moment, green lid closed, green lashes resting along the skin over the metatarsal of my little finger. And then it faded. I was still marked. Now I had to worry about Evan. And Lachish.

There were emergency vehicles gathering, blue and red

lights creating a stained glass effect on the nearby buildings. A fire truck pulled to the curb, brakes hissing. Voices
called; people raced here and there. I hoped that the paramedics standing at the ambulances had sufficient skills to
work with witches. Not all the city's EMTs had taken the
specialized training.

Nunez and I accepted Eli's weapons, and before we
could raise hands to help, he found a good handhold, slid
off the top, flipped over and through his arms and into a
swing, dropping free and landing in a crouch.

"Showoff," I muttered.

He gave me a self-satisfied grin and brushed his hands
together. Eli seldom deliberately displayed his skills and
combat readiness, but he was having fun, his body odor
heavy on victory pheromones, which were musky and
acrid, but he didn't swagger. Uncle Sam's best didn't need
to swagger.

He had to climb a tree to get a firing angle on the next
focal item. Once he was settled into a firing stance, I moved
to Evan and took both of his hands as Eli counted down.

"Three. Two. One."

The explosion was intense, stronger than the others,
as if they got worse as more and more of them went
offline. I ducked but kept my eyes open, watching Evan's
palms. Green eyes appeared in both palms, for half a
heartbeat. The lids were partially open.

I didn't know what it meant that both palms were
marked. It could be that he was under the power of the
two witches. Or was a target they were intent upon attacking. Or that they had spelled him already, as they had me.
There wasn't a single good reason I could come up with
for Evan to have witchy eyes in his palms.

Molly had said I was free of latent magics, but my palm
had displayed green eyes. I had to think the eyes were
linked to me, through the first scanning spell. But how
could the witches turn it off and on? Good question. Were
we all a danger to the conclave? Better question. Should we
stay away? Best question. And the answer was no. Together,
we could defeat anything a spell could throw at us. Yeah.
That.

Keeping my worries and conclusions to myself, I went to help Eli down from a perch much higher than the gazebo. He stretched down and gave Nunez the pistol, then motioned us two feet apart and dropped down. He landed, taking the fall on bent legs, a hand on Nunez's shoulder and one on mine. I stumbled, not expecting him to drop that way, and bit my cheek. Just a nick, which I ignored. I didn't even flinch. How could I in the presence of so much testosterone?

When my partner was in place for the third shot, I dropped to the ground by Lachish, who was struggling to resist Ailis's healing magic, struggling to break free of the painkilling sleep. I took both of her hands, turned them so I could see the palms, careful not to jar the broken arm, and whispered, "It's okay. It's a healing working. You broke your arm and leg. You're in pain. Let Ailis help you until I can get an ambulance." Oddly Lachish stopped struggling and relaxed.

"Thank you," Ailis said, her shoulders dropping.

"This explosion may be worse that the last one," I warned. "Can you cover us all in a ward?"

"On one!" Eli called out.

Ailis cursed with great force and even more imagination about donkeys and male body parts. I stuttered in laughter as a ward opened over us.

"Three."

I opened Lachish's fingers so I could see her palms.

"Two. One." The explosion was shocking, and I felt a concussive blast knock into the ward at the same moment that two green eyes appeared in Lachish's palms. Staring at me. The ward Ailis had raised shivered and shook, the energies blasting up in a shower of purple sparks. The eyes seemed to look around me and I closed the palms, fast.

The tree branch where Eli was stretched out in a shooter's stance fell with a crack. My partner rolled backward along the limb, tucked, pushed off with one foot, and rolled to the side. Another branch broke. Both limbs hit the ground. He leaped and landed, rolled again to his feet, the target pistol nowhere in sight, and a small subgun I hadn't even noticed on him, held at firing position. Above me,

Ailis's palms were marked with staring green eyes. She squeaked and the protective ward spluttered and fell.

I motioned to Eli to hold his open palms out. There was a faint gleam of green in both. His eyes held mine in the darkness as I heard what might have been laughter in the air. It wasn't his. And while it wasn't mad, maniacal laughter, like something from a serial killer TV show, it wasn't ordinary giggles from girls' night out either. It left a bad taste in my ears. So to speak. I opened Lachish's palms, and the eyes were gone. I smelled a hint of iron and salt and I knew that the witches responsible for this working had been watching, though from nearby or with the witch equivalent of a crystal ball, I didn't know.

Molly shouted, "The wards are all down! The offensive working is no longer active."

The paramedics trotted over, one with an oversized orange supply kit. They started to Evan first, but a man appeared in front of them with a small pop of sound and said, "See to the lady first, if you please." I felt the power of vampiric compulsion flow through the damaged yard. "I'll see to the gentleman. I'm a doctor," he added, sounding and looking perfectly human, probably to keep the human paramedics relaxed and calm.

Really? I thought. *Dr. Edmund Hartley.* But why not? He was old enough to have taken out a few years of his very, very long life to go to medical school. Of course, he might have attended in the seventeen hundreds. And of course, he didn't need medical training to heal.

Pushing outward with his compulsion, he said to the medical personnel, "Lachish Dutillet is a witch, so you'll want magical protection while you assess her and secure her for transport to Tulane University Hospital. The beautiful Ailis should be able to provide you with that assistance."

Ailis gave him a look that would have cured leather, but he ignored it. The two might have had a history. Interesting.

Tulane University Hospital was the only hospital in New Orleans that kept paranormal medical experts on contract. They also had medical and technical personnel who dealt with the needs of supernats and their injuries.

And they had, on at least one occasion, allowed vampires into the ER to treat dying patients.

Edmund turned to me. He was dressed in a black tuxedo with a burgundy hankie and cummerbund, and very shiny patent leather shoes. There was a faint five o'clock shadow along his jaw, which I thought might be the first time I had ever seen a vamp with ungroomed facial hair. Fangs dropping with a tiny *schnick*, he said, "I haven't fed tonight."

"Noted," I said, and pointed at Evan.

"As my mistress requires." The words were quite clear, despite being spoken around the fangs. He offered me a tiny bow that managed to come across as mocking.

Something that smelled like cinnamon with a hint of anise and . . . maybe chocolate mint wafted from Edmund. He smelled like a bakery. I said, "Alex and the Robere brothers will draw up the primo papers tomorrow. I'll approve them and get the signing witnessed."

"Agreed, my mistress. And then they may be stored at the Mithran Council Chambers along with all such legal writs."

I narrowed my eyes and answered without agreeing to that, "Heal your other master. Please."

Edmund gave a deeper bow and actually clicked his heels together, a military tradition that went back centuries, though no one but me might have heard the patent leather tap. He knelt beside Evan and pulled off his tux jacket, tossing it to the grass. With deft motions, he rolled up both sleeves of his pristine dress shirt. As if just seeing her, he offered Molly a truncated bow and, at the same moment, bit into his own left wrist with a quick, tearing action that almost seemed graceful. Or ritualistic.

He lifted Big Evan's head off the ground and held the bloodied flesh over Evan's mouth, allowing several ounces to dribble in. Vamp magic and witch healing magic grew on the air, competing and blending, like spices that weren't usually used together, but that somehow worked. The air took on a piquant tang, with a hint of red peppers.

Evan swallowed. His hands glowed green.

The hair on the back of my neck stood up.

"No!" The Gray Between exploded out of me. I threw myself at Edmund. Faster than the speed of sound. Faster than time. In the instant of the leap, in the moment of no time, I took it all in.

Edmund halted in the act of turning to me. Eli was swiveling with the subgun, pivoting on one heel, the other foot held up, stationary in the air. The green magics around Evan's hands were an unmoving cloud of gas and icy sparkles. Molly was frozen too, her hands reaching for Evan's face, her brow crinkled as if she knew something had just gone wrong. Really badly wrong. There were green clouds of gas on her hands as well, but on Molly, the spell was shot through with blackness. Her death magics had been activated.

As I leaped through time, my belly was already cramping, tearing, ripping along my side where something had never healed quite right. I caught Edmund by the shoulders, jerking him into my arms, into the bubble of time, with me. Whatever was happening, whatever spell had been activated in the instant before I leaped into the Gray Between of time, was still happening. Edmund's eyes vamped out. His taloned hands reached for me, gripped the back of my head. Jerked me to him. His head tipped back. Fangs struck at me, like a snake striking at prey.

CHAPTER 14

Deader Vampire

I whipped my body back and busted him in the mouth with my elbow. Not the best way to strike an opponent, but at close quarters it was all I had. The blow slammed his lips against his teeth and fangs. Ripped the inside of my elbow on a fang, mixing our blood. Magic wrenched through us both. His eyes went wider. He snarled.

Still moving, I threw Edmund away from me, my hands in his blood and mine. He slid from the bubble of time, into the night, hanging in thin air. I tumbled forward, beneath him, and came up on my hands and knees. Vomited blood in a scarlet gush. Nothing new there, not with Gray Between and its nasty during-effects and after-effects. My belly cramped in a molten fist of agony. Normal. Dying again . . .

I pushed to my feet and wiped my bloody mouth on my wrist. And looked at my left palm. A green eye was glowing in the center of it, the lid open and smeared with vampire blood and my blood. Mixing us together in the dark working. This was bad. But the vampire was now in real time and I wasn't. The spell was stuck in real time, in

Edmund's time, not whatever bubble of time the rest of me was stuck in.

"Crap." I had guessed right, in that singular instant before I grabbed my primo. This part of the layered and multipurpose spell was triggered by vamp blood and my blood at the same place and the same time as witches. Though the attacking working had probably been constructed with Leo in mind, not Edmund. Edmund, the only vamp here, had now been spelled to attack me, just as Gee had been.

I staggered back to Evan and looked at the working erupting out of him. Compared it to the working stuck in my palm. Tried to put it all together.

The two enemy witches had . . . what? Gotten a sample of my genetic material and used it to create a watching-working tied to me? Then they scanned my house, using it as a distraction so they could drop a DNA spell into me. Yeah. That felt right. Their initial scan had left a back door entry to my house. Using that, they put a similar watching spell in an air elemental gas spell, sent it inside the *hedge of thorns* ward that had been protecting the house. The Truebloods had breathed the spelled gasses. Their breath had carried it to their blood, and Edmund had done artificial resuscitation on them, probably getting the spell on him/in him that way. Making it worse, Evan had triggered the magical icons at my house, and then here, and gotten knocked loopy, getting more of the magics on him.

But the working on me, while it wasn't active when Mol scanned me, was still there. Hiding inside me? Yeah. Like the way a spider hides its eggs in its prey. And the moment my blood and vamp's blood were in the same place, inside a witch circle—or the remains of one—the main part of the attack was activated.

I leaned into Molly and checked her palms. Yeah. Same green magic crap. Lachish's hands and Ailis's hands were erupting green stuff too. So the spell had been transferred from one to the other the way one person with the flu might infect another, by touch or breathing. Or when the focal was tripped.

The spell—or part of it—appeared to be intended for us to turn on each other. It was an amazing spell, intricate, multilayered, specific, targeted on a genetic level and then targeted on a multivictim level.

I didn't know who the attackers were. I didn't know how to stop the spell. Except to get away from them all. To get Edmund away from them all.

Nausea flooded my mouth with saliva. The taste of blood and acid rose up my esophagus. I vomited again, but this time I felt something different. Something warm near my ear. Cold dripping down my neck. I touched the soft tissue of my throat, in front of and below my ear, and my fingers came away cold and sticky. Blood. Just a trickle.

Right at the place where Leo had bitten me when he tried to force a binding on me. Blood welling in the two spots where his fangs had bitten me. "Well, joy," I said. I didn't know if the blood was the effect of entering no time one time too many, or the effect of the attack spell, or some other mumbo-jumbo paranormal crapola. But whatever the reason, it wasn't going to be good.

I propped my hands on my knees to hold myself up. An unexpected shiver raced through me, raising the hair on my arms and legs in reaction to the cold. I would never be able to defeat Edmund in real time, not as sick as I was. So I pulled a pure wooden stake out of my bun, one with no trace of silver on it, and crab-walked over to him. I shoved it through his shirt into the sweet spot where his ribs came together, where the descending aorta—in both humans and vamps—was. His flesh in no time was rubbery and difficult to puncture. But I leaned into the strike, putting my weight behind it until the stake was buried deep. It wasn't a heart stick, so he should survive it.

I stood there, cramping like a son of a gun, until I saw his eyelids flicker. When I was able to stand upright against the cramps again, I rammed a shoulder into his belly, below the stake, and rolled him up into a fireman's carry. I was doing a lot of that lately. Maybe I needed to add more weights to my squat lifts.

Fighting nausea and vertigo, I carried the now-comatose

and paralyzed vampire off the property, down Eighth Street to St. Charles Avenue, where cars and people were unmoving, caught in no time. I trudged across the streetcar rails into the Garden District, and hooked a left onto Pryatania Street. My intent was to zigzag to the empty and former Clan Mearkanis Home. But my strength was draining away fast.

Stumbling, two blocks later, I turned again and made my way into the street to avoid a romantic couple frozen arm in arm, laughing, sightseeing along the white walls encircling Lafayette Cemetery Number One. The limestone and marble and whitewashed cement glowed in the night like a beacon. A sound that might have been humor rumbled within me. I was far enough away from the Elms to feel a bit safer and the irony was too much to ignore. I hobbled to the iron gate, which, strangely, was still open, and into the cemetery.

I passed what might have once been a guardhouse, but was now derelict, the roof never replaced after Katrina. The hurricane had left the city bankrupt and unrepaired, and the many cemeteries and their mausoleums and crypts and vaults open to vandalism. The concrete path was cracked and busted. Gang graffiti marked the resting places of the dead. But the family mausoleums still managed to impart that distinctly New Orleans flavor, standing cheek by jowl, with crosses and arched roofs and sun-faded silk flowers at the sealed entrances.

Near the middle of the burial grounds, I stepped off the path and into the narrow space between two humpbacked family crypts and dumped Edmund off my shoulder. And nearly fell on top of him as he left the no time of the Gray Between and almost landed. He was caught by normal time just above the ground, his white dress shirt stained scarlet, the stake buried in his lower chest. I dropped to the dirt-covered cement near him and placed a hand between his head and the cement riser. When I touched him, his body landed with a thump, his head in my hand. I laid it on the cracked and broken ground.

I let myself slide out of no time, into real time. The

smell of lime and urine and old, old, old death, combined with Edmund's blood-scent. I had bubbled time far too much in the last few days. I wondered what the repercussions to that were, and if I might reach the point someday very soon when I could no longer access no time. Well, I had lived without the ability once. I could do it again. Or it could kill me outright. There was that.

A bat flitted down between the crypts, did a little ungraceful, unballetic pirouette and flew back out. If I had felt a little more alive, I might have laughed again. Instead I let the Gray Between go, rolled to the side, and vomited. More blood fell from the spots in my neck, and this time when I put my fingers there, I felt small slits, the kind that fangs might leave if vamp blood didn't constrict the pierced blood vessels and close off bite wounds.

I pulled my cell, which was working again, and called Leo. His new secretary answered and I said, "Hey, Scrappy. Tell Leo to send help to the Lafayette Cemetery Number One. My new primo has been staked and I'm pretty sure I'm about to pass out." She tried to say something, but I interrupted, gave the mausoleum family name, and ended the call. Then I reached again for my powers and Beast shoved through me in a blinding rage. It was a tearing, stabbing, slicing, flesh-being-flayed-from-my-bones shift. I rolled away from the vampire, hearing my own rough scream in the night. And I was gone.

Claws tore through Jane clothes. Pushed out of Jane shoes. Pawpawpaw to darker shadow. Gathered paws beneath body, tight. Curled tail around body. Panting for breath. Heart racing away from big predator Beast could not see.

Beast was safe in space between human-dead-places. But felt wrong. Cold. *Hungered.*

Looked at vampire. *Edmund.* Was dead. Did not breathe. Heart did not beat.

Beast stretched out neck and sniffed vampire. Blood smelled fresh. Meat smelled good. But cold. Like meat from white box refrigerator. Sniffed again, lips pulled back to show killing teeth. Sucking in air over tongue and scent sacs in roof of mouth. *Scree* of sound. What Jane called fleh-men response. Smells rushed in. Mouth watered. Smelled *good*.

Was *hungry*.

But . . . was wrong to eat Edmund.

But Edmund was dead. Was good to eat dead. But not all dead. Jane would be mad if Beast ate Edmund. But Beast was cold. Felt *wrong*. Breath did not feel right. Heart did not feel right. Coldcoldcold. Heart rushing like rabbit into hole, with Beast chasing after.

Looked up at sky. Did not know what to do.

Bat flew into small space, chasing small biting things, too small to eat. *Mosquitoes*. Hate mosquitoes. Edmund smelled good to eat.

Pawed closer to Edmund body. Sniffed in small bursts of breath. Smelled *so good*. Could . . . just taste . . .

Thought about taste. About taste of vampire blood. Jane ate vampire blood. Made her well when she was sick. Made her strong when she was weak. Beast should be able to taste vampire blood too. But not eat meat. Thought about tasting and not eating. Was human way to think. Was hard to think human. Thoughts of right and wrong for humans. For Jane, though Jane was not human. Was confusing.

Pawed closer, until Beast side touched vampire side. Cold meat vampire. Cold Beast body. Stretched out neck and sniffed blood. Goodgoodgood blood. Cold, strong blood could fix cold Beast. Touched edge of lips to blood. And licked. *Blood so good*. Licked and licked. Licked all blood from wound. Tongue found tip of stake. Stopped. Thinking again. Wood in vampire blood stopped vampire from being . . . alive. Undead. But wood did not kill old vampires, only young vampires. Old vampires could live if wood came out.

Thought. Licked wound, pressing deep with tongue, until all blood was gone. Stake was still there. Rose on haunches and pressed jaw to Edmund belly. Gripped stake in killing teeth. Pulled stake. Dead flesh made sucking sound, as if trying to hold stake. Stake came free and Beast backed away, teeth in wood. Stake had Edmund blood on it. *Good blood.* Sat and held bloody stake in paws, licked. Was good. Beast shivered and was no longer cold. Licked all blood off stake.

Looked up at new smell of vampires. Shadows walked and stopped at opening between human-dead-place-buildings. Knew shadows of vampires. Snarled. *My stake!*

"*Allors,*" Leo said. "*Jusqu'à présent. Je ne le crois pas.*"

"Is that a stake?" Grégoire asked, pointing killing claw, what Jane called sword, at Beast.

Beast snarled again and let stake fall. But did not attack vampires. Felt good. Felt warm.

"Indeed it is," Leo said. "Was she eating him?"

Grégoire waved tip of sword at Beast and walked nearer.

Beast showed killing teeth. Growled. But vampire was not afraid. Laughed at Beast. Was bigger predator. Pressed Beast belly to ground. Beast backed slowly into darkness. Stayed down, smelling blood. Was blood on paws and pelt. When vampires did not follow, Beast stopped. Groomed paws with tongue. Was good blood. Beast felt warmer and warmer.

Watched as small, paler vampire knelt at side of Edmund, dead vampire. Deader vampire. Beast chuffed with amusement. *Deader vampire.*

"This shall be an interesting story, no doubt," said Grégoire.

Beast chuffed again. Felt good. Liked good vampire blood. Wanted more.

"We need to feed him, my friend."

"His master should feed him."

"His master is a puma." Grégoire made sound like laughter. "I fear she is more inclined to eat him than to save him."

Good vampire blood. Dead vampire meat.

Jane came awake inside Beast, beta to Beast's alpha. *Holy crap,* Jane thought. *Are you . . . drunk?*

Am warm. Can eat vampire meat?

No!

Snarled. *Jane is not good to Beast. Will not let Beast hunt cow in Edmund car. Will not let Beast eat Edmund.*

What? Never mind. Back away.

Beast snorted in disgust. Backed deep into darker shadows.

"*Merci,* Jane," Leo said.

Not Jane. Beast. Like vampire blood. Made Beast warm.

You were cold?

Was sick.

Jane went silent, thinking hard human thoughts. Beast did not listen. Jane was beta.

Leo dropped to knees beside Edmund. Held out wrist to Grégoire sword. Small pale vampire flicked point of steel over Leo skin in fast, killing strike with steel killing-claw. But cut only wrist. Sword pointed back at Beast. Good smell of vampire blood filled small space. Leo dribbled blood into Edmund mouth. Dribbled blood over stake wound. Smeared blood onto wound with fingers and stuck finger into wound.

Mosquitoes flew into space between small human-dead-places. Bats flew in. Leo made Grégoire cut wrist again and fed Edmund. Beast wanted to taste Leo blood, but Grégoire sword was pointed at Beast. Big steel killing claw. Was good hunter.

I don't have my gobag, Jane thought.

Beast sent Jane vision of Jane waking up in mud, smell of catfish all over her.

Not funny. And not happening in front of Leo and Grégoire. Let's get home.

Using darkness to hide movements, Beast slowly gathered self and shifted all weight to paws. Leaped from ground. Landed on top of rounded human-dead-place. Below, Grégoire and Leo were shouting but not in Jane language. Beast leaped to next roof and next and many more than five. Vampires followed, calling to Jane. *Am not Jane! Am Beast! Stupid foolish vampires. Did not feed Beast!* screamed into night.

Gathered big-cat power and leaped over three small

human-dead-places at one time, and then over wall. Landed
in limb of tree over street. Jumped to top of car Jane called
limo and then onto truck going past. Settled onto truck top,
claws spread and belly down for balance.

Jumped to more trucks, moving downstream near big
flowing river. Smelled water from river, strong and fast.
Jumped to street into darkest shadows and padded slowly
to Jane house. Wards were up, bright and silver and green,
and, in Jane eyes, red. Walked to front door and stood up
on hind legs. Extruded claw, rang bell. Heard Angie Baby
and Little Evan and smelled wolf. Alex opened door.

Beast leaped inside. Landed on wolf back. Sank claws
into white wolf. Bit down on wolf haunches. Wolf yelped,
growled, and rolled over, trapping Beast. Beast chuffed
with laughter and bit wolf. Play bite. Did not taste blood.
Wolf rolled again, making dog sounds of laughter and joy.
Wolf was heavy. Beast scratched and bit and rolled from
under wolf. Wolf coat was thick, good weapon against
big-cat killing teeth.

Played with wolf for long time, dodging Angie Baby and
EJ, who squealed and ran, feet making thumping noises on
wooden floor. Until Beast and wolf were panting and lying,
looking at each other. Wolf tongue hanging out of mouth,
dripping drool to floor. *Stupid wolf.* Thought for a moment.
Beast likes *stupid wolf.*

I like him too, Jane thought. *How weird is my life?*

Alex said, "If you two are finished roughhousing, I
need to get the kids to bed and tell you what I discovered.
Get out of the way, Kit-Kit. Jeez. It's a zoo in here." The
boy went upstairs, tugging witch kits with each hand. Beast
looked away from wolf and rested head on paws, heated
belly on wooden floor. Panting. Wolf still panting too. Kit-
Kit sat at wolf mouth near drool and curled up on wolf
paws. Closed eyes. Went to sleep.

Beast sighed heavy breath and closed eyes. *Vampire
blood is good blood.*

"Wake up, you two," Alex said. I need to update you."

Beast opened eyes. Wolf opened one eye. Like Leo
raised one eyebrow.

"Jane, are you alert enough to listen?"

I/we nodded Beast's head. Was stupid human movement.

"Okay," Alex said. "I'm not sure where I left Jane on the search for Reach. I tracked the cell he used to City Grounds Coffee Bar on West Dickens Avenue in Chicago. It was behind the counter where the staff put it because they assumed a customer would be back for it. No cameras on the doors, no vid of Reach. Coffee bar is near Oz Park, not too far from the lake, so lots of ways in and out. Dead end." Alex toed wolf. "Wake up, dog. I'm talking here."

Is not dog. Is wolf.

Wolf snorted and showed killing teeth to Alex.

Beast saw cell phone was glowing. Jane thought, *Alex is on speakerphone. Stand up and see who's on the other end.*

Beast stood and looked at cell. Was picture of man.

Captain America, Jane thought. *So Eli's on speaker. We're good.* Beast lay down again.

Alex said, "I've been studying about the Mings, trying to find what Ming of Mearkanis being alive might mean to the current political situation, the Witch Conclave, and the arrival of the European Vamps. I have a feeling that whoever is behind all this had no idea she would be found, and her discovery is throwing a monkey wrench into the plans."

"Roger that," Eli said.

"I've been looking at how the Mings got to this continent, and according to Reach's database, there's no record of the twin Ming sisters first arriving in the Americas. At some point they were owned by a Creole family of vamps by the name of Bondaille. Other than that, the records never existed or have been lost.

"There's no record of how Ming Zhane rose to Blood Master of Clan Glass. Ming Zoya became Blood Master of Clan Mearkanis, and that one is well documented."

Alex's words have no blood, Beast thought.

Boring, Jane agreed.

Wolf snuffled and rolled over to lie on back, belly in air, eyes on Kit-Kit, pawing at little cat. Beast wondered if wolf meat was good to eat. Jane thought, *Only if you want to turn me into a werewolf. I survived two bites and have no desire to risk it again. And his name is Brute.*

Like name Wolf better, Beast thought. *Wolf is Wolf like Beast is Beast.*

"The remains of the humans at the pit where Ming of Mearkanis was found have received official, legal, forensic autopsies and have been identified by comparing missing persons reports and dental records."

Beast's ear tabs twitched in interest and Jane moved into Beast eyes to stare out at Alex.

"Their names are Onus Rebarius Brown," he said, "age twenty-four when he went missing, and his girlfriend, Jesimine Ladasha Pirrie, age nineteen. No firm COD or TOD has been established, but the bone scarring and healing around wrists and ankles suggest they were shackled and alive for some time in the pit. *Scavenger depredation*," he emphasized, "took place postmortem, and may be interfering with the COD determination. Changing water tables are interfering with TOD."

Jane thought, *COD and TOD. Cause of death and time of death.*

"Local LEOs are not saying who or what they think killed the couple, but the chains suggest that they were kidnapped, possibly tortured, leaving mostly soft tissue damage, then drowned. And then the water table dropped, and animals got in somehow, and then the water table went back up. Maybe several times."

"But they think vampires?" Eli asked over the cell connection.

"They think weres of some sort."

Wolf snorted at words. Still upside down, he batted house cat with oversized paws. Kit-Kit batted back.

"Hmm," Eli said.

"Yeah. Anyway, I started researching the brooches and found the style was based on Egyptian history, in European and American revival jewelry and art from several decades in modern history. There's a maker's mark, and they were signed by an artist, so we know they were made by a local New Orleans jeweler, but there's no documented tie-in with the Mings, or with any of the witches or the vamps, and I don't think I'll find any."

"Copy," Eli said. "Jane, I'm not sure what happened with Edmund, with you doing that whole—" He stopped. "With you taking off that way."

Beast chuffed at Jane's amusement. Eli was about to say things on cell that might be overheard by ambush hunters.

"Lachish is at Tulane, surrounded by witches and cops and a doctor named Robere. Sound familiar?"

Beast yawned.

"She needs surgery on her leg and arm, and the good doctor has privileges there, so he'll be scrubbing in to assist, gratis. The MOC has offered his blood to help in healing, especially so that she can show up at the big wing-ding. I've already secured a wheelchair and ramps for the Elms, and the staff and family at the Elms are suddenly more agreeable to allowing cameras in-site. They want a price from YS for security upgrades. Evan is fine. Edmund donated enough blood that Molly and Ailis were able to finish his healing. He's a little tender, but he and Molly are on the way home."

"But the Witch Conclave is still on?" Alex asked.

"Roger that. But I think we should get a bloodhound and walk the grounds of the Elms. See if we can get a scent."

Beast's head went up. Snorted. Eli meant Beast to let Jane become ugly dog with good nose. Beast growled. Wolf turned over and tilted head, watching Beast. *Could use Wolf?* Beast asked Jane.

No. I think we need to shift and do it ourselves.

Beast snorted in disgust. Was good word, disgust. *Is stupid. Is prey move.*

Okay. It isn't smart. But we've done it before. Once. We survived.

Stupid, foolish, kit thing to do. But nodded head as humans would.

"She's in," Alex said. "I'll get her box of bones and put a steak on to sear."

"I'll be there in fifteen." The connection ended.

Beast and Jane followed Alex to Jane's room and stood in doorway, watching as Alex got chair and stood on it, feeling around on top shelf for box of bones and teeth. When he set it on floor he paused and looked at Beast. "I don't guess I could watch this ti—"

Beast snarled and growled, vibration loud in warning. Showed killing teeth.

"Right. Never mind. Forget I asked."

Beast growled again and Alex stink changed with fear. *Good fear smell.* Beast chuffed. Alex walked fast out of Jane room, closing door. Beast pushed on door with nose to make sure it was shut. Pushed small lock with nose. And went to bed, jumped on top. Jane's den was good den. Soft den. Good place for kittens. Jane did not reply, so Beast opened box with teeth. Picked out necklace of bloodhound teeth and bones. *Do not like ugly dog. But good nose.* Settled on bed and let Jane reach into bones and teeth and into snake at heart of all things.

Jane shifted, first into Jane, and then into ugly, hungry dog.

When Eli knocked on the bedroom door, I gave a friendly woof.

"You locked it," he said, the faint click telling me that the latch had been no concern for the Ranger. Eli stepped inside, and though I couldn't see well in this species' form, I smelled his exhaustion, tart and marginally sour. With the long ears and folds of loose skin, it was hard to see anything, and I shook myself, the flesh slapping, rippling, and sliding over deeper tissue. Eli held a leash and a Canine Service dog vest, and Beast crinkled up our nose at the smell of it, but I stepped off the mattress and sat, like a good dog.

Brute pushed into the room and stopped short. His head whipped back and forth, his nose scenting the air. He growled. A werewolf growl was much louder than Beast's, a vibration that swept into the walls and floor and made the house judder under me. I went utterly still.

Eli grabbed Brute by the ear and yanked back. The wolf snapped in the air and the Ranger made a move taught by

Uncle Sam's army. Brute yelped and ended up halfway back into the living room. Eli followed and shut the door with force, if quietly enough not to wake the kiddos. I heard him say, "You do not snap, were. That's a death sentence for your kind."

I walked to the leash and sniffed it. It smelled like me, and like another dog, a not me-dog. I remembered other dogs and a lone wolf werewolf we had hunted with. The dog part of my brain associated the memories and I lay down beside the harness, remembering the smells of that hunt.

Hunger pulled my mind away from the past. More hungry than usual, my having shifted twice without eating.

Want cow.

I know. I smell meat. I'm sure they fixed us a nice meal.

Ten minutes went by, according to my unreliable internal clock, before Eli walked back into the room. I snuffled at him for the scent of blood or werewolf saliva. I got nothing, which was good. If Brute bit Eli, it would have meant Eli and the Mercy Blade in bed together for a few days of magical healing, which would surely not sit well with Eli's überhetero tendencies. Even just a platonic, no-touch, no-tongue time in bed might send him over the edge. And Brute . . . As Eli had said. Brute would have been dead. There was no leniency for a were who bit a human. None at all. Automatic death sentence at the steel claws of the grindylows in the nation, and they had second sense when a human suffered a bite.

I whined softly as Eli knelt next to me.

He chuckled, the sound evil, and said, "He's fine. But he'll think twice about snapping around humans again." I whined again.

"He's okay. I'm okay. You're okay. Step in," he said, holding the harness out. I stepped into the harness and let him adjust the straps. "Let's go, Fido."

I butted him behind the knee and chuffed when his leg buckled. He laughed and led me to my steak dinner. The steak was cooked, but just enough to get the juices flowing, and it was so much more delicious and savory and smelled so much better than when I was Beast. I loved steak. I

licked the dish and raised my head, licking my drooping
jowls and the floor. I licked Eli's hand.

"Yeah," he said, cleaning his hand on his pants. "Right.
Let's go."

I leaped from the SUV to the ground at the Elms and
instantly stuck my nose in the air. And wanted to fall
down and roll on the ground from the intensity of it all.
The first time I shifted into a bloodhound, it had been like
being blindsided by an odoriferous Mack truck, and this
time was no different. Magic, blood, magic, anger, blood,
magic, Evan, Molly . . . I whined and Eli scratched behind
my ears. I leaned into him, sorry now that I'd tried to trip
him. He said something, but with my long ears flopping
down over my ear canals, my hearing was affected.

He scratched me again and I snuffled him. Eli smelled
good. *Like litter mate,* Beast thought. Eli jiggled the lead
and led me/us along the sidewalk and around behind the
house, where the scents were . . . intense. Amazing. I
took breaths in little chuffs.

A bloodhound's nose is more sensitive than any other
dog's in the canine kingdom, and, as with the first time I
took this form, it made my brain go into overdrive, identifying every scent and its breakdown components, cataloging
everything, noting associations and differences, calcu-
lating, parsing it all out into chemicals and pheromones
and—

"Fido? Let's go, girl."

"Fido is a male name," Nunez said. He smelled of spices
and coffee and sugar from donuts, and peanuts and chocolate from Snickers bars. He smelled *good.* I lifted my
head and snuffled his crotch. Nunez jumped back. Eli
pulled me away with a sharp flick of the lead. "Fido. Bad
girl." I chuffed and turned my head to him, remembering
that my nose wasn't supposed to take over. I was Jane. Jane
Yellowrock. Not a dog. Right. A skinwalker. But Nunez
still smelled good.

Eli led me through the backyard and to the first of the
exploded focal items. It smelled like magic and Evan and
vampire and blood and . . . And like Ming. I stopped, my

nose to the ground, snuffling and searching through the scent signatures. Ming. Ming's scent was here. Ming was a twin. Was I certain that it was Ming of Mearkanis? And why? I snuffled to the site and buried my nose in the ground. Sniffing, snuffling, analyzing. Remembering the stench of Ming in the small cage. Yes. Ming of Mearkanis. Her blood had been used in the creating of the iron icons. Iron and magic didn't mix, but if combined with vampire blood . . . Yeah. That changed everything. The dark magic was beginning to make sense.

I pulled to the next icon and snuffled it too. This one had no Evan smell, but scented of Lachish's sweat and urine and pain. The witch smell was strong here, a witch smell that had nothing to do with the witches I knew. It smelled of vampire, of Ming, and of the unknown witches. But I knew them now, the mother and daughter witches. The daughter was by far the most powerful of the two. The daughter was alpha of the pack. I followed the scent around the yard, to another place that smelled of gunfire and lead.

I remembered, in some odd part of my mind, that Eli had shot three of the places. Why did he shoot them? They couldn't die.

And then I remembered again. I was Jane. Eli was my partner. Eli shot the icons to disrupt the magics. Jane. I held to myself, pulling memories to me, memories of Brenda, one of my favorite house mothers. Memories of Eli and Alex, my family. Memories of Bruiser. Yes. I had myself now.

I found two more sites shot by Eli. They smelled the same, set by the same two stranger witches, women I would know instantly now, even in human form. I followed the scent of an enemy witch across the lawn to the side yard and found a place that smelled of witch and iron but no gunfire and no lead. I sat and looked up at Eli. And whined. He had a flashlight and shone it on the grass. "Got it," he muttered, and he pushed a small plastic army soldier, taped to a stick, into the grass.

I chuffed softly, spittle flying, and led the way to the next site, where I sat again. There were three unexploded magical focals altogether, one in each narrow side garden and one in front. That seemed important, but I couldn't remember why. I was Jane, but . . . I caught the scent again, on the sidewalk, and pulled Eli into a lope, tracking the scent down the street. Witches. Witches and vampire blood.

Nose to the sidewalk, I pulled hard, knowing, knowing, *knowing* the witches. One older, with bad bones, who ate too much fat, who smelled of sugar and sickness, and one younger who . . . smelled like Ming. Like Ming's blood and . . . *Crazy woman*, I thought. *Like a crazy woman*. And *Almost like an Onorio*.

I was Jane.

I snuffled to Eli. I had no way to tell him what I had discovered, and there was more I needed to learn, so I pulled harder. I needed to shift back while I still knew who I was, but . . . the smells pulled me forward. Along the sidewalk to an apartment building. I stopped and looked up at Eli.

"They came here?" he asked.

I woofed.

"We're on St. Charles and Second Street. The apartment building is eight stories."

I snuffled to the entrance and sat.

"The women went inside," he said.

I gave a human nod and it brought me back from an edge I hadn't known I was near. Back from bloodhound-nose-brain to human thoughts. I was Jane. I needed to shift. Fast. I had been a bloodhound before and, each time, my brain adjusted faster to the scent-brain. I realized that I could easily get stuck here, in a place with so many smells, in dog form.

"Just once or many times?"

I struggled to remember what we were talking about. I patted my right paw one time.

"Okay. So the witches came through here to throw us off. Let's go around the block. See if they came back out somewhere."

I *needed* to shift, but I also needed to follow the scents. They were rich and full and intense and amazing, and I put my nose to the ground and snuffled all around the building. The witches never came out.

"They got in a car here?" Eli asked. I snuffled and I

didn't look up. Eli said same words, but I pulled on lead, searching through smells. Eli talked as I snuffled down the sidewalk. Searching. Searching. *Learning.* Someone had dropped chili *here*. Someone had bled *here*. Two humans had mated at *this* tree. Someone had peed *here*. A squirrel had run *here*. I tried to follow the squirrel, but Eli forced me into the SUV. Nunez was driving. Wanted to smell Nunez's crotch, but Eli held me still. I chuffed and lay down. Memory of smells was wonderful, but Eli put burger in front of me. Burger smelling of pickles and ketchup and melted cheese. I wolfed it down. Was sooooo good.

CHAPTER 15

Dude Has Ugly Legs

Followed handler into house. Smelled . . . smelled *things*.
Smelled *people*. Smelled *witches*. Knew them, but not
how. Not where. Was important. And . . . sounds came in
fog of confusion. Was *important*.

Trotted to low thing with witches. Snuffled witch crotch
and . . . *knew* witch. Evan! Evan jumped with excitement!
Made sound like rabbit in brush! Barked with happiness!
Evan . . .

Angie. Little Evan. *Kits*. Smelled Eli. Alex. Molly and
Evan!

Tail wagged, body wagging too. *Happyhappyhappy!*
Snuffled Molly, asleep on couch. Had puppy in womb.
No. Had baby. *Godchild*. Angie. EJ. *Kits*.

With names, human words, came memories of . . .
Jane. I twisted my head to Eli and woofed softly.

"You're back?" he asked.

I dropped my head. Lifted it. And trotted to my room.
I pushed the door shut, but not before I heard him mutter,
"Thank God."

*   *   *

At nearly three thirty in the morning, I came out of my room, fully dressed and fully weaponed up, because the feel and smell of steel and silver and wood gave me a false sense of security. In the living room and kitchen I smelled coffee and witch and magic and . . . *Crap.*

I had never said it aloud, but I had a feeling that Beast kept part of the bloodhound's olfactory genetics each time I shifted back from it. That genetic stealing might be making it harder to shift from hound to human. No. Not saying that. Not thinking that. Instead, when I closed my door and Eli and Alex looked up at me, I put a hand on the holstered nine-mil and leaned my back to the door. I said, "The devil will wear mukluks and a fur bikini before I spend that much time in bloodhound form again."

"Roger that," Eli said, sounding laconic, but smelling vastly relieved. "You're okay?"

"Ducky. But it was too close. How long was I in dog form?"

"About six hours."

"Next time, we cut it to three. Maybe two."

"Good by me," he said, sounding better, smelling better.

"Molly and Evan are upstairs?"

"Sleeping. Evan said to keep your nose out of his privates." Eli laughed at me, but he had the decency to do it under his breath.

My face burned lightly with a flush of embarrassment. "Is he okay? Is Lachish okay?"

Eli said, "His legs are a little itchy and the skin feels tender. The hair hasn't grown back yet and Alex said he modeled his smooth calves for everyone."

"Dude has ugly legs," I muttered.

Eli said, "Lachish will be okay, barring side effects. Leo sent someone to feed her. The witches have set up a healing circle. Molly is fine."

We'd need to get the last names of the witches from Lachish. As soon as possible. "Have you heard anything about Edmund? I think I stabbed him."

Eli breathed another laugh and turned back to the kitchen. I heard oil sizzling and smelled the scent of pancakes cooking. Maple syrup. Chai with tiny piri-piri peppers in it. Eli had found the peppers at a market, this batch imported from Portugal, and he had been adding them to my spiced tea.

I followed him in. My mouth watered and my belly cramped—with hunger, not the sickness of the Gray Between time shifts. I used a lot of calories shifting, and shifting so many times had left me little more than skin and bones. I hadn't weighed, but my pants were hanging on my hipbones.

"Edmund will be fine," Eli said. "He's at HQ, being pampered, vamp-style."

Which meant with blood and wild and bloody sex. Ick. "Oh. Good." Worry slid off me like water down mountain stone, and I slipped into my chair as he placed three pancakes on my plate and poured on the syrup and melted butter. I sniffed first. I couldn't help myself. It was heaven. Digging in, I ate everything on the plate, and then three more platefuls. And bacon. A pound of bacon. And the entire pot of tea, with extra sugar and lots of heavy fat cream.

Out front, a motorcycle roared by. Moments later it returned at a much slower pace. I lifted my head, listening, as the sound of the engine again faded. I was either paranoid or I wanted my bike back. I hadn't known Bitsa was so ruined when it was damaged last. Dang it.

Need Bitsa, Beast thought. *Nose in air. Good smells.*

The bike didn't return and I went back to eating.

When I was finished, my belly was rounded against my pants and I felt marginally better. I checked Eli out, and saw that he was fully dressed, even down to the combat boots and weapons. Neither one of us had slept, but it looked as though he was ready for more fun and games.

"What did you learn?" Eli asked.

"Not much that relates to the witches, except that according to the scent patterns, they're mother and daughter. Lachish said she didn't know who the witches were, but she had to be lying. A mother-daughter team in the city, in her coven? She knew. And she didn't tell us."

"Lachish lied," Eli said, laconic. "Surprise, surprise. Probably thought she could handle it in-house and not have to turn it over the Enforcer of the vamps."

"It also opens up the possibility that Lachish is secretly working against the conclave." I gave a halfhearted shrug. "Not likely but we can't completely discount it."

Eli made gesture that said, *People are strange.*

"If you're up to driving," I said, "I'd like to go to vamp HQ and talk to Ming. The one in the cage, not the other one."

"I'll clean up the dishes," Alex said, "and then hit the sack."

I looked at him in surprise and then at his plate. He'd eaten like the still-teenaged boy he was and I hadn't even noticed. But he was acting like a grown-up. I said, "Cool. Thanks."

He shrugged. "The ward is up and you won't trigger it going out, so—" His tablet dinged and Alex snatched it up. "Oh yeah. Hang on. I got the witches' names." He keyed on three different tablets at once. "Oh yeah. Piece of cake. I got names and social media pages for a mother-daughter team who were at the witch circle where you were struck by lightning. I'd still like Lachish to verify, but until then, I sent the photos to your cells."

"Names?" I said.

"Tau and Marlene Nicaud."

I was tired beyond belief, but a fierce victory shot through me. We had IDs. And maybe a relationship that would lead us to motive. And then to stopping the witches.

"You done good, Kid," Eli said. And he scrubbed Alex's head in a noogie, what looked like true, if painful, affection.

Alex gave an abbreviated nod and looked away, but I could smell the pleasure in his scent. "I'll keep digging and send the info to your cells. Go on. Get stuff done." He made a little shooing motion with his fingers.

"SUV is at the curb," Eli said, leading the way to the door. Silently I followed.

The city that never said no to a party was still going strong, musicians on street corners, artists trying to attract the loitering tourists. More motorcycles sounded in the distance, like a whole club of them heading for Bourbon Street. I kept my eyes out the window and said, "Would you be so kind as to update me about my time as a dog?"

Eli said nothing for a long stretch of time, during which we passed a silver space rocket on the sidewalk, in front of a bar. Riding the rocket as if it were a bar bull was a half-naked woman, long purple wig hanging down her back, most of her boobs hanging out of the top part of a black corset, with garter straps on the bottom part of the corset, holding up golden-glittered fishnet stockings. She was also wearing a red sequined thong, and shaking her backside at the street while a bunch of drunk college boys applauded and a biker in a Saints helmet wolf-whistled. A local cop shook his head. Only in New Orleans.

Then Eli started talking, and as he did, the memories of the time as Beast and as a hound dog came back. I chuckled at the parts where I sniffed people's crotches, but really, it wasn't funny. It was scary. I had lost myself and Eli knew it. But I knew my partner. He wouldn't let me stay in dog form that long again.

And it was possible that all the shifting from species to species had helped with my healing. I ran my hands over my belly and down along my right side. No pain. No tenderness. No nausea. For a gal who had just nearly lost her mind into the olfactory sense of a bloodhound, I felt pretty dang good.

He finished the story with "And that is the story of Jane in bitch form."

I slanted a look at him without moving my head. "You've been waiting all night to get the chance to say that, haven't you?"

Eli's lips twitched. "Yes, I have. I also brought along pieces of one of the icons I shot, in case we need a vamp to sniff them."

"Smart. That saves you from a head smack for calling me names."

"Ohhh. I'm so relieved. I was shaking in my boots, babe."

* * *

We went through the usual security measures at the entrance, and Ro Moore, the self-proclaimed Alabama backwoods hillbilly, boxer, wrestler, and MMA cage fighter, did the pat-down, under the supervision of Brenda Rezk, the security person from Atlanta. It was professional and deft, and I said, "Thank you," when she was done, shaking my jacket back into place. As I readjusted my weapons, Derek Lee showed up. I hadn't seen Leo's other Enforcer and I knew that he and Eli needed to have a chat about what had happened at the Elms and in the cemetery with Edmund, but it would have to wait. "I'm here to see Ming of Mearkanis."

"Clan Mearkanis no longer exists," he said, his words clipped. "Ask for something else."

Derek and I'd had issues from time to time. Tonight, he was gonna be difficult and I didn't have the emotional fortitude to deal with it like a grown-up. Like Alex. Which was amusing. So I went for my go-to snark and looked Derek over, as insolently as I could. He was wearing a hand-stitched dress shirt, Italian lace-up dress shoes, and cuffed pants with a perfect half break. I know that kind of stuff now because I live in New Orleans and I hang with people who spend gazillions on clothes. His mouth went tight at the way I was looking him over, and I grinned at him, showing teeth as I stepped up to him, into his personal space, so my height would work for me. I tilted my head down, to his ear, and whispered, "I can handle this one of several ways. Eli and I can walk away and go to the scion room alone. I can go to Leo and tell him you're being a butt-head. Or I can kick your ass. Right here. Right now. In front of your people."

He stepped closer and whispered back, "You can try, little girl."

"Stop it," Eli said, shoving us apart. "What's wrong with you two?" He twisted his body so we were the width of his shoulders apart. I put another few feet between us, and Derek stepped back too. Formally, stiffly, as if passing along an order to a higher-ranked soldier, Eli said, "Lee. We need to see Ming Zoya, who was once Blood Master of Clan Mearkanis. Do you wish to lead the way?"

Derek frowned and blinked. "Yeah. . . . What just happened?"

"Were you at the Elms tonight?" I asked.

"Why?"

"Crap," I said, checking out my hands and his. They looked okay, but they might not be. "We got bigger problems than I thought." Not that I knew what do to about any of it. And then it hit me. "Hair," I said. "From the locker room shower drain. I always use the one on the end. They got my DNA here." That was where the witches who attacked me got the stuff that tied the spell to me. And they might have gotten other people's DNA the same way. Vamps. Blood-servants. Anyone. Everyone.

Eli's lips went tight as he processed that. "We got an inside man. In HQ. Someone with access to the women's locker, which means security and housekeeping."

"Which means," I said, "that they could have all our samples. Crap. We need to change the protocols and create a more stringent burn policy for everyone. Though it's clearly too late. Even the EVs could have our samples by now."

"We've been stupid," Derek said.

I pulled my cell and texted Molly the problem. To the others, I said, "Here's hoping Molly can come up with something to counteract DNA spells. And fast."

Derek shook his head as if thinking of the numbers of people in security and housekeeping who might have gone into the locker room. Or maybe thinking of the work that went into creating a new protocol. Silent, he led the way to the scion lair, which was reached by a circuitous route, up- and downstairs, through recently discovered hallways and, as best I had ever figured, the lair might actually be located between two floors, half in one and half in the other. I nodded to the security guy, who nodded back, one of the many new ones I hadn't gotten to know yet. He opened the door and we three went inside, into the smell of mixed vamp—almond, lily, and a tiny hint of rot.

Derek stayed with his back against the door and I sent him a quick, assessing look. He was staring down, frowning, thinking. He raised his hands and ran them over his buzzed scalp, his frown deepening. Eli and I went to the cages.

Ming-the-not-sane, not-Mearkanis, now technically just Ming Zoya, though she might not know that, was awake. She had been showered, cleaned up, fed a lot of blood, if her state of healing was any indication, and had been dressed in black silk, the kind of clothing her sister wore. She was curled up on a beanbag-type lounger, and, unlike her fellow caged vamp, Adrianna the nutso, Ming Zoya looked relatively coherent. Her black hair wasn't yet silken and long, and her scalp showed through in some places, but her face had regrown flesh and she looked mostly human, if a lot older yet than her twin.

Adrianna was dressed in skinny jeans and a halter top, with ballet slippers and a gold chain necklace, and was snuggled down with a furry-looking blanket that reminded me of a bearskin but was synthetic. Her blue eyes crinkled with humor and she laughed when she saw us. It was perfect laughter for a horror movie where the bad guy was a basement-dwelling, serial-killer clown.

Ming said calmly, "She laughs because of the scents you carry. One of you is both cat and dog and human. She finds that amusing."

Okay. That was interesting and unexpected. I asked, "You know what she's thinking or has she been talking?"

"She has spoken to me, but the English words are confused and make little sense, except for the punishments she will mete out to one she calls Jane Yellow Rock. It is an odd name, and I thought it was confusion too, until you arrived to visit with me. You are she?"

I belatedly realized that I had been rude by vamp standards and dipped deep for some formal phrases that would fix things. "Forgive me." That was always a good one to start out with. "I hadn't expected to see Ming Zoya of Mearkanis Clan so healed and well. I'm Jane Yellowrock, Enforcer, along with Derek Lee"—I indicated the man at the door—"for Leo Pellissier, Blood Master of New Orleans and the greater Southeast, with the exception of Florida. And this is my business partner in Yellowrock Securities, Eli Younger."

"Two humans in such positions of power?"

"We have our uses, ma'am," Eli said, snark subdued but strong on his scent.

"There was no offense intended."

Eli gave her a light nod. "No offense taken, ma'am." A bald-faced lie.

Ming gifted him with a slight smile. "With the exception of Florida," she quoted. "Leo has spread his borders."

I thought about the current events Ming had missed out on. I wanted answers, so maybe a little chatty quid pro quo would grease the wheels of an info exchange. "The Master of the City of Atlanta, Lucas de Allyon, created a vampire plague and infected several small holdings across the United States, then took them over without proper Blood Challenge. He was securing and expanding his power base against the protocols of the Vampira Carta. He came to New Orleans and challenged Leo. His Enforcer and I fought and the challenger died. Then I killed Lucas de Allyon in combat when he attacked outside the protocols of the Vampira Carta. Leo freed the masters de Allyon had infected, and his lab found a cure, which he offered freely."

Ming had watched me raptly as I spoke, her black eyes seeming calm and at rest, the way a kung fu master seems at rest just before he lops your head off with his bare hands. "Leo has never done anything for free," she said. "Much has transpired since I was taken."

"About that," I said before she could come up with questions about her clan. "Do you know who took you? Who held you? And what they were doing with you? What happened?"

Ming's lips turned up, but the expression never touched her eyes. "What do you know of my blood-servants, Benjamin and Riccard?"

So much for me steering the conversation.

Eli said, "My brother ran a search on them. They disappeared when you did."

Ming's face didn't change, but her scent did. Sorrow. Grief. And what might be stoicism. "And my heir?"

And here we go with the clan stuff I was trying to avoid.

"Your heir, Rafael Torrez, took over, aligned with a female vampire from Clan St. Martin." I pointed at my archenemy. "He started practicing black magic with the Damours, and was taking part in a blood-magic ceremony with witch children to sacrifice. He died at the hands of two of his men." I indicated Derek.

Ming inclined her head to show she had heard, her gaze on Adrianna. Her black eyes slowly, very, very slowly, vamped out. But her fangs were still up in her head, which meant she was in total control, far from what I had expected. Adrianna, however, vamped out fast and threw herself at the mesh that held her. Twisted steel mesh was a poor substitute for silver-plated steel, but it held her.

"I see," Ming said. "Rafael betrayed our clan and turned against the Master of the City. With *that* one?"

"Yes," I said.

"And you did not take *her* head?"

"I've killed her any number of times, including the time Rafe died, but Leo keeps bringing her back. Something about the European Vamps making a trip here soon. Or soon in vamp time. This century maybe."

Ming went silent, letting that settle inside while she watched Adrianna, who might have been listening. With my peripheral vision, I saw the other vamp throw herself onto the beanbag and stretch like a cat, her eyes on my partner, trying to attract Eli's attention, her fangs out and her boobs nearly so. Eli ignored her antics. Realizing that only Ming was actively watching her, Adrianna stuck out her tongue.

Ming said, "Rafael deserved his true-death. Leo and I will discuss the woman. If she bonded with my heir, who was then Blood Master of Clan Mearkanis, then she is mine to claim." Which was news to me, but was probably covered in the Carta or one of its codicils.

"Rafael's betrayal and death. How badly did they affect my clan?" Ming asked.

This was the sticky part, but I had a feeling that Ming Zoya had already guessed, just from my greeting to her, and was likely to prefer truth over anything else. Still, I spoke softly and with a grieving tone in my voice when I said, "A vampire war followed. Clan Mearkanis was disbanded following the conflict, as were three other clans who rebelled against Leo. Because it was believed that you were true-dead, your clan home was given to the witches in recompense for the Damour blood-family killing their children."

Ming drew in a breath, things taking place in the darkness of her eyes—calculations and games and machinations and politics. She said, "This is of interest. I thank you for the candid responses, no matter how distressing the reception. My sister is overly concerned about my state of mind, and underconcerned about my need for information. Your words will be useful during my discussions with the Master of the City."

Leo might be ticked off that I gave information to her, info that she might turn against him soon. Which made me smile. It was always a pleasure to frustrate the MOC.

Still watching Adrianna, Ming said, "The man who took me from my lair was known to me. His name was Antoine."

I drew in a breath, slowly, between my teeth. *Antoine.* Antoine Busho, or other spellings. The magic user who had read me the first time I came to New Orleans. He was *dead*. But . . . *Antoine* . . . Pieces began to fall into place in my brain. Rick had said that Marlene was Antoine's wife, way back when I met the magic user. And Antoine was part of Ming's being taken, kidnapped, tortured. Part of the spell that erupted in my palm, the spell that started all this crazy crap. And Marlene was his wife. And Tau . . . Tau was his daughter. The daughter of a magic user who had trained in a form that made him smell like something other than a witch. A shaman of some kind, maybe.

Ming said, "He had once been a chef of some repute, but his use of opiates had brought him low. He owned a diner where Benjamin and Riccard, my favorite blood-servants, often dined. Antoine was a magic user, of island and African descent, though his scent did not speak of witch. Because Benjamin and Riccard *trusted* him"—the scent of grief from rose from her—"*I trusted* him. He broke that trust, entered my lair, and pierced me with the point of a brooch. He had the assistance of Rafael and two Mithrans I did not see, whose scent I did not know."

The number of Mithrans, even in an over-vamp-populated city like NOLA, was fairly limited. But then, the helpful, betraying vamps might have been from Atlanta, paving the way for the attempted takeover. Or unaligned vamps from a backwater clan. Heck, it could be anyone, even Euro Vamps . . . Could they have started plotting and scheming so early on a visit? Easy answer: Yes. They lived for centuries. They connived with the long view in mind.

"The pin and the brooch were spelled," Ming continued, her voice strong but her grief unabated, "and when he threaded the pin through my flesh, I became compliant like a human who tastes Mithran blood and is addicted from the first moment. He cut my flesh and sprayed my blood throughout my lair, and overturned the furniture that it might appear I was taken by force, though I was agreeable to anything from the first moment I wore it. Even being put in a pit in a swamp, I was docile."

She looked up at me, her eyes still vamped out, empty of emotion, dark, cold, harsh. Scary as heck. "I do not know why I was taken or why I was kept alive, but I remember much, and more returns to me. Antoine drank from me and I was unable to cloud his mind while the pin of the spelled brooch was upon me. He asked me questions about the Pellissier clan and about Leo and about his son and I answered. I had no gift for beguilement while pierced by the brooch."

She transferred her gaze to Eli and it was as if a fifty-pound weight had been taken off my shoulders. She might not have been able to mesmerize humans while she was pinned, but she did now. And she was using that gift. "Eli. Derek. Don't look at her."

Both men flinched, hesitated, and turned away. No argument. How cool was that?

Ming said, "You spoil my entertainment, woman who smells of cat and dog. You are a shape-shifter?"

It was my turn to flinch and hesitate. But my secret wasn't

exactly a secret anymore. And if she knew what I was by my scent, then she might have met another skinwalker before. "Yes. You know of my kind." I made it a statement instead of a question, hoping she would elucidate.

Ming simply shrugged, which baited and hooked me. And she knew it. She was good at this. Without answering she went on. "The water had not risen in the pit at that time, and it was dry. Antoine gave me humans to drink upon, a different one each time. They were the homeless, the addicted, the outcast members of society. I drank and they were taken away. But—" Her dark eyes filled with tears, bloody and thin, and they ran in slow trails down her perfect skin. "Then he brought a stray animal. I did not wish to drink, but he commanded me. Every time he came he brought another one. I became sick. My blood dried up in my vessels. It was horrible, horrible, horrible." She didn't blink, didn't move, and yet the tears ran in steady streams to drip off her cheeks and onto the black silk she wore.

"He fed me *dogs*. He made me drink from *dogs* . . . I had forgotten. The brooch let me forget. The brooch kept me mesmerized and drugged and . . . But I now remember. *I remember*." Her tone said she was ready for vengeance, and she clenched her hands. She breathed, and it was a quaking breath, as if her lungs and throat wanted to collapse, and she breathed again, calming. "And then he vanished. Much . . . *much* . . . later, the girl came. She and another woman brought me two humans and chained them in the pit with me.

"I tried to be gentle with them, but it had been so long . . . I was so *hungry* . . . And the witch girl did not return for such a long time, long after I had drained the humans and killed them, after I ate their rotted flesh and sucked dry their bones." Ming blinked and took a breath, exhaled. I smelled blood on her breath this time, the scent of Katie, the most powerful vampire in New Orleans, and the only other one I knew of who had eaten dead flesh and survived. Katie hadn't been sane, even by vamp standards, in a long time, but she had kept her promise to feed Ming after she got here. Point to Katie.

"The girl drank from me then. But my mind was not

true. I do not know why she drank or what she gained from my words or my blood, except that something in her changed with each taste of me.

"She left the dead in the pit with me. And I ate." Ming closed her eyes. "Eventually she brought me more humans. One a month, on the full moon, when I was so starved that I had no control. These she threw in with me, into the water, where they thrashed and the stink of their fear was an aphrodisiac to me.

"I was mad. I drank as the Naturaleza drink, to the death. Of all of them. I killed."

I said nothing. What could I say?

Ming's unblinking eyes tracked to me. "I am free from Antoine. I drank from the girl, his daughter. Her magic was strong. Stronger than any I remember in all my life."

Of course it was. Because Tau was the daughter of two witches, so she had a fifty percent chance of being a double-gened witch like Angie Baby. *Crap. Crap, crap, crap.* This explained why the spells she threw were so complex and powerful. Like Angie, she could likely craft with her mind, with a single thought, without the work and mathematics that other witches needed to craft a successful working.

Ming asked, "The witches. They are dead?"

"Antoine is. Tau, not yet, but soon. She no longer has the brooches and can't trap another vampire. And I plan to . . ." *Kill her? No.* "To bring her to justice."

Ming thought about that for a while, her eyes transferring again to Adrianna, who was lying back on the bean-bag, her long legs up, feet propped on the mesh above her. Ming said, "You killed Antoine?"

"No. Leo's son, Immanuel, killed him. And then I killed Immanuel." Enough with the history lesson, I thought. "Would you recognize Tau and the other woman if I showed you photographs?"

Ming gave a single downward nod, and Eli held out his cell, with photos of the witches in question. On the screen were photos of Tau and Marlene Nicaud from social media. Ming turned away from Adrianna, and Ming's blackened gaze fell on the cell screen. "Yes," she said. Eli's eyes flicked to me and back and he paged through the last ones. "Tau. And this one. Mother and daughter," she said, her tone bitter. "They are the two who put humans in the pit with me. And to save myself, I killed the humans. Until then, I had never killed a human. Never."

"Would you recognize her magics if you saw them again?"

"Her magics, her scent, her person. Yes, and forever. Why do you ask?"

"Your words have been most helpful," Eli said.

"The trade was acceptable though dreadful, the memories harrowing," Ming said. "But it was fair. My past is mine again, no matter how horrible. Go away. Find the girl. Bring her to Leo. You are dismissed."

And for once I didn't mind the send-off. I wanted out of there too.

The door thumped and sealed. I pulled my cell. Without telling Eli what I was doing, I called Bruiser. When he answered I said, "I need to see the pit. Can you arrange a helicopter to take Eli and me?" When he said yes, I added, "I'll need to change into bloodhound form when we get there. I need to smell the pit." I ended the call.

Eli said, "I don't think this is a good idea."

"Me neither, but we need to know what the girl was up to. Her scent is . . . I don't know. Not right. Too strong, too angry, too something. I smelled it last night, but it's all mixed up in my human brain. I need to shift. I need to figure out what I figured out last night and then forgot when I shifted. And if she was drinking from a vampire, then she wanted the blood to give her power to do more than what we've seen so far." My fear was that she wanted to be able to control people—humans, witches, and especially vamps, all vamps—without sticking them with a pin.

I had changed clothes in the locker room and was wearing loose, baggy workout pants and a sweatshirt that would have fit Wrassler. I knew that for certain, because the shirt smelled like him. The big guy had lent me his own shift to shift in, which made me smile inside and out.

My bare feet were cold in the helo, and the lack of coms

was isolating but gave me time to think. I grew even more chilled when the copter set down. The rotors were still turning as Bruiser opened the side door and the chilly fall night air, filled with helo exhaust, swept inside. It was still dark, though the eastern horizon had grayed slightly when I stepped out onto the half-dried black mud of the landing site. The police were long gone, the scents telling me that they had left only recently, driving out of the Waddill Wildlife Refuge through the two-rut dirt road that bisected the property. The land smelled of swamp and frustrated humans and animals and birds. It also smelled of the Comite River, which flowed nearby.

Eli and Bruiser and I stepped into a metal johnboat and Bruiser shoved off, calling to the pilot, "Wait for us."

"Yes, sir," the pilot replied, lighting a cigar. Normally I loved the smell of cigar, but not with my nose so sensitive and the cigar so cheap. *Ick*.

Bruiser pulled the small engine's recoil starter, and the sputter filled the night, along with more exhaust, and I sneezed to clear my head of the foul stinks. As he steered us slowly through the wet hell of swamp at night, the air quickly cleared, leaving the swamp stink, of fish, gators, rotting vegetation, and stagnant water. When he finally turned off the small motor and beached us, the sky was lighting.

I had to get this done fast or risk staying in dog form all day. Not gonna happen. I wasn't going to endanger my memory and identity. Bruiser tied us off, and by prearrangement, he and Eli stepped off the boat, leaving me on it, silent, neither one arguing about my choice, which I appreciated.

I took up the fetish necklace and let myself drop into the meditative state that was easiest to shift from, trying to ignore the men's soft voices talking. I dropped down and down, and found the snake in the heart of the marrow. The genetic material from the bloodhound whose bones and teeth had been donated to the fetish necklace. Her accidental death had allowed me to use her RNA and DNA to assume her shape.

It didn't take nearly as long as it used to, to find the

coiled snake of bloodhound genetic code. Suddenly I was wrapped in the Gray Between, my bones sliding and snapping and painpainpain like being flayed alive.

I stepped from the boat, putting my front paws on land, my nose so full of wonderful smells that I nearly fell into the water when the johnboat slid away from shore while my back paws were still on the boat seat. Stupid. I leaped the rest of the way and Bruiser slipped a leash around my neck, presumably so that he would have a way to pull me back if I accidentally went swamp-swimming.

He led me over mud-crusted, muddy, and some semidry ground, my big paws tripping over ruts and a two-liter cola bottle full of human urine. Fortunately it was sealed with the screw-on cap. Unfortunately other humans hadn't been so kind and had relieved themselves behind trees, on bracken, and in the swamp water itself. The stink of human pee was everywhere.

I stopped and let the scents filter through my brain. There had been eight humans here, working up the crime scene. Seven were male, one was female. Each had his and her own particular scent pattern, and I was far better than I had been at differentiating them. I discovered that I could tell age range, race, health conditions, and that one of the men was sleeping with the woman. Dog noses were amazing.

Beneath the fresh scents were older ones, of Onorios and the humans who had helped to rescue Ming, all familiar from my Beast form. Some known intimately from my hound nose.

I opened my eyes and looked for Eli. I whined. As if able to read my mind even with me in dog shape, he reached into a thigh pocket of his cargo pants and removed a leather drawstring bag. He nursed the object inside to the lip of the bag without touching it, and dropped to his knees. I put my nose on the thing.

It smelled of iron, nitrocellulose, lead, lawn chemicals, magic and . . . the girl. I snuffled all over it, getting drool on it, but making sure I had the scent. I put my nose to the ground and began sniffing the patch of land in a grid pattern. My nose caught the scent instantly. She had been here. She been all over the site. But it had been a while.

I sniffed and learned and sniffed and . . . I understood. I froze, going as still as a vamp. Knowing. Knowing. I held the understanding inside me, my dog body still as a pointer, unmoving as the bits and pieces fell together. The scents filled my head, filled me. Filled everything and . . .

"Jane? It's nearly dawn. You need to shift."

I shook myself and whined. Looked up at man. At other man. Shook again, uncertain. Man held new scent pattern to my nose. I sniffed. Female, not Caucasian. Dog. *Big-cat.*

The part of me that was still Jane ripped aside the nose-suck and shoved the bloodhound away. I leaped to the side, ripping the leash out of Bruiser's hand, and raced to the boat. I jumped into the johnboat, sending it waffling on the water. Bracing my paws out, keeping my balance, I realized that I was trembling with cold. Even with my dog coat.

I reached into the Gray Between.

I pulled the oversized sweats on me just as it started to rain. I was colder than I should have been, shivering, but I could worry about that later. "Y'all! I got it. And it's bad!"

They scrambled into the boat and Bruiser started the engine with a single ripping jerk. Eli took one look at me and opened his gobag. He popped three hand warmers, tucked them under my arms and into my waistband, shook out a rain-shedding blanket, which he wrapped around me. "Thanks," I said over the boat roar.

The warmth hit me fast and I huddled into the blanket, holding in the heat from the chemical packs. He also opened two Snickers bars and four energy bars, and I ate, not talking, thinking. I had to address the being-too-cold thing, but there were more important things to discuss, the moment we were airborne. This time, Bruiser gave me some excellent ear protectors attached to a headset and I realized that he and Eli had been chatting privately on the trip to the wildlife refuge, chatting and leaving me out. I could worry about that later, adding to the rather long list of things to deal with when my life became normal. Whatever normal was.

I swallowed the last of the Snickers without tasting the chocolate and nuts, and felt more stable as I started in on the energy bars. "I got the scent of the girl witch," I said over the muted helo roar. "It was a mutating scent, fluctuating, morphing into something else."

"You saying she was a skinwalker, babe?"

I wish. "No." I looked at Bruiser. "She's a lot more like an Onorio."

Bruiser's eyes met mine for a shocked heartbeat and jerked away, thoughts racing behind his eyes, the vision reminiscent of Ming's eyes in her cage, too fast to follow. Even his scent was too fast to follow, and my nose was now spectacular by human norm.

"Bruiser?"

"Humans have attempted to become Onorio without a Mithran's approval, holding the Mithran captive. It has never been successful. Mithrans eventually compel the human to free them and then the humans die. A witch, damping a Mithran's ability to compel, attempting the same thing . . . If she had the formula . . . It might work. And she would be dangerous. Beyond dangerous."

I said, "Add it to her being a homogeneous witch, one with two witch genes, one from her father and one from her mother, then things get kinda freaky. And this witch chick is freaky. Bad, sick, nutso, got her panties in a wad, wants to blow up the world, mad über-supervillain freaky."

"Worse," I said. "Or maybe not worse but adding to the problem in ways I can't describe, there are other scents. Ming. Iron and salt. Other humans. Two in particular, male, who might be distantly related to her. Cousins. Maybe. Something like that."

I stuck my nose up and pulled in scents in with a *scree* of sound. "Problem. Put us down over there." I pointed. Bruiser relayed my orders to the pilot and the helo banked hard enough to throw me into the seat belt. He turned on the landing lights to reveal a small islet with tire tracks across it. Trusting the tracks, he set the bird down gingerly.

I stayed in the helo, wrapped in the blanket and heated by the hand warmers, but the guys got out. It was light enough out to see that there were a lot of gator slides on the muddy banks. Gators push with legs and clawed feet through muck to the edge of a water source and then push off, letting gravity slide them into the water. The trails were long and slithery. And wide. Big gators. I sniffed. "Humans. There." I pointed. "And dogs." I wrapped myself more in the blanket and Bruiser and Eli stepped to the muddy edge.

"Skull," Eli said, jutting with his chin because his hands were suddenly holding weapons. "There."

"Another," Bruiser said, pointing.

"I count three human skulls," Eli said, "that one shattered, probably by gator teeth and jaws." He took a number of photos of the crime scene. "Portions of several dog skulls. That one is fresh." He pointed, and took a last photograph.

"Feeding her dogs wasn't good enough. Tau wanted magic, and for that Ming needed human blood, I'm guessing at least once a month."

"Why did she leave the first two humans and none of the other bodies?" Eli asked.

I gave him a small shrug, tilting my head to the side, the gesture mostly hidden by the enfolding blanket. "Smell? The first two were bones already and underwater."

"And the new bodies floated while decomposing," Bruiser said, "and the smell of decomposition was horrible to her. Good supposition."

"Four on the surface," Eli said. "Concur. Likely more bones in the muck at the bottom. Let's go."

CHAPTER 16

Đang-Er-Sus?

Back inside the helo, Bruiser said to the pilot, "Pass along these coordinates to the sheriff's department and the detective handling the investigation of the pit."

"Yes, sir."

He switched off the pilot's access to our coms. "Jane? Love. . . . Clarify for me, please. Were the women here? Was Antoine?"

"Yes. All three. And two human males who were helping Tau bring humans here, but their scents had degraded from rain and the churning of the mud. I think . . . I *think* that I'd recognize them if I came into contact with them. If I was in bloodhound form. But I can't say for certain about in human form. There was something awful about their scents. Like drugs, maybe."

And the stink of Ming, starving and insane and raving. How many had she killed while trapped in the pit? How many were her fault? Any of them? I didn't know.

"So we can add murder to the long list of crimes committed by Tau and Marlene. The Witch Council of New

Orleans could turn over the crimes to the law enforcement authorities," Eli said.

"Or take them out themselves," Bruiser said.

"Or call in a hunter," Eli said.

I knew he meant me. Turning away, I stared out the window at the rapidly approaching New Orleans landscape. "What about the Onorio scent?" I asked.

"I'll have to ask the priestesses," Bruiser said. "I don't know. I've never heard of this before."

"The scent wasn't *just* Onorio," I said. "It leaned toward vampire. Maybe a new kind of vamp." Vamps had an uncanny desire to play with nature and create new things, things that were not bound by the usual strictures of vampdom: daylight, silver, blood, the devoveo. What if the double-gened witch had tapped into that desire in Ming and used it? The witch might have turned herself into anything. Something new. Something so powerful that . . . that I couldn't fight it. Couldn't fight *her.*

Eli pulled his cell and read aloud. "Alex found a last will and testament for Mildred and Eugene Nicaud, in 1957, who left four peacock pins to Simon Nicaud and his wife, Alva. Antoine Nicaud was their sole heir and he inherited the four brooches from his parents."

Four brooches. And Rick had said Antoine was originally from the Pedro Cays, islands south of Jamaica. Rick didn't know anything about Antoine's magic or training except he had maybe apprenticed to an African priestess.

Bethany was an African priestess. Bethany had bitten me, to heal me, once. She had access to every part of vamp central. She could have gone into the women's locker room and scraped my DNA out of the drain. But Bethany was nutso and I couldn't quite see her being so linear and driven.

Bruiser asked, "Are the names confirmed? Are there photographs of the brooches? Any proof whether they were sold?"

"Four brooches," I said. I had thought we were in the clear as to the brooches and the witches' ability to control vamps. I closed my eyes, imagining all the crazy spells they could throw with the two brooches.

Bruiser nodded. "Do we have any insurance listings to confirm where the missing brooches are now?"

"Alex is searching," Eli said.

"If she still has them," I said, "and if she is what I think she is, then we're in big trouble. Tell Alex to check marriage license for Marlene and birth records for Tau. A will for Antoine. Text Molly and have her get to Lachish, right now, about Marlene and Tau Nicaud. She can't play games anymore. If we're right, and Tau is the daughter of Marlene and Antoine's wife, then she might carry two witch genes." *Like Angie Baby,* I thought again. "Meaning that she is beyond scary, crazy powerful. She could be a magical nuclear bomb waiting to go off. And, after drinking blood from a vamp who had been eating rotting human flesh, probably just crazy."

Eli bundled me into the limo and turned on the heat. Both men turned their backs so I could dress in my own clothes, but I pulled the warm sweatshirt back over my street clothes for the extra warmth and comforting scent. As I dressed, Alex texted more info on the brooches. Eli read and told us, "No records on sale or insurance, but that doesn't mean anything. It's possible that all four were spelled or that only two were spelled. Alex checked probate and found that Marlene Nicaud was left two brooches and the girl was left two. The women received the brooches about six months ago." He looked up at me. "That gave them six months to learn how to use the brooches. Six months to bleed Ming of Mearkanis, who we found because the brooch we had tracked to the brooch on Ming. Which means that we could use the two brooches we have to track the other two."

Bruiser chuckled and the two men exchanged a complicated fist bump of victory. I said, "Unless that's what they want you to do." The men dropped fists, considering. "In which case you would be walking into a trap and go boom."

"True," Bruiser said. "And it also means that this started long before you got to NOLA, Jane. So Antoine's original plan would have been in place before you killed Immanuel. Which means that plan, whatever it was in the beginning, was taken over and subsumed by Tau and Marlene. But it might still be in effect, like a second trap we could walk into unaware, at any time. We need to find Tau and Marlene. Get Alex to do property searches and credit—"

"Being done as we fly," Eli said.

I added, "They have DNA from . . . maybe all of us." My cell buzzed with a text and I said, "Molly." It was a reply to the thread where I asked her about breaking DNA spells. She had texted, and I read aloud, "Piece of cake. Antigenetic spells were some of the first defensive workings ever made. I can put together a couple dozen in a couple hours."

Bruiser nodded, turning his unfocused gaze out to the sun, rising over the flat wet world in a wash of gold and pinks.

It was after dawn when we reached home and I was exhausted. I needed to stuff myself on food, needed to sleep, but the house was full and noisy when we entered, and I had a feeling sleep wasn't going to be mine today, not here. Before the door even closed I spun on a heel, leaving Eli inside, and jogged back to the limo. "Bunk at your place?"

Bruiser opened the door, his eyes warm. "My bed is far more comfortable than a bunk."

I fell inside and the door closed. "True," I said. "But right now I'd take the floor if the place was quiet."

Bruiser's lips turned up in a smile I didn't see often. "I don't think we've ever done it on the floor— Well, nearly." He tapped the limo floor with his toe. "*Nearly.* On this floor." A low-key thrill ran through me, but before I could reply he pressed the limo intercom and said, "I have an order to be picked up at Stanley Restaurant on St. Ann Street."

"Yes, sir," the driver said. "Shall I go in and pick it up, sir?"

"Yes, please."

"The Stanley?" I perked up.

That odd, heated look was still on Bruiser's face, his eyes a warm brown like melting milk chocolate. "Yes."

I breathed out, *"Breaux Bridge Benedict?"*

He nodded.

"Ohhh. Oh my. Creole breakfast potatoes?"

He nodded again and said, "Pecan-smoked bacon and eggs Stanley. A carafe of coffee for me and a carafe of tea for you. And pancakes with vanilla ice cream and all three side options."

I closed my eyes, my mouth watering. And then, eyes still closed, my lips turned up. "You knew I was coming to your place, didn't you?"

"I had very, *very* high hopes."

The sound I made was helpless and laughing all at one. "We really should do it on the floor. At least once. Or twice."

Bruiser's arms slid around me and he pulled me to him across the seat.

We reached the restaurant before anything could progress to the floor, and then Bruiser's apartment before anything could progress to the floor, and then, because I was beyond starving, we ate before anything could progress to the floor of the apartment. And then . . . I fell asleep.

Later, I felt Bruiser crawl in beside me and pull me close, spooning. The stubble of his beard was rough on my shoulder, and his chest was Onorio-hot against my back. His body smelled of Onorio, his new, spicy scent that I was still getting used to, and the faint, familiar citrus of his cologne. His breath smelled of pancakes and bacon. *Bacon* . . . Sleep took me again.

When I woke next, it wasn't to be dragged to the floor, but to far more delightful pursuits on the mattress. Bruiser was right. His bed was much more comfortable than a bunk. Afterward, I panted against his shoulder, "We're still . . . doing it . . . on the limo . . . floor someday."

Gasping, he said, "God yes . . . Someday. Soon . . . When I can feel my feet again."

An hour after nightfall, I walked out of my bedroom dressed in worn jeans tucked into old green Lucchese boots, and a men's tailored white dress shirt with the sleeves rolled up. I was wearing multiple leather arm-bands, each pressed with various logos: the company logo, Have Stakes—Will Travel, Yellowrock Securities, and my name. The one with my name was inset with tiny pieces of turquoise. I also wore my sterling-over-titanium gor-get and my gold nugget necklace on its doubled gold chains.

Most important, every piece of my weaponry was visi-ble, strapped outside my shirt and atop my jeans and in my boots, from the two matching-scarlet-gripped Walther PK .380s beneath each shoulder and the H&K nine-mils on each thigh rig, to the multiple vamp-killers in sheaths at my belt and on my thighs, to the stakes in multiple tiny sheaths and in my bun. The Benelli M4 Super 90 shotgun rode in its spine rig, collapsible stock extended and stick-ing up behind the nape of my neck as protection from rear vamp attack. All of them in the brand spanking new Kydex holsters and the new weapons rigs.

Everyone in the living room stopped dead when I walked in, heels clomping. I let them look. And I grinned slowly, showing teeth. Kit-Kit spat at me, her hair standing out in fear. She spun and raced into the butler's pantry, to safety.

The .380s were loaded with standard ammo. The nine-mils were loaded with silver. The Benelli was loaded with six rounds, each round hand-packed silver fléchettes, loaded for vamp. Half of the stakes were solid sterling silver. Half were wood. If a vamp was working with the witches, I was ready to take him down.

Angie Baby said, her voice a breath of sound, "Aunt Jaaane." She was sitting in the small wingback chair she had chosen before, her Cherokee doll in her lap, her red-gold curls falling around her. "You look dangerous."

Little Evan echoed, "Dang-er-sus." Then he threw his arms into the air and shouted, "Gun! I wanna play guns!"

I glared at the toddler and said, "No. Do you understand me? No guns. Not now. Not ever."

His lips quivered, blue eyes filling with tears. "You got guns."

"Yes. And what am I?"

"Dang-er-sus?"

"Yes." I leaned in, letting him see the threat that I was. He leaned back into his father's chest and Big Evan put his arms around his son. "I am not a nice person," I said. "I am dangerous. I kill bad people. You are *not* like me. You don't *need* guns. You have magic. And that is way better than guns."

Both kids stared at me for a few uncomfortable heartbeats and then turned to their parents.

"Listen to your aunt Jane," Big Evan said, his face showing no emotion.

I nodded and looked to my partners. For once Eli had not read my mind. He was wearing a suit. And his mouth was hanging open. "I thought," he said, "that we were attending the dress rehearsal for the security arrangements at the Elms tonight."

"We are. So, shouldn't you be in your fighting leathers?" I asked.

"I thought—" He stopped.

"You thought I'd refuse to wear my new leathers. You thought I'd go all fashion ball gown on them. Or wear one of Madame Melisende's jackets and only a few weapons. You got it partly right, the part about me not ruining my new leathers, but you overthought it. We got multiple enemies. I'm dressing for enemies. Go get casual."

I looked at the Kid in his new suit, the one he was expected to wear when he ran the security system that he had set up today while I slept and would give a test run on tonight. He'd ruin the suit if he had to climb around. I shook my head. "You too. Jeans and a shirt." When neither of them moved, I clapped my hands once and said, "Make it snappy, boys."

They both headed for the stairs at speed. Alex whispered, "I told you so."

"Shut up," Eli whispered back.

A heartbeat later I heard Edmund's car shut off in the side yard, and he stepped inside. I had never seen Edmund in blue jeans and a white tailored shirt. With the sleeves rolled up. On some level it really bothered me that Edmund had read my mind better than Eli had, but I didn't let it show on my face.

He glanced at me, took in my wardrobe choices, and said, "Copycat." The accusation made me feel marginally better, which might have been his intention. He gave me a shallow bow and produced a small box. The kind jewelry once came in from high-end stores. Much more formally, he asked, "My mistress. May I present your goddaughter a gift?"

"What kind of gift?" I could help the suspicion in my tone. He was a vamp, after all, and Angie had marked her face with his blood when she swore to him.

"When I was human, I had a daughter. She passed of the bloody flux while I was in devoveo, and her belongings were kept by a Mithran friend. Little has survived the ages, but this one thing. I would offer it to Angelina in recognition and acknowledgment for her promise to me and proof that I will not allow the blood-oath she made to me to become effective until she is twenty-one. And as testimony and witness of my fealty to her, as proof that I will protect her for as long as she lives." He held my eyes, his own full of entreaty. Edmund's body smelled of purpose and resolve, like a sweet scent of distant jasmine, carried on a night wind, twined with the scent of copper. If integrity had a scent, this was it. Strangely the mixed scent of human blood from his early feedings didn't detract from that.

I gestured to the box; the rotting velvet fell to ash as he lifted the top away. The scent of age, old walnut wood, ancient illness, and dried tears wafted out as the light fell inside. Two tarnished metal rings had been affixed to the wooden sides so long ago that verdigris marred the wood.

New satin ribbons had been tied to each. The ribbons then passed through specially made loops in a velvet cushion, which was new also. The ribbons held the cushion in place and also secured a tiny gold ring, centered with a faceted peridot. The setting was made of tiny hands, holding the jewel. It was delicate and pretty.

It was petty of me, but I leaned in and sniffed. Then I put my hand on the ring. There was no tingle of magic that might have been meant to ensnare a young witch. This wasn't a trick. I tilted my head and said, "Dang. You're just being nice."

He gave me a small, human smile. "It isn't impossible for us." But he sounded wry and cautious. And perhaps a bit sad. I considered the ring. His daughter's ring. How difficult and momentous it must be to give away something so precious. "If her parents don't mind, I'm good with it."

Angie piped up, "Does this mean I have a boyfriend?"

"No." The word was flat, icy, and powerful.

Edmund pivoted on one foot to face Molly, whom I had paid no attention to until now. She was sitting on the far end of the couch, her hands holding her belly, her face a mask of some emotion I couldn't even name, something cold and hard and maybe even deadly. I felt the faint thrill of magics race along my skin, raising the hairs on my arms beneath my leather armbands. *Death magics.*

"I never had a boyfriend," Angie said.

"Mol," Big Evan said, his tone gentle and warning all at once.

Edmund swiveled his head to me, turning too far. He clearly didn't feel the trace of magic, didn't know how great his danger, but he had heard the threat in her single word. I shook my head without looking at him but stepped to his side, putting a hand on his shoulder, ready to pull him behind me if needed.

"Molly," Big Evan said again.

Angie Baby slid from the chair and walked calmly to her mother. She put both hands over her mother's and squeezed. Molly closed her eyes and forced herself to take a breath. It wasn't magic. It wasn't anything paranormal. It was mother and daughter and that connection I would never have and didn't remember from my own youth. Wet heat prickled under my eyelids as Molly slid her hands free and wrapped herself around Angie, holding her close.

Edmund dropped away from my hand and landed on his knees, offering the box to Molly. "There is nothing here but my honor," he said. "My honor is all I have left of who I was, and I would not sell it at any cost. But I would give it. I would promise it to you and to yours."

"Why?" Molly asked. "That makes no sense for a fanghe—a Mithran."

"The priestess Sabina has divined much about the state of the world and about our species. She has said that my life is wrapped inextricably with you and yours," he said to Molly. "And with my mistress."

That was news to me. "Did she get around to saying why?" I asked.

"All she said were nonsense syllables, perhaps in her mother tongue."

"And they were?"

"Bubo-bubo," he said. "Senseless."

But it wasn't senseless, nor was it in her mother tongue. It was the scientific name for the Eurasian eagle owl. I had flown in its shape once, for a chance to sit in a tree and listen in on a vamp *gather*.

Later Sabina had seen me in the tree and she spoke to that owl. It had been eerie enough to make me want to lift wings and fly far away. She said something like "I know not if you are real, or prophecy, or the mad imaginings of an old, old sinner." My flight feathers shivered and my taloned feet danced on the limb. "If you are prophecy, if you are the breath of God on my stained and darkened soul, then know this, and take my words back with you to paradise. We still seek forgiveness. We still search for absolution."

Much later even after that, she had said of the raptor, "It came to me, at a time of gathering and blood, when we put Katherine to earth to heal. It cried out its lonely call to me, a bird of the night, a bird of a different place and time. The owl has long been a harbinger of change, of danger, of loss. You are that beast of change and loss. That harbinger of bitter defeat. Of true-death."

Go, me. I was part of a prophecy. My life was weirder and weirder. Molly was watching me as if reading my mind and I flashed her a grin and shrugged, hoping to throw her off my train of thoughts. But Edmund's words were enough to make me believe him. I said to Molly. "He'd make a pretty watchdog."

Edmund inhaled a breath that he hadn't bothered with until now and said, "I am a far better protector than a *dog*. Or even a werewolf. And I have pledged you my honor."

"Y'all are all angst and indecision and drama queens, worse than a bunch of old men on a street corner." Pointing at Molly, I said, "You deal with this. Get yourself together and chill. And make nice-nice with the fanghead. I'll be back later and I expect you to be one happy family." I pointed at Angie. "You. No vamp boyfriends until you are at least twenty-one years old. He's your protector, not your honey bunch." Angie frowned mutinously and I frowned right back. "Don't make me go all big-cat on you." I pointed at Evan. "You are one cool dude. Keep things together and don't let them kill each other or blow up my house once I leave."

Evan might have smiled beneath his fried beard. The fire had burned off a lot, but he was still hairy enough that it was difficult to tell.

My business partners clattered back into the room, dressed in jeans. Or Alex clattered and Eli glided. He had been hanging around the corner with a weapon drawn. I said, "We have a lot to debrief before we all leave, so let's stop this here.

"Any new thoughts on why Antoine kept Ming prisoner?" I asked my little group. "I mean originally, before his daughter took over."

Edmund rose to his feet and said, "Antoine kidnapped Ming near the time that Immanuel, the Damours, Adrianna, and others were to make a play for Leo's Blood Master status. I believe that is one reason why Adrianna and Rafael became Anamchara and allied with the Damours is that they intended to challenge him to a blood duel. Had they won that challenge, there would have been all-out war between the Mithrans and witches all across the colonies. Such a war would have played into the hands of the Europeans. Perhaps that very thing was part of *their* plan, and the shaman Antoine was being coerced or maneuvered by them."

I said, "Yeah, yeah, we've been over and over this. He had Ming. He knew where the Damours were. He went to kill Immanuel and died instead."

Edmund said, "You killed Immanuel, but you didn't save Antoine. Or the other female witch. They may believe that you were responsible for Antoine's death. And also that their fellow witches are fools for aligning with the Mithrans. They may wish to halt any such parley and drag us back into war. There is seldom only one reason for treachery, but many, interlaced and tangled."

Eli said, "I get the vengeance angle. So they kept Ming alive but stoned, feeding her humans when they could, biding their time for revenge against Jane and the witches who 'let it happen'"—his hands made little quotations around the phrase—"and the vamps who started it all."

I said, "Our problem is the timeline. The women have had Ming for months. Why did they wait to hit me?"

"Changing someone into something vampish, but not a vamp, someone capable of beginning and possibly winning a war with vamps, might take time," Eli said.

"No," I said. "It happened to Bruiser in days."

"But," Edmund said, "they didn't have a priestess to make it happen in the proper time."

"And they might have had to wait on probate on Antoine's estate to get the second brooch," Alex said. "And the third and fourth brooches, which we haven't added into the equation."

I nodded. "Okay. We're all on the same page, meaning we still don't know enough. Next subject. Bruiser hasn't sent a text or called about the girl smelling like Onorio."

"And there's nothing," Alex said, "in the files or histories about female Onorios at all."

"Fine. Molly, do you have the anti-DNA charms?" She nodded. "Good. I'll have Leo's CPA send you a check." When her lips parted, I said, "What? You thought those were favors for me? Heck no. You made big bucks, baby." Molly ducked her head and blushed, delight glimmering in her eyes.

"We're late," I said to the Youngers, "and so are you," I said to Edmund and Molly. "Lachish isn't going to get well by tomorrow night on modern medicine alone. You need to get to Tulane to donate blood to Lachish and add your magics to her healing. We need to get the security set up at the Elms. We have a conclave to put together." And with the new charms, we might just pull it off. "Let's all get crackin'."

In the SUV, the powerful engine rumbling under the hood, I said, "Update."

Eli pulled away from the curb, the lights of New Orleans casting neon glares on the windows, a group of tourists walking down the street, laughing and smelling of alcohol. A motorbike roared past, a vibrant blue crotch rocket, the exhaust foul, as if it ran too rich. He said, "You are one scary chick. I like it."

"Get a room," Alex said, fingers beating hard on the tablet's keyboard.

"*Ewww.* He's like my brother."

"Fine. Buy pompoms and do some calisthenics for each other, bur shut up and listen. About an hour ago, I found clear and current pics of the women, and the young one is hot. Hot and crazy. And you know what they say about crazy women."

"No," I purred. "Do tell. . . ."

He looked up at my tone and quickly back down, hiding a smile. "They make the best bosses."

"Good save. Insulting, but a good save."

"Sending pics to your phones," he grouched.

"How goes the background checks on the Elms' servers, cooks, delivery people, and all the others?"

Alex began telling me everything, about the staff.

*Eeee*verything. The rest of the drive was tedious and boring, but, in its own way, just as important as weapons practice and workouts.

Eli and the Kid were pure wizards with electronics. They had a system set up, refined, tested, rerefined, and powered down in minutes, all the while charming the ladies and a few of the men who made it a point to come around and watch or to ask questions. Amalie, however, was less than pleased with the results of our last visit, and seemed inclined to blame Yellowrock Securities for the damage to the gardens from the icon explosions.

Overhearing her comments, Alex suggested that she contact our lawyer, or better yet, Leo's lawyer, but that YS couldn't be held responsible for the actions of a third party, outside the time limits of our contract. That we were being paid to provide security for the event, not the days leading up to it. And that perhaps she could consider how many lawsuits, and defensive spells gone haywire, might have resulted from the same situation had we not discovered the trap several days early. She went away dissatisfied with the financial burden placed on her to get the gardens repaired in such short order, but placated with the thought that greater disaster had been averted.

While I was glad that the Kid was growing up, I was less happy with the thought that we were missing something. And that the explosions we had triggered with no loss of life had been secondary to a far greater plan of attack yet to come. Or worse, had been intended to lure us into a false state of undeserved triumph. It was all coming together and it was too easy. Nothing in my time in New Orleans had been easy. Which meant it was all going to break loose and soon.

There were things contained in the subbasements at vamp central that were far more dangerous than the witches, the vamps, or me. Was I looking in the wrong direction for the problems? Blinded by the expected? I didn't think so. It felt as if I was on the right track. The early attack on the Elms was either an accident or a plan triggered too soon, or it had been intended to get the Truebloods and me out of the way just before the Witch Conclave, when it was too late to change security plans. That would have left Leo without a trained Enforcer and made it easier to kill him.

I hoped that, for once, there wasn't a deeper motive or multiple aims or a multilevel plan, and that the witches had one purpose only. Hoped that our witches were too young to have layered goals and century-long discriminations. That their hatreds would be short-term hatreds.

Hating the Truebloods and the other witches for being willing to parley with the vamps.

Hating me. For living when Antoine had died.

Hating Leo. Because his son killed their father/husband.

CHAPTER 17

Namaste. Oops, Vamps Don't Have Souls. Never Mind.

"I have some home addresses for the Nicaud women," Alex said as we crawled back into the SUV, "four, to be exact. They moved around a lot. I tracked the last one down just this second. Sending them to your cells, along with GPS and sat pics."

The Nicauds lived in the Lower Ninth Ward, on Lamarche Street. The Lower Ninth Ward had been the hardest hit by Hurricane Katrina, large stretches of the neighborhood under eight feet of water for days. The largest numbers of deaths took place there, human and pet. And the Lower Ninth had received the least amount of revitalization money, which is to say, little beyond tearing down and hauling off the most uninhabitable buildings and homes. There were still boarded-up homes and empty housing lots, little opportunity, and fewer jobs.

Since the last time Google drove through, with its rotating camera, preserving the world for online viewers, things had changed on Lamarche Street, and not in a good way. Eli drove past the first address and turned around in the intersection of Florida Avenue, driving back slowly. Half a block up he cut the lights and backed into the cracked drive of an empty lot.

The Nicauds' most recent address was a weathered brick Creole cottage, two rooms wide, the house visible in the security light of the house next door. The cottage was traditionally symmetrical, with two front doors and two front windows, the shutters closed over each, with smoke damage showing behind and plywood hammered over them. The steeply pitched, side-gabled roof had seen the hand of firemen's axes as they tried to open a way to control the fire that had destroyed the inside. Someone had tacked a blue tarp over the damage. "There's a light on inside," Eli said. "Two figures, adult-sized, human, moving around."

He had a mono-ocular on to preserve the night vision in the other eye should something explode and temporarily blind him. He was flipping back and forth between low-light and infrared, studying the house.

"Looks like a brazier and an oil lamp. Both figures are male. Wait. Under the eaves on the second floor, there's another figure. Supine. Maybe on a cot." He studied the view for a while. "We could check it out."

I nodded. "Give your brother the keys and let's go pay them a little visit." I opened the door, and the scents of the place hit me like a wet blanket wrapped around a sledgehammer. Water from the river. Water standing on the rain-soaked ground. Old smoke, that peculiar, vile stench of a burned-out house. Food cooking over an open flame, maybe a chicken. The stink from an outdoor latrine. Sweat. Unwashed male. Familiar males. I'd smelled them before. And riding over the stinks was the pong of sex and the reek of fear and pain and . . .

A memory shoved up through me like a clawed fist. *My father, beside me on the floor, dead, his blood cooling. My mother, on the floor as well, the white man's shadow riding her. The smells. The smell of pain and sex.* I moved so fast the world blurred. When I stopped, it was to find myself on the narrow front porch, Eli's hand on my arm, the Benelli against my shoulder.

"Jane. Wait," he murmured.

Pain ratcheted through my bones and settled in my fingers and my jaw. I hissed at Eli, lips snarled back to show killing teeth. My eyes were glowing gold, reflected in his.

He yanked back his hand and held it up, telling me to stop. Or to be peaceful.

Peace is human concept. Not predator concept, Beast thought.

"There's a woman in pain in this house," I said. "I smell her blood and the men's—" I stopped, unable to go on. "They hurt her."

"Are you absolutely . . . completely certain she's been hurt? That she's not there of her own free will?"

"I—" I stopped. "Yes."

"Is it Tau or her mother?"

"No. The scent is human. A young female."

Eli's voice went cold, expressionless, what I had come to know as his battle voice. He looked over the house, whispered, "Saw something like this in a little village in . . . elsewhere. Two men with a woman captive, upstairs, bound and gagged. Squatters. Had 'em a woman too beaten to fight anymore." He made a waffling motion with his hand. "Not saying the situations are the same. This girl could be here by choice, but . . ."

I didn't react to the change in his scent except to say, "How'd you handle it?"

"Small group at the front. Small group at the back. Fast entry, quick clear. The targets didn't have time to draw weapons." He hesitated. "Wasn't supposed to be action, just recon. We had a female with us. When the stairs were cleared, she went up. Came back with the woman."

"And?"

Something that could never have been called a smile ghosted across his face. "Two casualties of war. One female rescued and taken to Uncle Sam's finest medics. Last I heard she was studying to be a nurse."

"Repercussions?"

"Not everything made it into the reports that night. Let's be smart," Eli said. "Let me clear the area."

I raised my head and sniffed the air. With Beast-hearing, I heard the girl whimper. Her scent was human. Broken. Sick. I growled when I heard her whimper. From inside a man shouted, "Shut up, bitch, or I'll give you something to cry about." I heard the laughter of two men. And the sound of soft sobs from upstairs, all loud enough that even Eli could hear. "She isn't here of her own free will," I growled. "I know what rape smells like."

"Not disagreeing. Just saying let's be smart. One minute more. Two at the most. The men are downstairs. Not hurting her right now." Even more soft, he repeated. "Let me clear the area."

I jerked my chin at him and said, "No explosive smell here," my voice an octave lower, rumbling.

He nodded and said, "When I'm done, ready to enter, I'll give a whippoorwill bird call. You know it?" I jerked my head down to say yes and Eli asked, "Can you get the door open fast?"

I showed blunt human teeth, attached the M4's shoulder strap, and slung the shotgun back. I reached out and inserted my clawed, knobby fingers under the edge of the plywood. Instead of my having to pull it, making an ungodly noise, it simply opened about two inches. The plywood had been secured to the shutter and to the door, making it all one single piece, held on by a simple door chain on the inside. I grinned at Eli and showed my teeth again. "Stupid humans."

Using his mini flash, he cleared the door of physical, mechanical, and explosive booby traps, then cleared the front porch, making sure there were no booby traps there. Even nonexplosive traps could be deadly and I had raced up here without a plan. *Stupid Jane/Beast.*

Eli leaped off the porch; I followed his progress by the slight swish of his legs through the unmown weeds and grasses. I waited. Looked at the SUV. Growled softly, though Alex couldn't hear me.

And realized two things. I hadn't told Eli who the two men were. And I had half shifted on the way across the street. I gazed at my feet. They still fit in the boots. I scrunched my toes, which curled in the toes of the Luccheses. Human-shaped still. Yet another new half form. Now that I was thinking clearer, I pushed the shotgun farther around back and repositioned two vamp-killers for easy access, unseating the weapons from their new hard-plastic holsters. The blades were shorter, but they had really stout tangs and hilts and rounded pommels, good for use as weapons themselves.

A whippoorwill called, the sound lonely. I ripped the plywood, the shutter, and the door off its hinges. The chain popped free, the stench of fire, unwashed male, and fainter, the fading, ancient scents of Tau and Marlene, roiling out. Before the assemblage fell to the porch, I was inside. Weapons drawn, blades back, against my lower arms. Moving Beast-fast.

The man in front of me caught sight of me. Started to scream. Began to pull a gun from his pants. I brought my right arm up from my hip. Caught him under the jaw with the pommel. An uppercut. Easy to dodge, easy to just fall away from. But his jaw crunched, blood flew. I stepped over him as he dropped.

The man behind him was holding a weapon in a street-style grip, out to the side. *Stupid*. I whirled. The other pommel took him in the cheek. Roundhouse. I/Beast whipped inside the gun hand, which went wide. Whirled. Caught him a backhanded fist to the jaw on the same side. Whipped my blade. Instead of killing him, I slammed the blade down through his lower arm, slicing between the arm bones with a killing claw, slashing down, cutting nerves and tendons as he fell.

He was out cold, so I performed the same treatment on his other arm. *Predator can no longer hurt human girls.* I/we ignored Eli, standing in the darkened doorway, the scent of shock leaching from his skin. I went back to the first man. Beast guiding my hand, I cut down his arms the same way.

Sounding far too casual, Eli said, "They'll bleed out if you leave them that way. Cops might get involved."

I snorted, looking the men over. I blinked. Seeing what I had done. Arterial blood was pumping from both men, wide pools of blood forming beneath them, splattering on the fire-blackened walls with each pulse. My own heart raced. My breath came too fast, uneven, hurting my chest with each inhalation. "Oh . . . crap." The words were still Beast-deep, rough and grating.

There were shoes nearby, two pair of work boots, long laces on each. With the bloody blade, I cut the laces free, and wiped and sheathed the vamp-killer on a cloth nearby. Working fast, I created makeshift tourniquets with the laces and dirty spoons lying on the scorched table nearby. The bleeding stopped, but not before I got it all over myself.

I rose and looked at Eli, still standing in the doorway. Too relaxed, too nonchalant. But he smelled of uncertainty, doubt. I inspected at the men on the floor. My voice still deep, half Beast, half human, I said, "In my tribe, rape was very rare. Women held the power and the land. Men were warriors and hunters. When they . . . *misbehaved* . . . they were given to War Women. Who meted out judgment." I toed the hand nearest. "I'll . . . I'll see if some willing fanghead will offer them blood. But no matter what, they won't will be able to hurt a woman again. Ever."

"And you're sure they raped the woman upstairs?" He nodded to the darkness up the narrow steps, barely visible in the oil lantern light. Questioning my judgment.

My voice dropped even lower. "I smell her on them. They stink of her blood and pain and fear, not fun and games."

Eli nodded at that, musing. His scent altered to acceptance. "Good enough for me. Do we free the girl and leave the mess or call the police? And if we call the cops, do we wait?"

I bent to sniff closer, recognizing something I'd have realized sooner if I hadn't been so caught up in memories and rage. "Tau," I said. "They smelled like Tau and Marlene. They helped to care for Ming of Mearkanis in the pit. Brothers, half brothers. Maybe I should have kept them conscious and questioned them before I . . ." *Before I cut them up.* Beast withdrew from the forefront of my mind, prowling away. Satisfied. But I wasn't. I looked down at my hands. The hands of a killer. A maimer.

A memory flashed before me, of a blade sliding slow, down through the bones of an arm as he jerked and thrashed. Heard a man screaming. Saw blood flash, crimson against white flesh. Then it was gone. And I knew that I—or my grandmother—had done this exact thing before. When I was five. When I helped to torture and kill the men who raped my mother and killed my father.

Eli said shortly, "Shit happens in battle. You don't think. You just *do*. And if you're lucky, you survive to fight another day."

But this was now, and . . . I was guilty. I knew it. Something inside me tightened and twisted, tangling up. "Call the police," I pointed to the grimy ancient flip phone cell near the cooking brazier. "On that. I'll free the girl."

"I'll free her. She needs to know a man saved her. And your face is kinda scary right now."

I touched my jaw with my knobby fingers and felt pelt. Upper and lower canines too long for cat or human. I grunted. Blinked. Saw again the ancient memory of the man I had helped to kill, so long ago. Bucking against the blades. I had just punished these two men, in part, because of the murder and rape that were nearly two hundred years gone. As if the little girl I had been was still alive and well inside me.

"Don't touch anything," Eli added. "We won't be staying."

He dialed 911, gave the dispatcher the address, and, without identifying himself, gave a quick description of what to expect, ending with the words, "There's a girl upstairs. She's been held captive. Used. We're setting her free, but she won't be able to walk. She needs care." Eli wiped the cell free of prints and set it down where he'd found it, the dispatcher's voice asking questions to the empty air.

He went up the stairs and the girl began a panicked moaning, a muffled "Hunh-hunh-hunh" behind a gag.

"It's okay," Eli said. "I'm here to set you free. Not to hurt you. An ambulance is on the way. You're safe now." And he said it again. And again. Over and over. When he came back down the stairs, he was grim and smelled of fury and impotence. The human girl was free and crying, her voice hoarse and dry. In the distance sounded sirens. Eli looked around and said, "You were right." He analyzed the scene. The men. "Totally right about everything. There's no sign of female habitation down here. She's been a prisoner. Nothing here but porn mags and video games."

"No electricity," I said, thinking clearly again. "As if they're squatting in their mama's house? Weird."

Eli and I left through the doorless front opening, stepped over the door, and raced to the SUV. Alex had the vehicle running and pulled out of the empty drive before we could close the doors. At a sedate pace, he crossed the next intersection and then turned left on the one after. Weaving through the silent streets, he headed uptown, back to the French Quarter, passing cop cars, an ambulance, and two Harleys ridden by local bike gang members. I missed Bitsa fiercely, but I also knew that missing the bike was just one way of not thinking about the girl, tied to the bed, at the mercy of the men.

I looked away, out the window, into the night. We had come to track Tau and Marlene. And instead of finding them, I had cut up their . . . brothers? Sons? Whatever. "We could have questioned them," I said again. "About Tau. And Marlene."

"I take it that whatever went down in there wasn't on the action plan for the night?" Alex asked.

"No," Eli replied. "And we lost the chance to learn something. But Janie saved a kidnapped girl. Sometimes, even in the middle of war, we do God's work, no matter what."

I thought about those words as I stared out the window. War Women. We do God's work, his vengeance. Whether he wants us to or not. I reached into myself and found the memory of Jane, the human-looking part of myself, of ourselves, though I was quite certain that I had never been human. Not at all.

I climbed across the seat and into the back of the SUV, where I found towels, washcloths, and a bottle of water in a rucksack. I stripped, washed up, and redressed in stretchy pants and a tee. I also found my human shape and let myself flow back into it. It hurt this time, as if in direct proportion to the previous, painless half shift, the agony ripping along my nerves like tiny knives cutting through me, scoring my bones. When I came to myself, I was gasping, grunting softly.

In the backseat, Eli asked, "You okay, Janie?" overly unconcerned.

"Ducky," I managed, sounding human. I wiped my boots as well as I was able and pulled them on too. My stomach growled and I said, "I could eat."

"Pulling into a Popeyes right now," Alex said. "Bucket of chicken and all the fixings coming up."

"Make mine grilled," Eli said, "yours too." He was cleaning my weapons and rigs and sheaths free of blood. When we got home, he'd do a further cleaning with chemical compounds that would eat away at any DNA evidence. Under a Woods light, they might show up as having been exposed to body fluids, but I was a vamp killer. One might expect body fluids.

"Yeah, yeah, yeah," Alex said.

Once we finished eating, we drove into the night and checked the other addresses listed in the Nicaud women's records. We found less than nothing. They might have lived at any of the places at one time, but they had taken off, leaving old scent patterns but no forwarding addresses. With nothing else to do and equipment to clean, we headed back to the house. The wards were up and the lights were on when we got there, and we trooped through, the sting of recognition a reminder of what it would have been like had the ward not been set to allow us entrance, and we tried to enter. Crispy critter YS peeps.

Evan was sitting in the recliner when we entered, and watched us as we scattered to different tasks. Me, to wash and bleach my shirt, jeans, and towels. Evan stopped me halfway through the utility room door with the words "Where's Molly?"

I stopped and backed three feet into the living room. "Say what?" Which was when I caught the smell of magic and frustration. The trip through the ward had blunted my receptors.

"She told me you had texted her to meet you. But from her absence, I gather that was a lie. She never showed up, did she?"

Carefully, choosing words meant to be honest but innocuous, I said, "No. I didn't text her. I haven't seen her." Molly had lied to Evan before, to do something she knew he would consider to be too dangerous for the mother of his children to do alone. And I was thinking about Molly's addiction to death magic. . . .

"Molly has a natural ability to find trouble," Eli said. So much for innocuous.

Suddenly something came to me, the way thoughts come to you when you aren't looking for them. Molly had never touched the brooches, had shown no interest in them, which was really odd for my curious friend. "Where are the brooches? The two we have?"

Evan's head came up fast and he and Eli dove for the weapons room, opening the bookshelf door. The smell of vamp and steel and gun oil filled the room. Eli didn't blow out a relieved sigh when he opened the sack and the foil-wrapped brooches tumbled out onto Edmund's bed, but his shoulders did relax a hint.

Evan took one and unfolded the foil, revealing the green stones. I took the brooch free of the foil and sniffed it. "Nothing," I said. Evan took it and instantly jumped back two feet, ramming Eli, cursing a blue streak, and dropping the pin as if he had stuck his fingers into a light socket. Overhead I heard a vague thump as Eli leaned around him and picked the pin up with no problem. Evan glared at it, saying, "It's being used."

Angie Baby stuck her head around the corner of the bookshelf opening, saw us and all the weapons on the walls, and said, "Coolio!" Just like me. Dang it.

This time Evan cursed under his breath. Molly would be ticked that the secret location of our weapons room had now been irrevocably revealed to the little witch. Aloud, he said, "You will *not* tell your brother."

Angie shrugged and said, "Okay, Daddy. But the witches aren't using the brooches. They're just using their power and the jew-lery is tied to them, like the black thing is tied to Aunt Jane."

"Jew-el-ry. What black thing?"

"Ummm . . ." Angie said, uncertain. "Aunt Jane gots a black witchy thing inside her. It's not dangerous. Well . . . not right now."

"There's nothing I can do about," I said. "When things settle down we can address my little problems."

"We know where Tau and Marlene went when they left the Elms after booby-trapping it. I tracked them from the apartment building."

Our heads snapped up and we all saw Molly standing in the doorway. She looked exhausted.

"Where the . . . *blue blazes* have you been?" Evan shouted, clearly trying not to cuss in front of his daughter.

"We? I?" I said.

"And I saw the residue of Tau's magic," Mol added. "But let me get Angie to bed before we talk."

"*Back* to bed," Evan said, pointing out how late it was.

Molly nodded and herded her daughter up the stairs as we followed her out of the weapons room. Eli put the brooches away and locked up. Edmund was standing in the center of the living room, still dressed in jeans and a very expensive, tailored shirt. He had his hands in his pockets, aping human better than most vamps. I narrowed my eyes at him, putting together the unmatched pronouns. Molly had been with Edmund.

I gave him my best human scowl and ignored his interest in the bloody clothes I was taking to the utility space that backed up to my bathroom. I started a load of clothes with bleach, the chlorine strong enough to make me sneeze. The jeans would be a few shades lighter, but at least they would have nothing for a crime scene tech to find. I pulled off my boots and put them in a bucket, spritzing them with a mixture of water and soap and scrubbing the soles with a stiff brush before rinsing them. Edmund hung at the door, watching.

Finally he said, "Shame on you, wasting all that lovely blood."

A small snicker escaped me and I sat back on my butt, looking up at him. "I didn't kill anyone."

"I never said you did. However, I would make a far superior hunting partner than Eli and the boy."

I thought about the scene we had made. About how a vamp might have immobilized the men with his mind, drained them to anemia and weakness, freed and physically healed the woman upstairs, while easing her mind into a peaceful state, then called her attackers to follow him and keep them out of trouble forever. And I wouldn't have to carry with me the memory that I had maimed the two men. Along with the other memories of things I wish I hadn't done. I sighed and finished rinsing my shoes, stood, and tossed my socks into the washer. He had a point. I hated that. "Free will, even for the bad guys I hurt. They didn't have to kidnap and torture a woman. And the Youngers are my partners."

"And I am your primo."

"Okay. Noted."

Edmund gave me a military-like nod of acknowledgment and followed me back into the living room, where I fell into a chair and closed my eyes. Moments later, Edmund served us tea, decaffeinated chai with all the proper trimmings—linen serving napkins, silver teaspoons, a china plate with cookies on it, and sugar and creamer. And humongous stoneware mugs. I laughed even before I saw my mug, because it said so much about my life, the juxtaposition of cheap tchotchkes and antique-expensive-fancy. The mug fell into the former category, new, candy-apple red, and it had a saying on it. "Namaste. Oops, vamps don't have souls. Never mind."

Edmund leaned over and sprayed a large upside-down cone of dairy creamer on top of my tea. I met the eyes of my primo as I accepted my mug. "Thank you. For the big mugs and the silliness. I needed both."

"It is my greatest pleasure to hear you laugh, my mistress."

Alex said, "I'd say, 'Get a room,' but I'm having to say that too much. Besides, I think the modern snark would be lost on the fangy guy. Good cookies, dude." He bent over multiple tablets at his table-desk, not syncing them up to the main screen.

Molly tapped down the stairs as Edmund finished serving the rest of the cookies and tea and coffee. She stopped in the doorway, capturing Ed's gaze. "Is there anyone else, anywhere, anytime, who takes precedence over your vow to Jane, to us, and to our children?"

Edmund stood military straight, his hands open at his sides, managing to look vulnerable, despite the fact that he was a blood-drinking killing machine. "No time, not anywhere, not any other person, save my wife and daughter, both long dead these many centuries."

"Good," Molly said. "I've worked with Tau. I've seen her magic, though it was while she was hiding her true power. I saw the signature of it then, felt its resonance. And I've seen it now, after she finished drinking from Ming. She's like Angie. She's homogeneous. Her father and her mother both carried the witch gene on the X chromosomes."

My breath hitched. Molly was very close to letting a vampire into her biggest, most dangerous secrets, which was why she had clarified his loyalties. *Gotcha.* "Antoine didn't smell like a witch," I said.

"Recessive genes," she replied without looking my way, her eyes on her husband. The big man nodded once, very slightly, accepting the risk she was taking, the secrets she was close to sharing. "I touched her magic in the Elms' backyard. I know the *feel* of that magic. As soon as Jane told us she lost the scent at the apartment building, Edmund and I went there. Every chance I've had, I've followed the magical traces." She gave her husband a tiny smile. "Not alone. I'm not stupid."

Evan looked at the servile-appearing vamp, who did not meet his eyes.

"That iron and salt odor you smelled at the pit where they held Ming?" Mol looked at me now. "It was Tau after she drank from Ming in huge quantities. Over and over. Tau isn't a vamp, but she's no longer just a superwitch. She's the closest thing to an Onorio and probably more magically powerful than anything ever. Tonight I caught a glimpse of her while I was using a *sight* working. When she isn't using her gift, her magics aren't witch magic, not anymore. When they're at rest, they look and feel like the magics on Bruiser, except that they flicker like toxic flames, green and ebony. She used the brooches to keep Ming compliant. But she also used them to change herself into something else."

I placed the half-empty mug on the small table nearest and thought about the scents I had picked up from the witches, some that—knowing this—made sense. I pulled my official cell, called Bruiser, and gave him the information.

He said, "I've been talking to the outclan priestesses. They call Tau a *senza onore*. Loosely translated to dark honor or without honor. There hasn't been one in a thousand years. This is . . . Be careful, Jane."

He disconnected and I stared at the dark screen, putting it all together. *Senza onore* . . . Bethany, one of the outclan priestesses, was on my short list of inside men for getting the witches my DNA material and the DNA of anyone at HQ. I said, "Tau became a *senza onore*, which I'm guessing is a dark Onorio."

Alex said, "Translation sites say it means *without honor* in Italian."

I had no idea what it all meant except that the Witch Conclave had to be called off. I checked the time on the cell. The city was already full of witches. Lachish had been healed enough to get around in a wheelchair or with crutches. Leo was prepped. He'd never call it off. It was far too late. He'd expect me to pull security measures out of my hat like rabbits. I asked Molly, "Where did you see the witch?"

Molly pulled her husband down beside her on the sofa and Big Evan gathered her close. She leaned into him, their bodies making a nest for her baby bump. "You're gonna love this, Jane," Mol said, her eyes closing. "And maybe I should have opened with this, but . . ." She sighed, and I could smell the fatigue on her exhaled breath. "Tau was outside the Elms. Riding a brilliant blue motorcycle, one of those foreign ones with a lot of aluminum and a molded plasticized body."

"A crotch rocket," I said, remembering the sounds of the high-pitched engines several times. They had been watching me, keeping track. Probably through the magics in my left hand. I looked at my palm. Nothing there. Didn't mean that I was free of magic. I wondered how many blue bikes were in New Orleans and the surrounding area.

Alex stated emphatically, "There's not a single record of Tau owning a bike. But . . ." His fingers tapped whirlwind-fast on a tablet. "There were other witches in the circle where you were struck by lightning. Maybe one of them has a bike. I've done a search on them in case one of them was offering sanctuary and assistance to the Nicauds. But I haven't looked for a bike. Or a bike maybe owned by one of their friends or family members. This will take a while. It would help if I knew the make."

Molly shook her head. She didn't know.

Before we left, the Truebloods turned in, safe behind the upgraded ward, one so powerful that even antitank missiles couldn't penetrate it. Air elemental spells could still penetrate, but not without setting off a big honking alarm now. Evan and Mol hadn't been able to make a magical filter working large enough to cover the house.

Alex turned in as well, taking the necessary tablets to bed with him to continue the search for conspirators. Eli, Edmund, and I made a trip to vamp HQ, to fill Leo in on the problems in the hope that the MOC might, maybe, put off his participation in the big witch hoedown. Not likely. Not likely at all.

CHAPTER 18

Leo Has a Type?

"You believe, then, that this superwitch, Tau, has a plan to compel the witches and Mithrans into war and kill whoever is left alive. Or undead," Leo said, adjusting his cuffs and looking himself over in a long cheval mirror beside his desk. "Something of the like was to be expected, of course. Witches have always been notoriously sly and unpredictable. Unlike Mithrans, who can drink of a subject or scion to determine reliability and loyalty, and to compel that loyalty when needed." He ran a hand down his flat stomach and turned to see himself from every angle. Satisfied, he removed solid gold cuff links, not the sterling silver ones he might have worn to show his power to Mithrans, and dropped them in a velvet bag held by one of his valets, whom I had seen but never met.

Lawrence Hefner was English, with a south London accent, according to Edmund. He wasn't exactly a blood-servant, nor was he a blood-slave. He was more of a rarity in the vamp world, a human in that strange position of salaried specialist who did not drink vamp blood beyond that which was necessary to be trusted. Larry, who had sniffed at me when I called him that, drew the strings of the bag tight and placed it carefully on Leo's desk. Leo's shirt was a modern blend, both wrinkle-free, soft, and heavy-starched-looking all at once, tailored to show Leo's trim form and the muscles beneath. Modern tech fashions were pretty cool.

But as I stood there, Leo unbuttoned the shirt, pulled it from the tuxedo pants, and tossed it at Larry. I blinked. Twice. I hadn't seen Leo shirtless in . . . well, never. At least not any time when he wasn't bloody and damaged. This was different. His once-olive skin was pale and scarred, the kind of scars that indicated damage no human would have survived. Dozens of life-threatening injuries. Beneath it, lithe muscles flexed as he took another shirt from Larry and pulled it on. This one was linen, the cut loose across the shoulders. As he buttoned it, I met Bruiser's gaze. His eyes twinkled, his expression an understated amusement, as if to say, *Yes. He's pretty. I know. I remember seeing him strip off a shirt before.*

I realized that there was a reason Leo had us meet here, while he was dressing. He was showing off. I shook my head at Bruiser as if to say, *Oh. My. Gosh. Really? Really!* Bruiser's eyes went to laughter and he looked away, at the rug beneath his feet, as if to hide his expression.

"Yes," I said to Leo, bringing my attention back to the conversation and away from the silent communication with my sugar lump. "This very situation we're facing *has* to be why there's a schism between vamps and witches. Because a small group of determined, powerful, prepared witches could ambush and destroy a larger, better-armed group of vamps." Leo lifted an eyebrow at me in disdain. "In a heartbeat," I said. "No matter how fast a well-fed vamp might compel or mesmerize them, witches can work in daylight and from a distance. If the witches ever decide to take over the paranormal world, vamps are screwed. Especially when fighting a *senza onore* witch." Leo knew all this. Dang it.

"Hmm. What do you think, Lawrence?" Leo asked, ignoring everything I had just said.

"I prefer the other, milord. The fabric, while not traditional, will provide comfort in a stressful situation, and should you take off your tuxedo suit coat for some reason, the lines of that dress shirt are more appealing."

"I tend to agree. Now, what about the silks and the cummerbund?"

Now he was just messing with me. I was tired, worn, it was nearly dawn, the day of the Witch Conclave. I sat down. Without permission. Larry sniffed at me again. So I put my feet up on the desk and crossed my boots at the ankles. And yawned. Larry turned his back on me, clearly scandalized.

Leo laughed. "I depend upon my Enforcer to care for me," he said. He took in the entire office, which was tightly packed with too many people, all watching him dress or carefully looking elsewhere. His gaze finally settled on Bruiser and Edmund, who had stepped up behind me, in some kind of unspoken accord. Leo's face went tight and hard, his scent peppery in the crowded room. "Even a *senza onore witch*," he said, emphasizing the words, "will not stop this parley. It is essential to the survival of the city and to my clan and my bloodline. It is essential to every Mithran and witch and human in the land. And it *will* take place." He gestured to the door. "Everyone out. Except the Enforcers and the Onorio." He glanced at Eli. "And that one."

The room cleared fast, and as the door closed, Leo said, "My Enforcer and the Onorios shall all be in attendance. I will be quite safe at the conclave."

I said, "But *no one else* will be."

His shirt hanging open, Leo faced me, piercing me with his eyes. His power buffeted me, cold and potent, raising the hairs on the back of my neck. I realized then that he was blood-flushed. He'd been drinking, and drinking deeply, from all the clan blood-masters and from the Son of Darkness in the lowest subbasement. The feel of his power along my flesh made me want to drop my feet to the floor and put my back to the wall, but to Leo, that would have appeared to be a defensive move, would have suggested that I was afraid, would have made me lose face in the presence of my enemies. So I stayed where I was, drawing on Beast to keep my breath and heart rate low and the stink of my fear inside me.

Leo's tone was low, but every word was enunciated clearly, as if to drive it into the top of my skull like a nail. "If I die, there will be war among the Mithrans in New Orleans. All your friends will die. All the witches will die. Hundreds of humans will die in the immediate fallout. Within twenty-four hours. And after that bloodbath, the Europeans will walk in unopposed. At that time, *thousands* will die and the military will come in and destroy everything that registers on the psy-meter. Every*thing* and every*one*. It will be war and utter devastation."

I knew all this. We all did.

Leo went on. "The United States military has laid plans for this. They are called *contingency plans*." He flicked that stabbing gaze up at Eli. "You will tell me that you have heard of such things."

Eli was silent for the space of several breaths, and without looking up at him, I knew he was weighing loyalties between Uncle Sam and family. When he spoke, however, his voice was sure and certain. "Yes, sir. I have."

Leo pulled his eyes back to me. "Therefore, you will keep me alive, for I am all that stands between all that you hold dear and a horror and ethnic cleansing that has not been seen in this hemisphere since the native tribal peoples were decimated and the population of the Amazon River disappeared in blood and disease and horror."

Copying my partner, I said, "Yes, sir."

Leo said, "The people I assign shall be yours to command. You will keep the peace. You will keep us all alive. It is your *job*." I nodded and he said, "Make it so."

With that pithy *Star Trek* order, Leo left the room. I stood up fast and shook off the effects of the magical demands. In the hallway, Larry met Leo, trailing after, talking about the benefits of scarlet silks versus total black.

Derek Lee wandered over and I turned my attention to him. "You got one day," I said. "I want Ming of Mearkanis fed and dressed in finery. Get her jeweled up and her hair done. Make sure she's not just presentable but a hundred ten percent. Not saying we'll need her, but if Tau shows up, Ming could be the weapon we need to bring her down."

"Why do you think that?" Derek asked.

"She isn't pinned anymore. If she's fed as well as Leo, has fed on Leo's blood, they'll have a link, which might benefit us in case of a fight. And she might recognize the witch magic faster than anyone else."

Derek gave a head-tilt shrug, not agreeing or disagreeing with my reasoning, but accepting the order.

"Find Katie a safe place, not at her house, and make sure there are plenty of humans and loyal vamps to protect her and the kids. Set it up like a presidential security team, with observers and shooters in the high points all around. Protocol Stupid Move." I had named it that because it was used only when we were backed into a corner so deep that any move at all was likely to kill us all.

"As to the conclave, make sure Grégoire is armed but pretty. He'll be our final backup on-site.

"Make sure this place is locked down. I don't want an ant to crawl along the street without you knowing about it and it being made dead."

"Yes, ma'am, Legs." Derek saluted, which I didn't think he had ever done. If there was a slight trace of snide in Derek's tone or gesture, letting me know he had seen my reaction to Leo's naked chest, I ignored it. A girl was allowed to admire. And then feel stupid for it.

Before I left, I made three calls to specific members of the HQ security team, with additional orders I told no one else. Anything Leo was involved with had a way going FUBARed, and I wanted a net to catch us, just in case. They would be inside the ward, on the grounds, and would make sure there were no magical icons buried in the ground. They would also be there, ready to follow orders at a moment's notice.

Beyond drained, depleted, and worn slap-out, I slept at Bruiser's, beneath the framed bacon shirt, held in Bruiser's arms, and woke up around noon, alone in the bed. I stretched like a big-cat, arms and legs moving in a long sinuous curve of muscle and tendon, and, silently, I slipped into the bath for a hot shower. Afterward, I pulled on the T-shirt he had worn while we ate a late dinner on the gallery, watching the world pass by. It had ended up between me and the burned persimmon couch in his living room, when we made love. The first time. The knit now smelled of his cologne, vaguely of Creole-Cajun fusion spices, and of him, heated and hungry for things other than food. I held the cloth to my nose and breathed in, holding his scent close. His odor was still changing, though by increments now, instead of by leaps and bounds as it did after he was changed from blood-servant to Onorio.

Feeling content, I checked the time and my messages. Everything was going according to plan, the Witch Conclave was going perfectly, the Youngers had everything in hand, everyone was doing his and her jobs, and I had some time to relax. *Ducky*. It paid to have minions. Not that I'd ever call the Youngers or Derek Lee that. I'm not stupid all the time.

I combed out my hair, leaving it to dry down my back before braiding it. I had learned my lesson about putting my hair up wet. In the Louisiana humidity, hair could stay wet all day, all night, and all the next day, if not allowed to air. I also brushed my teeth and left my toothbrush next to his. It was weird to see it there, next to my comb, my body oil, my face cream, which he had bought for me, and my lipstick. All in his apartment. Just weird.

I left the bath to catch the scent of shrimp and grits from Café Amelie and beignets with chicory coffee from Café du Monde. And tea made by Bruiser. He made great tea, especially for breakfast, strong enough to kick-start a mule. I liked a good strong tea, but Bruiser's idea of breakfast tea was way more British than mine, which is to say, way more strong.

I heard him moving in the kitchen nook and followed him there, to climb up on one of the three white bar chairs. I rested one elbow on the bar and my head on my lower arm as I thumbed through the texts awaiting me. Again, nothing urgent. I put away the cell and looked up at my sorta boyfriend. He was shirtless and barefoot, wearing my favorite thin linen-weave pants that hung low on his hips. "Can I hire you as my full-time chef?" I thought for a moment and added, "And lover?"

"You want me for a gigolo?" He placed a ladylike cup of tea beside my elbow and shared a half smile with me.

I let him see the satisfaction in my eyes. "You *are* uniquely qualified for the position."

"Which position?" he inquired, his eyes heating as if he remembered several from last night.

I picked up my teacup in both hands and brought it to my mouth. The steam curled around my face, warm and soothing. "All of them?"

He pulled a serving spoon from a round utensil holder and opened a food-delivery container. As he dished up a late breakfast, he gestured to his shirt on me. "Is it a theme for us? Bacon?" he asked. I pulled out the tee and read it upside down. It was a tee I had bought for him at the touristy shop after seeing it hanging in the store window. It had a big raindrop on it and garish letters reading, I LOVE NOLA RAIN. IT SOUNDS LIKE BACON FRYING.

"Could be worse," I said. "It could read Life Without Bacon."

"True." He dished up shrimp and grits into a china pasta bowl and set a plate of beignets between us. He leaned on the bar and dipped a spoon into his own bowl of spiced breakfast, and we ate several bites in companionable silence. "Shall I have that shirt framed too?" he asked.

"Eh." I swallowed peppery grits and sipped my tea, which was a breakfast blend strong enough to bend iron bars and leap a locomotive, perfect for the spices. "Too much bacon might spoil the décor."

He laughed and leaned farther across the bar to cup my head in his hand and claim my mouth as his own. An hour later, I went home to a nearly empty house. Molly and Evan were at the conclave, talking and voting, along with every other witch in town. Eli and Alex were at the conclave monitoring the witches' security arrangements. The kids were in the safe house where Katie was sleeping, guarded by Derek's most experienced men, the last members of Team Vodka. And by Brute. How weird was my life when I was grateful to have a werewolf guarding my godchildren?

Edmund was sleeping somewhere. Bruiser was at HQ making sure everything was okay there. I hadn't been alone in the house in months, and the silence that had once been peaceful was unnerving. So I pulled out all three of my new fighting leathers and tried them on to decide which one to wear. Based on color. On style. Tried out all the color-coded custom Kydex holsters on the new weapons rigs. Badass. Totally badass.

And then I braided my hair and went through my meager collection of makeup to choose what I would wear with my ensemble. *I am such a* girl.

Two hours before dusk, I received the call from Molly and Big Evan. It should have come before I left Bruiser's and I had been pacing the floors waiting. "We have approval," Molly said.

"You sound less than excited," I said.

"You try to get agreement between a couple hundred witches on *any*thing and see how excited you are afterward. It took an hour before they could decide to update the rules on the national council—which hadn't been updated in over a hundred years, about the time the first telephone lines crossed the nation. Then there were another several hours of wrangling on the need to update the rules on witch behavior and mores, and another hour on who was to enforce those rules and—" I could almost see Molly rubbing her forehead. "All that was before lunch, which was served late because the Seattle coven insisted on a thorough cleansing of the kitchen, in a spiritual sense, not with Comet and elbow grease, though that might have been considered too at some point. And then they had to purify all the copper pots the food was prepared in. And let me tell you, the stink of frankincense, yarrow, and white sage is awful on the air."

"And?"

"And then, about three p.m., we began to discuss the fanghead situation. And we just got the vote. Leo's in. His proposal for rapprochement has been approved without any substantive changes to the wording or the reparations. The mayor and the governor have been notified and will be here for a live, remote, glad-handing photo shoot for the late-evening news.

"Leo will need to be here in time for his speech at seven thirty, to be followed by more speechifying, and a late supper at eight thirty or nine. Can you make it happen?"

"Piece a' cake," I said. And crossed my fingers.

I notified everyone about the arrangements by phone call, not text. No way was I leaving anything in the hands of electronics. When everyone was notified, I decided on the new scarlet leathers. Seemed all I needed to get out of my unexpected girly mood and into action was a definite time and date for the vamp festivities. My last line in each call was "Wear the anti-DNA charms I had messengered over. Do *not* forget."

I powdered up, because the weather was muggy and leather meant sweating no matter what. Over the unscented body powder I pulled on a stretchy knit cami top and undies, and then matching stretchy knit socks. My former combat socks didn't work anymore. If I had to shift into a half form, I needed room for my feet to grow in width, room for my claws. I slid into the leather pants and snugged up the clasps and ties to get them tight, but not so fitted I couldn't move when needed. Then the jacket, the rich, scarlet leather so gorgeous I wanted to pet it. They still smelled strong, but I wasn't a walking, talking olfactory ad for cow skin. And I looked freaking fantastic.

My cell made a burbling sound and I bent to pick it up. The leathers squeaked, which wasn't good. Vamps had very good ears. Something to remember if I needed to go silent. I opened the cell and read a text from Alex. He had found a witch whose child owned a crotch rocket. A blue Kawasaki. Worse, the teenager was a budding witch too.

I pulled the guest list, and the young witch's name wasn't on the list. But . . . Yeah, but. Tau might have killed her to get the bike. Might have allied with the witch or her mom. Too many mights and might nots. But before I could worry too much, Alex sent another text—*the young witch safe at home.*

I sent a quick text back, putting together the idea of a witch on a motorbike. There were dozens of places a witchy attack might be made upon Leo in the next few hours, but only one place where an attack might take place on the witches and Leo too. I weaponed up and strapped on my silver-plated titanium chain-mail gorget to protect my throat, and layered on the fancy gold-and-citrine gorget over it. When the horn tooted outside, I left the house, looking like a demon from hell. A well-armed demon from hell.

I climbed into the SUV that was my ride and greeted the driver. Wrassler said, "Looking good, Legs. Looking good." I buckled in and he proceeded to update me on the security measures at HQ. Which gave me time to think.

At HQ things were going according to plan. Between them, Wrassler and Derek had every possible means of attack buttoned up at the vamp council chambers. The building across the street, from which an easy armed attack had once taken place, had been commandeered, and armed personnel walked the halls. Men and women with bullet-resistant shields lined the porte cochere, the shields overlapped to protect Leo's passage from doorway to the limo. The three limos each had mapped out differing routes to take. Motorcycle escort was in place. NOPD had been notified of the passage of the MOC and the potential for problems.

I scanned the bikes as I waited under the porte cochere, and not one was brilliant blue. They were all white, and the riders wore white riding leathers, so we could keep track of them as Leo's security. I sought out the three bikes whose riders wore red helmets and black riding leathers. One at a time, they lifted a hand to me. I nodded back. They were my backup plan if it all FUBARed as spectacularly as I feared.

The three Onorios stepped out of the doorway, heads swiveling, checking for danger. They were decked out in fighting leathers like mine, but all in black. None of them were weaponed up, at least not that I could see, though I was quite sure they wore enough blades on them to start a good-sized butcher shop.

Leo followed the Onorios, dressed in evening wear. He and Larry had decided to go with a solid black-and-white color scheme, the tux, cummerbund, tie, and lapel silk all in black. The shirt was the trim white one he had tossed at the valet. He ducked into the armored limo and sat, his eyes on me.

Ming Zoya, formerly of Mearkanis, came next out the door, wearing finery that could only have been put together by Madame Melisende, a blend of elegance and class that was uniquely Ming. The outfit had to be something left over from her time as clan Blood Master. She wore yards of scarlet silk to her ankles, embroidered with peonies and brightly colored birds. Feathers, dyed to match the dress, trailed below her waist and around her body, in a train of some sort down her back. She wore black shoes, like flip-flops but not made of plastic or foam, rather made of something with no flex. Her long black hair was up in magnificent braids and coils and curls, her lips and talons painted to match the silk. She smelled of blood. A lot of blood. And she looked young and beautiful and powerful, as unlike the thing that had come up from the water of the pit as it was possible to look. A different being entirely. Ming of Mearkanis was here under the slim possibility that she might recognize the witches' magic before anyone else. She was our canary in the mine. If she started acting weird, compliant, anything at all out of whatever was ordinary for her, then the Nicauds might be near. Ming made it to her limo without incident.

Girrard DiMercy and Grégoire slid into the last limo in line before I could get a good look at them. One Onorio stepped into each limo.

Everyone was perfect and everything had been done according to plan. There was no reason to feel a sense of impending doom. No one could see under the roofed porte cochere without a drone. At this point we were all safe. Of course, we were about to hit the streets and that safety level was about to change totally. My heart raced.

Everything from the moment Leo left the building made us a target.

I caught a familiar scent. I stopped, one hand raised to do . . . something. I turned, following the scent with my nose. An odor that I had last smelled when I was dying on the floor of the sparring room/gym. *Here.* At vamp central. I pivoted slowly and followed the scent. It led back into vamp HQ, from inside. I held up a finger, telling Bruiser to close up the limos and wait. I pulled a nine-mil and a vamp-killer and strode through the phalanx of confused security personnel, into the chambers. I got a glimpse of a female in the gray uniform of housekeeping. She tucked her head and ran for the elevator.

Beast shoved her speed into me. I raced across the small space and inserted a hand into the crack as the door tried to close. The woman backed into the corner of the small trap and curled into herself. Her arms crossed her body and she slowly sank to the floor. Beast and I analyzed her together. She was pretty, in a blond, blue-eyed, victim-prey kind of way. I had seen her in the gym footage, mopping my blood off the floor of the gym when Gee stabbed me. I had my traitor, the person who had given enemies my blood or hair or tissues to use in spells against me. And it wasn't the outclan priestess who had bitten me when I first arrived here. It was a human.

"Why?" I asked, seeing my eyes glowing bright yellow in the metal of the trap.

She risked a look up at me and then back down. She shook her head. "I was stupid."

And I couldn't disagree. She was dumb enough to bring her scent where she knew I'd be. She should have run. "Stupid how?" I asked.

"In every way a girl can be."

Which sounded as though it was going to be a long story, one best told to a vamp, with blood and compulsion and all that stuff. "Never mind." I put away my weapons and fisted my hands. I walked into the elevator, letting my boots clomp in the small space. Behind me men and women gathered, watching. Behind me, someone held open the doors.

"What do they have planned?" I asked her.

"I don't know," she said, sounding miserable. "They didn't tell me." She risked a glance up at me, her pretty eyes full of tears. "Just that he would die. And I wouldn't have to pass him in the hallways like he's some kind of king and not even see me. After what we did together." She caved in on herself and added, "I gave up everything for him. Everything." And the weeping became a waterfall.

What did I do to be surrounded by so many weepy humans? I backed out of the elevator and caught sight of Scrappy, Leo's new secretary, and Del, Leo's new primo. I hadn't seen much of Del recently and we exchanged nods. "She was Leo's pet for a while?"

Del's mouth hardened in a line as she looked over the girl. Except for the height, they were dead ringers for each other. "Before my time."

I thought about Grégoire. And Katie. Blondes. "Leo has a type?"

"It's fluid. Currently he is chasing blondes."

"Get someone to bleed and read her and send anything pertinent to Alex and Eli."

"I'll see to it, Enforcer," Del said.

Yeah. My order, sanctioned by the authority given me by the man who had hurt this poor pitiful girl. Who would likely slide into more blood and sex slavery. "See if you can find someone with a lot of finesse. And then see if they can break her addiction." When Del looked at me in amusement, I added, "Try," making that an order too.

I entered Leo's limo and a security person closed the door. "Problems?" Bruiser asked.

I frowned at Leo. "One of his castoffs was working with the Nicaud witches. You really need to keep it in your pants."

Up front, Wrassler made a choked sound. No one spoke. Leo's eyebrow rose, just the one. There were multiple emotions in the elegant gesture—amusement at me, a trace of anger at the woman's betrayal, a steely-eyed promise of retaliation at my lack of proper etiquette. "Keep it in my pants . . ."

"Yeah. Your need to tap everything that moves causes nothing but problems."

Leo said stiffly, "I have taken your recommendations under advisement."

Which said and meant absolutely nothing. I just frowned back at him before looking around the limo. "Everyone got your anti-DNA charms?"

"We all have them," Leo said, sounding almost snappish.

The motorcycles pulled out in a roar and Leo's limo followed them, turning right. Ming's turned left, and Grégoire's turned right and then pulled away from us, each limo taking a different route.

As my worries increased, we drove through the streets of the French Quarter and down St. Charles Avenue, toward the Elms Mansion and Gardens. All three limos arrived without incident. All the motorbikes arrived safely. Even the traffic cooperated and not a single motorcycle came near any of us, except the ones ridden by Leo's security as they zigged and zagged through traffic, keeping watch. Everything was perfect.

Heck. It didn't even rain. When the other shoe drops, it's gonna be a kicker. Ha-ha, I thought as we reached the Elms. Wrassler, driving the limo that Leo and I were in, pulled into a parking space on a side street, one guarded by a police officer in charge of traffic cones. There was no press. In a city like New Orleans, a gathering of two hundred unknowns was nothing, and Leo's appearance hadn't been publicized.

I gave Bruiser a communications headset before I slid out of the limo. I rearranged the stakes in my bun from travel-position to higher, into a tall silver, garnet, and ashwood halo, adjusted my weapons, and wished there had been time to oil and wear my slightly squeaky leathers for a month. But a girl can't have everything. With Beast-sight, I took in the house and the surrounding area. Everything glowed with witch magics, reflected in windows across the street, in the paint jobs of the limos. Here, where we needed it just as much as, or more than, under the porte cochere, there was no phalanx of armored shields. No.

Such precautions would have made Leo look weak. My unease grew.

The motorcycle escort pulled in and dismounted fast. They lined up, providing a passageway of bodies for Leo to walk through. If someone shot at Leo, they'd more likely hit one of his humans. Which ticked me off, but that was the ugly truth of the blood-servant life.

Bruiser followed me, and together we flanked Leo's door as he slid, elegant and graceful, from the leather seat. Leo breathed in my scent, which let me know how much he liked the trace of alarm that was coming from my pores. I thought about smacking him, but this wasn't the time or place to depend on snark.

Ming slipped from the next limo, petite and delicate and powerful, to be flanked by the Robere twins. "I feel nothing," she said to Leo across the short distance. "No taste of the magics used against me." Which meant the enemy witches were probably saving whatever attack they were planning for when we were all inside and had no room to maneuver whatsoever. Just ducky.

Grégoire and the Mercy Blade stepped lightly from the third limo and joined us. Both of the narrow-waisted men were dressed in silks and satins and leather thigh-high boots, Gee in a gold-color brocade that looked vaguely familiar, and that contrasted with his hair. Grégoire wore black, something like what Zorro might have worn, though without the demi-mask, to contrast with Gee's. And then I got it. They were wearing each other's clothes. They had shared. How . . . cute. I kept my lips in a neutral position, not allowing my face to show my amusement, which would have been a good way to get sliced and diced. The two made a fetching set of bookends—deadly, dangerous, lovely book ends. The witches would swoon at the sight of the pretty, pretty boys.

I had worried that since Gee had been spelled once before, he might be again, but Molly and Evan had given him an extra trinket, Christmas-tree-shaped, that was pinned to his lapel. If he was on the bad end of a magical attack, all the little Christmas tree lights would light up. That and the anti-DNA charm were good enough for me.

I wanted his ability with a sword tonight, and if his tree lights lit up, I'd just bonk him on the head and knock him out. I had mad skills that way. I had no Christmas tree charm, but I wore a charm like the others, my leathers were spelled to withstand all sorts of magical attacks, and with my Beast Early Warning System I had enough protection. Totally enough.

Bruiser and I, with Leo between us, walked through the line of security toward the front of the house with its unarmored, stained-glass-windowed front doors. Our cadre didn't look like a show of force to non-Mithrans, but it was. We were dangerous enough to defeat most any attack. Or so I had told myself.

Evan was standing in the doorway, silhouetted by the lights within. The witches must have been watching for us to arrive, because the ward dropped with a shower of black, silver, and crimson motes of power, and a falling rush of flaming energies. The conclave witches had to lower the ward so that we might enter, and this was the best time of all to attack, when the defenses were down and people were in motion. But nothing happened as we filed in and our outside security took up their places. No green magics. No explosions. No iron and water scent. No warning from Ming. Nada.

My black-helmeted backup precautions took their places on the porch and nodded to me as we passed. They didn't appear to be armed, but they all were. Heavily.

The door closed behind us all and the ward went back up with a prickle of magics that would have made my hair stand on end if it wasn't braided so tightly and plastered to my head. The magics rising over the house and grounds made me want to sneeze. The Elms was warded so completely that looking at the crisscrossed energies was like looking at a scarlet sun. Even humans could see the magics.

Evan bowed to Leo. "Welcome to the National Council of Witches, sir. The council has passed *all* of the accords."

"Ahhh," Leo said. "A momentous day indeed."

"Yes, sir. This way, please?" He extended an arm to show us the way, and I moved out in front. As I passed Evan, I presented him with a leather booklet containing a single written page, the titles of the vamps to be introduced. Under cover of the move, he pressed something into my right hand. I looked down and saw a lump of clear yellow, amber, and brown. A sticky note was stuck to it. I pocketed it for a later read.

Waiting still for that other shoe, I led the way into the ballroom, where the witches would hear the vamp trio's titles announced. The smells hit me first. If I had hoped to tease out the one scent of the Kawasaki-riding *senza onore* witch, I was sadly mistaken. The stink of magic burned my nasal passages, mingled with the awful mashed-up scents of perfume, scented body sprays and lotions, fabric softener in their clothes, hair spray, sweat, bad breath, toothpaste, and the food odors from their lunches. I managed not to gag or wrinkle my nose at the blended stench, but it was a near thing.

We filed in and onto the low dais in the ballroom corner, across from the entrance, where the speech-giving was taking place. No one jumped us. No one threw magic. No one even looked dangerous. Mostly they looked like middle-aged women of various cultures and ethnic backgrounds, most of whom could have used a fashion makeover centered on what not to wear. Ever. But they looked uniformly pleasant, if tired. No one even frowned at us.

Evan opened the booklet I had given to him. Vamp titles were always too long, too complicated, and boring to anyone but them, so the fangheads had agreed to trim the titles that would mean nothing to the gathered witches anyway. He cleared his voice as he scanned the page, and I checked out the hidden cameras and the positioning of the exits, the mansion and gardens so heavily warded that no one and nothing could get in or out. I hoped that we didn't have a fire.

Evan introduced the vamps in order of importance, from least to most significant, "Ming Zoya, former Blood Master of Clan Mearkanis, currently third in line to the position of Master of the City of New Orleans." Which was news to me. Ming might have been elevated because of something about the vamp war, or Leo had promoted her to make her look more important to the witches gathered here. There could be a dozen overlapping reasons for her promotion. She was sniffing the air, searching out the witches, but from her body language, she was having less success in finding the *senza onore* than I had.

Evan went on, reading from the small booklet. "Grégoire, Blood Master of Clan Arceneau, of the court of Charles the Wise, fifth of his line, in the Valois Dynasty. Second in line to the position of Master of the City of New Orleans."

Grégoire bowed and smiled and looked for all the world like a fifteen-year-old boy dressed up for cosplay at a local faire or for a part in a school play. Pretty. Vivacious. But the sword at his hip was real and he wasn't afraid to use it. While he was being charming, I pulled the small thing that Evan had given me. It was about the size and shape of a goose egg, lightweight, with a faintly resinous scent. I put my right hand behind my back and explored the lump with my fingers as Evan continued.

"Leonard Eugène Zacharie Pellissier, Mithran Blood Master of the City of New Orleans and the Southeastern United States, with the exception of Florida." All three bowed and Leo's bow was the least deep. It all meant something to the vamps, but nothing to the witches. In fact, the vamps might be insulting the witches to pieces and they would never know it. The Onorios stood to the sides, the Roberes on one end, at the windows, Bruiser with me.

I spotted Eli in his new leathers, looking spiffy, eyes intense, his jacket unzipped for easy access to the weapons he was wearing beneath, but his body appeared relaxed and easy. As if everything was okay.

It had never occurred to me that there would *not* be an attack. But . . . I had to consider the possibility that the *senza onore* witches had planted all the magic they had in the yard, and that once it exploded, they were out of witchy firepower. I managed a deep breath at the thought. It was possible that we'd blown up all they had up and that everything was going to be hunky-dory. That possibility had never seriously crossed my mind.

Leo lifted his head from the bow, took a breath that made his nostrils move, inhaling the mingled scents.

"Many thanks for allowing me to speak with your *gather*.
Our species have been divided, and divided again, with
war and discord and fear, when we Mithrans came from
witches and owe our magic to them. It is my hope that the
Witch Council of the United States of America will heed
my plea and accept my offer of reconciliation and peace.
I know you have been presented with my offer of resolu-
tion and restitution, and have had an opportunity to discuss it. I am here now to answer any questions . . ."

Yada yada yada.

I took another breath that didn't hurt and only then
noticed that I'd been holding myself ready for battle. I put
my hands together, shielding the thing the thing Evan had
given me with my left, and glanced down. It was a lump
of yellow, brown, and rusty-iron-colored stuff, a vaguely
ovoid blob of nothing much at all. The note said:

> Lump of burned iron-dust from two of the icons.
>   Encased in melted frankincense.
>   Mixed with an Everhart-Trueblood spell.
>   These three things encase the brooch that was in the
> pit with Ming.

Holy crap. It didn't feel like magic, but it had to con-
tain some pretty major hoodoo.

A small arrow at the bottom of the note suggested that
there was something written on the other side. I flipped
the small paper over to see smaller print.

> This will get three beings through the wards.
>   Once out, they can't get back in.
>   It *may* do other things against the ones who used the
> brooch on Ming.
>   We inserted a . . . a *backatcha* working in the frank-
> incense.
>   It hasn't been tested. It hasn't flown.

I held in a smile. When Molly created a new spell that
flunked when tested, she folded it into a paper airplane
and few it across the room. "It hasn't flown" was an

attempt at humor. I pocketed the blob and turned my attention back to the rest of the ballroom. Evan was standing near Eli. The witch caught my eye and I nodded once, very slightly. His beard, which he had trimmed short after the burning, moved, suggesting that he might have smiled back.

The Q and A had started and Leo was answering with as much honesty as I had ever heard, though anyone who had ever listened to vamps dicker could hear the places where he fudged or talked around or answered a different question from the one that had been asked. Of course, he was so charming that he got away with it most of the time. As long as he didn't try to compel them, we were all good and they wouldn't fry him into a strip of vamp-flavored jerky.

Things moved from boring toward conclusion pretty fast. Until a witch asked, "We understand that a Mithran contingent from Europe is expected soon. If we sign your accord, how would their presence in the city affect us?"

Leo actually offered a small bow to her, in recognition of one who got the political implications. The woman nodded back. She was short and middle-aged, with broad hips and hair dyed in strips of pink, burgundy, cerise, and purple. The hair was braided and hung long, maybe longer than my own. "Madame is wise and politically astute with her query," Leo said. "There are many ways to consider such a question, and I wish to be perspicuous and candid with this issue, so forgive my verbosity. Such wordiness is frowned upon in these modern times of hashtags and sound bites, but I must offer a complete answer.

"The Mithrans of Europe have no love of witches. The Parisian War between our species in the third century AD left the remaining Mithrans with . . ." Leo smiled. ". . . anger issues."

The witches tittered.

I had to guess the vamps had lost that battle.

"There are Parisian survivors among the Europeans," he continued, "and if they still cherish violent intentions against witches, there might be . . . difficulties. And if they come with violent intent against the Americas-based

Mithrans, instead of peaceful ones, there is the possibility of . . . shall we say, more than verbal discord?" Leo paused and clasped his hands behind his back. He dropped his head, his posture so professorial that it was disconcerting. I had to wonder if Leo had been an actor in his earlier life. Or a professor. "If they choose violence here, war between the European and the New Orleans Mithran factions becomes more likely.

"It has been my purpose," he said, staring at the dais and his patent leather shoe tops, shining black in the ballroom lights, "and my intent to keep the humans and witches of this city safe from all discord between the factions."

"Not safe from the Damours who killed our children?" the woman asked, her soft voice carrying through the abruptly silent room.

"This requires a tale not oft told, of the world as it was in the days of slavery," Leo said. "And the slave revolt in Saint Domingue, what is now Haiti, and an evil clan of Naturaleza vampires who were also witches."

An explosion sounded, juddering through the floor. The vamps were instantly holding bladed weapons. Eli was holding a handgun, and his head snapped to me. Bruiser sprinted to the front door, the other Onorios spilt, one Robere twin to the Chaperone's Alcove and its entrances to the back and side of the house, and the other to the doorway to the Louis XVI Room. Eli tilted his head, listening to the aftershocks and echoes, and said, "Outside the ward. Within a block. Similar to the ones in the yard." Belatedly the witches began to stand.

"That was outside the ward," Lachish said. "We are utterly safe." She looked down her nose at the vamps and said, "Put away your weap—"

Something clattered and thumped upstairs. Overhead. As if falling and landing on the floor. *"Alex,"* I said. Alex had set up his equipment in a small room off the stairway. I was halfway up the stairs, moving at Beast-speed, when Leo and Bruiser passed me, their bodies pops of air and blurs of color.

Leo was kneeling at the Kid's side, fingers pressed to

his neck at the carotid. My heart plummeted. "He is not dead," Leo said, "but I smell his blood."

"Alive," I shouted down the stairs to Eli, who was standing halfway down, guarding access to the front entrance, the ballroom, and the stairs, weaponed up like a ninja in his new spelled leathers. Guarding our exit, knowing that we were better able to help Alex right now than he was, when he had to want to be up here with his brother. "Out cold," I added, watching Leo's medically proficient examination. His fingers came away bloody. "Head wound, but it doesn't appear major."

Eli didn't reply, but I smelled his relief as if he'd been standing right beside me. I searched out and found Bruiser, who was entering the closed upper rooms with impunity, rooms set aside for family and privacy. The explosion might have been outside the ward, but Alex was inside and down. Something was wrong.

To Leo, I said, "I don't see magics." I eased into the room, clearing the closet and window nook and under the tiny desk. I was holding a vamp-killer in my left hand and the blob in my right. "No witches, no magics."

"A candlestick is the culprit," Leo said, his fingers growing bloodier as they crawled through Alex's hair. "When he wakes, I will see that he is fed to mitigate any possibility of brain damage."

"They hid here," I said, coming back to the closet and tucking my head within. Something touched my face, like a spiderweb in the dark, a feathery brush of . . . *magic*. I wrenched my body out, tripping on my own feet. "Magic!" I shouted. A sneeze slammed through me. *Witch magic. A lot of magic.* Something thumped my left hand, no more than a fist bump of force.

Everything happened fast. Pain ripped out of my palm and green magics swept out from the closet to me, instantly coating my body, the floor, Leo, and Alex. A fast blur of flaming green. I cursed and shook my hand, but green flames roared up, shaped for an instant like an eye. My left hand caught fire, flaring with green flames. The pain was instantaneous. I staggered back a step, mouth open to suck in a breath that burned in my lungs. The anti-DNA charm sizzled and died, not built to withstand such intensity.

On pure instinct, I dropped my weapons, pulled the blob from my pocket, and slammed it into my left palm. The flames on my hand went out. The heat in my chest cooled. The pain *stopped*. The remnant flames raced up my spelled fighting leathers and died, but . . . my hand. I gasped and swallowed back a scream. My hand was blistered and weeping. I opened my fist and the pain flared back, so I closed it on the blob again. But I had seen enough. The flesh was coming off in small wrinkled, water-engorged strips, leaving the muscles beneath visible and raw. My poor hands, hurt again. This New Orleans gig was proving more damaging, more often, than I had ever expected.

Around me, the green magic boiled on the floor, spitting and spattering, like water poured into a red-hot pot. No one but me had caught fire. The spell had been targeted to me. That was a relief and a surprise, but I'd take it. I just had to get out of here before the spell touched my skin again and burned me to a crisp. With my booted foot, I flipped up the vamp-killer, which had landed at my feet, and caught it.

Leo's fine-boned fingers were still in Alex's hair. Bloody but unmoving. As if pressed gently against the perimeters of the wound to slow the bleeding.

"Jane?" Bruiser asked. He was standing at the door, weapons out, including a sword I seldom saw him carry. He hadn't been carrying a sword in the limo and I had to assume he'd secreted one on the premises. "You're hurt."

"Yeah," I said. "I triggered something, but this put it out." I showed him the hand holding the blob. "Unfortunately it's still active. Can you see it?"

Bruiser shook his head. "No." But there was a strange look on his face, confusion, maybe. And he sniffed as if something smelled unpleasant.

"Are *you* okay?" I asked him.

"I . . . I don't know." He knelt by Leo, into the green, low-lying spell-mist. Tilted his head.

"Jane?" Eli called.

I heard more sizzling. My brain clicked back on. The anti-DNA charms were going out all at once.

There was no way that anyone could have known that I would be the one to trigger the spell. No way to know when the targeted spell had been put in the closet, but under ordinary conditions, it wasn't a place I should have even entered. The chance of me entering the closet, even with Alex injured, was minimal. I was missing something. The green spell was still pouring out around my feet, filling the room. I was missing something. Something big.

"Jane!" Eli called, soft, but edgy. "Leo?"

Leo lifted one hand to his face. Opened his mouth. And he licked his bloody fingers. His head swiveled from Alex up to me, that inhuman oddly jointed way they move when they don't care if they look human. From his place on the floor Leo's gaze swallowed me. *Fastfastfast*, he vamped out. Eyes bloodred with pupils blown, huge and black. Green flames danced in his eyes. Leo's fangs *schnicked* down. He rocketed up, talons reaching for me.

I'd been wrong. The spell hadn't been aimed only at me.

CHAPTER 19

A Billowing Gust of Fiery Death

With no thought at all, I bonked Leo on the head with the hilt of the vamp-killer. Hard. Leo fell like a human. Into the rising, flaming cloud of glowing green vapor-based spell that was rising all around me, but wasn't touching my skin again. Yet. Not through the spelled leathers and with the blob in my hand. "Bruiser, what—?"

But he was kneeling exactly as I'd seen him last, head down and tilted. Staring at Alex. Not moving except for a slow, shallow breath. And he hadn't reacted to me putting Leo down. So to speak.

I whipped my head and took the working in, Beast-sight making the magics glow in brilliant greens and silvers, now flowing out of the room and into the hallway like a slow-moving, developing flood. Heading for the stairs. Understanding came in an instant.

This spell, whatever it was intended to do, other than burn me to death, make Leo bonkers, and freeze Bruiser, was being carried on flaming green air, a vapor that would pass through my clothes eventually, and burn me alive. And it could pass through all defensive *hedge* wards where any witch who used the protection would breathe it. Even vamps had to breathe to speak and would inhale the spell, which was likely how Leo got hit. He had breathed in to speak to me. So had Bruiser, who was breathing normally when he dropped into the mist. The spell was multifaceted and multipurpose and I had no idea what all it might do or what it was based on. We were so screwed.

Worse. *I* had done this. When I stuck my head in the closet, when I touched that spiderweb stuff. I had somehow ignited the green magics. Like det cord, flaming too fast to catch. Like an explosion out of the closet, a billowing gust of fiery death.

A small, rational part of my mind told me that something so sophisticated probably had a dozen possible triggers. But the rest of me wasn't listening. And the working was still flowing out of the closet. I closed the closet door, but the spell raced through the cracks, barely slowed.

"Jane!" Eli shouted this time, and I heard his feet on the stairs.

Beast flooded me with another shot of adrenaline. "Problem," I said softly, not wanting my voice to carry to the ballroom. "Spell. Stay put." Eli halted, but I could smell his tension, a rising tide of violence that had nowhere to go.

I tried again to put the blob away and this time my hand stayed flameless. But as I released my grip, I ripped the flesh off my palm, leaving it clinging to the blob. I made a choked sound of agony. Beast shot painkilling endorphins through me, damping the pain and making me weirdly euphoric, while standing in the middle of a spell with a skinless hand. I rubbed the peeled strip of flesh off the blob and onto my leathers, tucked it all into my pocket, and sheathed the vamp-killer. Pulled a wooden stake with my good hand. Leo was already moving, trying to wake. His body was submerged and encased in green flames. His eyes popped open. Green pupils, face mad with rage.

I staked him. I'd done it before and he had lived. This was only wood, not silver, so I figured he'd be ticked off but would live to undeath again and without the drama of the last time. He went still, his eyes glazed over in what looked like real death. The magics crawled all over him, writhing, trying to wake him.

I spoke again to Eli, loud enough to carry, forcing my voice to be calm and controlled, despite the pain. "Spell activated. Booby trap in the closet. Minor injury to my hand. Made Leo unstable. He's out of commission. Bruiser is motionless. And—" I took in the second story. The hallway was filling with green gas, low down, heavier than air. "Tell the witches a dark magic spell is on the way down the stairs. To do some magical whammy and put it out, and ward against air."

"Roger that. Alex?"

"Spell had no effect so far as I can tell. I'll bring him down."

I smelled more than heard Eli move down the stairs, a faint change in the potency of the scent patterns. By one arm, I pulled Leo out of the small room and into a bathroom. I rolled him over and into the tub, and double-checked the stake's placement, midabdomen, where the descending aorta was, in a human. I gave it a little push to secure it and wiped his blood off along my wounded, skinless hand. Residual pain decreased and the oily-looking flesh seemed to grow more opaque in the first hint of healing. I rubbed every drop of the leftover blood into my skin and then wiped off on a fancy, tasseled hand towel and tossed it over the currently dead vamp, hiding the stake.

Leo was strong enough to get free if someone came in and pulled the stake loose, or if the magics in the house made it happen, or if it worked free somehow. I didn't carry silver handcuffs. Note to self. If I survived this, I'd get me a pair of them. I locked Leo in the small room and wedged a chair under the knob. He could get out of the bathroom easily, but at least I'd hear him do so.

Back in the security room, I bent into the gas, careful to keep my face above it, and rolled Alex up onto my shoulder. I paused to look over the security console, which was now little more than shattered plastic, broken screens, and fried wires, dancing with green flames. So much for knowing what was going on throughout the house. I raced back down the stairs, through the six inches of spell that was flowing down them like a river and pooling at the bottom of the stairway, hearing the sounds of furniture breaking and shouts. I dumped the Kid—still breathing—onto a champagne-toned sofa in the Louis XVI Room at the front of the house; the settee was above the floor enough to have him breathing real air. I rose upright, feeling unexpectedly breathless and a strain in my thigh muscles. I huffed a breath and stepped to the entrance. Brandon stood there, back to the door, staring at nothing with much the same expression as Bruiser wore upstairs. I had a feeling Brian was out of it too. I scanned the wide foyer and up the stairs and back toward the ballroom, taking it all in.

Some smaller part of me was analyzing and adding up the factors: Skinwalker burns. Vamps go crazy. Onorios freeze. Minor witch charms fizzle out. Humans and witches had to be in there somewhere.

Green flaming magics roiled across the floor from the stairs, but also were in free fall through the stairway opening and straight down. It clung to the ceiling and across, to slide down the walls. The spell was growing in speed and in volume, seemingly feeding on itself. Or feeding on the people in the house. *Skinwalker burns. Vamps go crazy. Onorios freeze. Humans and witches . . .* Yeah. The magics had to be getting their power from somewhere and we were as likely a source as any. I was too tired for the minimal exertion. I had a feeling that we could be used up and left drained. Maybe that was the intent of the spell. Tau had become a *senze onore . . .* and that might be a psychic and metabolic vampire. She was stealing the life and energy from us all.

I waded through the mist toward the ballroom entrance. The witches were screaming incantations in English, Celtic, French, and Latin, a jumbled auditory mass. The burn of their magic was heated and icy on the skin of my hands and face, a dozen workings flying at the same time, skidding and skipping over the green mist like flat pebbles over a pond. But the spell was still flowing in around my knees, unchecked. My strength was failing, despite Beast

shooting me full of the good stuff. But her gifts, even added
to my normal skinwalker powers, wouldn't be enough. Not
for long.

I took in the ballroom with a single breath. Beast filled
my head and my senses and evaluating as only a predator
can, by scent. And she smelled blood. It was spattered in
arcs and small pools on the parquet wood floor. The stink
of the mixed blood was witchy, human, vamp, Onorio, and
Mercy Blade, tasting acrid on my/our tongue as I tried to
figure who was hurt. The reek of mixed-species blood
bubbled in the green spell as if heated, the stench cooking
up a miasma of terror and rising anger in the melee.

Visually the place was a wreck. Tables and chairs had
been overturned and scattered. Witches and the human
plus-ones were huddled under wards and *hedges*. Green
energies encased ceiling, floors, and walls, licking out and
up. I stepped just inside the opening and slid my back
against the wall, behind Brian, where he stood, unmoving, a sword pointing at the floor, his face slack. I studied
the long room. Locating prey and predators. And I didn't
see attacking witches anywhere. What I saw was vamps
fighting.

Grégoire was closest to me, vamped out, whirling like
a dervish through the rising magics, his sword keeping a
wide swath of room open around him. But he didn't seem
to have any opponents at the moment. Gee DiMercy was
bleeding, a smeared trail of evaporating, floral-scented
blood leading to his hiding spot under the baby grand
piano. I smelled his flesh burning, the stink of singed
feathers, and his magics were glowing with some kind of
protection, but he couldn't heal himself and I couldn't tell
how bad he was injured. I had no idea why the green spell
burned Gee and me and not the others, but when I got a
long vacation I'd try to figure it out.

Beast chuffed at the thought.

Ming, also vamped, had bloodied fangs. She had bitten someone. Not good, if it was a witch or human. She
was holding two knives, like short swords. Standing atop
a small table in the nook called the Chaperone's Alcove.

She was barefoot now, beneath the scarlet dress, which was hitched into the feathered train.

Evan and Molly were huddled together beneath her *hedge 2.0* ward, in the narrow place between the fancy bar and the liquor cabinet behind it. Their heads were, so far, above the rising mist, their hands working their magics, probably trying to use the filter magic Evan had come up with to stop the vapor working from entering. They were safe. Safe-*ish*. For the moment.

Eli was on the bar, two weapons drawn, one aimed at Grégoire, one on Ming. Neither vamp seemed to have noticed him. His legs weren't on fire and his leathers weren't scorched, but he looked tired, as if he'd been in-country for a week with no sleep.

The other witches were protected under various *hedge of thorns* wards, except for Lachish. She walked toward Grégoire, her hands up, holding a ball of pale golden light. Within it, red motes of power zipped and swirled. She raised her hands as if to throw it at Grégoire.

I shouted, "No! Lachish, they're spelled by witches!"

She hesitated and I took my chance. From behind, I dove around Brian, pulling the blob, holding it in both hands before me. I threw my entire body at Grégoire's feet, sliding across the elegant parquet through the spell. Holding my breath. Behind the blob. I didn't catch fire, the blob protecting me in the Trueblood-Everhart working.

I took Grégoire out like a batter taking out home base. Except that I grabbed his feet as he toppled over me. Pressed the blob against the back of his knee. He landed on my back. All the breath left my body at once in an *oof* of sound and pain. I closed my lungs down, refusing them the breath they so desperately wanted. Grégoire rolled over me to the floor. His swords clashed once, just missing me. I spun and whipped the blob to Grégoire's head in a half-roundhouse, half-uppercut move I seldom used except in the dojo as a feint, sparring. I clocked the vamp once on the temple. His head knocked back. With my good hand, I staked him too, midcenter abdomen, nonlethal to such an old vamp. The green magics in his eyes flickered and died. He was out. I'd need two pairs of silver handcuffs.

I rolled to my feet and caught a breath, coughing. I held a hand out to Lachish to keep her from using the spell, but she had already let the heat of it wisp away.

That left Ming. "Eli!" I managed between coughs. "Standard ammo." I pointed at the table in the alcove. "Take her out!" The report of the nine-mil overrode my last two words. A three-tap. The shots echoed through the house. Ming fell, one hole in her cheek that seemed to enter at an upward angle, two in her heart. The heart shots would be an easy heal. The head shot, if it hit the brain, would take longer.

All around the room, the green flames fell. The vapor dying to little more than an oily film on the floor. And I couldn't see why, unless the spell had burned itself out. And I didn't think I'd be so lucky. I coughed and leaned on the bar beside Eli, who was breathing just fine and dandy. I sucked in air and lowered my head between my hands, trying to restore my spent energy.

I turned and rested my bruised back on the bar. Seconds passed. Silence filled the room. A waiting emptiness. Witches watching. Maybe the mist had been intended to kill the vamps, and now that they were technically out of action, it was over.

Lachish stepped back. Slowly the witches began to drop the various wards they were using. Molly dropped her *hedge*. "Son of a witch on a switch," she whispered, and shook herself like a wet dog after a long rain. "Here," she said, handing me two charms, carved from unstained wood. "The bear is for healing, the fish is to deflect violent spell attack."

"What the . . .," Evan said. His eyes went wide. Staring behind me.

Without thought, I pivoted. Freeing a vamp-killer and a nine-mil from their holsters. Marlene was dancing on the stairway from the second floor, visible about midway up. She was wearing transparent red harem pants and a flaring silky skirt over them, with a flaring, beaded tunic, and her bare feet drummed on the floor in a four-four rhythm. *Marlene Nicaud was inside with the witches.* Had been inside all day. No wonder everything had gone to hell in a handbasket.

"She was not here when I cleared the house this morning before the ward was set," Eli said.

"Obfuscation spells," I suggested. "Good ones." Eli cursed softly and I said, "Even money says she was in the closet and I triggered the spell. We might lose the final payment on the witch contract unless we discover a hidden room or something that Amalie didn't disclose, where the witches hid."

He chuckled coldly as I returned my weight to my feet and tried to find my balance. "Long as we get away intact, I don't care about the money, babe." I heard *shinck*s, and *click*s and *clack*s, metallic and otherwise. The stink of gun oil wafted from him too. He was checking and laying out weapons on the bar top. He had clearly hidden a stash beneath the bar.

"Yeah. Totally, my brother." I pushed away from the bar and raised my voice. "Lachish. They're coming. They were upstairs, hidden in the family quarters or a hidden room." She cursed too, but the words were a spell she was readying.

"Come to think of it," I said again to Eli, "we may have to exist on PB and J for a while. I may not get paid for Leo's part either."

"Why's that?" Eli asked as if we were playing checkers and not facing death by burning or asphyxiating on magical gas.

"This was my fight to protect Leo—who I staked. His people—one who I staked, and another you shot at my direct order. I think I broke my contract."

"Dang, babe. That sounds like a great story for the hot tub."

"We have a hot tub?"

"We survive this, I'm buying us one."

I chuffed. I had only a few moments before Marlene was in the room with us. I explained the spell to Lachish and she called out orders to her people. Lachish's witches snapped up personal wards again and took places for a full circle—witches standing shoulder to shoulder, in an actual circle. They began a working that sparked the air blue and purple. It looked aggressive and dangerous. Go, Lachish.

Mixed magics sizzled on the air like burning meat. My left palm, holding the blob, broke open again to leak down my wrist. My hand ached, but I didn't let go of Evan's gift. The pain that had been muted by Leo's blood screamed back, working through the cracks of my fingers where the air touched the burned flesh. If Marlene was here, Tau was close behind. And the spell was stronger now than before. The Nicauds had been scoping out the place and the occupants, a tactical maneuver, similar to the icons in the yard, to see what we had and how we'd use it. They were one step, or maybe three steps, ahead of us all the way.

The red-dressed witch appeared in the doorway. The magics on the air were suddenly so strong they skidded on my damaged skin like hot asphalt and broken glass. Tactical maneuvers . . . Were the Nicauds former military? That wasn't in the dossiers prepared by the Kid.

As if reading my mind, Eli said, "This isn't going down like attrition warfare, where success is quantified by enemy killed or disabled, weapons and infrastructure destroyed, and territory occupied. This is going down like a game. A video game."

"Like the ones we found at the Nicauds' old house."

"Yeah. We've missed something. Our intel is bad."

"A game run by a cat," I said. "Cat and mouse. Play with the mouse. Maybe hurt it a little. Let it go, let it think it was free. Then pounce again." I knew diddly-squat about video games, but I knew cats. I patted the bar and Eli leaped to the top as I stepped away, across the room, spreading us as targets. Grégoire's body was now between Eli and the Truebloods and me. Molly, who had been listening to the byplay, nodded at me, looked at her husband, and snapped up her ward, which was a darker tint than before, likely modified on the fly for gaseous spells.

"Options?" Eli asked.

"Not much. We have to keep the spell contained and not let it into the streets. Let's see what the witches can do. We're not dying. Yet."

"You're worse than Uncle Sam."

A laugh startled out of me, despite the danger, and I chuckled the words "You wound me."

Marlene's dance rhythm mutated, the vibration through the floor, a pounding ethnic beat that had elements of tribal American, African, and island. She moved into the room with balletic grace, the way lava moved. Swirling down a hill, taking everything with it. She was dark-skinned, with a mass of hair that coiled and curled down her back, a turban over her head. Full-lipped, with a broad nose. Wide, glistening eyes. Skin gleaming ruddy in the red magics that spun from her.

She performed a rippling dance step that started at her feet and undulated up her body to her head. A move that was part of the spell, directing it with her will and gestures.

Flames of power flared out from the witch, fire tipped with the pale spring green of her daughter's workings. Smelling of iron and salt and scorched wood. Everything happened at one, in overlapping segments of time or maybe intersecting segments of my awareness.

Magics and energies slid along my skin. Kissing it. Promising pain unimaginable, except that hadn't happened. The leathers were spelled against magics, even ones as strong as the green vapor spell. So as long as I kept my clothes on, and I didn't simply asphyxiate on the gasses, I was good. My partner wasn't good, however. He was fighting a cough. His skin had gone pale as if he was ready to knock on death's door.

I tossed him the two charms Molly had given me and instantly he looked better. We shared a nod. Lachish's huge witch circle at the back of the room was so full of power it was nearly black with the energies.

I clenched the blob. *Stupid name,* Beast thought. Which made me laugh, a sound more like a frustrated sob. The Nicauds' spell was growing, stretching, slipping over the working at the back of the ballroom like oil over water, coating it entirely. It was also leaching my own energies as I breathed, feeding the vapor spell.

A human male hiding behind a table in the hallway slumped to the floor with a thump, unbreathing, his energy drained. A busboy racing down the hallway to get away, fell, and tumbled. *Crap.* That changed everything. The Nicuads were now willing to hurt everyone, human, witches, vamps, me. The only tactic I could think of was to drop the outer wards and evacuate the mansion. Which would take the spell and the fight out into the street and hurt the bystanders and then the first responders.

Run. Hide. Jane is stupid, Beast thought.

Yeah, I thought back.

All this thinking in less than two breaths. My head was swimming. Eli staggered on the bar top.

Already, outside, I heard sirens. Someone, probably one of our sharpshooter teams, had spotted something through the windows and had called police backup and ambulance. But the first responders couldn't be let in, even if they could get in through the outer house ward. Things in here were beyond unstable. Anything I did might put the victims in greater danger. Flying by the seat of my pants and bashing heads didn't sound like a good solution to this. I didn't know what to do.

Eli crouched upright on the bar, still high above the fog, and maneuvered so he was between Marlene and the Truebloods. I fingered the blob, gripping and releasing, the pain in my burned hand easing again. Trying to think. Trying to decide on . . . anything.

Tau entered the room, delicate and tiny, like a tree nymph, with glorious hair, full and curly, standing out as Angie's did when her magic was high, in a nimbus of power that writhed and snaked. There was an old myth about a woman—a goddess? A demon?—with a head full of snakes. Had *she* been a double-gened witch, her myth gaining power through the ages into a deity? Tau wore a green dress, a floral watercolor print in emerald, mint, and misty-sage green. She danced like her mother in style, but where her mother moved like molten earth, Tau moved like water, flooding the room with her magics.

As if a dam had broken, the green power of the working boiled up from the floor and walls and raged higher in the room, falling from overhead, from the height of the doorway, rising again on the floor. Filling the ballroom like a deluge, expanding like the sea through a broken dike, flowing through the doorways, down the walls, a waterfall of power that eddied and shifted into whirlpools of rainbows. The vapor magic flowed into the working at the back of the room. Quickly the magics were waist high. A witch inside started to scream and writhe, slapping at her own skin as if bees were stinging her. Lachish's huge protective ward began to crack.

To the side, Molly whispered, *"Carraig,"* in the lilting tone of her family's oldest wards, in Irish Gaelic. Her own ward hardened yet again, but it wasn't the same power signature as the one Evan had made in the yard. They had little air left. Several of other witches knew a working to keep out air, but not enough of them and the circle at the back thinned. More witches fell inside the ward.

The protective circle fell with a shower of sparks and a sizzle of power that was instantly swept up by the green misty flames.

Doors slammed shut throughout the house, a resounding multidimensional whamwhamwham of sound and vibration. In Beast-sight, the entrance to the ballroom and every doorway leading out, now glowed with blacklight magic. Exactly like the magic Angie Baby used. Frustration and fear gathered in my throat, wanting to be screamed out. The Nicauds had just added their own wards to the one the Witch Conclave had created. If I had wanted to escape, I should have done it before now.

The witches broke up and raised smaller wards, in small groups. Or tried to. The green mist began to suck the energy out of them. All but Molly's ward.

"Molly?"

"Got this," she said.

"Good to hear." I lifted my arms. The green magics

were up to my chest, and ankle high on Eli. He might not
be able to see the magics, but he had deduced how they
worked. The flaming pool was now tipped in black, stinging, burning my hands.

Molly pressed her fingers through her ward, toward
the dancing witches, saying, *"Múchtóir dóiteáin. Múch."*

Marlene staggered. Tau threw out her hand at Molly
and said, *"Confuto. Retardo."*

Molly's offensive working exploded in a scattering of
scarlet sparks. Molly dropped like the dead. Evan caught her
and her reinforced *hedge 2.0* brightened over them, glowing
red and blue. Half of it was now Evan's magics. *Dang.* One
more use of magic and he'd be permanently out of the closet.
My godchildren would be forevermore in danger.

"Jane," Eli demanded. "Options."

"Eli," I whispered. "Take the shot."

He fired. But the weapon clicked oddly. Misfire. With
his off hand, and a second weapon, Eli took another shot.
It too misfired. The spells of the green mist were multilayered and multipurpose. Eli cursed softly and, in a single motion, pulled a knife, throwing at Tau. The whirling
blade stopped in the air and fell with a sound of shattering steel.

The Nicauds turned at the sound. Marlene snarled
when she saw the broken blade. Ignoring the human on
the bar as useless, she looked at me and said some word I
didn't recognize. "Now, my daughter," she said, and
whirled something around her head. In Beast vision it
looked like two electric stones tied together with a length
of black magic rope, a spelled bolo, one of those things
horsemen used to trap horses, if they didn't care if the
horse broke a leg. It whipped through the air. Once . . .

Tau danced to Grégoire on the floor.

Twice . . . The bolo spell whirled.

Marlene aimed her gaze at me.

Someone called my name, the voice broken, full of
pain.

Three times . . . Marlene released it. The magical rope
slid from her fingers.

"Jump!" I shouted.

Time slowed down, that situational awareness that sometimes gives battle the consistency of taffy. In a single motion, I caught my breath, set the weapons on the bar, and again dove through the fog, sliding under the piano. My hands caught on fire again. My face burned. My hair smoked. But as I slid through the mist and into the blue magics of Gee's personal protection, the flames on me were snuffed.

The bolo hit the bar, just behind where I had stood, wrapping around it and through it, cutting the antique burled wood into four equal-sized chunks of smoking kindling. At my shout, Eli had leaped and landed on top of the Trueblood's hardened ward. *That was close.*

Marlene screamed in fury. Whirled to follow my movement. And threw a second bolo spell at me.

Still sliding across the floor, I bowled into Girrard DiMercy, picking up his slight form as I rolled over my burden and to my feet on the far side of the piano. The bolo was wrapped around nothing but air, about a foot away from my skin. It fell to the floor in a shower of blue as I placed Gee on top of the piano. We were both coughing and full of the stink of burned hair, skin, and feathers. His voice a pale imitation of its usual power, Gee said. "I didn't know if you would hear me. Not after—"

"I heard."

Eli jumped back onto the broken bar. And threw another knife at Tau, who ignored him and his broken blade. But trying to buy me some time.

Marlene threw another spell at me. It spat when it hit Gee's magics and fell. Marlene screamed in fury. With her attention on me, conclave witches were abandoning ship, turning their attention to getting through the black, woven wards on all the doors. It was just occurring to them that they were trapped. Tau hit one with a knockout spell and the woman simply crumpled to the floor. Tau laughed and hit another.

Gee's face was blistered. Neck and hands raw. Burned before he opened whatever magics he had used to shield himself. Magics that had let me in. Another thing to think about later. His burns weren't quite as bad as my own, but they were bad enough. There were slashes in his throat. Two fang slashes.

I remembered Ming's bloody fangs. She had clearly attacked him. He wiped both hands through the blood of his throat and onto me, on my face and my injured hand. The pain instantly eased and beneath the blood I saw actual skin on my palm. "What—?"

Beneath Marlene's screams, Gee said what I had thought only moments before. "We two are the only ones burned. We two who are goddess born. My blood, a drop of Ming's blood, and your blood upon the weapon made by your friends." He closed my healed fist around the blob, which appeared in his bloody fingers, stolen from my pocket as if by prestidigitation. "You are protected now. You must protect the children. Always." His eyes closed as he slumped on the piano.

I turned back to the ballroom. Marlene's anger had fueled the green flames all around her. Red fire danced over her body, licking but not burning.

Beyond her, Tau pulled something from her bodice, but her back was to me, and I couldn't see what it was, except it was small. She said what sounded like *"Meus es tu."* And she struck down with her hand. Down onto Grégoire, who still lay on the floor. Magics ballooned out around him like a black flower blooming through the green.

That couldn't be good.

Tau turned to the witches and pointed at them, accusing. "You didn't help us when we asked, when we *begged*."

Marlene hunched in, her angry screams echoing away. Tears had tracked down her face, leaving black mascara trails in her makeup. In Cajun patois, she said, "You. You di'n' stop the fanged devils when we show you proof of they evil. You done hid you heads in de sand and let dem take our young, you did. My Antoine, him die because you refuse him help. Now you pay."

"Now you pay!" Tau echoed. She clapped her hands together twice and said, *"Maintenant. Vous tuerez. Assassiner."*

I understood the last word, just as Grégoire stood. He moved the way a marionette did when a puppeteer pulled it upright on its strings. He was still vamped out. There was a peacock pin stuck into his chest, just inches above the stake I'd stuck in him. Grégoire opened his vamped-out eyes. The black of the pupils were filled with green flames. He had a sword in each hand. Face slack. He stared at the wall.

Tau smiled and twirled her fingers.

Grégoire spun and raised his swords to Tau like an offering. She slid her thumbs along the steel. Her blood slicked down across the blades. The vamp staggered toward the Truebloods. One sword lifted above Molly and Evan's ward.

"Assassiner," Tau repeated.

Kitssss. Beast reached inside and ripped her claws through the Gray Between.

The world swirled and roared around me. The gray magics erupted out. And then died. I lost my footing as an unfamiliar pain slammed into my chest, stealing my breath. I caught myself on the bar, not sure how I'd gotten there. Not sure what had happened. Except that my chest was aching as if I'd taken a hit. I glanced down and saw a scuff in the scarlet leather jacket. Yeah. Somehow, in the Gray Between, I'd been spell-stabbed. The leather/Dyneema/ chain-mail counterspells had protected me.

Eli's weapons were laid in a row on the bar, like a line of death, but nothing he had on hand had worked. He looked like death warmed over, face greenish, fingers trembling. I grabbed up my vamp-killer and raised it across my body in the Spanish Circle's cross-guard.

Grégoire spun past me, knocking my clumsy block, sending my blade spinning across the room. His sword circled, a flashy move in preparation to cut Molly's ward.

The blade fell and sliced through the energies like a hot knife through butter. The magics sizzled and spat and fell.

Lachish dropped her ward for half a second, and threw the orb of magics she had gathered once before. It wasn't the tightly shaped weapon it had been, but it also wasn't weak.

It hit Grégoire, cutting like a scissors through his marionette strings. He fell in a heap. The magics slithered like snakes up his body and inside, crawling through the hole in his belly where the stake still rested. I hoped Lachish hadn't just killed Leo's boy toy and best fighter, but I also didn't have time to help him now, because Leo walked back through the door from the stairway. The stake was still in his chest. He too had a brooch in his flesh, pinned through his throat.

"Oh, crap," I breathed. Leo had been left upstairs, incapacitated. With *them* . . .

Tau sidled up to him in a four-beat step, step-step-turning-step-step, as if she shared a dance with him. She yanked the stake out of him. Vamp blood splattered and Tau licked the stake. Leo looked at her and laughed.

Okay. Not good.

Ming slid off the small table and onto the floor, standing. Unlike Grégoire and Leo, Ming had no pin. Maybe she didn't need one. Maybe she had been under the control of Tau for so long that she was biddable just by the pulse of magic. My bringing her as my ace in the hole suddenly looked a lot less brilliant. She walked with the snake-spine-slither of the vamp on the prowl, head swiveling too far to the left and too far to the right. Hunting.

Ming set her eyes on Lachish. Leo set his eyes on Molly. Grégoire mewled, where he lay on the floor, and tried to stand. There was too much magic. That's what had happened to the Gray Between. I was surrounded by the green mist. It was on my clothes, on my skin, in my hair. It was interfering with everything. And if I couldn't get to the Gray Between, I couldn't shift, couldn't heal, and for certain couldn't bubble time.

I repocketed the blob and raced to the nearest Onorio. I tore his leather jacket open to find enough blades to run that good-sized butcher shop. I took three, a long sword in my right hand and two in my left, the blades held forward and back, like a helicopter blade. I cut through the bloody blob with all three steel blades, coating the edges with the mixed blood, smeared there by Gee, and with magics. Then I raced to Tau. And I cut her.

CHAPTER 20

In the Blood of My Enemy

She threw up her arm in a defensive gesture, shock on her face. Her defensive spell was too late to stop all damage, as if defensive magics hadn't been prepared for. As if was no one was supposed to fight back with mundane weapons.

Stupid girl, Beast thought as my blades slid through the rising wards, cutting.

It wasn't a killing strike. Her raw power was enough to stop the edges of the swords long before that. But it was enough. Maybe. Moving in Beast-speed, I watched as two of my circling blades cut along her raised arm, shallow enough to do no long-term damage, but deep enough to hurt like a son of a gun. Taking her blood with them. Anointing my blades, the same way she had anointed Grégoire's, because, for sure, blood had been part of the Nicauds' dark working.

Killing claws in the blood of my enemy, Beast screamed inside me. The sound came out of my throat, a puma's fighting scream of rage.

Tau screamed back, the sound a shrieking peal of anguish, so close to a vampire's death scream it was hard to determine the difference. She dropped to the floor beneath an emerald ward, hard as diamond, cradling her arm. Her mother rushed to her and slid into the ward as if it were made of water, already muttering incantations of healing.

I slashed my helicopter blades through the mist in the air, and the green fog we were breathing parted. Gathered. Tightened into tight, irregular, balls of dull green, like sleet. Congealed and hardened. The solidified mist fell to the floor, raining down with slight pings. The air cleared instantly except around Tau and her mother, where the mist grew more dense and then settled on their personal wards like a layer of glue. Score one for blood-magic used against a blood-magic user by a nonmagic user. That had to be record of some kind.

The edge of one blade I had used on the air was coated with a gummy slime. I tossed it out of the way, to land with a clang in the corner. I still had two blood blades. I raced to Leo.

Yanking his arm, I whirled him around and pulled back my right arm. I stabbed Leo in the center of his abdomen, exactly where the stake had been. "Molly!" I called. As the blade slid from Leo's undead flesh, I plucked the brooch free and whipped it through the air to Evan.

His ward parted and closed again with an audible snap, the brooch in his hand. Beside him, Molly was waking again, her hands going to her belly.

Something hit me, in the same spot where the scarlet leathers had been nicked. I looked down to see another scrape. Something hit me again, a little to the left, but hard enough this time to hurt. Green energies swarmed in front of my face, a confused-looking mass of undirected power.

Tau had thrown a spell at me. The magics had impacted my leathers, rebounded, and gathered themselves. In front of my eyes, her working reshaped itself. And shot back. The spell hit Tau, who fell again. Silent this time, her screaming having stopped cold.

Gee. He had wiped his blood all over me and all over the blob. Somehow he had warded me. Or my clothes.

Or . . . added to the spells on my leathers that protected me against magical attack. Yeah. *That.*

I whipped my head back to Leo. The green in his eyes fluttered like flames in a wind, and vanished. He blinked once and his pupils constricted. His fangs clicked back. "My Jane. What . . . ?" He looked down and his eyes widened in a purely human gesture. "You stabbed me? *Mon Dieu!*" Oddly enough, he sounded surprised, maybe even traumatized at the reality.

"Yep. After I staked you. That's why you feel so crappy. You can thank me later." I put an Onorio blade in his hand and said, "I figured it out. The young witch's blood"—I pointed at the bloody blade—"is also Ming's blood, because she's, in a way, Ming's scion."

And then it hit me. Every working of the Nicauds was blood-based. And their blood or Ming's blood was disruptive to the workings. "It's also powering the spells she's using," I said. "Bringing Ming? Was an act of genius."

"But of course, *mon amour.*" Leo flipped the short sword, testing its balance. *"Je suis brillante."* He had just taken credit for my idea. Of course. He lunged into the fight, taking on Ming. Marlene stepped away from her daughter and threw a red-hued spell at Lachish. Lachish and two other witches, standing in a triangle, shielded against the attack spell and threw one of their own, coating Marlene in a cocoon of magics that looked like spun pearl, if pearl came alive and vibrated with might.

Tau was on her knees, under a ward, picking apart her own spell, as if peeling tar off her body.

Now was my chance to obey Gee, his words still ringing in my head. *You must protect the children. Always.* Molly's children. I tapped on the mixed magic ward and Evan looked around before dropping it. I grabbed the True-bloods and hauled them bodily out of the ballroom, through the Chaperone's Alcove, and the short hallway through the office. With another swipe of the Tau-bloodied, vamp-killer short sword, I cut through the black-light wards, and we all raced out the side door.

The couple looked like crap, but there was no blood and I didn't smell amniotic fluid. However, Molly's fancy dress was blackened and ruined, and I didn't want to know what had happened to it. I pressed the blob into Evan's hands. "You said it could take three people out of the ward. Baby makes three, in my book. Go. Tell the ones out front to be ready for anything."

"Fine. You take this, then." Careful not to touch the two brooches together and knock me out again, he handed me the brooch that had been in Leo's flesh, still tacky with vamp blood. I skimmed it into the small pocket where the blob had rested.

Before either of them could reply, I shoved them through the witch *hedge of thorns* and into the side yard, to safety. In the same motion, I ripped at the Gray Between and Beast forced a half form onto me in a wrenching of bones that left me huddled in a mewling heap on the small porch.

"Are you okay?" someone asked.

"What about us?" another voice complained.

I made it to my feet, the toes of my combat boots now massive, my paws pushing out the sides, which had been made to change shape with them. I had to say that they looked really weird with the extra width. I caught a breath, aching in every part of me, as I tried to straighten my back.

Behind me, the waitstaff, the chef, the sommelier, and a few others huddled on the small stoop. They had followed me out through the sword-sliced Nicaud door ward and now all were pressed back at the sight of me, squishing each other tight against the house, and because there was only one blob, they were still trapped. "You're out of the house on the porch," I said. "That's all I got."

"What the hell are you?" the chef asked.

I chuffed a laugh and sprinted back through the door just as Beast bubbled time.

My belly cramped and tore. I stumbled and a knobby knee hit the floor before I could catch myself on the office desk. I knocked papers off in a flying shuffle that caught in the air the moment they slid away from my time bubble. I held my gut with a hand as I pushed upright again and felt something new in my belly. A depression ran along my right side, a space where the muscle had ripped and left only soft tissue like a hole in a foam pillow. It ran from my ribs down to my hipbone, soft and slightly spongy, as if something was missing like a part of my abdominal wall and muscle. I chuffed in disquiet, and the sound was growly.

Holding my side, I stalked through the house, my narrow waist and wide hips moving with a catlike roll, despite the missing parts. The sounds from the ballroom were echoing, heavy, deep, and vibrating painfully on my ears. The magics had a sound too, a rustling, shushing sound like fire reaching for dry leaves high in a tree. And the room ahead was glowing a reddish shade, different from the greenish one when I left only a moment ago in real time.

I stopped in the doorway. In real time, the ballroom was on fire. The walls were burning, a green fire that was paused midway, licking up the draperies. Black and red smoke billowed into a separate working, the form of which I couldn't yet see. The parquet flooring was blackened and heated beneath my boots. Amalie was going to be one unhappy hostess. And the Witch Conclave would never get their security deposit back.

But there was something symbolic about the fire. Fire was used to cleanse, purify, sanctify. Just as I had once cleaned my soul home of Gee's blue watching eyes, the Nicauds were cleansing the witches and the vamps. But their form of cleansing was brought about with blood and suffering and the kidnapping and draining of a vampire and the deaths of many humans who had been dumped in a swamp. This was using evil against evil, and that was never successful.

The Nicaud witches were standing back to back, throwing fireballs at their enemies. The workings were about the size of softballs and they were being tossed underhanded, the orbs looking like red glitter that had been pasted over celery-green spherical Christmas tree ornaments, with a hint of black in the centers. There were three in the air and two about to impact witch wards. A sixth had smashed onto the ward of the woman who had asked Leo the good questions. Her ward was falling and her skin was burned, second-degree blisters weeping and breaking. The attacking sphere was in the act of changing shape, spreading out. Flames licked to her, as if hungry to taste her flesh, ready to wrap the witch up in a binding of fiery pain. Three other witches were down and burning. It was no longer Gee and me burning. Now it was everyone. The rest of the witches had retreated to the Chaperone's Alcove and the doors to the rest of the house, where they were working to remove the Nicauds' sealing ward.

Leo and Grégoire were engaging the Nicauds, one on either side, and appeared to be in the act of batting the fireballs aside with bloodied swords. Ming stood by the vamps, her eyes still green with flames but not reacting to anything. Her body displayed a number of wounds, suggesting that the fighting vamps had cut her each time they needed fresh blood on their blades. There was something horrible and evil about that, but I couldn't deal with the thought of a blood-sucking vamp victim who should be rescued. Again. Who had been made into a victim by witches and now by her own kind. Maybe I could fix it later. Tomorrow, Tara.

I went inside the ballroom and considered all the people and my options. I could try to take them all outside, one by one or even two by two, and stack them up on a porch. I could try to put out the fire with buckets of water. But all that would take *time* I didn't have. Not with my belly cramping so badly. So it looked as though I'd have to do this the hard way, flying by the seat of my pants like always. One day it was gonna get me killed. I wondered if today was that day.

I stepped to the dark working that was about to land on the wise witch and poked it with my blade, bringing it into my time. The working fell to the floor and darkened. Like a dried-out shriveled fruit, maybe. *Good enough.* I poked all the Nicauds' attacking spell orbs that were hanging in the air and watched them fall. Not like fruit. More like rotting water balloons.

I turned my Nicaud-bloodied blade across my body and cut through the Nicauds' ward, stepping up to Marlene. Pressed the point into her neck, just deep enough to draw blood and make her gasp when she felt it, I wrapped my other hand around her waist and pulled her in. She left real time and entered the bubble with me.

"Move, try a spell, and I'll cut through your neck and out the other side." My voice had become a growl in the half form and my mouth felt wrong, making it hard to form words. "Then I'll cut out, forward, and take out your esophagus, trachea, jugulars, and carotids. You'll bleed out in seconds." Marlene swallowed, the sound loud in the odd vibrations of bubbled time. She spread her fingers and raised her hands.

"What dis is?" she asked. "What you do?" Her tone changed and she said, "You stop time!"

I pulled her even closer. "We're going out the front door. You are going to be quiet. Totally silent. You are going to walk the whole way without stumbling or tripping or trying to get away." I took a breath and caught the scent of her blood.

I'd miscalculated. Maybe a lot. Before I could exhale, Marlene shoved back against me, allowing the blade to slice through her flesh. Her blood splattered over me, and into her working. The magics whipped out black and brilliant blue, the bolo spell. It shouldn't have worked in the bubble of time. It should have been inert. Instead the black strands wrapped around me, and the electric balls pressed to my spine. I stopped. Just . . . stopped.

Marlene kept one hand on me and swiveled her head, staring through the energies of the Gray Between. But when she spoke, it wasn't about my magics or the fact that time was stopped. She said, "You de one what hurt my boys."

"Yeah," I said, not backing down even though it might be smarter to keep my mouth shut. "They raped that girl. They deserved way worse."

My arms were bound tightly against me. My fingers began to tingle as the bolo did its work, tightening, its magic binding into me, despite the magics on the leathers. My sword slid to the floor. Guns didn't work in the Gray Between. I couldn't get to a bladed weapon. But I had my claws. . . .

"Dey. My. Boys. Unnerstan? *Mine!*"

I nodded, unable to do anything but agree.

"You like de one what kill my Antoine. Evil like dat . . . dat *animal*."

Yes, I thought. *Skinwalker. But not spear-finger or liver-eater. Not u'tlun'ta.*

Marlene slid one of the sterling stakes out of my hair and pulled me across the room, my feet following an unspoken command to obey her actions, the bolo spell forcing me to comply. But my body wasn't acting with a normal sense of balance and I tripped over something on the floor. Swayed drunkenly.

Marlene stabbed Grégoire with the silver stake. "No," I tried to say, but the word was stuck in my throat with the gathering tears. They filled my eyes and I blinked against them. She removed a second stake and stabbed Ming. She pulled me to Leo and repeated the motion. "Hem you pick up," she said, patting my arms, releasing the binding on them. But before I could react, the bolo tightened on my chest, making it difficult to breathe.

Unable to refuse, I bent at the knees and lifted Leo over my shoulder. My breath whooshed out of me in a pained grunt. My belly tore again. Leo made a soft breathy sound, too low for anyone but me to hear, and went still, his blood trickling down my back. But he didn't move or resist.

Worse, I had a feeling I was bleeding internally. The working was leaching away my energy. I was dead on my feet. Leo and I were both in bad shape.

Lastly, Marlene pulled me to her daughter and took my hand, forcing me to touch her. I nearly fell to my knees as my strength was depleted. Bubbling time for two—four now—was not a wise move.

Tau gasped and looked around. "What—? Mama?"

"We gots what we come for. Let's go."

"What is *that*?" Tau pointed at me.

"Dat dere a monster carrying a monster. We use dem both."

Together we four walked out of the burning room, out of the house. The three security types who I had positioned on the front porch before the ward went back up were frozen in real time. Ro Moore, Brenda Rezak, and Wrassler, facing the front door, armed, holding weapons.

I tried to reach out and touch one of them, but I didn't make it before Marlene grabbed my knobby fingers and yanked back on them. Dislocating my fingers. I dropped to my knees and vomited all over the porch and dropped Leo with a thump that sounded slow and basso. I landed on him. The bolo spell bound me tighter, cutting into my skin where it touched. I smelled my blood on the air. Marlene didn't let go of me or my fingers or her daughter. She kicked me, her foot finding the torn place in my belly with unerring accuracy.

I retched and tasted blood, but used the time to assess my options. I was still tied up in the bolo spell. I didn't know what the working did, other than cut into me and make me agreeable to most anything they ordered, which was bad enough, but could become a lot worse, fast. I didn't have the blob anymore. But I did have the brooch. And Leo's blood. And the bolo might work differently in no time. Like, maybe I could get out of it. Somehow.

Marlene studied the witch ward and laughed. She said to her daughter, "Don' let go of dis monster. But put out your hand. Break dis ward. Dis nothing for you power."

I lifted the hand on the witch's off side—the not broken hand—and checked for the brooch. Still there. Then I eased my fingers between Leo's body and mine and got two fingertips and my thumb around the silver stake. His belly was in bad shape, numerous cuts, punctures, and what felt like intestines (assuming vamps have intestines?) pushing up at the nexus of the wounds. The stink of silver-tainted vamp blood assailed my nostrils, revolting on my tortured stomach.

I gagged again, and the tearing sensation in my belly doubled me over on the porch floor.

Leo smells wrong. Smells like meat, two days dead, Beast thought. *Or like Son of Darkness with silver inside.*

Which would be about right. To prepare for tonight, Leo had gotten blood-full, probably blood-drunk at one point. And he had surely squeezed out a few drops of the good stuff belonging to the oldest of all vamps to sip on. And now Leo was full of silver, just like the SoD.

I pulled the stake out of Leo's belly and set it on the

porch floor, careful to not let it *tink* or thump down, in a darker shadow. Just as carefully I extruded my bloody claws and cut the Morse code for SOS into the porch floor. Three dots, three dashes, three dots.

As I carved, Tau inspected the structure of the magical working ward, fingers running over the energies frozen in no time. In the Gray Between, the striations and overlapping flaps of the ward looked like geometric forms—triangles and polygons made of light. Tau pressed her fingers into a faint, narrow crack between two angles and ripped a small hole. She placed one hand over the hole. Black electricity blossomed out of her palm. The rent in the red ward stretched and pulled.

I twisted my body and scratched the SOS again, just in case Eli didn't get it the first time. I wiped my bloody fingers over the porch, hoping that someone was around to smell what had happened and track us. Or they might at least see the blood and the SOS and figure out it was something bad. I went back to kneading my belly, feeling the torn muscle like mush beneath my fingers. It was bad. Real bad. But . . . I felt Leo's weight shift, just a millimeter or so. His fingers tapped on my back. Tap, tap, tap. Scratch, scratch, scratch. Tap, tap, tap. SOS. Leo had seen me leave the note and was letting me know he was less incapacitated than the witches and I had thought. But how to use that?

With her other hand, Tau widened the hole, her palm sliding over the ward in a large oval, and pressed outward. A segment separated and fell into the yard like an egg-shaped door.

Leo was tugging on the bolo spell. How could he even do that? Then, *Ooooh yeah*. It was likely made with blood magic. Tau's blood. Which was Ming's blood. Ming had sworn to Leo. Ming's blood was Leo's blood. Ming's magic was Leo's magic. That would have been a great thing to understand before this. But . . . I was betting that neither one of us had had the time to figure that out or decide how to use it. The bolo loosened and slid on my body. I hissed with electric shock.

Marlene yanked on my broken fingers, the pain pulling me to my feet, and Leo with me, through the opening and into the night. The bright lights, flashing red and blue, streetlights, vehicle headlights, neon in windows, all seemed to smear across my retinas like lights in slo-mo camera footage, long swirling swaths of brightness on the dark of a New Orleans night.

There were police officers everywhere and Leo's security people, including Derek, who should have been elsewhere, not that I blamed him for deserting one post for where the action was. We passed close to him, and I used my drunken staggering to get close. I flicked my good fingers at Derek's face, seeing the blood fly from my fingertips and stop, hanging on the air. In real time, Derek would get hit and know that something was wrong.

Still in the Gray Between, we walked down the street, me weaving, the strength leaving my body along with a blood trail to follow. Leo's hands bumped against my butt with each step, over and over, and I knew that he was enjoying the ride. I lurched off the sidewalk onto the street and landed hard on my heel, my shoulder ramming up at him. He almost gasped when my shoulder thrust into his solar plexus. But my gut tore just a bit more.

Jane, must shift back, Beast thought.

"I have to stop," I said aloud.

"No," Marlene said, jiggling my dislocated fingers.

My throat made a strangled noise of pain. "Then I'll die, right here." I let myself fall to my knees again. They were taking a beating tonight. "I have to stop . . ." I paused, thinking through what I was going to say, knowing it had to be something that didn't let them start to figure out how to bubble time. No way could I let these two figure out how to do that. So I lied about one thing on my person that I could do without, lied to gain us some time. Lied to keep my secret. Lied to give Leo access to the one thing I could offer. The one thing I had refused to offer, ever. Until now. "I have to stop using the gorget. It only gets an hour of time per person. It needs . . . um . . . sunlight to replenish it."

"What dis gorget is?"

"On my neck. The gold-and-citrine necklace. It's what lets me change time. It has to spend time in sunlight to stay . . . charged." Charged? I was so lame.

Marlene yanked the gold gorget, forcing me forward and down to my knees again with the violence of the ripping. The clasp broke and scored the nape of my neck. Blood welled to the surface of my skin. An offering, if Leo could figure that out. I felt Leo slowly lift a hand and wipe my blood. I knew he was licking his fingers. And for once I wasn't irritated that he took my blood. I didn't have much strength left and I needed him to be fast and strong. A master vamp who got the drop on a witch could bend her mind so fast she'd never see it coming. Leo took some more blood and I turned our bodies away from the witches so they wouldn't see.

Deep inside, Beast growled, a low vibration of warning. I felt Leo's mind near mine, a shadow in my soul home. My first thought was that he was trying to bind me again. My second thought was a realization that he was stealing power from my soul home. He had been there once, not that long ago, chained to me. And maybe that allowed him access to the spiritual power stored there. Or maybe the mere fact that I offered him my blood gave him access, the same way blood magic worked when the sacrifice was willing. The cavern space went dim and the flames in the fire pit lowered, growing cold.

I could feel Leo growing stronger. He tasted my blood again. I thought about telling him to stop, but . . . the bolo spell was trying to kill me. His fingers tangled in the bolo spell and loosed it from my torso. I managed a single full, deep breath. Relief flooded through me.

Leo took a drop of my blood. Funny how anything that saved my butt was okay, even things that had only recently repulsed me. Leo with some of my blood. A vamp knocking out some witches.

"Dis t'ing got no magic in it," Marlene said. "But I sell it and make us some money."

"I have to stop," I whispered, the warning to Leo. And the Gray Between slid to the side and disappeared.

Leo struck.

I felt him push off me, vamp-fast. Before I could even blink, he had both witches, their throats in his fists, his fangs in Tau's. Neither one moved. Neither one protested. I fell over onto the sidewalk, landing with a slight bounce. Tau smiled and sighed, sexual arousal in the tone, and leaking from her pores. She wrapped her arms around Leo's shoulders. Onorios cannot be bound, but blood-drunk, clearly, was another matter.

Marlene simply stood there, gazing off into the night. This was why the witches had not taken over the world and killed off the vamps. The vamps might have little recourse against their magic, but the witches had absolutely no defense against the mind-blowing compulsion of a master vamp. In a way, they were evenly matched in this war that been going on for millennia. If Leo got the accords signed after this massive snafu, he'd have a huge edge over the EVs.

"Drop the rope working you have upon her, *ma chérie*. The woman is no danger to us."

The bolo fell away with a soft sizzle of sound. I closed my eyes, not wanting to watch Leo bind Marlene against her will. Making Tau love him and desire him. Forever. It was illegal. It was immoral. It stole their free will. But I just couldn't care about two people who wanted me dead.

Through the ground I felt the vibrations of people running toward us. Eli and Bruiser and the two Onorios reached us first. Bruiser slid his arms under me and lifted me. "Get her home. To the rock garden," he said. He kissed my forehead, his lips burning hot. And he passed me to Eli. My head lolled on my partner's shoulder, the stink of fear and relief so strong in his pores it was rank.

An SUV pulled up, a short distance away, the head-lights visible through small buildings. We were no longer on St. Charles Avenue, but just off Loyola Avenue, in an area of town where cemeteries were on either side of the street. We were actually inside one cemetery, however, and I caught a glimpse of the mausoleum belonging to H. Meyer. The crypt was constructed of brick covered with cement, shaped to look like stone. There were once-white marble architectural elements and a pediment on top. If the concrete parts of the burial place had ever been painted or whitewashed, the pigments were long gone. Low beds of white clover grew everywhere between the resting places of the long dead, and taller weeds pushed through the broken concrete walks. Bracken and more weeds grew from the walls and roofs of even older crypts. Neglect and decay and useless decadence. There was no one to keep the place of the dead nice, not anymore. It was falling to ruin.

Eli carried me past the Haynes' resting place, the O'Haras', and eventually on to Sixth Street. He strapped me into the SUV, which smelled of Youngers and Truebloods and home. He got in, started the engine, and I let my head fall to his shoulder.

When I woke, the sun was nothing more than a gray shadow, still to rise, a promise of heat and humidity. I was in my own bed, with Angie Baby curled into the curve of my totally human body.

Kitsss, Beast thought. And *Den. Safe den. Want kitsss.*

Eli opened the door and said, "How did you get away from the guards?"

My godchild giggled and snuggled closer to me, her arms around my neck. "Aunt Jane needed me. She feels better now." Later, I felt Molly lift Angie away, and I smelled breakfast on the air. But I was too tired to care, even about food. Alone in my bed, I rolled over and let sleep claim me.

Much, much later, Eli came to my room again and cleared his throat. Then again. And then over and over until I grunted that I was awake. He said, "The witch/vamp accords were signed this morning before dawn. Leo has his deal."

I grunted again, hoping he'd go away so I could go back to sleep, but then I remembered I had a question. I grunted again, something might have been "Nicauds?"

Eli said, "In court with a full coven of the more powerful witches in the U.S. They broke enough witch law to see them confined somewhere for decades. Or to have their magic stripped forever."

"They can do that? Take magic?" I asked, though it came out scratchy, sounding like a cat with dry heaves.

"I overheard some stuff. So I think so. Not sure." I didn't reply, and he said, "We got paid."

Which was good. I grunted one last time, "Ducky. Go away."

He did.

I slid back into dreams, a sweet relief spreading through me, gentle fingers of hope in its tail. If we could do this—the we of vamps and witches and YS—there was nothing we couldn't accomplish.

EPILOGUE

Two days later, I woke in my bed, the smell of fresh sheets and the jojoba oil Bruiser had given me telling me that I was okay, or as okay as I could be under the circumstances. I also smelled Bruiser's scent and I stretched out an arm to find his place empty, and cold. He hadn't slept here, but he had been here. His citrusy cologne was fading on the air. He hadn't been gone long.

I didn't know what had happened in the aftermath of the cemetery, except that I had found my fully human form and been taken home. At some point, I had been fed by Edmund. Clearly I had been showered and someone had somehow gotten me into my jammies.

I remembered the smell of magics and Angie Baby. And later, the sound of angry voices. I remembered Leo, on the other side of the door, sounding concerned and then sounding irritated, saying, "She should be told that the witches signed the accords. We are aligned. I must tell her."

And Bruiser's voice as he told his once-master that he couldn't come into my bedroom, couldn't wake me up, and that was final. And Eli, telling Leo, "I've already informed Jane. She said, 'Ducky,' and went back to sleep. No, you can't wake her. No, I do not work for you. I work with Jane. No. No."

At the sound of the confrontation, I had smiled in the dim light.

I remembered food—soup—being spooned into my mouth. Water through a bendy straw.

I also remembered pain. And the respite from pain.

And now I was awake, feeling stiff and sore and deeply rested. And there wasn't any reason to put it off really. Either I was healed or I wasn't. And if I wasn't, I'd have to shift into Beast a few times, and maybe into some other animals, to find the parts of me that went missing when I bubbled time so much in the last week.

I pulled my arm to me and placed my open, healed fingers on my abdomen. I had skin, not pelt. I slid my hands up and down, discovering that I was my usual human shape and size. The hole in my side where my external oblique muscles should be was . . . better. Not so deep. Not painful. But I wasn't totally okay.

And I still had a dark mote of power inside me, attached to my heart, one that would kill me if I tried to rip it out.

But all in all, things were pretty okay, considering.

The door cracked open and the scent of Angie, Little Evan, and Brute filled the room. "Aunt Jane?" Angie stage-whispered. "You still sleeping?"

"You still weepin'?" Little Evan echoed.

"Shhh. Mama says we can't wake her up if she's still sleeping."

I chuckled softly and said, "I'm awake. Come on in."

"Aunt Jane's awake," Angie shouted to the rest of the house. "She's not dead!"

"She not dead!" Little Evan said.

"You woke her up, didn't you?" Bruiser said.

"No. Uncle Bruiser! She was awake."

"No, Unca Buse!"

The three, and a werewolf, traipsed in. My mattress moved like an earthquake as Brute leaped up. The kids took his action as permission and followed, Angie snuggling into my left arm and EJ into my right. Brute claimed the bottom half of my bed, on top of my feet, but he was werewolf warm and I didn't mind.

I smelled my honey bunch at the door and knew without looking that he was standing there, watching us all. Smiling. Yeah. I could smell his smile. How cool was that?

A moment later the grindylow jumped up on the bed and raced around like a furry, fuzzy green ferret, chittering madly, before she leaped onto Brute and burrowed into his hair. I had wondered where the creature slept.

I closed my eyes and might have even gone back to sleep if Eli hadn't forced me up and out of bed, by the crafty device of putting a steak on the grill out back and leaving the side door open. Evil man. But then I realized that if I added steak to the picture, I would be the happiest person on the face of the Earth. So I gathered up my godchildren and my menagerie and rolled off the bed, seeking the rest of the Yellowrock Clan.

Read on for a special preview of the first book
in Faith Hunter's Soulwood series,

BLOOD OF THE EARTH

Coming in August 2016 from Roc.

Edgy and not sure why, I carried the basket of laundry off the back porch. I hung my T-shirts and overalls on the front line of my old-fashioned solar clothes dryer, two long skirts on the outer line, and what my mama called my intimate attire on the line between, where no one could see them from the driveway. I didn't want another visit by Brother Ephraim or Elder Ebenezer about my wanton ways. Or even another courting attempt from Joshua Purdy. Or worse, a visit from Ernest Jackson Jr., the preacher. So far I'd kept him out of my house, but there would come a time when he'd bring help and try to force his way in. It was getting tiresome having to chase churchmen off my land at the business end of a shotgun, and at some point God's Cloud of Glory Church would bring enough reinforcements that I couldn't stand against them. It was a battle I was preparing for, one I knew I'd likely lose, but I would go down fighting, one way or another.

The breeze freshened, sending my wet skirts rippling as if alive on the line where they hung. Red, gold, and brown leaves skittered across the three acres of newly cut grass. Branches overhead cracked, clacked, and groaned with the wind, leaves rustling as if whispering some dread tiding. The chill fall air had been perfect for birdsong; squirrels had been racing up and down the trees, stealing nuts and hiding them for the coming winter. I'd seen a big black bear this morning chewing on acorns halfway up the hill.

Standing in the cool breeze, I studied my woods, listening, feeling, tasting the unease that had prickled at my flesh for the last few months, ever since Jane Yellowrock had come visiting and turned my life upside down. She was the one responsible for the recent repeated visits by the churchmen. The Cherokee vampire hunter was the one who had brought all the changes, even if it hadn't been intentional. She had come hunting a missing vampire, and because she was good at her job—maybe the best ever—she had succeeded. She had also managed to save over a hundred children from God's Cloud.

Maybe it had been worth it all—helping all the children—but I was the one paying the price, not her. She was long gone and I was alone in the fight for my life. Even the woods knew things were different.

Sunlight dappled the earth; cabbages, gourds, pumpkins, and winter squash were bursting with color in the garden. A muscadine vine running up the nearest tree, tangling in the branches, was dropping the last of the ripe fruit. I smelled my wood fire on the air and hints of that applecrisp chill that meant a change of seasons, the sliding toward a hard, cold autumn. I tilted my head, listening to the wind, smelling the breeze, feeling the forest through the soles of my bare feet. There was no one on my property except the wild critters—creatures who belonged on Soulwood land—and nothing else that I could sense. But the hundred fifty acres of woods bordering the flatland around the house, up the steep hill and down into the gorge, had been whispering all day. Something was not right.

In the distance, I heard a crow call a warning, sharp with distress. The squirrels ducked into hiding, suddenly invisible. The feral cat I had been feeding darted under the shrubs, her black head and multicolored body fading into the shadows. The trees murmured restlessly.

I didn't know what it meant, but I listened anyway. I always listened to my woods, and the gnawing, whispering sense of danger, injury, and damage was like sandpaper abrading my skin, making me jumpy, disturbing my sleep, even if I didn't know what it was.

I reached out to it, to the woods, reached with my mind, with my magic. Silently, I asked it, *What? What is it?*

There was no answer. There never was. But as if the forest knew that it had my attention, the wind died and the whispering leaves fell still. I caught my breath at the strange hush, not even daring to blink. But nothing happened. No sound, no movement. After an uncomfortable length of time, I lifted the empty wash basket and stepped away from the clotheslines, turning and turning, my feet on the cool grass, my gaze cast up and inward, but I could sense no direct threat despite the chill bumps rising on my skin. *What?* I asked. An eerie fear grew in me, racing up my spine like spiders with sharp tiny feet. Something was coming. Something that reminded me of Jane, but subtly different. Something was coming that might hurt me. Again. My woods knew.

From down the hill I heard the sound of a vehicle climbing the mountain's narrow, single-lane, rutted road. It wasn't the clang of Ebenezer's rattletrap Ford truck, or the steady drone of Joshua's newer Toyota long bed. It wasn't the high-pitched motor of a hunter's all-terrain vehicle. It was a car, straining up the twisty Deer Creek mountain.

My house was the last one, just below the crest of the hill. The wind whooshed down again, icy and cutting, a downdraft that bowed the trees. They swayed in the wind, branches scrubbing. Sighing. Muttering, too low to hear.

It could be a customer making the drive to Soulwood for my teas or veggies or herbal mixes. Or it could be some kind of conflict. The woods said it was the latter. I trusted my woods.

I raced back inside my cabin, dropping the empty basket, placing John's old single-shot bolt-action shotgun near the refrigerator under a pile of folded blankets. His lever-action carbine .30–30 Winchester went near the front window. I shoved the small Smith & Wesson .32 into the bib of my coveralls, hoping I didn't shoot myself if I had to draw it fast. I picked up the double-barrel break-action shotgun and checked the ammo. Both barrels held three-inch shells. The contact area of the latch was worn and needed to be replaced, but at close range I wasn't going to miss. I might dislocate my shoulder, but if I hit them, the trespassers would be a while in healing too.

I debated for a second on switching out the standard shot shells for salt or birdshot, but the woods' disharmony seemed to be growing, a particular and abrasive itch under my skin. I snapped the gun closed and pulled back my long hair into an elastic to keep it out of my way.

Peeking out the blinds, I saw a four-door sedan coming to a stop beside John's old Chevy C10 truck. Two people inside, a man and a woman.

Strangers, I thought. Not from God's Cloud of Glory, the church I'd grown up in. Not a local vehicle. And no dogs anymore to check them out for me with noses and senses humans no longer had. Just three small graves at the edge of the woods and a month of grief buried with them.

A man stepped out of the driver's side, black haired, dark eyed. Maybe Cherokee or Creek if he was a mountain native, though his features didn't seem tribal. I'd never seen a Frenchman or a Spaniard, so maybe one of those Mediterranean countries. He was tall, maybe six feet, but not dressed like a farmer. More citified, in black pants, starched shirt, tie, and jacket. He had a cell phone in his pocket, sticking out just a little. Western boots, old and well cared for. There was something about the way he moved, feline and graceful. Not a farmer or a God's Cloud preacher. Not enough bulk for the first one, not enough righteous determination in his expression or bearing for the other. But something said he wasn't a customer here to buy my herbal teas or fresh vegetables.

He opened the passenger door for the other occupant and a woman stepped out. Petite, with black skin and wildly curly, long black hair. Her clothes billowed in the cool breeze and she put her face into the wind as if sniffing. Like the man, her movements were nimble, like a dancer's, and somehow feral, as if she had never been tamed, though I couldn't have said why I got that impression.

Around the house, my woods moaned in the sharp wind, branches clattering like old bones, anxious, but I could see nothing about the couple that would say danger. They looked like any other city folk who might come looking for Soulwood Farm, and yet . . . not. Different. As they approached the house, they passed the tall length of flagpole in the middle of the raised beds of the front yard and started up the seven steps to the porch. And then I realized why they moved and felt all wrong. There was a weapon bulge at the man's shoulder, beneath his jacket. In a single smooth motion, I braced the bolt-action shotgun against my shoulder, rammed open the door and pointed the business end of the gun at the trespassers.

"Whaddya want?" I demanded, drawing on my childhood God's Cloud dialect. They came to a halt at the third step, too close to for me to miss, too far away for them to disarm me safely. The man raised his hands like he was asking for peace, but the little woman hissed. She drew back her lips in a snarl and growled at me. I knew cats. This was a cat. A cat in human form—a werecat of some kind. A devil, according to the Church. I trained the barrel on her, midcenter, just like John had showed me the first time he'd put the gun in my hands. As I aimed, I took a single step so my back was against the doorjamb to keep me from getting bowled over or from breaking a shoulder when I fired.

"Paka, no," the man said. The words were gentle, the touch to her arm tender. I had never seen a man touch a woman like that, and my hands jiggled the shotgun in surprise before I caught myself. The woman's snarl subsided and she leaned into the man, just like one of my cats might. His arm went around her, and he smoothed her hair back, watching me as I watched them. Alert, taking in everything about me and my home, the man lifted his nose in the air to sniff the scents of my land, his delicate nasal folds widening and contracting. Alien. So alien, these two.

"What do you want?" I asked again, this time with no Church accent, and with the grammar I'd learned from the city-folk customers at the vegetable stand and from reading my once-forbidden and much-loved library books.

"I'm Special Agent Rick LaFleur, with PsyLED, and this is Paka. Jane Yellowrock sent us to you, Ms. Ingram," the man said.

Of course this new problem was related to Jane. Nothing in my whole life had gone right since she darkened my door.

ABOUT THE AUTHOR

Faith Hunter is the *New York Times* bestselling author of the Jane Yellowrock series, including *Dark Heir*, *Broken Soul*, and *Black Arts*; the Soulwood series, set in the world of Jane Yellowrock; and the Rogue Mage series.

CONNECT ONLINE

faithunter.net
facebook.com/official.faith.hunter
twitter.com/hunterfaith

ALSO AVAILABLE IN THE
NEW YORK TIMES BESTSELLING
JANE YELLOWROCK SERIES
FROM

Faith Hunter

Dark Heir

For centuries, the extremely powerful and ruthless vampire witches of the European Council have wandered the Earth, controlling governments, fostering war, creating political conflict, and often leaving absolute destruction in their wake. One of the strongest of them is set to create some havoc in the city of New Orleans, and it's definitely personal.

Jane is tasked with tracking him down. With the help of a tech wiz and an ex-Army ranger, her partners in Yellowrock Securities, she'll have to put everything on the line, and hope it's enough. Things are about to get real hard in the Big Easy.

Available wherever books are sold or at
penguin.com

R0222

THE *NEW YORK TIMES* BESTSELLING JANE YELLOWROCK SERIES FROM

Faith Hunter

Praise for the Jane Yellowrock novels:

"There is nothing as satisfying as the first time reading a Jane Yellowrock novel."
—Fresh Fiction

"Jane is the best urban fantasy heroine around."
—Night Owl Reviews